PRAISE FOR

"Clever, word-drunk, and falling-down funny . . . Robertson is a moral writer and a bitingly intelligent one, a man who writes with penetrating insight of what needs to be written about: beauty, truth and goodness."

—*The Globe and Mail*

"Introducing Ray Robertson to American readers is long over-due. One of Canada's finest younger novelists, there is no better Robertson novel to start with than *Moody Food*, a textured, evocative tale of life, love, music, and inebriation in the late 1960s. Infused by the legend of Gram Parsons (here fictionalized as a draft-dodging American musician named Thomas Graham), *Moody Food* charts the grand schemes and off-kilter dreams of the Woodstock Nation's northern enclave in Toronto's hippie ghetto of Yorkville. If we thought America owned the counter-culture, *Moody Food* tells us otherwise, and does so with a wise eye on the beautiful and absurd in all of us. This is a funny, generous, touching novel by a writer of genuine gifts."

—*Richard Currey (author of Fatal Light, Lost Highway)*

" . . . his characters are as engaging as they are vivid. The spell of his barroom yarn never lets up . . . Burning question: Will Ray Robertson and his book make the cover of *Rolling Stone*?"

—*Montreal Gazette*

"Riotous and tender, funny and sad, *Moody Food* is as good an elegy for the counterculture as we've seen. The question, 'What if someone were to write a 60's rock novel worthy of its subject' need no longer be asked.

—*Books in Canada*

"A giant jukebox of a book, *Moody Food* is the moveable feast of that Found Generation which evolved into the mythic Hippie Nations. Canadian wunderkind Ray Robertson has written a syncopated celebration packed with pure peddle-steel sex and fiddle-assaults on the soul, with moans, weeps, and rainy day Delta blues that make a broken heart seem like an attractive option. Mr. Robertson is the Jerry Lee Lewis of North American Letters and he makes writing a book seem like ringing a bell."

--*Chuck Kinder (author of Honeymooners and The Last Mountain Dancer)*

"*Moody Food* has the vibrancy of *The Sun Also Rises,* but instead of Pamplona, we have Toronto's Yorkville in the 1960's. It's a tale of idealism gone awry, of dreams going off the rails, of life catching up with those who live it at too rapid a pace. Robertson's ability to catch the mood of the times is uncanny. *Moody Food* simply bursts with the life of the street."

—*London Free Press*

"Ray Robertson is one of Canada's finest novelists."

—*Ottawa Express*

"Among the most talented of a younger flight of Canadian novelists."

—*Owen Sound Sun Times*

RAY ROBERTSON

MOODY FOOD

SANTA FE WRITERS PROJECT

Santa Fe Writers Project, SFWP and colophon are trademarks.

National Library of Canada Cataloguing in Publication

Robertson, Ray
   Moody food / Ray Robertson.

   I. Title

PS8585.O3219MM66 2003   C813'.54   C2002-904259-3
PS9199.3.R5319M66 2003

Cover design: Bill Douglas at The Bang
Printed and bound in Canada

Published in the United States by
Santa Fe Writers Project
SFWP ISBN: 097767990X

Visit SFWP's website: www.sfwp.com and literary journal: www.sfwp.org

TRANS   10 9 8 7 6 5 4 3 2 1

Mara Mara Mara

HOT BURRITO #1

Give me some music; music, moody food
Of us that trade in love.

one

Chicken-legged Thomas Graham, all white flesh and thirteen years old, in the huddle, on one knee, giving out the signals, in charge.

Mid-signal call, Thomas puts his mouth to the earhole of the helmet next to him, helmet belonging to Gary "Fat Man" Jones, Thomas's best friend and sure-handed fullback. Whispers:

"Hear that? Hear the cheerleaders?"

"Jesus, Thomas, everybody's looking, finish calling the play."

"Listen. That's three-part harmony. They're doing three-part harmony."

"Thomas—"

"Forget the words, don't even listen to the words. Just listen to the harmony. Just listen to the music."

"Hey, Graham, what's the fucking play?"

"Thomas . . ."

"Uh, right . . . 48 flanker split left, halfback off tackle right."

"On what, asshole?"

"Two. On two."

"Break."

And on two the halfback plunges left just like he's supposed to behind a tackle blowing spit and exploding left and a pulling guard chomping down hard on his mouthpiece pulling hard left just like he's supposed to do too. Doesn't much matter, though. The quarterback forgot to give the halfback the ball.

And Thomas Graham, football tucked underneath his arm, runs the other way, runs alone right, runs for his life, runs right into a wall of half of Jackson Central High's opposition that afternoon, the All-Mississippi high-school runners-up of the year before, the Oxford Panthers.

Hit high, hit low, hit hard, loudly hit, the ball pops loose at first point of pounding contact and sputters uselessly out of bounds, Thomas's collarbone snapping in two in the process as easy as someone keeping time to a catchy tune snapping happy his fingers.

On his back, arms and legs splayed, the bars of his helmet stuffed full of home-field turf and with a mouth full of blood and broken teeth like Chicklets floating in warm red syrup: "Oh, that's pretty," Thomas says, the cheerleaders on the sideline hitting all the high notes now, really cheering their boys on.

"That is just so pretty," he says.

1.

I MET THOMAS GRAHAM in a bank. He was withdrawing, I was depositing.

Fall hadn't managed to elbow out of its way yet all the humidity and baking haze of September lingering summer, but I'd decided to brave heatstroke anyway and broken out my buckskin jacket and slid into the friendly snug of my favourite pair of Levis. Impossible, I've always maintained, to be the best you can be when you're not wearing pants. Maybe this is northern prejudice, or maybe I'm just unnaturally sensitive about my legs. Anyway, there I was in my jacket and jeans.

And there was Thomas. In white cowboy boots and a red silk shirt with a little silver cross peeking out underneath, all topped off with a white jacket covered with a green sequined pot plant, a couple of sparkling acid cubes, and a pair of woman's breasts. The jacket glowed, I swear, and I'd had nothing stronger that morning than a cup of coffee. He was also the only other guy in the bank in blue jeans and with hair hanging down past his collar.

They'd given him some kind of form to get started on while he waited in line, and he was squinting and grinning at the thing like it was written in a language he couldn't quite understand but for some reason was getting quite a kick out of anyway. Probably high, I thought. He looked up at me from the piece of paper and blew a few brown strands of hair out of his eyes.

"Now that, sir, is one *fine* article of clothing," he said, lifting a long thin finger, pointing at my fringed jacket.

It took me a second to recover from the jolt of his southern accent. "There's a place over near Kensington Market," I said. "Good stuff. Cheap, too."

"Much obliged," he said. Using the pen he'd been given by the bank, he scribbled down what I'd just told him on the back of his hand. Information recorded, "Thomas Graham," he said, offering his hand.

"Bill Hansen."

"Pleased to meet you, Bill."

A blue-haired teller signalled that it was Thomas's turn at the counter. Thomas gave me a wink and loped right up. "Afternoon, ma'am," he said.

Later, after counting out my $23.50 monthy loan payment and signing my receipt, I noticed Thomas with the teller and some obviously important higher-up at the bank—he had to be important: he was balding and wearing an expensive suit—joking and laughing like old friends. At one point the man in the suit actually clasped Thomas by the shoulder to give him a paternal squeeze. My own teller sourly tore off her part of the carbon receipt and didn't thank me for being part of the Royal Bank family.

I had to walk right past him to escape the bank's partitioned maze, and Thomas turned away from the two behind the counter and put a hand on my arm. "Hey, Buckskin Bill," he said, "Uncle Owsley says thanks for the tip." He stuck out his hand. "See you around?"

"Sure," I said.

I smiled, shook his hand, and didn't open my fist until I was well down Avenue Road.

When I did: two tabs of Owsley acid. Everyone who prided himself on being in the know knew about Owsley Stanley, the mad chemist of San Francisco's Haight-Ashbury. But here I was actually holding a couple of his legendary powder kegs.

Won't Christine be blown away? I thought. And wait until I tell her about the guy who gave them to me.

2.

OKAY, JUST A LITTLE background music: Toronto, 1965 in particular.

For anyone starting to let his hair grow long and wanting to hear some good music and maybe even check out some of that free-love action you'd read about going down in places like California, that would basically mean Yorkville, just north of Bloor Street. No more than three blocks in all, Yorkville was our very own city within a city, every street, alley, and low-rent hippie-converted building bursting with the sounds of loud music and the sweet smell of incense and overflowing with like-minded friendly, freaky faces. There was the Inn on the Parking Lot, the Riverboat, the Mynah Bird, the Penny Farthing—coffee shops and folk clubs, basically—where you could listen to Joni Mitchell and Ian and Sylvia and a million others no one has ever heard of since. Everyone drank lots of coffee and smoked plenty of cigarettes and you could play chess outside if the weather was nice and there was pot if you wanted it and all the girls, it seemed, were eighteen years old and tall and thin with the kindest eyes and long dark hair and none of them wore bras even if there really wasn't all that much love going on, free or otherwise.

But maybe that was just me. As a University of Toronto second-year dropout of no fixed major working part-time at a second-hand bookstore with no guitar-strumming ability of my own, I wasn't on anybody's love-to-love-you-baby list. At least not until Christine showed up one day at Making Waves.

The Making Waves Bookstore wasn't much more than the entire first floor of a paint-peeling Victorian house near the corner of Brunswick and Harbord crammed to the walls with the owner, Kelorn Simpson's, own book collection, most of it accumulated over twenty years of academic gypsydom. Kelorn was a fiftysomething psychedelicized Ph.D. in English literature with a framed degree from Oxford and dual portraits of Virginia Woolf and Timothy Leary hanging over the front counter to prove it. She was also near-messianic in her need to educate, physically and otherwise, the young female undergraduates who would drift into the bookstore from the university just a few blocks away, as well as reluctant as hell to sell any of her books. Which is how I started working for her in the first place.

After she saw how disappointed I was when she barely even looked at the cardboard box I brought by full of an entire semester's worth of practically new books, and then how pissed off I became when she wouldn't sell me her City Lights Pocket Book copy of *Howl* (a cute girl in black leotards with jet-black hair and no makeup in my Modern American Poetry class told me to read it when I'd asked her out to a Varsity Blues hockey game; she also declined my invitation to the hockey game), Kelorn made me take off my coat and gloves, poured me a cup of mint tea, asked why I needed money so badly that I wanted to sell all my books, and why I wanted to read Allen Ginsberg.

After I told her about the cute girl with the jet-black hair and how I'd dropped out of U of T a few months before and how the bank was calling in my loan and how I'd have to move back in with my parents in Etobicoke soon if I didn't get a job, Kelorn asked me if I wanted to work at the bookstore.

"Doing what?" I asked.

"Nothing."

"You want to pay me to do nothing."

"Practically nothing," she said. "Open and close up when I'm busy. Brew a pot of tea now and then. Help out the customers."

"But you don't sell anything. How am I supposed to help out the customers?"

Kelorn set down her cup of tea on the counter. "You're not buying anything and I'm offering to help you, aren't I?"

"So when people come in you want me to offer them jobs working here?"

Leaning a heavy arm on the countertop, the massive collection of beads, religious medallions, and junk jewellery hanging around her neck set swinging and crashing against each other as she shifted her weight, "I thought you said you needed a job," she said. At an even six feet and with a figure that now—thirty years on and my own 28-inch waist as much a memory as my 8-track collection— can be charitably called Rubenesque, Kelorn, I came to find out, had a way of stopping the talking when there just wasn't anything worth left to say.

I told her I'd take the job. Told her thanks.

On my way out the door she called out my name and fluttered the copy of *Howl* across the room. "An advance against your salary," she said.

I put the book in my pocket and said thanks again.

"And one more thing, Bill?" she said.

"Yeah?"

"Beatnik girls don't go to hockey games."

Days at the bookstore, nights prowling around Yorkville, and my hair grew longer and winter into spring. I'd stare outside at the leaves bursting their buds while upstairs Samantha or Roxanne or Gretchen, the very same girls who wouldn't have given me a second look across the room in Introduction to Philosophy 101, writhed away under Kelorn's experienced hands before shuffling downstairs from her top-floor apartment wearing freshly fucked-flushed faces and carrying Woolf's *A Room of One's Own* and Norman O. Brown's *Life Against Death*, the building blocks of Kelorn's very own Great Books course.

But I managed to keep up on the rent on my room and shared bath on Huron Street near the university and not fall too far behind on my bank loan, and even when I couldn't afford to or didn't feel like getting high, the music around the clubs was usually good and the girls, if unattainable, even more beautiful than the summer before. And the guitars chimed away while we all waited around for what was going to happen next.

When I'd go back home to Etobicoke to visit, my mother would plead with me to cut my hair and my father would read aloud from the pulpit of his easy chair any one of an increasing number of editorials starting to show up in the *Toronto Daily Star* or *Toronto Telegram* about "the moral decay of our young" and "the pied pipers of popular music leading our younger generation headfirst into the hazards of political anarchy and sexual promiscuity" and I'd play right along, as if I'd just come back from a six-hour orgy and was way too tired to go into it, couldn't even be bothered to defend me and all my raging pagan friends.

Truth was, though, never having to go to the barber any more and hearing some good tunes and getting high once in a while aside, when, I wondered, was some of that moral decay going to come my way?

I wasn't then and am not now what you'd call a big reader. The hundreds of spines I must have cracked over the counter of Making Waves and the book-crammed cases lining the walls of this Tilbury farmhouse were and are liars both, making everybody and even myself sometimes think I just might be someone who knows something about something. But, then as now, I simply like the feel of being close to so much dedicated conviction and craft, surrounded at every turn by walls and walls of clean black type. Maybe because mine was the first generation to get plunked down in front of the TV whenever mum wanted a quick and easy kiddy-break, eyelids begin to hang heavy and attention span flickers before too many pages manage to get turned.

Or maybe I just wasn't intended to be one of those who know or think or feel too much, my place the place of steady but plain beat-keeping. But sitting here tonight, a lazy yellow lab by the name of Monty sleeping on the kitchen floor at my feet, maybe a mere metronome is not the worst thing a person can be. Because flip the coin of too much and the other side always comes up too little. Always.

But the next best thing to actually knowing what you're talking about is memorizing a few good lines and trotting them out at just the right moment. Like when Christine came into the store for the first time wanting to buy one of Kelorn's recently acquired treasures, a Viking first edition of Kerouac's *On the Road*.

"You're telling me you've got to ask the owner for permission to sell me this book?" she said.

"I'm saying I can ask her when she gets back if she wants to sell it, but I don't think she will."

"Come outside with me for a second," she said, opening the shop door, tinkling its bell. Seeing me hesitate behind the desk, "C'mon," she said.

It was only the first week of April and we both had our hands buried in the pockets of our jeans. But the afternoon sun was warm on my face and the air was beginning to smell more and more like a full-out blooming was only waiting for the right moment to spring.

"What does that say up there?" she said, pointing at the sign over the door to the shop.

"Okay, I get your point, but I've still got to—"

"No. What does that sign say?"

"Making Waves Bookstore."

"Exactly," she said, pulling the pen out of my shirt pocket and scribbling something on a piece of paper she'd taken out of her beaded shoulder bag. "Stores sell things. This is a store.

Therefore, the owner will sell me the book. Here's my number. Get her to call me with a price."

She stuck the pen back in my pocket, flashed me a peace sign, and departed down Harbord. Wonderfully long, at least my five-foot-ten, and handsome more than merely pretty with a Yorkville-unfashionable stubbly bald head and strong, sharp features and intense brown eyes, I was glad Kelorn wasn't there.

"Why do you want the Kerouac?" I called out after her.

She turned around.

Hesitating only a moment, "Because," she said, "the only people for me are the mad ones, the ones who are mad to live, mad to talk, mad to be saved, desirous of—"

"—of everything at the same time," I took over, finishing Kerouac's sentence for her, "the ones who never yawn or say a commonplace thing, but burn, burn, burn."

The girl smiled. Impressed or maybe only amused, I wasn't sure. But she smiled.

"You give me a call, too," she said. "I'm playing a gig at the Bohemian Embassy tomorrow night and you can come by my place before if you feel like it and, you know, whatever."

I said maybe I would, okay, maybe, yeah, and put her number in my pocket and the Kerouac under the counter and made myself a fresh pot of mint tea. I liked the sound of whatever. Whatever, I thought, just might be what I'd been looking for.

And time cannot mist out this. How, from the next day's first but not last furious fucking, to how Christine, moments after completion of the inaugural act, took a drink of water from a glass on the floor beside her mattress and leaned over as if to post-coital kiss but, instead, patiently passed cool water from her mouth to mine, everything she did in bed—to me, to herself, to us—seemed wholly holy natural, yet, at the same time, shatteringly erotic, every hungry gesticulation body-stirring earthy. And later, after her solo acoustic act between poetry readings at the Bohemian Embassy, all night long all that I didn't know yet about all the things a man and woman stoked by a little hash and a lot of just-met lust can do to and for one another.

But you've flipped through the magazines and seen a late-night cable movie or two, and even if it feels like it at the time, no two people ever invent sex, so no need here to blather on and on about what went where and who wailed what. But to this day, never again like that. Never. Aching muscles, for instance, where I didn't even know I had any. And coming to work straight from spending the night at her place and within an hour having to go and jerk off in the bathroom because Christine getting herself off with her nimble fingers while straddling me back-ward all I could see, hear, taste, smell. Et cetera, et cetera, all known positions and speeds.

And it was fun having a girlfriend again. Christine was smart and hip and always knew about all the musicians and authors you were supposed to listen to and read that it usually took Canadian hippies a year after the fact to discover. Because as much as it might not have felt like it, Yorkville was still Toronto, and Toronto was still Canada, the kind of place where it had been a crime ten years before to drink a beer in your own backyard.

Thanks to Christine, though, I was probably the first one in the audience able to sing along with her Fred Neil covers, and I even had my own copy of *Last Exit to Brooklyn* before Kelorn did. And the fact that Christine played Yorkville so much meant that I had something to do with my evenings, a legitimate reason to sit around all night drinking espressos with a step out the back door at the break for a quick jay. And that, for a while, for most of that summer, enough.

Then, late one night early in September, after one of Christine's shows—just before I met Thomas, in fact—after organic banana bread from Yorkville's combination head shop and munchie mart, the Grab Bag, and after fifteen minutes of fairly predictable lovemaking, Christine shook her head no to our usual post-doing-it doobie, left the bed, and leaned out my small room's small window that looked directly onto the bricked wall of the house next door.

The stifling heat all the more so for the kiln-sized dimensions of my room, I decided to attribute the lackluster shows Christine, even by her own admission, had been mailing in of late as well as our own recent less-than-banshee-like coupling—even my own heavier than usual toking—to the same sweaty source. Just as soon as this damn heat and humidity lifts. . . . I sparked up, the joint's tiny orange end the room's only light.

"What do you *want*, Bill?" Christine said, head still hanging out the window. I could just make out the soft white outline of her bare ass and legs softly glowing in the dark, her long back and all the rest of her curving gently upward into the hot black night filling up the room.

"For you to bring that gorgeous body of yours back to bed and smoke some of this fine dope with me."

"I mean," she said, as if she hadn't heard me, "what do you want out of life? What do you really want?"

I inhaled, held, swallowed, breathed out. "In terms of what?" I said.

"In terms of . . . I don't know. Like, where do you think you'll be twenty years from now?"

"Geez, Chris, I have a hard enough time trying to imagine what I'm going to wear to work tomorrow."

"Does that bother you?" she said.

"No."

"Really?"

"I don't know."

She came back from the window and sat down on the edge of the bed, took the joint and toked. Her beautiful pear-shaped breasts hung down dipping away from each other left and right, slightly defeated and depressed looking drooping there like two ends of a fleshy frown.

"They say Dylan's gone electric for good," she said.

"Yeah."

"Maybe I should go electric," she said, passing me back the joint. "What do you think?"

"Well, that depends, I guess."

"On what."

"On whether you want to. I mean, do you want to start playing electric guitar with a band?"

She took back the spliff before I'd had a chance to put it to my lips, inhaled deeply and didn't pass it back. After a while, "I guess that's the problem, then, isn't it?" she said.

"What is?"

"I guess I don't know what I want."

Naked arm around naked shoulder, I pulled her gently to me, eased us both down on the bed and under the thin white sheet, all the covers the sweltering room would allow.

"Wait until the fall," I said. "Nobody knows what to do or think in this damn heat." I crushed out the roach and kissed her on top of her bristly head goodnight.

But it was too hot to sleep lying there so close together so we separated and clung to opposite sides of the bed. And even then neither of us could seem to drop off, even with my little rotating General Electric fan going full blast. So we sparked up another joint and sat cross-legged on the bed with our backs to the cool white plaster wall listening to Dylan's latest, *Highway 61 Revisited*.

And Dylan, it seemed, sure had gone electric. That thin, wild mercury sound right through until morning, the September sun blazing back up and creeping down the alley between my house and the next, the light and the heat and the fierce music charging out of the speakers for just a moment almost one.

He woke up with money all around him, nickels, dimes, quarters, and even a few crumpled dollar bills, all of it surrounding him on the warm morning mattress, a few of the smaller coins sticking to his arms, the imprint of their designs only now beginning to fade as he sat up at last, allowing them all to slowly fall away.

Open-stage Saturday nights at The Steer mean Sunday morning hangovers so intense that blinking equals wincing and not all that much you can do about it but gently close your eyes and try not to breathe too hard and lie there silent and still until extreme thirst, hunger, or the need to urinate absolutely necessitates getting up.

But worth it, though.

Easing himself back down on the mattress, rolling over out of the line of direct sunlight pouring through the window, Thomas manages a sliver of a smile.

Oh yes, worth it.

The toughest, shit-kickingist country and western bar in the state of California circa 1965 is the Steer, located in the city of Industry, California. The sign on the highway states that Industry is twenty-four miles east of Hollywood, but it's actually approximately 100 million miles away. This is Redneck Country. Work, death, and then, the Good Lord willing, heaven.

Sitting by himself at the back of the club drinking his own pitcher of Budweiser with only his guitar on the chair next to him for company, Thomas Graham waits for his turn at the microphone. Thomas Graham in blue satin bell-bottoms, white rattlesnake-skin cowboy boots, and a genuine Nudie jacket from Nudie's Rodeo Tailors decorated with hand-sewn sequins in the shape of acid cubes, a woman's ripe bosom, a green marijuana leaf climbing up each arm, and a flaming red cross emblazoned across the back.

Finally, after the guy in the wheelchair singing "I Walk the Line" and the trio of grandmothers doing an a cappella version of "Ruby, Don't Take Your Love to Town," the bored MC in the white Stetson chewing away at his Redman with a clipboard in one hand and the mike in the other announces, "Okay, next up, Thomas Graham. Are you out there, Thomas?"

The long walk from the back of the bar to centre stage gets the hooting and wolf-whistling and calls to "Get a haircut!" started. By the time he's settled himself on the wooden stool and tuned his instrument and adjusted the microphone, it's hard to hear the guitar introduction to his first song over the noise from the crowd.

Not waiting for the audience to quiet down, Thomas sings the opening verse, then another, then goes into the chorus, but with about as much luck at being heard as before. A couple of people think they might actually recognize the song this faggy long-haired hippie is playing, though, and slow down their ruckus long enough to place what it is.

It's all the opening Thomas needs.

One or two, or maybe even a few, actually begin to really hear him now, but most quit their cackling and hollering just to identify "More and More," the Webb Pierce song barely audible just below the clamour of the crowd. Webb is pure Nashville, one of the big boys, a fat white guy in a crewcut with eight Cadillacs and a guitar-shaped swimming pool. At least this Graham guy knows enough to know a good song.

But before the next number is even halfway over, no more hooting or hollering and all eyes and ears aimed at Thomas singing a Hank Williams song and letting everyone in the universe know he's so lonesome he could cry. And he could, too, any fool could hear that. Just listen to that boy sing.

Like a back rub on the brain.

Like drinking velvet out of a glass.

Like hearing God hum.

Thomas finishes up with a recent Bob Dylan tune, "Subterranean Homesick Blues," a mile-a-minute bluesy thing with slightly surreal sputtered lyrics that no one in this dark, smelly bar would have ever thought they'd be nodding their heads along to even if you had sworn to them on their momma's tattered black Bible they would be twenty-five minutes before. And then a gentlemanly, "Thank you, everyone, for listening, and goodnight," and Thomas slinks across the beer-puddled floor back to his table by the washrooms.

Before he can refill his glass from what's left of his warm pitcher of beer, darkness at the edge of his table in the form of three very large men in overalls and scuffed, steel-toed workboots. The Trimar he'd gobbled down an hour before he'd arrived at the club is really starting to kick in now, and Thomas wonders whether he's seeing triple. Animal tranquilizers, after all, have been known to do so such things.

The one Thomas thinks is in the middle leans his baseball mitt–sized hands (car grease under every nail) on the edge of the table and slowly zooms his hairy face in close.

"Me and my buddies here, we were gonna take you out back and kick your ass," he says. "But you sing real nice so we wanna buy you a beer instead."

A white reptile-skinned cowboy boot scrapes a chair away from the table.

"Only if you boys will do me the honour," Thomas says, making room so his three new friends can sit right down.

3.

"I MEAN, I'M UP there trying to be cool about it, but it's my show, right? You've seen my set a hundred times, Bill, you know I always take requests and try to encourage everybody to get involved. But this guy just wouldn't stop. I mean, at the end of every song he's, like, 'Merle Haggard! Wanda Jackson! Jimmie Rodgers!'"

I'd had to miss Christine's Tuesday night gig at the Riverboat because of inventory at Making Waves—believe me, taking inventory at a bookstore that rarely ever sells a book is no eight-hour day—and we'd made plans to rendezvous at my place after the show. Christine was striding up and down the length of my tiny room.

"And then, just when I thought I'd caught a break after he got up and split after the first set and I'm just starting back up again, just getting into 'I Ain't Marching Any More,' the front door bursts open and here he comes again. But this time he's not alone, this time he's got three of those go-go dancing bimbos from the Mynah Bird with him. And of course he somehow manages to get them all settled in at the same table he had before, right in front."

"*Three* of them?" I said.

The Mynah Bird was a certified Yorkville hippie hangout, but with a strip club exterior for the entire street to see, the club's owner one day deciding that what he really needed to separate his place from all the others jockeying for our coffee money along the avenue were several bikini-clad dancing girls shaking and shimmying in a second-storey glass booth out front.

Christine stopped her pacing.

"Feeling like you really missed out on something, Bill? Maybe if you had been there tonight you could have taken one of them off Mr. Shitkicker's hands."

"No, no, I'm only saying I'm surprised that—"

Christine resumed her pacing.

"So then it starts all over," she said. "'Lovely, lovely, why that's just lovely, but how about a little Miss Patsy Cline now, darlin'? I just know you could do the old girl justice.'"

"Hey, this guy," I said, "is he tall and about our age, maybe a little older? Brown hair, white cowboy boots? Like the guy I told you about I met at the bank?"

Christine didn't hear a word I said.

"So by now I've about had it. I finish up the song I'm doing, put down my guitar, and walk off twenty minutes before the set's supposed to be over. Go right to the very back of the club to sit by myself for a while and have a smoke and get my head together, you know?"

I nodded.

"And I'm almost starting to wind down when over walks one of the Mynah bunnies in her four-inch heels with a message and a cup of coffee that I didn't order. 'Thomas wants you to know he thinks you've got a lovely voice and wonders if he can borrow your guitar.' I take a sip of the coffee and almost gag—the thing is half coffee and half whisky—and tell her he's welcome to my guitar but that the owner doesn't let audience members up on stage except during the Monday night hootenanny. 'Groovy,' she says, and hops off back to their table. In the time it takes me to light a new cigarette there he is on stage tuning my guitar."

Christine was at the window now sitting on the sill, trying to find the moon way up there somewhere between my building and the next.

"And then what?" I said.

Giving up on the moon, she came over and sat down beside me on the bed.

"And then the funniest thing happened," she said.

"Did he finally get to do his country thing?"

"Yeah, but . . . no. I mean, that's the weird part. I'm not quite sure *what* he did. I mean, it definitely sounded like country—you could definitely call it country, I guess. But also, I don't know . . . religious, like gospel music or something. But not in a churchy way, you know? I don't know how to explain it."

"What was it called? Was it his own tune?"

"After he was done he said it was a Hank Williams song. And I don't know Hank Williams from Adam, but I don't think any country singer ever sounded like that."

"Did he say what the name of it was?"

"'I'll Never Get Out of This World Alive.'"

Christine got up from the bed and fished out of her purse the clear plastic overnight bag she carried with her whenever she was staying over.

"And then what happened?" I said.

"Just what I told Miss Universe would happen. Bernie came out from the kitchen and saw that somebody else besides me was up on stage and told him to get off, that open stage was Monday night, and not to do it again."

"What did this guy say? Did he get mad?"

Christine had her hand on the door knob to my room. The shared bathroom was at the end of the hall. "No," she said. "Not at all, actually. He just set down my guitar, shook Bernie's hand, told him, 'You've got one wonderful place here, sir,' and asked the waitress for a round of coffee and tea and espresso, whatever anybody was having. For the entire house."

"Get out of here."

"For everybody in the place."

We both smiled.

"And I got this."

Back to the dresser and out of her purse, a single red rose.

"Where'd you get that?" I said.

"After I'd finished my whisky and coffee—"

I started laughing.

"I had to!" she said, laughing along. "If Bernie had found out somebody'd smuggled in booze and that I—"

"Okay, okay," I said, holding up my hand.

She looked down at the rose. "After I shot the shit with Bernie for a while and was halfway out the door, guess who comes running up the stairs after me?"

"*He* gave you the rose?" I said.

"Uh huh. 'For a fine country lady, whether she knows it or not.'"

It had to be the same guy I'd run into at the bank the week before, I thought. It just had to be.

Christine stuck the rose between her teeth and fluttered her eyes her hick-glamorous best.

I took the rose back out.

"Hurry up and brush, you fine country lady. Your country boyfriend's got another ten hours of inventory to do tomorrow."

After we'd surprised ourselves with the first really raunchy, eye-to-eye, good-and-grinding screw we'd managed in a while, I got up to light a candle and brought back to bed with me the gift Thomas had slipped me at the bank.

"Do you think it's the real thing?" Christine said. She was up on one elbow holding the covers to her neck with one hand and the two tabs of acid in the palm of the other. Fall had finally fell. Although a sauna in the summer, my room was like a morgue even on the earliest of autumn nights. Christine pulled the blankets higher and tighter.

"I don't know," I said, "but this guy strikes me as the sort to be pretty serious about his drugs."

"And it doesn't look like he's hurting for bread," she said.

We both looked down at the acid.

In spite of our fairly regular toking habits we were both, all things considered, pretty tame users. Heroin, coke, and speed were as yet mostly just ugly gossip around Yorkville, and LSD only a little less so because you never heard of anybody getting hooked. But you'd hear stories. Bad trips, flashbacks, permanent brain damage. . . .

Christine and I kept looking at the acid.

"What do you want to do?" she said.

"I don't know. What do you want to do?"

We were both naked, and the sweet stink of sex was still in the air. And this was the real deal, after all, authentic Owsley LSD. But even if I didn't know why, all I really wanted to do at that moment was take Christine ice-skating and hold hands and buy her a hot chocolate when she got cold and go around and around until we both got tired. I think she must have been thinking something like the same thing.

"I'm not saying it wouldn't be fun," she said. "But you do have to go to work tomorrow. You've got a long day."

"And you were going to get an early start looking for that new guitar."

"And I'm not saying no as in never, just not right now, you know?"

"I know," I said. "I know exactly what you mean."

I jumped out of bed and put the acid back in the bottom of the silver sugar canister I used for my stash, blew out the candle, and slid back in; wrapped myself around Christine like a hungry python around its next unsuspecting meal.

"Oh, God, your feet are like ice!"

"C'mon, baby, keep your man warm."

"Get those feet off of—"

"C'mon, baby, give your man a little—"

Leg-kicking and giggling and wrestling under the sheets, laughing and squealing filling up the tiny room. Soon, all calm there, all cuddling and quiet, just me and my girl.

4.

"UNDERSTAND, NOW, I wasn't born with the taste of ashes in my mouth or the sound of two-part harmony fuzz-tone honky-tonk never not echoing in my ears. I've only come to know and accept and even love these things as the necessary small suffering to be endured for being the self-appointed chronicler in song of all our lost days and nights after much contemplation on the life and times of our Lord Almighty, Jesus Christ, the original sweetheart of the rodeo himself, Amen."

Let's get this straight right from the start. The guy got me with the way he talked.

And how he'd look up from the jukebox, his face red with excitement over the song coming up next or maybe just flushed from all the booze or maybe simply bathed in the light of the machine or maybe all of these things all at once, and say, "Buckskin, I want you to meet Mr. George Jones, the King of the Broken Hearts"—dusty old George Jones, the saddest man alive, moaning his ten-cent tale of loneliness and betrayal into every corner of the nearly deserted barroom—I knew I was being let in on something I never knew was there before, was being baptized into my new friend's world with a shot of bourbon on the side whether I wanted to be or not.

The guy got me with the way he worshipped.

But talking a nice line and getting somebody good and loaded and laying it on thick about a bunch of country and western tunes shouldn't be enough to make any rational person really believe that what the world needs now is more steel guitars and that "When they pulled poor old long-gone Hank Williams out of that Cadillac Coup deVille on New Year's Day, 1953, that wasn't an overdose, friend, that was a sacrifice." Even if in the beginning is the word, a miraculous deed now and then never hurt anybody's chances of being born again.

After I'd finally bumped into him again coming out of the Mynah Bird and the single beer we'd agreed upon led to another and then another—all bought by him in appreciation for me turning him on to the shop where he'd gotten his beat-up brown leather jacket—the slippery slope of one-too-many wobbly-pops put me, at Thomas's instigation and against my better judgement, in the back seat of a taxi headed for the Canada Tavern, one of Toronto's nastier east-end bars. We smoked pot and They—our parents and all the other ungroovy grown-up types—drank alcohol. Thomas did both. Lots and lots of both.

Once we got where we were going, Thomas rapid-ordered so many glasses of draft beer that the waiter started bringing them over every ten minutes without us even asking. He also never gave anyone else a chance to play the jukebox. Now I understood why we were in the kind of bar where brush cuts were the "in" thing and George Armstrong, the Maple Leafs' star centre, was a bigger deal than George Harrison. I might not have known that Hogtown had its very own Hank Williams–listening portion of the population, but Thomas sure did, and he was determined to give me a crash course in all things twangy.

After so many rounds of Labatt 50 I lost track, Thomas apparently decided he could trust me and pushed a dime across the beer-puddled table.

"Three chances at bliss for ten cents," he said. "You find a better deal than that, I strongly suggest you take it."

As soon as I slipped the coin into the jukebox the previous song wound up and another 45 did not immediately drop down to take its place. Great. The bar was now a church and I was at the organ, my people ready to worship. I speed-read the hand-printed label for each two-sided record, desperate for a familiar name, every second I stood there staring at the blinking machine the room's silence seeming to grow that much louder. Except for the bands and tunes Thomas had played, almost every title drew an absolute blank, the jukebox a multicoloured blinking phonebook for a town I'd never even heard of. I punched in the letters and numbers to the only songs I recognized. If the dime Thomas had given was some kind of test of my country soul, I'd flunked big time.

"Eight Days a Week" came blaring out of the speakers, the same tune that had been playing on the cabby's AM radio on the way over to the bar, then another Beatles' song, and then "Shakin' All Over" by Canada's own the Guess Who. Whether I'd let Thomas down or not, I'd done my CHUM Chart Top Ten best to keep the room humming. I leaned back in my seat and sipped at my beer without being able to help tapping my fingers on the tabletop. Then it was all over, my eight and a half minutes of fame all done, and one of the half-dozen or so soused seniors drinking by himself throughout the bar lurched to the juke and clanked in a dime and we were back to acoustic guitars and stand-up basses and no one was apparently worse for my rock and roll detour.

Thomas hadn't said anything the entire time my tunes had played and didn't say anything later when we pulled up the collars on our coats and hit Queen Street. It must have rained while we'd been inside the bar. The 1 a.m. deserted street gleamed that post-storm shine that, aided by a few streetlights, can make even big-city blacktop look clean. Outside a boarded-up coin laundry, Thomas wordlessly pulled me by the jacket inside the door front. Crunchy brown leaves and old newspapers swirled around at our feet. He let go of my coat, closed his eyes, tapped a simple mid-tempo beat with his foot, and tested the entranceway's echo with a long hum.

Then Thomas sang; wrapped images and words I'd never heard used in a song before around a melody that had me seeing colours, I mean literal fucking colours: early morning, morning-after grey; deep, dark browns; sharp, midnight blacks. Later on I realized that the tune he'd sung was one of his own, "A Quality of Loss," but right then and there all I cared about was the light show.

He gave me his coat to wear and I gave him mine and we started walking again.

5.

I FORCED OPEN MY eyes and blinked several times and looked up from my third refill of coffee and wondered how I was going to get through a full day of work at the bookstore. Again. A few weeks after our first, another long night travelling the Thomas Graham Direct Express to Country Soul Enlightment had me wishing the conductor looked half as bad as his only passenger felt.

"Don't you ever get tired?" I said.

Thomas smiled, picked up the glass container of sugar off the tabletop, and started pouring it into my cup. "Say when," he said.

My reflexes weren't quite what they'd been sixteen sleepless hours before. I *saw* too much white powder going into my cup, but it took a few seconds for brain to tell mouth to tell him to stop.

"Stop!" I said.

He beamed wide again and stopped pouring. "Ole Buckskin," he said.

I'd never met anyone who smiled so much. Even as hippies we weren't supposed to be this happy. There was a war on in Vietnam, after all, and people somewhere I couldn't find on a map if their next meal depended on it were starving.

Thomas brushed aside some of the long hair hanging in front of his face and threw both arms behind him on the back of the red plastic booth we'd been trying to come down in for the last hour; took in the Wednesday morning breakfast crowd with ear-to-ear satisfaction like it was anything but what it was.

The Niagara was just the sort of meatloaf-special-with-your-choice-of-rice-pudding-or-green-Jell-O-for-dessert greasy spoon I would've walked by a thousand times without ever once going in. I wasn't a vegetarian yet like Christine, but she was working on it and had me down to an occasional tuna fish sandwich for lunch and whatever my mother happened to be serving whenever I'd go home (refusing to get a haircut and having a bald girlfriend were one thing, not eating my mum's roast beef dinner a whole other level of rebellion all together). But it wasn't only the low-end surf and turf the place specialized in that made me nervous.

There were cops here. The fuzz. The Man. *Pigs*. And lots of them, too. The way they kept pouring through the door and greeting each other, the place might have been some kind of police hangout. And aside from the obvious principle of the matter, here was Thomas with a pocket full of very illegal goodies and him set upon greeting every pot-bellied pair of Toronto's finest with a loud and clear, "Good morning, officers, fine day, isn't it?" This, in spite of my repeated knocking against his shins with the end of my black Beatle boots and several useless throat clearings that only succeeded in making me sound like an operatic asthmatic. Throw in his suspiciously slippery Southern delivery and you might as well put the cuffs on us right here and now and let us make our one phone call from the restaurant payphone. "Hello, Christine? You know the money you've been saving up for that new Gibson you've had your eye on? Well . . ."

But nothing happened. The cops just said good morning right back at Thomas and ordered up their coffee and ham and eggs and sucked deep at the long night's last cigarette and joked and laughed and argued about the Maple Leafs over greasy-fingered shared sports pages and one at a time eventually left the same way they came to return to wives and children relieved to see husbands and fathers safe and sound and at home again from another night of protecting our fair city.

A little after 10 a.m. and the last cop gone, the restaurant basically ours now and the breakfast specials already thinking about turning into lunch specials, and me already ten minutes late opening up Making Waves, "Are you crazy, man?" I said. "I don't know what the deal is where you're from, but up here you don't mess around with the Man because the Man will mess around with you. Got it?"

Thomas kept smiling into his empty coffee cup with a heavy-lidded gaze that said he just now might be ready to finally come down and cash it in for the night. Or was it for the day? Anyway, lucky Thomas, I thought.

Because even if I'd only forfeited another night's sleep in return for another lesson in all things country soulful—tonight's class conducted cross-legged on the floor of my room, cross-eyed drunk on a bottle of Old Grandad, listening to the collected works of Buck Owens and his Buckaroos—once again Thomas was off to bed and I was off to work and the onset of morning-after crankiness said this just didn't seem particularly fair. Also, maybe I had long hair and my very own roach clip, but I was also my parents' son whether I wanted anybody to know it or not and had never been late for a day of work in my life. Until I met Thomas, that was.

Slowly raising his eyes from the table, "Everyone says all we need is love, Buckskin," he said. "All incense and peppermints and hugs for all the one-eyed teddy bears and your momma and daddy holding hands as they tuck you into bed every night and you safe at home forever. But what we need, what we really need . . ."

His voice trailed off and he wrapped his hand tight around his cup, squeezed it hard like he wanted to make sure it was really there. "What we really need is more *give*. Because love, that's hard. That's real hard."

Sometimes it was like this. Sometimes this was all there was, all he could see, hear, think, breathe; every nerve end in his body encoded right down to the bone with it, every cell inside stuffed straight through until it felt like it was all he'd ever been, would be. Drink smoke snort shoot swallow and still, there it is. Play guitar and sing every song you know until your fingers bleed at the tips and it hurts your throat to swallow and at the end of it, staring right back at you, there it is.

The screen door slams shut with a hard, wood-to-wood summer whack and Becky screams across the lawn and through the small forest of trees everyone has always called Dream of Pines, "Thomas, come here now, Thomas, please, come here now!"

Thomas knows the only thing his sister hates more than being around him and all his dumb twelve-year-old friends is asking her little brother for anything, so he drops the football and tells his friends to go home and tears off toward the house. The Grahams have the biggest lawn in Jackson—it takes two coloured men all day to cut every green inch—but Thomas is up on the front porch before his sister has to call out a second time.

Panting, dry-mouthed, "What?" he says.

Graham family flesh clamped tight to Graham family flesh, her little brother's hand in hers seems to calm Becky, to give her resolve. "Let's go and see Momma," she says.

Their father, as usual, is away on business in Memphis. Selma, the elderly Negro woman who'd served as nanny for both Becky and Thomas, is at her sister's house in town. It's only a little after three on a cloudless July afternoon, but Selma has drawn all the curtains just like Mrs. Graham asks her to do whenever Mr. Graham isn't at home to shout, "Open up those goddamn windows, Selma, and let some fresh air and light into this godforsaken tomb!" and the entire antebellum house is foggy with dark except for here and there the yellow glow of a floor lamp and an occasional slice of dusty sunlight somehow managing to sneak in past the heavy drapes.

Thomas and his sister slowly climb the twisting stairs to the third floor. At the end of the dark hallway, at the closed door of his mother's room, Thomas pulls back, hesitates. But his sister, saying nothing, but with tears in her eyes, turns the crystal door handle and tugs him hard inside.

Blink (eyes adjusting to the unlit room), and inside no different than it ever is. A gallery of framed ghost photographs of long-gone Gibsons, Thomas's mother's people. The well-stocked liquor cabinet on wheels parked in the corner. His mother's leather-bound Bible on top of the bureau beside two brass buttons, a single piece of green silk, and her ever-present silver comb. Her bedside pharmacy, pills and capsules every colour of the rainbow. And, of course, Thomas's mother herself, lovely pale lovely Mrs. Caroline Graham. Almost fifteen years to the day of her coming-out party and still any debutante's dream with her small slim feet, light summer dress of crimson, and all that combed-a-hundred-times-a-night brown hair splashed all over the pillow under her gently resting head.

Blink again (eyes seeing everything now), and not the smell of gin or freshly cut lilacs (all so ordinary, all so familiar) but something else, something different, something . . .

See: An empty pill bottle on the bedspread and the discarded white cap and piece of cotton beside it.

See: A creeping black stain soaking through the blanket and red dress below the folded white hands.

See: A blood-smudged razor blade lying by itself on the wooden floor.

See blink stare blink scream and break free of sister Becky's hand and through the doorway and down the stairs and out the front door and back outside again toward Dream of Pines and into the bright light of saving daylight and run run run, Thomas, run until the green green grass of home is gone daddy gone. You run, Thomas. You keep on running, boy.

6.

KELORN AND I USUALLY took turns picking what got played on the record player at Making Waves. The fake-walnut and permanently smudged turntable and speakers she'd lugged into the store one day from a yard sale a few doors down weren't that much of an improvement on the Sears and Roebuck system I'd received for my thirteenth birthday, but even if through no fault of his own Dylan sounded even more pinched-nosed nasal than he normally did you were usually able to make out most of the words and could always hum along. And no matter what, music swallowed up an afternoon's unwanted hours better than any double-talking philosopher blathering on and on about the non-existence of time ever could.

Even if I wasn't a player like Christine or Thomas, I'd Jailhouse Rocked as a hormone-hopping teenybopper, found out from the Weavers which side of the class struggle I was on as a properly alienated high-schooler, and even heard it all brought back home by the Byrds doing sagacious Dylan when they'd sent everyone onto the dance floor to the toe-tapping sounds of the chimes of freedom flashing. Music meant something.

But, Kelorn was beginning to wonder, what exactly was the meaning of this Hank Williams character I'd started playing non-stop at the shop?

Democracy really is such a nice idea, especially the brand of breezy affairs that Kelorn insisted govern Making Waves. Although she owned the store and I was clearly her employee and she my boss, deepest hippie equality technically ruled the day. So we split up the number of hours to be put in at the shop, divided down the middle the work that had to get done, and even divvied up the amount of time each was allowed on the hi-fi.

But there comes a time in every progressive theory of human affairs when the one who signs the cheques can only hear "I'm So

Lonesome I Could Cry" spun so many times before the plug gets pulled and it's back to the boss's Fugs and Joan Baez records with a little Mozart thrown in when she happens to be laying somebody new and feeling a little lovey. That day came for us when I'd returned to work from meeting Christine at Café El Patio for a macrobiotic lunch and Kelorn had apparently forgotten about my scheduled all-day Friday allotment of playing time. Ian and Sylvia pleading in their "Song for Canada" for all us True North types to try to get along meant that Hank wasn't asking "Why Don't You Love Me Like You Used to Do?"

"Dearest Christine," Kelorn said, tinkling doorbell lifting her head from Spengler's mammoth *Decline of the West*. "And what did my favourite employee treat you to today?"

Hug hug, kiss kiss, all in the appropriate lip-to-cheek European fashion I'd never learned to feel all that comfortable with. Christine and Kelorn had hit it off as soon as I'd introduced them. I knew everything was going to be fine when Kelorn sold Christine the copy of Kerouac's *On the Road* she'd wanted.

"Hey, what's the deal?" I said, heading right for the hi-fi.

"Your only employee gave me another lecture I didn't ask to hear," Christine said. "This time on the difference between—let me get this straight—the Bakersfield Sound and the Nashville Sound."

"My goodness," Kelorn said, shutting her book and resting her hands on top. "And I didn't even know there was any."

Hank's "Six More Miles to the Graveyard" restored to its rightful place on the record player, "You two can kid around all you want," I said, "but if it wasn't for people like Buck Owens keeping the Fender Telecaster and that freight train sound alive you can bet that Nashville and all those bastards like Owen Bradley would have poisoned every honest country record getting made right now with his goddamn strings and choirs."

A goateed guy in black horn-rimmed glasses with a slightly constipated look on his face was sitting with legs crossed and perfect posture on the couch by the gas stove near the back of the shop and making no secret of the difficulties he was having concentrating on Nietzsche's *The Birth of Tragedy* while Hank merely swam through an ocean of razor blades of suffering to tell the world all about it while a grieving pedal-steel guitar mournfully complemented his every utterance of suffocating melancholia. Oh, that was all. Every thirty seconds or so the little geek would look up at the record player and frown. Finally he slammed the book shut and stormed out the door, making sure to shake his head a couple of disappointed times as he threw his long red scarf over his shoulder.

I dinged the door open again and yelled after him, "'The existence of the world is justified only as an aesthetic phenomenon!' Look it up, buddy! Believe me, it's in there!" I'd never been so happy to have read the first five pages of a book before. I closed the door to the afternoon chill and turned around triumphant.

Not to a hero's greeting, though.

"What?" I said, beating them both to the punch.

"Bill," Kelorn said, "I think I've been about as understanding as you could expect me to be about this whole . . . cowboy period you're going through, but when it starts to interfere with—"

"Cowboys!" I said. "You know, that's exactly the sort of stereotype Thomas says you can expect from the supposedly progressive Left. I mean, I thought our whole generation was about breaking down the doors of the old ways of thinking, not reinforcing them. I thought we were supposed to be about getting rid of all life-inhibiting labels."

Life-inhibiting labels. This from a man who only a month before would have had a difficult time getting worked up over anything other than having enough pot left over in the bottom of his stash for one more good fatty at 3 a.m. and not a pack of matches in the house.

"Now that we're on the subject," Kelorn said, "it would be nice if every other sentence that came out of your mouth these days wasn't directly attributed to Thomas."

"That's bullshit, Kelorn," I said. "You just don't like Thomas."

Too much her even-tempered self to take the bait, "I hardly know Thomas, Bill, you know that. Thomas isn't the problem."

"Well, then, what is the problem?"

"The problem is that when you start making the book-store an unpleasant environment for our patrons, you force me to act like some taskmaster and tell you to cool it. And I don't like doing that, Bill. I *won't* do that."

"That guy wasn't even trying to hear the music," I said. "He thought he knew exactly what country music was all about, that it was just a bunch of two-chord songs for bigoted hayseeds who don't know any better, end of story. If he'd only put down his book for ten seconds and paid a little attention to the way the Drifting Cowboys accented Hank's every—"

Christine pulled on the hood of her parka and left. No good-bye, no thanks-for-lunch peck, nothing.

I looked at Kelorn like I really didn't get it.

"For goodness sake, Bill, go and talk to her."

"Did I just miss something?" I said. I really didn't get it.

Kelorn wouldn't even look at me; just carefully took my record off the turntable and put it back in its jacket.

"Maybe I should go see what's wrong," I said.

Christine wasn't trying to get away from me, but she wasn't slow-ing down any either. I got lucky with a red light at Spadina and finally caught up.

"Hey," I said, grabbing onto her arm.

Twisting away, "Hey, what?"

"Hey, what's the big deal?"

"She's right, you know," she said.

"Kelorn? About what? That guy in the shop? He was a jerk."

"How come you never help me put up posters any more? You never even come see me play any more."

"I do. I do still come and see you play."

"Once in the last two weeks. At the Riverboat, last Tuesday. And you and Thomas were both so drunk you yakked through my entire set."

"That's not true," I said. Wasn't it? I was so loaded that night I honestly couldn't remember.

"And it's like we never talk about anything any more but Thomas and country music, country music and Thomas."

"But you said you were starting to like some of it."

"I am. I mean, I do like some of it—I can see what you see in it—but that's not the point."

"Well, what is the point then?"

The light was green now, but we stayed where we were.

"All you ever do any more is hang out with Thomas and get loaded," she said.

"Since when did you get so hung up about getting wasted once in a while? Thomas knows a lot about something I'm interested in right now and I like talking to him about it, so what's the problem? He's informative."

"You're starting to wear each other's clothes, Bill."

That, at that very moment, underneath my jean jacket, I had on a powder blue, crushed velvet cowboy shirt Thomas had lent me didn't stop my machismo meter from going off the chart. Way off. I frowned and locked my fingers behind my head and looked up at the sky like I'd seen my dad do a thousand times when my mum would say he was spending too much time on the golf course and not enough with his family.

"So this is what this is all about," I said. "You're mad because I want to spend some time with my friends and not every minute with you."

"Asshole," she said. And off she went again.

Relationship late bloomer that I was, I was thankful to Christine for a lot of first-time things. But feeling like a complete shit for saying nasty stuff you don't really mean definitely wasn't one of them. I stood on the edge of the curb trying to figure out the best way to apologize long enough that by the time I broke into a trot after her the light was red and I had to play matador with a herd of snarling, horn-farting cars. I managed to make it across the street in one piece, apologizing the entire hop-scotching way, and overtook her after a short sprint.

"I'm sorry," I said.

Silence.

Try again. "I really am. Really."

Silence.

If at first you don't succeed . . . "And I promise I'll go see your set this week. And that I'll keep quiet."

She stopped.

"This isn't about me, Bill. This isn't about you doing something to make me happy."

"I thought you wanted me to—"

"What I want is for you not to forget about what makes *you* happy."

"I am happy."

"You're obsessed. There's a difference."

"Hey, y'all." Oblivious to both the hurricane he was walking into and the fact that he was at the very eye of it, waving and waltzing our way down Hoskins Avenue, here came Thomas. I felt like running.

But by the time Christine had coolly received his kiss on the cheek she couldn't stop laughing and I started to laugh along with her. Thomas didn't have a clue what was going on but didn't want to miss out on whatever was so funny, so then he started laughing too, first in little breathy sniggers but then full-out howling just like us, even if he still didn't know why.

"Come on now, y'all, what?" he managed.

"Thomas," Christine said, "who put that . . ." That was it, no more.

"Come on, really, what?" he said. By now, we all had tears in our eyes.

It was up to me to finish the job. "Who put that . . . black electrical tape on your head!" All of us roared.

Thomas adjusted the two brown paper bags he had under each arm and placed a finger to his head and smiled like it was the most natural thing in the world to have a huge sheath of white gauze stuck to your forehead with half a roll of electrician's tape to keep it in place. Then he gave us the story.

"So I finally get my pants on and grab my boots and shirt and am almost out the window and on the roof when the damn window comes down on my head just as I'm climbing out."

"So it wasn't her boyfriend who did this to you?" Christine said.

"No! His window!"

More hysterics.

"But who . . . ?" I said, pointing to his forehead.

Thomas touched his head again. "Well, I just bought some supplies from the Grab Bag on the way home and did it myself. And not too bad a job if I do say so. I've seen worse."

We all laughed again, though somewhat like sane people this time. By now Christine and I had our arms wrapped around each other's waists.

"What's in the bags?" I said.

Slowly pulling an album out of one of the sacks, "This, my friends," he said, "is a little something I just picked up." Tenderly holding the record out for our inspection, he could have been a proud father presenting his precious first born.

I thought I felt Christine edge back a little into her earlier sulk when she realized it was an album, but after she saw what Thomas had bought, Woody Guthrie's *Dust Bowl Ballads*, her face softened.

"Woody," she said.

"Woody Guthrie, indeed, Miss Christine," Thomas said. "And all because of you."

"Me?"

"Yes, ma'am, you. After your fine performance last Tuesday I simply could not get those songs of his out of my mind." Turning to me, "Remember how impressed I was by them that night, Buckskin?"

"Oh, yeah," I said. Yeah, right.

"But . . . Woody Guthrie's not country," Christine said.

Thomas sighed, he literally sighed.

"You know," he said, talking to us but looking across the street at a white-leotarded girl in a purple, fringed miniskirt getting on the back of a motorcycle and wrapping her arms around the driver's waist, "it makes me sad to hear you say that." He looked back at Christine, his eyes locked on hers.

"Sometimes I wish there wasn't any such thing as country music any more, wish there wasn't anything called folk music or rock music or the blues or anything. What I've always dreamed of is what I like to call Interstellar North American Music, a heaven-sent musical hybrid fusing together all honest forms of sound into one great big soulful stew. Just music, understand, just one kind of music—good music."

We all turned around at the squeal of tires to watch the motor-cycle with the miniskirted girl noisily take off.

"Because when I heard you and your guitar doing '1913 Massacre' the other night at the Riverboat, Miss Christine, I was moved like everybody else who was there that night was moved. And I knew right then and there that I wanted Mr. Woody Guthrie to be part of my musical family. I *knew* it."

Pulling me closer, "What's in the other bag?" Christine asked.

"This," he said, holding up the other package, "I have because I was hoping that maybe later tonight I could convince Buckskin here to let me come by his place and sample this record album of fine music. And if he lets me—and maybe if he could convince you to come by and help me get to know your Woody boy a little bit better—maybe we could all three of us share a little . . ."

Out of the paper bag a bottle of 100-proof mescal, a little white worm floating all by its lonely self on the clear-glass bottom.

Christine took the bottle from him and inspected the green chicken carrying a red spear on the label, the unfamiliar Spanish. She handed it back. "Jesus, where did you . . ."

"Well, Buckskin mentioned the other night that he'd never had a chance to sample mescal's not-insignificant charm. So I got a hold of a friend of mine who talked to a buddy of his and . . ." Thomas smiled, shrugged.

"Thomas," I said, "how is it that you've managed to live in Toronto for two months but have already made more friends than I have in twenty years?"

He handed Christine the Guthrie album and me the bottle of mescal. Draping an arm around each of us, "Not *real* friends," he said.

Pick a city, any town or city, pick any place there while you're at it, too (a tarpaper shrimper's shack in Biloxi, Mississippi; a polished dormitory room in Harvard Square; a poorly heated small room at the top of the stairs of a subdivided Victorian house on a tree-lined Toronto side street); pick the people gathered there, pick the time of night, pick the circumstances that brought everyone together.

Regardless: Thomas Graham, rolling, pouring, playing.

The consummate madman host leans into one of his guests— even if always on the road, always the master of ceremonies wherever he goes—and politely inquires, "Another hit? Top off your drink? Care to hear that song again?" And whatever the answer given, invariably, Yes, Yes, Yes.

There are no spectators when Thomas runs the room. No way to know, for instance, when his slightly perspiring face will without warning loom large right there in front of yours imploring stillness and concentration because, just between you and him, this is something you really don't want to miss.

"The tune's called 'Ramblin' Man,' Hank Williams is the artist, the year is 1951, but let's forget about all of that for a minute and just go nice and slow and try to hear what's there, all right? Because we've got all the time in the world, don't we? And even if we didn't, this is where we're supposed to be anyway because this is where we are right now. Okay, let's give it a shot, here we go, cheers. Now, what you've got to do first is dig the steel guitar that starts things

off. It's right out of the chute, just a little acoustic strumming and then BOOM! there it is, so get ready for it. You all set? You ready? Okay. All right."

Needle penetrates record and, as promised, three or four seconds of muted minor chording before a screeching steel-guitar run that sounds like the brake-slamming final tragic seconds before a train wreck set to music.

And because there is no chorus or even an instrumental break to the song, only one long chugging uninterrupted confession of how, happy or sad, heaven or hell bound, when the Good Lord made Hank, He made a ramblin' man, Thomas comes close to whisper in one ear while Hank continues to sing in the other. Moves right in so tight and has his mouth so close to your ear that his breath on your earlobe sends goose bumps up and down both arms. He speaks slowly. He speaks clearly.

"'Luke the Drifter' is what it said on the single when this song was first released. The name was a pseudonym Hank used for some of his so-called 'devotional' songs. But every song Hank Williams ever recorded was a devotional song. He was twenty-nine years old going on a hundred but he never made it to thirty. But Hank Williams did not die in vain, friend. He died for me. He died for you. He died for all of us. This much we know. This much is not in doubt."

His mouth so close now, the whisky on his breath dampens your ear, tingles your nose.

"The only question is," he says, "is anybody listening?"

With another screeching steel-guitar line "Ramblin' Man" crashes to an end the same savage way it began. You wonder where this universe of quiet came from. You wonder where it's been hiding all this time.

7.

THAT I DIDN'T KNOW how to play the drums apparently wasn't going to be a problem.

"I've seen you keep time to a jukebox with your butt planted on a barstool all night about a million times," Thomas said. "We'll just sit you down behind a drum kit and you'll barely even know the difference."

The main thing was that I was the only person he'd met since moving to Toronto who really understood "where my head is at, vision-wise, what I'm shooting for on the white soul concept level." Canada, Thomas explained, was the absolutely perfect non-prejudicial place for the launch of his sensibility-shaking movement of musical pioneering because of its basically blank cultural slate. Being a good Canadian, I chose to take this as the compliment it was intended as. Also, he said, he knew he could trust me.

"When the bullets start flying I know you'll cover my back, Buckskin." We were at our usual sobering-up back-corner table downstairs at the Riverboat. "When things begin to get heavy I don't want to have to worry about the guy standing next to me in the trenches."

And now that he'd deemed it time to put together a band and start spreading the gospel of the rich musical medley that was Interstellar North American Music, Thomas had decided that not only would I make a fine drummer but that Christine, with her beautiful singing voice, would fit in very nicely on high-harmony vocals. She'd have to play bass, though, he insisted. Besides the pedal steel, Thomas had always heard only one guitar in his head when he envisioned the kind of sound he wanted, and that guitar was his.

"Christine doesn't play bass," I said.

"I only hear one guitar, Bill," he said firmly, holding up a single finger. I tried to explain to him how he'd sort of missed my point.

Since the night at my place spent listening to Thomas's Woody Guthrie album over the shared bottle of mescal, Christine, it was true, was well on her way to gaining a deeper appreciation of all things twangy. And even if more inclined toward, say, the guitar, mandolin, and high-harmony approach of the Louvin Brothers rather than the straight-ahead fiddle and Telecaster assault of Buck Owens, it wasn't too long before Charlie and Ira's "Cash on the Barrelhead" began popping up in her shows right there between Woody's familiar "Union Made" and "This Land Is Your Land." But, I tried to point out to Thomas, Christine's coming around to the idea that folk music and hillbilly duets were actually country cousins didn't mean she was about to lay down her acoustic Martin and her own solo career just so she could pick up an electric bass and join his band.

"*Our* band, Buckskin," he said.

"Yeah, okay, our band," I said, putting on the patient smile one saves up for young children, the mentally ill, and the very religious. "But you don't get it. Christine's not going to—"

"Christine sure cares one heck of a lot for you, doesn't she, Buckskin?"

I paused. "What do you mean?" I said.

"C'mon, now," he said. "That woman of yours, she loves her Buckskin Bill."

I was a little confused, and it wasn't just the ten or twenty glasses of beer. "Yeah, okay. So?"

"Nothing, that's all. She sure loves him, though. Do anything for him, I expect."

I set down my coffee. "I'm not going to ask Christine to do something she doesn't want to do, if that's what you're getting at."

"I wouldn't dream of it, Buckskin. All a man can do is lead a horse to water."

Before I could object that my girlfriend wasn't a horse to be led anywhere by anyone, a waitress flipped on every light in the room. Thomas already had his sunglasses on. I clenched my eyes tight against the light and frisked my shirt and coat pockets. Since I'd started hanging out with Thomas, a good pair of dark shades had become an indispensable accessory. I finally found mine and jammed them over my ears.

The waitress stopped several feet short before getting to our table, probably something to do with wanting to have as little as possible to do with two clearly intoxicated men in matching red silk cowboy shirts wearing sunglasses inside in the middle of November.

"Five minutes," she said.

I nodded politely and thought about how although it had only been a few months since Thomas had shown up in town, it seemed like a whole other lifetime ago that I was just an incon-spicuous hippie boyfriend of a local folk singer who could usually get a coffee after closing time and nurse it in peace until the floors got swept and the tables wiped down. But maybe, I told myself, it wasn't just Thomas Graham guilt by association.

Ever since some of my more politically active long-haired brethren, Christine among them, had started slapping posters around the village and making noise in the newspapers about getting Yorkville shut down to all the exhaust-choking cars full of button-downed oglers hoping to get a good look at an honest-to-goodness hippie, the cop presence had picked up noticeably. Not quite "Move along, move along, young man," but enough that they would've loved to have busted a popular hipster hangout like the Riverboat for having a single cup of coffee on a table a few minutes after hours.

I turned back to Thomas. The smile of before had been replaced by the deep pout I'd come to recognize whenever he didn't get what he wanted.

"What?" I said.

"You never asked me the name of our band."

I knew I'd have to give in eventually. "Okay. What's the name of our band?"

He waited a second or two for dramatic effect. Then, taking off his glasses, leaning across the table, "The Duckhead Secret Society," he said.

I smiled like I knew he'd want me to and clinked his raised cup with mine.

More than the goofy name, though, I wondered at the unblemished whites of his eyes, unaffected as always by whatever amount of booze or pot we took in or whatever hour it happened to be. I didn't dare take off my glasses. Thomas could keep looking at me all night if he wanted to, but he'd still only see nothing but himself looking right back at him.

8.

FOR THE TIME BEING it was easier not to tell Thomas no. He might have wanted to argue, he probably would have sulked, and, more than likely, I thought, the idea of an absolute rookie rhythm-maker like me keeping the beat for whatever the hell the Duckhead Secret Society turned out to be probably wouldn't last much past tomorrow morning's hangover. And besides, we were well into phase two of my Interstellar North American Musical Apprenticeship by now and I didn't want to run the risk of doing anything that might disturb my studies. That more than anything else kept me silent on the subject of Christine and me joining Thomas's band. Trust me, once Little Richard is introduced directly into your bloodstream, you'd be amazed at all the things you'll do to make sure the medicine keeps coming.

And not just the ivory-pounding Georgia Peach, either. A Chuck Berry disc, in fact, was the first classic rock and roll record Thomas stuck in my hand, the first roots music changeup he threw my way. Because once I was lost but now I am found, and so where are all the shimmering harmonies, the softly moaning pedal steel, the weeping fiddle? So much electricity and so little bittersweet subtlety surely must add up to an impure teenybopper art form that all of us musically enlightened ones should turn our properly self-righteous noses up at, right? Wrong.

"I think your colour wheel needs a little filling in, Buckskin," Thomas said, hand-delivering to my door his own lovingly beat-up copy of 1959's *Chuck Berry Is on Top* LP.

"You're saying you think I should listen to more black music?" I said.

"Skin colour's got nothing to do with it. The Good Lord gave you ten toes to tap and two feet to dance with and it goes against His will not to use them."

"Isn't this kid's music?" I said, scanning the track listing.

Thomas raised an eyebrow; looked me over as if an offensive odour had begun to emanate from my body. He shut his eyes before he spoke.

"Because the head bone is connected to the hip bone, and the hip bone is connected to the feet bones, the high lonesome sound of a freight train blowing its sad midnight way through the middle of town on a frosty November night is, in fact, the exact same train that earlier that sunny afternoon clippety-clop chugged in perfect 4/4 rock and roll rhythm right past some dreary fool standing by himself by the side of that same set of tracks."

"Uhm . . ."

Opening his eyes, "Just listen to the record," he said, heading down the stairs.

9.

AND WHAT DO you know. Chuck Berry *could* play a guitar like he was ringing a bell.

Boom pop, boom boom pop, boom pop, boom boom pop, the drumsticks Thomas had given me a few days before and two pillows on my bed coming together to keep surprisingly good time to any number of raging rock and roll tunes, wopbobpaloobopa-wopbamboom black boy Little Richard neck and neck with piano-pummelling white boy Jerry Lee Lewis for the title of my all-time drumming favourite so far.

Boom pop, boom boom pop, boom pop, boom boom pop.

10.

"YOU?" Kelorn said.

"Yeah, me," I said. "What's so hard to believe about that?"

The blowout between us of a few weeks before was by now long forgotten, me admitting that my yelling at Making Waves customers was not a sound business practice, Kelorn agreeing to let me have my full rootsy turn on the store turntable. Little Richard, therefore, in all his shrieking glory, implored Lucille to please come back where she belonged while Kelorn indexed a fat stack of new Making Waves volumes and I climbed up and down the room's rolling wooden ladder, shelving this newest arrival under POETRY and that one under POLITICAL SELF-DEFENCE.

Under the latter heading were several copies of the *Manual for Draft-Age Immigrants to Canada*, the only book you could always count on taking home with you from Making Waves, a how-to-avoid-the-U.S.-draft guide published by a small Canadian press that Kelorn always made sure to have in stock and that was always gratis to whoever was legit in their need. Every week more and more nervous-looking guys my age and even younger with a variety of American accents were dropping by the shop. The word was starting to get out that having a moral conscience wasn't considered a crime in Canada and that the Making Waves Bookstore at 189 Harbord was a good place to find out how to keep your hands ethically clean and Vietnamese shrapnel out of your ass.

"Sometimes it seems like everybody I meet is a musician, so why not me?" I said. "Besides, it's fun, you know? Bashing away for a couple hours is a good way to blow off steam. Almost as good as sex."

"Now, don't start getting weird on me, Bill," Kelorn said.

I looked at the clock on the wall and saw that it was close to six, nearly quitting time. Christine was coming by to pick me up to grab something to eat, but I was going to have to talk my way out of the movie we'd planned for after. Although I'd known for a couple of days now that tonight was going to be the night Thomas unveiled the rehearsal space he'd rented, a room on the third floor of a four-storey Victorian full of a bunch of other bands and located right smack dab between the Mynah Bird and the Penny Farthing, I'd neglected to tell Christine not only about Thomas's bass-playing plans for her but also my own recent pillow-whacking drumming workouts. Mine was and still is, I guess, a mind not of the particularly confrontational kind, especially if things are rolling along just fine. But I'd tell her. Sooner or later.

But sooner or later always eventually becomes right now, and right now right now meant Christine coming through the door of the shop and kissing me on the lips and Kelorn on the cheek and asking if she could put a poster up in the front window.

"Certainly, dear. Where are you playing?" Kelorn said.

"It's not for me," Christine said, scotch-taping the hand-drawn flyer to the inside of the window. "It's the Diggers. They're organizing a 'Shut Down Yorkville' campaign because of all the traffic and pollution and stuff. Do you know what that fascist

Lamport said about Yorkville in the paper yesterday? 'Frankly, I'd like to see it become a shopping centre.' That's an actual quote, I'm not kidding you. A shopping centre. Over my dead body, you fat, bourgeois pig, over my dead body."

A quick explanation and a guilty confession.

The Yorkville Diggers were the Toronto arm of Haight-Ashbury's Diggers, hippie do-gooders who worked hard to get free clothes, food, and medical attention to the swelling number of Yorkville's penniless. Now the Diggers wanted city controller Allan Lamport and Mayor William Dennison to make the village clean and safe again by designating it an automobile-free zone. While they were at it, they also wanted the powers-that-were to get rid of all the cops who'd started hanging around and to basically give Yorkville back to us, the kids, the ones who'd turned the developers and the politicians in their back pockets onto the idea of it being such a swell place to begin with. Those are the facts.

The truth of the matter was that as much as the idea of a pack of drooling businessmen stumbling all over each other in the fight to see who would be the first to bulldoze down the village to make way for upscale shopping boutiques and exclusive dog-grooming salons bothered me just as much as it did Christine, the light of pure indignation that burned in her dark brown eyes whenever she raged on about some injustice or another was matched only by the hot flush of moral fervour that came to her cheeks, her accusing, clenched jaw and fight-ready fists illustrating wonderfully well that she damn well believed every word she said. So, okay: Christine thrilled me with the way she could hate. And sometimes I even wondered whether, if somehow I were given the choice, I wouldn't retain just a few slimy businessmen on the side if eliminating all the evil in the world would mean never seeing her so angry and so beautiful ever again.

"Maybe Bill and Thomas can lend their support to the cause in song," Kelorn said.

Poster plastered, Christine put the rest of the pile and her roll of tape on the counter and accepted the cup of tea Kelorn pushed her way. Kelorn's smile catching, Christine blew on her tea and began to cool down herself. Cutting her eyes my way, "Don't tell me Thomas has got you writing songs with him now," she said.

"Oh, I'm afraid it goes beyond that, my dear," Kelorn said. "Thomas has enlisted Bill as—get ready for it, now—his drummer."

I scurried up the ladder with the last of the unshelved books like a dog-treed squirrel. What the hell had I been thinking? Me, a musician. Pretentious asshole.

But before *Zen Buddhism: Selected Writings of D.T. Suzuki* was spinewise upward in its proper place, Christine laughed warmly and predicted that I'd make a fine drummer. But of course she would. Christine despised the bad and loved the good and therefore was altogether good herself. And Christine loved me. Christine loved Bill. I jumped down from the ladder five steps from the floor.

"I'm not saying I'll be any good at it right away," I said. "But it's really a gas, you know? And I'm willing to work, I'm ready to put in the time. And Thomas, he's got a kit waiting for me over at where he's rented us a rehearsal space and he says he's going to give me an extra key so I can go over there and practise any time I want. And maybe"—it was all coming out now, flood of relief flooding—"you could come by sometime and, you know, jam with us." *Jam.* Hot damn, I really did feel like a musician now. "I mean, if you're into it."

And not for Thomas's sake but for my own, this last invitation. Because whatever feels good you want your closest ones to share. You see a sunset of particular postcard beauty and you wish she was there to see it with you, simple as that.

Finishing her cup of tea and gathering up her posters, "Maybe," she said. "Why don't we check out your drums and have a look at this space tonight after we eat."

"Okay," I said. Everything really does work out in the end if you procrastinate long enough, I thought.

Goodbyes and see-you-tomorrows said, but before we could ding the doorbell on our way out, "Oh, I almost forgot, hold on a sec'," Kelorn called out. She went to the shelves and came back with a copy of the *Manual for Draft-Age Immigrants to Canada*. "Give this to Thomas when you see him, will you?"

"Thomas?" I said. "What for?" Thomas was one of the lucky ones, was 4-F—an irregular heartbeat—had told me so over our very first beer.

"I ran into him at the Grab Bag the other day and he said someone who lived downstairs from him wanted a copy. Insisted on paying for it, too. Practically forced me to take the money."

I took the book, and Christine and I headed off hand in hand, the protest posters in her free hand, the book for Thomas's friend in mine.

11.

ROOT VEGETABLE COUSCOUS sitting in both our bellies nicely, the fiery Tunisian red sauce that went along with it helping to keep us warm underneath our jackets, Christine and I strolled a lovers' stroll down freshly snow-dusted Bloor Street tight to each other's hip.

"So you haven't actually seen this place Thomas has rented?" she said.

"Nope, tonight's the night."

"But you say it's big enough for an entire band to practise in?"

"It's great, isn't it? And we're going to need every inch of it, believe me. Besides Thomas and me, eventually there'll be a steel guitarist and a bass player. Plus, Thomas says we're going to want to get a big Hammond B-3 organ sound sometimes, so we'll need space for that, too."

Not seeing us but right there anyway down Bloor at Avenue Road, coming out the front door of the Park Plaza Hotel, there was Thomas.

"Blonde or brunette?" I asked.

Christine laughed. "What makes you so sure she's not a redhead?"

"Maybe she is," I said. Thomas wasn't so far away we couldn't have yelled out his name and caught up, but we lagged behind on purpose to keep on being just the two of us.

"Well, whoever she is, it's not anybody we know," Christine said. "That place is ritzy. Like, fifty bucks a night, minimum."

We both considered this for a moment.

"Hey, where *does* Thomas get all his dough from, anyway?" Christine said.

"I don't know. I never asked."

"I mean, the way he's always paying for all of us whenever we go out? And the rehearsal space and the drums he got for you? He doesn't work—I've never even heard him mention having to get a job."

"He said the drums were a used set he bought off somebody in the village," I said. "And the rent he's paying on the place is cheap, lots of bands use it to play there."

"But it costs something, right?"

"Well, yeah." We walked in silence some more.

"Boo!"

Thomas leapt out in front of us from around the darkened corner of the Park Plaza, screaming and waving both hands in the air like some kind of psychotic windmill. Seeing us knocked back and scattered apart over the sidewalk, he let his arms fall to his sides and smiled.

"Got you two, didn't I?" he said.

Heart still pounding but at least out of my throat now, "Yeah, you got us," I said.

"Christ, Thomas," Christine said.

"Ah, come on now, y'all, I was only having a little fun."

Knowing that Christine was justifiably a little more sensitive to men lunging out of the dark at her than me, even in jest, I grabbed her hand again, gave it a squeeze, and nodded up at the hotel. "Who's your rich friend?" I said.

Thomas looked up high himself; after the briefest contemplation, let the cold wind deliver a carefully blown pucker to some unknown room on some undetermined floor. Kiss delivered, "Like my Uncle Pen used to say, 'A gentleman never kisses and tells.'"

Christine shook her head but couldn't resist a slight smile. "It sounds like this Uncle Pen of yours is quite a guy," she said.

I already knew all about Uncle Pen, had heard over our first beers together how Thomas, an only child, had been brought up by his uncle after both of his parents had been killed in a head-on car wreck when he was a still a baby.

"Rest his sweet soul, indeed he was, Miss Christine, indeed he was."

"Your uncle," Christine said, "he's passed on?"

"To a better world than this one almost four years now."

"I thought you said you worked on his farm this past summer picking cotton to help get the cash to move up here," I said.

Thomas shifted his weight from one cowboy boot to the other, lifted his eyes above the roof of the Park Plaza.

"I did, I did work on his farm this summer," he said. "It's just that it's not his farm any more. You see, the bank, they came in and foreclosed on his place before he died. Two rainless summers in a row and that was that. You call some place home for twenty years and with a couple strokes of a pen by a big-city lawyer you're working for your neighbour down the road."

Christine and I both shook our heads.

"A family by the name of the Hannahs, they own the place now. But everybody still calls it Uncle Pen's farm. And every summer after he had that heart attack, I hired myself out to the Hannahs so I could be close to Uncle Pen again. The morning dew on that cotton in those fields and the hot dust from the combine in the afternoon sun were as much a part of the old boy as anything else."

In spite of all his talk about scorching Mississippi summers, standing there on the street corner made it feel even colder than it was. Putting my hands in my coat pockets, I remembered the book Kelorn had given me.

"Almost forgot, here," I said, handing it over.

Thomas took the book. Stared at it.

"Kelorn said you wanted a copy," I said. "For your friend, she said."

"Oh, right," he said, folding the slim book in two and sticking it in his back pocket. "Thanks. Thanks a lot. I'll make sure he gets it. I know he'll really appreciate it." He reached for his wallet. "Here, let me give you some—"

"You already paid her."

Wallet halfway out, "I did?"

"She said you did."

"Oh, yeah," he said, pushing it back. "Now I remember."

"C'mon you two, let's go," Christine said. "And I hope this place you rented is better heated than Bill's room. I almost had to wear my clothes to bed last night."

The big grin was back on Thomas's face.

"No need to worry about that, Miss Christine. We're well-heated, well-stocked, and fully soundproof. I think you're going to find things most accommodating. I dare say y'all are going to learn to just love it there."

12.

IT WAS A LIVING room–sized room with a scuffed hardwood floor and there weren't any windows. There was a pair of rickety, glass-paned French doors along the back wall that led to a black metal balcony, and hundreds of yellow, pink, and brown cardboard egg cartons had been carefully stapled to all four walls to make sure Thomas's music stayed in and that of all the other bands in the building stayed out. There were musical instruments everywhere you looked and a Panasonic seven-inch reel-to-reel recording machine and two stand-up microphones in the middle of the floor. And there was no smoking allowed. When Christine reached into her shoulder bag as she toured her way around from drum kit to electric guitar to fiddle, Thomas was one step ahead of her.

"Miss Christine, I'm sorry, but I must insist, no."

One hand absently rummaging around in her purse for her pack, the other running a careful finger along the body of an aged mandolin in its worn black case, Christine looked up a little startled.

"Sorry," she said, pulling her hand back from the instrument. "It's just that it's so beautiful. It's a mandolin, right?"

Explaining what he'd really meant, how smoking was very dangerous in an old house like this, "But you can look at, touch, and play anything in this room you want," Thomas said. "Nothing would please me more, in fact."

Christine didn't need any more encouragement. She picked up the mandolin and brought it low against her body like an undersized guitar. Thomas placed two fingers underneath its neck and gently raised the instrument upward, chest-high, where it was intended to be played.

"You have good taste, Miss Christine. This is a Gibson F-5, the same kind Bill Monroe made famous in the twenties."

"Are they that old?" she said.

"This one is."

Christine lost for the moment trying to adjust her fingers to the tiny fretboard and its tightly tuned strings, Thomas caught me staring at the black drum kit on the other side of the room and nodded me over.

I knew I should have wanted to sit right down and start bashing away—as much fun as it had been, pounding on my pillows and mattress at home was definitely starting to lose its beginner's charm—but all at once I was trembling eleven years old again and petrified to kiss Tracy Linden behind the gym bleachers my first ever kiss on the lips because, my God, I realized I had absolutely no idea what I was supposed to do. And what if I went ahead and just did it anyway but mangled it all so badly—my nose in her eye; my lips too hard, too soft—that she rips herself away from me and I am known to every girl for all time everywhere as Bill "The Kissing Geek" Hansen? A first kiss, after all, is forever.

"Nice," I said, risking a timid forefinger touch to the crash cymbal.

"Nothing special," he said, "pretty much your basic snare, tom-tom, floor tom setup. Should get the job done, though. And may the Good Lord keep you from the temptation to play ten-minute drum solos, Amen."

I smiled and gave the cymbal another light rap.

Thomas picked the drumsticks off the snare. "Feel like having a go?" he said.

Christine stopped moving her fingers over the strings of the mandolin and everything all of a sudden just a little too quiet. She looked over at Thomas offering me the sticks and I moved my eyes from her to him to the door of the studio, wishing I were somehow on its other side and down the stairs and back home alone in my room.

Laying the mandolin back in its case, "So, Thomas, what's the deal?" Christine said. "Where'd you get the money for this place and all this great stuff?"

Now Thomas was the one with his eyes darting toward the door. But only for an instant. He carefully placed the sticks back on top of the drums and cleared his throat.

"Well, I was going to let y'all in on this sooner or later, but I figured we'd be a little further down the road as a group. But you've got a right to know and I guess now's as good a time as any."

Picking up on the words *we* and *group*, Christine caught my eye but I looked right back at Thomas.

"You see, in the South," he said, "there's a long tradition of someone in the community who's not actually an artist themself lending what they do have—money, basically—to help out someone else who God has blessed with talent and vision. It's like in medieval times, kings and queens giving the cats who wrote the symphonies a salary to live on so they could do their thing. You've got to understand, the South is still a very feudal place."

"You've got a patron?" I said.

"No, *we've* got a patron," he answered. "Me, you, Christine—the band, Buckskin, The Duckhead Secret Society."

This time more than a mere attempt at making puzzled eye contact. "Me?" Christine said.

"But who?" I interrupted. "Who's bankrolling us? I mean you—who's bankrolling you?"

Thomas put a finger to his lips and shook his head.

"That is the one and only condition our benefactor has demanded in return for his generous support. Complete anonymity. Rest assured, there is total understanding and an absolute, mutual respect between our camp and him regarding artistic priorities and objectives in terms of what Interstellar North American Music is all about and what we all want it to accomplish. But for reasons he obviously feels are important, only I know who signs the cheques."

"You're getting all this money from somebody you don't even know?" Christine said. The tone of her voice tasting more like a challenge than an actual question, I worried how Thomas was going to take it. But at least she wasn't thinking about what he'd meant by talking about her and the band any more.

But Thomas wasn't angry at all, just sat down on the paint-chipped white radiator and rested his hands on his knees. "It's like this," he said.

"One day not long before I came up here and met y'all, I'm playing for spare change in front of the post office back home in Jackson when along comes this old-timer in the most beautiful white suit you ever saw hobbling up to drop off a letter. But instead of doing his business and being on his way, he ends up standing there leaning on his cane in that hundred-degree heat watching and listening to me play. Even when I finally say to him, 'Afternoon, sir,' he doesn't blink, just whacks his cane a couple times on the pavement and lifts it off the ground and jabs it in the direction of my guitar like he wants to hear another song.

"I'm no nostalgia act, but it's just me and him so I think what the heck, I'll make the old boy's day, give him what he wants. A little Red Foley, a little Johnny Horton—you know, hits from the forties and early fifties. But I'm no more than a quarter of the way through 'The Battle of New Orleans' when the old man raps that cane of his harder than he has yet and barks out at me, 'If I wanted to listen to the goddamn radio, boy, I'd listen to the goddamn radio! Tell me something I don't already know!'

"And right then and there I knew that he knew. *I knew*. So of course I go right into Interstellar North American Music overdrive and let it all hang out, give him the whole white soul royal treatment I knew he'd so deeply appreciate and understand. How long we were together there under that sun I can't honestly say. Long enough that I couldn't keep my lids open any longer because of the sweat pouring down my face and stinging my eyes. And when I finally opened them back up, the old man was gone. And I went home knowing that everything—*everything*—was going to be all right."

Thomas leaned back against the wall and closed his eyes.

Christine and I looked at each other. "But what about the money?" she said.

"Yeah," I said, "what about the money?"

Thomas slowly reopened his eyes. He looked surprised he was here with us and not back in Mississippi.

"In my tip jar there was a business card with a P.O. Box number on it and on the other side a short note from the old man saying for me to send him a bill whenever I needed to buy something to help spread the word of my music."

Christine and I were thinking the same thing, but, as usual, she was the one to say it.

"That's it?" she said.

"I don't know what you mean, Miss Christine."

"I mean, you're saying that all you've got to do to rent a studio like this or buy any instrument or new piece of equipment is mail off an invoice to this guy you met only that once and that's it?"

"Well, yeah, that about sums it up," Thomas said.

Christine looked at the floor. I looked at the drum kit. Thomas kept looking from Christine to me and back, no idea at all why we weren't as thrilled with the whole arrangement as he was.

I tapped the crash cymbal again, but all it did was make a little noise for not very long at all, and then everything was like it was before.

But then Thomas finally saw the light, finally had us both figured out. He put his arm around my shoulder and held out a hand to Christine. I gave her a nervous glance and she did what he wanted.

"You two," he said, pulling me closer, squeezing Christine's hand. "That is why y'all are Thomas's all-time favourite couple, do you know that? You are, you really are." We both lobbed back toothy grins in return for the compliment. Whatever the hell it meant.

"But don't you two worry a lick about that old man, you hear? He's gonna be fine, just fine. Because he's rich, you see? More money than one man ever needs—more money than he'll ever know what to do with, believe me. And I don't have to remind either of you of what the Good Book says about a rich man, the eye of a needle, and a camel. Because what that old man is doing is helping himself pass through that needle."

Thomas drew me tighter to him and was squeezing Christine's hand so hard I could tell he was hurting her.

"Soul by proxy," he said. "Friends, we are soul by proxy."

If the wrinkled apparition hunched over his cane in the doorway hadn't materialized, I think Thomas might have started sobbing for joy. Or crushed Christine's hand.

Spotting the old man, though, "Scotty!" Thomas shouted. He let go of Christine and me and rushed toward the door. In a shabby dark suit with a sick-looking yellow daffodil wilting out of his top button and carrying a beat-up black violin case and a brown paper shopping bag full of newspapers and scribbled-on legal paper sticking out of the top, Scotty definitely wasn't the millionaire old-timer of Thomas's story.

Six-feet-and-then-some Thomas tenderly entwined his arm with the diminutive old man's. "Buckskin, Miss Christine, I'd like you to meet Mr. Scotty Robinson. Scotty, sir, this is—"

"Save it, hippie boy," the old man interrupted, "there'll be plenty of time for that nonsense later." He broke free of Thomas's arm, pivoted on his feet, and looked up high and right at him. The old man's eyes were watery but almost as glimmering ice blue as Thomas's.

"Are you still going to buy me a beer tonight or are you going to turn out to be just another one of these goddamn fast-food people who believes that a promise made to a decorated war veteran isn't worth the breeze it was blown on?"

Turning to us, "What do y'all say we go out and do a little celebrating our first night all together at the studio?" Thomas said. "We can start practising tomorrow."

The two of them on that side of the room and Christine and I over on the other, it didn't seem like such a bad idea to keep it that way.

"I'm buying, y'all," Thomas added. Then, leaving off the "y'all," he repeated what he'd just said, this time speaking slowly and right into the old man's face.

"Now that's more like it," he replied. Motioning to Christine and me, "You two come along, too." Jabbing his thumb up at the towering Thomas, "You wouldn't leave a defenceless senior citizen all alone with this maniac, would you?"

After running around Mississippi on business all week, Thomas's father couldn't be expected to be the one to take him and his sister. Saturday mornings are for eighteen holes at the Rattlesnake Golf and Country Club and maybe afterwards a few drinks and a late lunch. And Christ, even then it's not just fun and games—how many times did a deal with a new supplier get made at the Nineteenth Hole over the third highball of the afternoon? His mother, of course, being a good Southern lady, doesn't know how to drive, and even though the maid, Selma, does, how would it look to have a Negro steering one of your two brand new '54 Cadillacs down main street in the middle of the afternoon?

No, it's for situations like this that Thomas's father keeps one-armed Jimmy Bowman, a retired Jackson policeman, on call as the family driver. Every Saturday morning Mr. Bowman comes by the Graham house at 9:15 sharp to take Thomas and Becky on their weekly shopping trip.

Miss Becky insists upon being driven, first, to Teen World Junction for this week's must-have outfit, followed by at least an hour at Rankin Footwear for a new pair of shoes to match. Accessories from Perkins Fashions and a basket full of cosmetics at Spencers' Drugstore and her usual hot fudge sundae at the Soda Works conclude the trip, Mr. Bowman patiently taking Miss Becky wherever she wants to go and waiting in the car out front until she decides it's time to move along. Her younger brother isn't anywhere near as demanding.

Before chauffeuring Miss Becky to the first of her many stops, Mr. Bowman drops Thomas off on the sidewalk in front of the Sound Shop, usually just as the young clerk inside is unlocking the front door and yawning his way through his first cup of coffee. When Mr. Bowman reappears with the Cadillac a few hours later, a spent Becky in the back seat surrounded by her small mountain of packages, Thomas climbs in beside her and sits there quiet and still the entire ride home with a neat stack of 45s on his lap and his eyes fixed directly on the road ahead.

Home—the car refuelled, washed, and returned to the garage, Mr. Bowman paid by Selma for his morning's labour—Thomas and his sister go to their respective rooms, Becky slowly, the sheen on today's purchases already beginning to fade, Thomas quickly, having to remind himself twice on his way up the stairs that running is not allowed in the house (his father, when he's home, with the belt and temper to confirm it). First Thomas's and then Becky's bedroom doors shut tight. Selma, in the kitchen downstairs washing fresh strawberries for dinner tonight, softly hums to herself an old gospel song, apart from the sound of cold running water and the ticking of the grandfather clock in the front room, the old house's only noise.

Thomas locks his bedroom door and heads right for the record player. Placing the first disc on the turntable, he carefully sets the needle down and sits on the floor cross-legged in front of the speakers and waits.

First he just listens, lets the record play, allows the music to engulf him like the foaming wild August waves he wades into every summer at the family cottage at Myrtle Beach.

Song done—Thomas's absolute favourite of the moment, Hillbilly Cat Elvis and his "That's All Right Mama"—he puts the arm back at the beginning and this time tries to really hear all that's there, to get a feel for how the whole thing manages to fit together so magically, so completely, to sound so unbelievably reined-in reckless.

Before picking up his Fender from its case to begin the long task of attempting to work his way through Scotty Moore's electric guitar lines, Thomas takes a short break and sits studying the picture of Elvis on the record sleeve. Eventually he sets the needle back down again and stands in front of the full-length mirror hanging on the door to his walk-in closet with his acoustic guitar strapped over his shoulder waiting for the sound of Moore's sharp Fender trebling to get things started and his own body stirring. He doesn't have to wait long.

Bill Black's steady stand-up bass-slapping starts right in soon after Scotty does and straightaway Thomas is swivelling his hips and shaking his hands and knees and snarling at the girls in the front row just like Elvis himself did last spring when Thomas saw him at the City Auditorium.

"That's All Right Mama" finishes up with Thomas on the edge of the stage staring deep into the adoring eyes of Debbie McDonald, the prettiest girl in his grade seven class, Thomas pitching his guitar over his shoulder and leaving the crazed audience dying for the favour of just one more.

For the next who-knows-how-many hours Thomas is back on the floor in front of the hi-fi, cradling the unplugged electric white Fender in his lap and working away on the lead to the song as best as his eleven-year-old fingers will allow. A little after six o'clock Selma knocks softly but insistently in steady little rap-taps on his door.

"Thomas."

Thomas lifts his head from the guitar.

Selma doesn't bother knocking again, knows that he's listening.

"Thomas, your daddy called from his club and he'll be home any minute now so you put your records and things away and start getting ready for supper now, you hear? You don't need to wear no tie tonight, your jacket and good pants'll do, it's just gonna be you *and Miss Becky and your daddy. Your momma's still not feeling too well but she's gonna be just fine so don't you worry."*

Thomas goes back to his guitar.

Not wanting to raise her voice for fear of disturbing Mrs. Graham resting in her own room at the other end of the hall, Selma comes closer to the bedroom door, her cheek pressed right against the wood.

"You know how your daddy don't like for you children to make him late in getting his supper, now."

Thomas presses the strings of the guitar harder.

"Thomas, you know how he hates it."

His little fingers flying up and down the fretboard now, desperate for the secret of how Scotty does it, Thomas begins to scat along with Elvis as the song reaches its end for the umpteenth time that day, his own picking and singing almost managing to drown Selma out.

"Ah da-da-dee-dee-dee-dee."

"Thomas . . ."

Both of them hear the crunch of hot gravel under the tires of Thomas's father's Cadillac tearing into the driveway.

"Thomas . . ."

"Dee-dee-dee-dee-dee."

13.

AND WHAT A HAPPY ragtag crew we must have made! Learning to play together, learning how to get along, learning all about that most elusive of lost chords, life. Ta dah! And weren't we all on the way to Interstellar North American Music worship right out of the gate, right off the bat, just like that? Sorry to disappoint.

More than a week after we'd first toured the studio, Christine still didn't know she'd been conscripted into the band, Thomas still didn't know she didn't know, and I was still too petrified to let anyone hear me play the drums. But at least I was playing. I knew I didn't have a clue what I was doing, but it felt good to do it anyway, too good to stop. All I could hear was the thunder of the musical gods, not my own puny little hallelujahs.

Somehow I always managed to find an excuse not to be in the studio whenever Thomas said he would be—overtime at work, I'd plead, or girlfriend stuff, or fighting off the beginning of a bad cold, or whatever other untruth happened to be lying around and handy. Then Thomas himself actually got sick—the flimsy leather jacket he'd been wearing since the fall no match for his first real sample of Canadian winter—and at least for a little while I didn't have to listen to him gripe about how the band hadn't started rehearsing yet. To try to provide a little cheer, I lied to him over the phone and said I'd made an extra studio key for Christine and that she was there almost every night working away on improving her chops on the bass, an instrument it turned out she'd played in her high school's senior band. Thomas sneezed and said she should be, that we had a lot of work ahead of us.

Through a plugged nose, "Next week we start, Buckskin. Rain or shine, the ball gets put in play next week."

I said I couldn't have been more excited and told him to drink lots of liquids and get plenty of rest.

14.

WHEN I SAY THAT no one heard me play, that's not quite right. Maybe Scotty was deaf and didn't actually listen to me, but he was there in the studio almost every night I was, hunched over the rickety green card table Thomas had set up in the corner as a sort of break space for the band, working away as usual on his poetry. Here, he'd carry on not that much differently than he did at the Riverboat, where he rubbed wrinkled elbows with us hippies, or at his own favourite watering hole, the Palm Grove Lounge, the downstairs drinking arm of the Embassy Tavern.

Ramming open the door of the studio with the rubber end of his cane, Scotty would nod/scowl at me behind the drums like he was reluctantly bestowing permission for me to continue playing and without a word shuffle off to the card table. Impeccably slovenly dressed as always—antiquated suit jacket, egg yolk–spattered tie, beat-up black Oxfords—he'd carefully unpack his out-of-tune violin and the contents of his paper sack onto the table. Today's *Toronto Daily Star*; a wide variety of different coloured pens, each for performing a different editorial task; and paper. Lots and lots of paper. And every long, legal-sized piece covered top to bottom with Scotty's indecipherable chicken scratch poetry. Only his customary glass of draft beer was missing. He managed to make do with a small silver flask full of cheap scotch from which he'd periodically nip before returning to the inside pocket of his jacket.

The first time he burst into the room while I was practising I froze in mid–drum roll, caught in the act, like there I was with my dick in my hand and half the world was watching. He barely even acknowledged me, merely undid the bottom button on his suit jacket, sat down at the table, and got down to work putting his portable office in order. He finally turned around in his grey metal chair.

"You think you're going to disturb me or something?" he said.

I knew he was expert at reading lips. "How'd you know I wasn't playing?" I said.

Slapping the sole of one of his Oxfords against the hardwood floor a couple of times to make his point, "I'm deaf, not dead, you know," he said. "And don't you or anybody else ever forget it, either."

With that, he swivelled back around and began to furiously scratch out line after line of apparently unworthy verse. Run or drum? The ball was clearly in my court.

I played.

It was like when I was a kid and it was two o'clock in the morning and I was downstairs in the family room with the *Late, Late Show* turned way down low so my parents wouldn't know I was awake, wondering why Ellen Simpson liked Jack Tate better than she liked me. Although Snowball, our family Westy, had never, as far as I knew, known the triple-heartburn package of lust, jealousy, and complete and utter self-doubt that makes up a fourteen-year-old's definition of love, having him beside me at the other end of that couch felt good. Even if he was sound asleep on his back with all four white furry legs stuck straight up in the air. Snowball was *there*. And sometimes that's not only enough, that's exactly what is needed.

So I played. And Scotty slashed with his red pen. And I played. And Scotty scribbled with his blue pen. And I played. And Scotty pulled from his flask, wiped his mouth on his coat sleeve, and read what he'd just written. And I played.

A half an hour in he swung around in his chair.

"Slow that down a little and you might actually have something there," he said.

Naturally I stopped playing. Of course he let me have it.

"If that's your idea of slowing it down, Thomas is in a lot worse shape than I thought."

"You can feel it that much?" I said. "Just through the vibrations?"

"Enough to know that a waltz doesn't sound like a goddamn jackhammer."

I stared down between my feet at a black boot smudge on the floor and wondered how many drummers have ever been bawled out by a deaf guy. While I sat there trying to figure out a way to tell Thomas that he'd have to find another percussionist, I looked up to see Scotty's feet moving together to some sort of rhythm.

Left Oxford tap tap, right Oxford tap; left Oxford tap tap, right Oxford tap.

Imagine my surprise, then, when I realized it was me—me—making those old shoes move. Imagine. Go on, try.

15.

BY THE TIME THOMAS got over his cold it was almost Christmas and the Duckhead Secret Society was just going to have to wait. Phlegm-free and vertical again, with both cowboy boots firmly planted on the ground, Thomas didn't take the news that his entire rhythm section was going to be spending the next several days at the homes of their respective relatives in quite the generous spirit of the season I'd hoped. It was the day before the night before Christmas and we were at the nearly deserted Riverboat for what I, at least, was calling a goodbye cup of coffee. We'd agreed to meet at two that afternoon and he'd showed up a half-hour late. He must have been at it since early that morning because he was already as juiced as I'd ever seen him. I ignored the coffee he bought me spiked with his own whisky. Drunks at Christmas-time always depressed me. Still do.

"Don't think I don't understand that you and Miss Christine have obligations that have got to be fulfilled," he said. "Don't think that because of my unfortunate orphaned condition I'm not sympathetic to the duties of kin. Because I am, Buckskin, believe me, I am. Let there be no misunderstanding between us on this point." He laid five cold fingers across my hand and leaned across the table, obviously his cool-headed feverish old self again. I nodded back as heartfelt as I could muster in the hope of breaking free of his cadaver's touch and getting one step closer to the door.

Because it was Christmas! In spite of how counter-culturally uncool it sounded, well . . . it was Christmas!

I wanted to taste my mum's hot mincemeat tarts with a plop of homemade whipped cream on top and see her in her old blue cardigan, the one with the bottom button missing, the one she alway wore around the house whenever she was in a serious baking state. I wanted to drink hot apple cider and watch *Bonanza* and *Gunsmoke* and *The Fugitive* on TV with my dad and get bugged at the smog of cherry smoke from his pipe filling up the downstairs rec room. I wanted to sleep in my old room again and not get up until noon and wear my green leather high-school football jacket and take long walks with Snowball after lunch and leave tracks in the freshly fallen snow down by the creek and maybe afterwards take a nap on the couch in the basement in front of the fireplace. I wanted to go home for Christmas.

"All of these family matters are legitimate and true," Thomas said, "all of this I admit to you as absolutely valid, one hundred percent, all of it. But I ask you this, here's the thing I want you to really, really think about: Even if there are unavoidable responsibilities that you two have, why should this mean that what we've got going here has to go to hell in a handbasket just because of it?"

Thomas stopped his pitch just long enough to turn around and two-finger motion to the waitress for another couple of coffees, although I'd barely touched mine and he definitely didn't need another. In deference to my dad picking me up at my place in less than an hour, I waved the order away behind Thomas's back. The girl, tie-dyed and long-haired and maybe nineteen, smiled at me and seemed thankful for the change in plans. Mincemeat tarts and pipe smoke and a childhood dog pal of her own, I thought.

"Listen," he said, "here's what you do, here's what you and Miss Christine both do. Tomorrow night, each of you shoots on up there to your parents' place and drops off your presents and has a glass of eggnog with the folks and kisses your mama on the cheek and shakes your daddy's hand and does what every good boy and girl is supposed to do. That's only what's right and proper, and you're going to do it, and that's the way it should be. Okay. That's settled. But that's tomorrow night. Tonight, well, tonight—"

"I already told you, Thomas, Christine's gone."

"But she'll be back. I mean, she's—"

"She left this morning on the train with her mum and dad and little sister to spend the holidays with her brother and his wife in Montreal. She won't be back until sometime late next week."

Thomas opened his mouth like he was going to say something, but his lips fell shut before anything managed to come out. He took a long, greedy pull from his coffee and whisky. I felt bad for him, saw how disappointed he was, but Thomas always seemed to get what he wanted and maybe not getting it for a change might not be such a horrible thing.

"Look, thanks for the caffeine," I said. "But I've still got to pack before my old man shows up." I took a last drink to try to make some kind of appreciative dent. Our waitress was busy piling chairs on top of tables.

Thomas looked up from the empty cup still in his hand. In a quieter voice than I was used to, "But what about us?" he said. "What about the Duckhead Secret Society?"

"We're coming back, Thomas," I said. "We're not going away forever."

"Sure," he said. He looked like a miserable little boy being left behind for summer vacation by all his neighbourhood buddies.

"Are you going to be all right?" I said. I knew he wasn't going back to Mississippi for the holidays—"No money to get me there, and now that Uncle Pen's gone, not much reason to go"—and I worried at the idea of him hanging around Yorkville feeling sorry for himself with too much time on his hands. But I had to go. My dad would be honking the horn of the station wagon in front of my place any time now. I really had to go.

"I'll be okay," he said.

"Are you sure?"

"I'll be fine."

All of the chairs except ours up on the tables now, the waitress was making time wiping down the counter area waiting for us to finish up.

"Hey, I've got an idea," I said.

He lifted his eyes.

"Come home with me."

He looked back down at his cup. "That's your idea?"

"Sure, why not? You'll eat some home-cooked food for a change, sleep in a nice clean bed, and we'll both just kick back for a few days. Do us both some good. By the time Christine gets back we'll be all charged up and ready to go. What do you say?"

Thomas managed a tiny smile and stood up; put his hand on my shoulder.

"Thank you," he said. "I appreciate the offer. I do."

"But no?"

"But no. But thank you, Buckskin, I mean it."

"What are you going to do then?" I said. "Nobody wants to spend Christmas all by themselves. And Yorkville's going to be a ghost town. C'mon, come home with me. It'll be fun."

"No," he said. "Thank you, but no."

He slowly pulled on his jacket.

"Don't you worry about me," he said. "I'm going to be fine. I'm going to be just fine."

Mississippi born and raised there, Memphis boarded and schooled there, Harvard, Massachusetts, one semester and too much of Professor Leary's LSD dropped and dropped out there, sunny, southern California where anybody who knew anything knew it was all going down down there. The new music. A new way of relating. A new way of being. New age . . .

Yeah Yeah Yeah. Far out. Out of sight. Groovy. Although, to be honest, some interesting sounds and even a few soulful souls if you can manage to avoid the peace sign–cramped fingers poking in your face everywhere you turn. But no twangy promised land, that's for sure. And this a good lesson to remember. For the kingdom of Interstellar North American Music lies within you, Thomas, not anywhere out there anyhow. Remember to remember this.

But Joshua Tree. If he'd never come to L.A. he never would have heard of Joshua Tree. From a guy at a hoot night at the Troubadour between tokes of a shared joint between sets.

"If you want to get out of the city for a while and blow your mind, man, drop a tab and dig the desert sky at night. Go on out to Joshua Tree, you've never seen anything like it. Take 105 east for, like, two hours, then wait for the sun to go down and get out there in the middle of the desert and see something you've never seen before. Blow your fucking mind, man."

And it did. It does. It still does. Even just imagining it. Even this far away and a bunch of freezing Canadian months since the last time there.

Getting ready to go, it always goes like this: score, fill up the tank of the Harley, and cruise by Ciro's to see who wants to be this weekend's old lady. Thomas is no player—not yet, anyway—but he's got a nice smile and is six-foot slinky good looking in those spacy neon cowboy threads of his, and yeah, the guy can play, no doubt about that. What the women dig most, though, is that Thomas is such an absolute gentleman, a real psychedelicate courteous cat right smack dab in the middle of Freakville, USA, the Sunset Strip, insisting on having whoever ends up riding on the back of his bike out to the desert for the weekend with him hold on to his entire stash, saying, as he helps her put on her helmet, "It's just easier this way, darlin'. Trusting somebody is just so much easier."

Thomas has called ahead and reserved his usual room at the Joshua Tree Inn, room #8—double bed, no TV, $13.50 a night—and he and she check in, get their key, and share the shower and a bar of soap to scrub the road out of their pores. Afterwards, don't bother dressing, roll a doobie or two, and kick back on top of the sheets passing the joint back and forth waiting for the sun to go down and the moon to come up and the stars over Joshua Tree to begin to do their thing.

And if nodding off for a bit, only for a bit, eventually waking up in a panic like it's the first morning of the first day of an eight-year-old's holy grail of a summer vacation. Whip on your clothes, jump on the Harley, and race off into the night in search of a place to get close to the earth next to an honest-to-goodness Joshua tree with only a single headlight to get you there and every one of the billions and billions of stars and planets God has breathed so alive tonight spearing holes of burning silver in the map of blackness behind them. Ride right into the middle of the desert darkness looking for that perfect spot in the sand. Ride and ride like you know exactly where you're going.

16.

IT WASN'T CHRISTMAS any more, just 1966 and January and cold, the piney corpses of December 25 dumped out on every freezing curb. But in spite of the snow on all the rooftops and the slush in the streets and the razor-blade winds, everybody was back and the village was its shimmy-shaking old self again, a familiar feeling of Yorkville-imminent anticipation bubbling in the pit my stomach just like it did every time I came back.

Within three hours of my return to town I'd had a big greasy breakfast by myself at Webster's, bought the newest Byrds album, *Turn! Turn! Turn!* at Record World with a pocket full of Christmas money I was determined to get rid of as quickly as possible, dropped by next door at Mont Blanc and scored a nickel bag of weed and played a game of chess with one of the waitresses, worked my way down Yorkville Avenue and stopped in for a cup of coffee and hellos at the Purple Onion, Jacques' Place, and the Mynah Bird, and, finally, when I couldn't wait any longer, dropped a dime in a payphone and dialed Thomas's number.

"Hello?"

"Thomas!"

"Buckskin!"

"Hey."

"Hey, yourself. Let's get together, buddy, let's get this show of ours on the road. These fingers of mine are practically falling off from uselessness. Meet you at the studio in an hour?"

"I'm here, I'm in the village."

"Even better. See you in ten?"

"Christine called me this morning at my parents. Her train gets in at five. I'm supposed to meet her at her place."

"So leave her a note and tell her where we'll be."

"I'll see you soon."

"Looking forward to it, Buckskin."

And so was I. Right up through when I'd slapped a hurriedly scribbled see-you-at-the-rehearsal-space-love-Bill note onto Christine's door and rushed right over, icy breath like idling-car emission as I jogged the entire way. Right up until I literally had my key in the studio door.

Maybe it was the buzz of being back in the village. Maybe it was the three quick coffees. But hearing Thomas tuning up inside, the all-of-a-sudden roller-coaster ride in my stomach told my head that something wasn't right. But I'd already turned the key in the lock, and the old warped, wooden door slowly opened up on its own power.

"Buckskin," Thomas said, looking up from his guitar, "good to see you again, brother. And, hey, I was thinking, this is great, this works out just fine. Finally we can get a bass in the hands of that woman of yours while we're all in the same room together. It looks like we're actually going to get the Duckhead Secret Society off the ground after all."

Now I remembered.

Thomas and I shook hands and stepped out onto the icy balcony and I rolled us a joint and we got caught up. I tried to pay attention, but had a few other things on my mind.

Like never having so much as even hinted to Christine how I'd had the gall to commit her to being a bass-playing backup singer in the service of Interstellar North American Music. Like having fed Thomas a steady diet of outright lies for several weeks about Christine's bass-playing progress and her own excitement over getting down to the serious work of giving the world the jump-start to the spirit it needed. Like wondering whether hopping over the balcony and into the street might be a more effective getaway than simply running out the front door when Thomas or Christine or anybody other than stone-deaf

Scotty demanded an on-the-spot demonstration of my drum-ming abilities.

A half an hour later Christine showed up with a long, deep kiss for me for a greeting and I rolled us another fat one and we all got caught up all over again. The weed was good; I was almost persuaded by its wonderful reason-wrecking effect that everything was going to work out wonderfully and not to worry so much because everything was going to work out just fine and not to worry so much because everything was going to work out wonderfully and . . . Then Thomas sucked a last toke from the joint and flicked the fluttering roach three storeys down onto Yorkville Avenue.

"You two about ready?" he said.

Christine returned Thomas's big smile and then some with her stoned own. "I'm already spaced, you guys go ahead. Besides, it's freezing out here." On her way back inside she pulled me close by the front of my jacket and gave me another long kiss, this time with enough tongue that it felt as if she was looking for something she'd lost in there. She closed the rickety French doors behind her as tight as she could to the cold and near darkness, although it was only a little after six o'clock.

Thomas put a bare hand on my shoulder. He never wore gloves, no matter how cold it got. "It's time, Buckskin," he said.

I tried to smile his smile back, but he could see it was only a try, not the easy real thing. He placed his other hand on my other shoulder and moved his face closer to mine.

"No BS, buddy," he said. "Straight up, now, no humming or hawing, right on down the line. What's troubling you?"

I didn't know what else to say, so I told him the truth. When I was all done, had nothing else to apologize for, he dropped his arms to his sides and smiled.

How can he just smile? I thought. What the hell was there to possibly smile about? Always a tight fit out on the balcony, Thomas was facing the studio, me the street, and I watched an enormous plough push a small mountain of dirty snow up onto the curb. I knew we were opposed to traffic in the village, but were we for or against snowploughs? I didn't know. Christine would have.

"You worry too much, Buckskin. You leave the worrying to me."

"But Christine isn't going to play with us, she just isn't. Although why it has to be her and why we can't get someone else who—"

He raised his hand for me to stop. "Miss Christine is essential. This is how it has to be."

He peeked over my shoulder. The harsh fluorescent light inside the studio bathed his face in spite of itself almost tender, a false moonlight soft. He put an arm around my shoulder, turned me around, and creaked open the French doors.

Sitting beside Scotty at the card table, Christine welcomed me inside with crossed arms and a look of feigned amusement. The two girls on the other side of the room giggled away like toe-tickled five-year-olds and were clearly seriously baked, not to mention unseasonably miniskirted with knee-high brown suede boots and matching belly button–cropped black turtlenecks so tight to their long skinny bodies you could almost see ribs poking through the thin, dark cotton. One of them was sloppily playing around with the bass while the other unsuccessfully tried to stop her hiccuping with three fingers to her lips.

"You didn't mention in the note you left me that I was supposed to bring a date tonight, Bill," Christine said.

I frowned and looked to Thomas for an explanation, but he was busy showing the taller girl some chord changes on the bass.

"You know as much about this as I do," I said, sitting down at the table.

"Oh, well, in that case, let me fill you in, then," she said. "Jupiter—that's Jupiter right over there in the black miniskirt, you might have noticed her already—she's one of the go-go dancers from the Mynah Bird I was telling you about that were with Thomas the night I met him at the Riverboat, remember? Well, Jupiter is now not only a go-go dancer, she's also the bass player in your band. In fact, considering that you two are going to be working together pretty closely over the next several months, it might be a good idea for you to go over there and get acquainted."

"Chris—"

"No, really, the bass and drums are the backbone of any successful group, anybody can tell you that. And I bet you two are going to make one tight little rhythm section."

"Chris—"

"Really, you should at least say hello. Jupiter," she called out, voice all high-pitched ten-year-old false girlie, "oh, Jupiter, sweetheart, this is Bill. Bill, Jupiter."

Jupiter slowly raised her eyes from the psychedelic miracle of all these really far-out sounds floating up from her fingertips and tried to focus. Eventually finding me in her sightlines, "Bill," she said, her voice a 45 record playing at 33 1/3. "Heeeyyy Biillll."

Christine turned to me in her chair and smiled. When Scotty joined in on the grinning grilling, I'd had enough.

"Thomas," I said, standing up, "we need to talk."

"Just a second, Buckskin. I think Jupiter here's almost got a handle on 'Tiger by the Tail.'"

"*Now*, Thomas. Outside." I didn't wait around to hear his answer, went out on the balcony and waited. Before I had time to roll the doobie I was telling myself I shouldn't, he was standing there beside me.

"What is this shit?" I said.

Hurt, offended, confused; he managed to convey all three.

"Buckskin, I don't—"

"Oh, fuck that, man."

Just like I never used the word *God* unless I was almost on the point of cumming, I reserved the word *man* for when I was righteously pissed off.

"I know what you're trying to do," I said. "And not only is it not going to work, it's screwing with my woman's head, which means that it's screwing with mine. If you think strapping a bass guitar onto some stoned chick—"

"You mean Jupiter?"

"Yeah, Thomas, I mean Jupiter. If you think you can make my girlfriend jealous enough to do what you want her to do and get her to join your fucking band then you're deluded."

"Buckskin . . ."

"Don't Buckskin me, man. And not only that, but how dare you try to come between Christine and me? There are certain things you don't fuck around with, certain things—"

Three quick raps on the glass balcony door spun us both around. The other miniskirted girl opened up the door far enough to be heard over the wind.

"Thomas, Jupiter's crying," she said. "That other girl, she . . . Jupiter's crying, Thomas."

And, sure enough, Jupiter *was* crying—more like shrieking, actually—as well as being slumped over the card table. She stopped sobbing long enough to look up at Thomas and me—a rainbow of dark makeup running down her face—and then began bawling all over again, burying those lovely cheekbones and lips in her folded arms on the table. Scotty stuffed his papers into his sack and grabbed his violin case.

"Peace and love, my ass," he said.

He slammed the door shut behind him and was soon followed by the still-weeping and unsteady Jupiter, aided by her friend. Near the door Jupiter once again stopped crying and looked at Thomas. Thomas gave her the biggest grin I'd seen him deliver yet, and at this she ran out of the room howling. Her friend hesitated on the doorstep like she wanted to say something, but the sound of Jupiter clickety-clacketying down the stairs sent her running after her.

"What did you give that girl?" I said.

"Nothing I haven't taken twenty times myself," Thomas answered.

"Yeah, well, she also probably weighs about forty pounds less than you and you've also probably taken more trips than she's had hot baths. You better go and make sure she's all right, man. You're responsible for her. If anything goes wrong with her out there tonight, you're accountable."

"Get behind the drums, Bill," Christine said. She was sitting on the Fender amp with the bass strapped over her shoulder, pick in hand.

It took me a couple of seconds to register what I was seeing. "What are you doing?" I said.

"What does it look like I'm doing?" she said. Thomas picked up his twelve-string Gretsch and took his place beside his own amplifier.

"Are we plugging in, Miss Christine?"

"Not yet. It's been a while since I've played one of these. It's not brain surgery, but let's see how it goes."

"You say when," he said.

I felt like I was the one who'd dropped the acid. I decided to go and make sure Jupiter and her friend weren't lying in a snowdrift somewhere. It seemed like the only thing to do that made any sense.

"Where are you going?" Christine said.

"Somebody's got to check up on those two." I cut my eyes Thomas's way but he had his head down, busy trying to get his guitar in tune.

"You go out that door, don't bother coming back," she said.

I hesitated a second.

"I think you smoked too much grass," I said.

"I mean it, Bill." She bowed her head to her instrument and studied the placement of her fingers up and down its long neck, slowly moving them back and forth across the four thick strings like a cautious spider. "Hey, here's one our music teacher in high school taught us that you should know, Thomas."

Thomas listened to her play. Nodding his head to the emerging beat, watching her fingers coax out the song's hesitant rhythm, he began strumming his guitar. In less than a minute the two of them weren't two any more but one, filling the air with something that just a moment before hadn't existed. So pleasantly lost they looked there in their playing, it felt like they'd forgotten about me. They *had* forgotten about me.

I sat down behind the drums, decided brushes were the better choice, and joined in.

Christ, it's just like fucking, I thought. You wonder when and how it'll ever happen and how you'll pull it off, and then one day, without warning, you're doing it, you're fucking, you're actually fucking. We found a comfortable rhythm and kept it. Eventually the chorus came and, after a little fumbling around, we got that down too, then went right back to the beginning and started all over again.

After a while, over top of the tune, comfortable enough now in keeping the beat to speak, "Hey, what's this thing called, anyway?" I said.

Christine kept concentrating, kept her eyes on her instrument. Thomas came over beside my drum kit.

Still playing, "'Wild Mountain Thyme,'" he said. "Just an old, old song every musician knows. And now you know it too, Buckskin."

two

17.

WHY ME?

Christine, okay, maybe. Thomas's voice was a medium tenor but in a wavering, aching sort of way, hers womanly high but strong and throaty, and he must have heard that right from the get-go when he'd listened to her sing at the Riverboat. He always claimed that two- and three-part harmonies were a big part of the sound he was after, so there you go, there was that. And he also knew that she was talented and would be able to pick up the bass easily enough, and that that would kill two birds right there.

But I couldn't sing, had to work hard just to be adequate on my assigned instrument, and had never even wanted to be up on stage before. And forget about us being friends; friendship doesn't even enter into it. He said he could trust me and could count on me to cover his ass when the going got rough and all the bosom-buddy rest of it, but Thomas didn't need my flesh. What Thomas was after was something else entirely.

I say this now, of course, claim to know this now, but even then I think I knew it. Thirty years on, getting saved and being seduced still really aren't all that much different. An unsaved soul is still a virgin of the heart. Either way, it's just as good for the seducer as it is for the seduced. Maybe better, when you really think about it.

Like I said, I think I knew this then. But even if I did, I didn't care. Who wanted to be a virgin in 1966? Who wants to be one now?

18.

I STILL KEPT the shelves well stocked and swept the floor clean at Making Waves, and Christine still punched in the amount tendered at her day job, working cash at Sam the Record Man, but mostly we rehearsed. Nearly every night for almost two months,

Christine and Thomas and I would trek our way through the cold and climb the three flights of stairs to the studio and wipe our feet at the door and say hello and tune up and get down to business.

Sometimes we'd share a single joint out on the balcony after a couple of busy hours, and once in a while, if we felt particularly good about what we'd been doing, would go downstairs and knock on the door of one of the other studios and pass a doobie back and forth with some of the other musicians. But except for Scotty working away at the corner card table and faithfully ignoring us, for most of the winter we didn't see much of anyone but ourselves.

For Christine and me, not only our new instruments to master, but, more, having to get used to the shared pulse of group playing, learning how to dance to the delicate rhythms of collaborative strumming, plucking, drumming. The difference between playing by yourself and playing with even one other, I soon learned, was large enough that it was almost wrong to think of the two as even being separate parts of the same thing. Think of sex: even halfway through their initial go at it, everyone's a genuis lover all by themselves. But it takes time, patience, and lots and lots of practise to learn how to make love.

19.

MAYBE IT WAS our growing confidence—I myself was particularly proud of the mock train-track brush strokes I was now laying down with ease on "Folsom Prison Blues"—but late one night, walking home to my place after rehearsal, Christine and I were both thinking the same thing. Love is like this, and if for nothing else, for this alone, is good.

"I think things are going okay," I said. "Overall, I mean."

"Oh, God, yes. I mean, if we listened to the tapes from that first week . . ."

"Thank God, no—"

"No, no, I know, I know."

Christine carried the mandolin case in one hand and had one of my hands clamped tightly in the other. As usual when we came home from the studio so late, we owned Bloor Street. As thick with people as Yorkville was after midnight, even as the snow fell in sheets sideways and the February winds ricocheted up and down the avenue, most of the rest of Toronto after ten in the evening was abandoned sidewalks, deserted streets, six-o'clock-shut shops. Every street light stood at attention, dutifully burning away for our benefit only; every set of traffic lights kept its lonely vigil for our simple amusement, a bit of flashing diversion thoughtfully supplied just to break up the monotony of everywhere winter white.

"But I'd say we're pretty tight now," I said.

"Oh, yeah, we're getting there, we're definitely getting there."

A blast of snow and wind came barrelling down Bloor, and both of us instinctively lowered our heads.

"It's just . . ."

"Yeah?" Christine said.

"It's just, I don't know, by this point, I kind of thought . . ."

"Yeah?"

"I don't know, I just kind of thought that by this point there'd be . . ."

"What, you mean you thought by this point there'd be . . . ?"

"You know, something . . ."

"Something more?"

"Something more."

"That by this point we'd be doing something more than just trying to sound like Thomas's record collection."

"Yeah."

"Yeah."

Although there weren't any cars and we were close to being home and out of the cold and into the warm again, at least as warm as my room ever got in the wintertime, we stopped at a red light near our street, near Huron.

"I mean, it's not like I'm not having a good time," I said.

"I know, me too," Christine said. "It's fun. You know if it wasn't I wouldn't still be doing it." She laughed, but she meant it. I laughed because I knew that she did.

"It's just that . . ."

"There's got to be more."

"There's got to be more. Because otherwise . . ."

"What's the point?"

"We should talk to Thomas," I said.

"Just to see what his plans are."

"Just to see what . . ."

"The point is."

Christine pulled the loose end of my scarf tight and tucked it into my coat and did up the top button. Hand in hand once again, we crossed the street without bothering to look both ways. There really wasn't any need to—there never was at that time of night—but I remember how we crossed without even looking once. Funny how I remember that now.

20.

THOMAS WAS SITTING with his back to me in a metal chair by the card table, silently tuning his guitar. I tightened the head on the snare drum and cleared my throat.

"Hey, Thomas."

"Uh huh." He always had a tough time keeping his Gibson twelve-string in tune.

"Christine and I were talking the other day and were kind of wondering when you were thinking about doing some, I don't know, original stuff. You know, some of your own songs."

He stopped messing around with the acoustic and turned around in his seat. I waited for him to say something. He didn't, so I said, "No big deal. We just thought it might be cool to try something new. You know, like some of the ones you were talking about when we first met. Some"—I gave a little drum roll and cymbal crash—"Interstellar North American Music."

He just sat there for a couple of seconds.

"And Miss Christine," he said, "she feels this way, too? You two are in agreement on this?"

"Sure."

He stood up, walked over to the drum kit, and knelt down beside me. On one knee. Strumming something I'd never heard him play before but never looking down at his instrument, only up at me, "Buckskin," he said, "you've made me a very happy man."

I took this as a yes and tried to concentrate on figuring out where this new tune of his was going. But really, all I could think was, Get up off your knee, Thomas. Anybody walks in here, they're going to think you're proposing to me or something.

Christ, man, I thought, get up. Get *up*.

21.

THOMAS FOUND HIMSELF a permanent old lady, Christine got busted, and Kelorn—who never failed to remind me that "Love isn't for hoarding, Bill" whenever I'd ask why I hadn't seen last month's sweet young thing around lately—was having girlfriend problems. And we really started practising, doubling, occasionally even tripling our usual rehearsal time of a couple hours a night so as not to drown under the deluge of original tunes Thomas had us swimming in.

At the moment, though, most of my attention and concern was directed toward dealing with the fallout from Christine's being charged with causing mischief and resisting arrest while attending a small, peaceful sit-in protesting the yahoo tourists clogging up Yorkville with their cars.

"Did I tell you how much Christine's fines could come to? *If* she gets off with just a fine?"

"Yes, you did," Kelorn said.

We'd just gotten in a fresh batch of the *Manual for Draft-Age Immigrants to Canada* and I was taking them out of the box and clearing a place for them on the counter. We didn't even bother to shelve them any more. Some weeks it wasn't unusual to go through ten or fifteen copies.

"*If* she gets probation and *if* they don't manage to jerk her around and lay down a sentence. I mean, think about it. Jail time! For sitting around in a circle holding up some signs!"

Kelorn unplugged the whistling tea kettle.

"Bill, dear, I know, I know, you already—"

"What's the word, goddammit! What's the goddamn word!"

Hunched over the old desk at the rear of the shop, Scotty cursed the poem in front of him one more time—"One word, dammit! All I'm asking for is one goddamn word!"—and ran a bony white hand through his surprisingly thick mop of silver hair. I kept my mouth shut and placed a single finger to my lips to make sure Kelorn did the same.

The first time I'd been witness to one of Scotty's profanity-laced invocations to the poetry gods at the studio and innocently asked whether he needed some help, he'd spat back at me, "What makes you think I was talking to you, hippie boy?" We were the only two in the room at the time, but he'd made his point. The next time he screamed out demanding to know what rhymed with "epoch" and meant "love, dammit, the very root of the whole putrid lie," I lowered my head and banged out the approximate rhythm to the Ferlin Husky song I was practising. Eventually he stopped yelling and I found the beat. There's a lesson to be learned here, I thought, although I never did get around to figuring out what it was.

I'd invited Scotty along with me to work that morning in an attempt to help him break free of the writer's block he'd been suffering from for the last couple of weeks—and which, in turn, the band had been suffering from because of Scotty's near-constant poetic pissing and moaning from his usual spot at the corner card table—but it looked like the change-of-pace tonic I'd suggested wasn't going down so well.

Scotty jammed the last scrap of paper into his shopping bag, bundled up his thick black overcoat, picked up his violin case, and hobbled toward the door, the nose-hair-bristling reek of the mothballs he kept in his coat pockets to combat the mildewy stink of his basement apartment overcoming the store's aroma of mint tea. Turning to Kelorn and me behind the counter, he lifted his cane and pointed.

"Homer never wrote a goddamn line hanging out in some hippie commune," he said.

I raised an open palm goodbye. "See you around, Scotty," I said.

"Nice to meet you, Mr. Robinson," Kelorn added. "Please come and see us again any time you like." Scotty slammed the door closed behind him, in the process ringing its bell loud enough that even he might have been able to hear it.

I resumed my rant—Me: "So it's a crime to sit in the street but it's not a crime for some creep from the suburbs to race up and down that same street in a filthy, polluting automobile hassling half the women who live there and endangering the lives of everyone else?" Her: "I know, Bill, dear, I know"—until Kelorn's own recent reason for worry moped into the shop, a nineteen-year-old

French major by the name of Susan who wanted to quit the university, move in with Kelorn, and dedicate the rest of her life to working at Making Waves.

Susan jingled the bell over the door just like Scotty had a couple of minutes before, but this time only the tiniest of tinkles. Scotty might have been nuts, okay, but the way he entered and left a room, you knew that he knew what he was doing, even if no one else did. Susan creaked open the door an inch at a time, as if she was entering a haunted house. Stood there wiping her boots on the carpet and brushing the snow off her coat for what seemed like an hour.

Of course, Kelorn gave her a big hug, made her take off her coat and gloves and set them out over by the stove to dry, insisted that she have a cup of tea to warm up, and asked her all about her philosophy mid-term. But it was over. Whenever Susan wasn't intensely studying the knotty patterns on the hardwood floor, her pleading attempts to make eye contact with Kelorn were politely but firmly undercut by Kelorn immediately shifting her eyes and the conversation my way.

Eventually, into one of several swelling pockets of painful silence—painful for Susan and painful for me; Kelorn herself seemed quite comfortable with the idea of spending the rest of the afternoon expertly avoiding Susan's eyes and amiably chatting away about Cartesian duality and competing modern theories of the mind-body problem—"Kelorn?" Susan said. "Can we please talk?"

"Why, of course, dear, what is it?"

"I mean alone. Can we please go somewhere and . . . be alone and talk?"

Kelorn laughed. "My goodness, you're going to give poor Bill here such a terrible complex, I'm sure."

"That's okay," I said, going for my coat on the peg behind the counter. "I feel like getting some fresh air anyway." Sometimes the decision to walk directly into a snowstorm is easy.

"Don't be silly, Bill," Kelorn said. "You've only gotten back from lunch less than an hour ago. Besides, I want us to get to work moving the poetry section like we'd discussed."

"Kelorn, please," Susan said. "We need to talk."

"Well, by all means let's talk, then," Kelorn said. "Only, if you mean about what we've talked about several times already, there's really not that much more to say, is there? We were friends when we met, then we were something else, and now we're friends again. If you think of it that way, it's all very simple, isn't it?" She smiled directly into the storm of Susan's face, but the bad weather of before began to really come down. A grown woman crying without making a sound, not a single, sobbing sound, this is grief. Even just to look at. I stared down at the floor, one arm still stuck in my coat.

Kelorn rested her hand on top of one of Susan's. "Now, dear. Wouldn't it be silly for us to get needlessly all worked up and to sacrifice our friendship just because we've moved on to a different kind of friendship?" Kelorn smiled and gave the younger woman's hand a squeeze.

Susan couldn't answer. Didn't have to. Her silence and wet face answered for her. She tore her hand free from Kelorn's and stalked to the rear of the shop and snapped up her coat and gloves and was banging the door closed behind her before she'd even bothered to put them on. I let the ringing of the bell die away before I said anything.

"It's not your fault," I said. "I mean, she knew what she was getting into."

Kelorn was standing at the front window, had pulled aside the curtain to watch Susan disappear down Harbord through the falling snow. "She knew she was getting into what?" she said.

"You know, that long-term relationships aren't your thing, that you're into free love. You told her all that right from the start, right?"

Kelorn dropped the curtain but didn't turn around.

"You've never heard me use that term," she said.

"What term?"

"Free love."

"No, but—"

"I've never used it because there isn't any such thing."

"Okay, but—"

"There never has been," she said, "and there never will be."

22.

BY THE END OF MARCH we were coming close to making Thomas's songs our own. Real close. Part country, part rock, part something it was hard to put your finger on, for lack of any other way of putting it, we simply referred to "Dream of Pines" and "One O'clock in the Morning" and "Lilies by the Side of the Highway" and all the rest of them as Duckhead music. None of us, not even Thomas, knew what the definitively right recipe was yet, but all of us knew that we'd know it when we tasted it. We also knew we were getting close. Real close. I knew because I could almost see it.

Christine and I would trudge home from work and try to grab a couple hours of sleep at my place before heading over to the studio to meet up with Thomas and Heather, Thomas's new girlfriend. While we tuned up, Thomas would go around the room like some kind of degenerate football coach minutes before opening kick off, handing out little white diet pills to help keep us awake and alert. Christine gave them a shot but decided they made her jumpy the next day. I happily reported no such side effects. It wasn't too long before I realized that the pills worked just as well first thing in the morning.

Gee, instant energy, get-up-and-go in a tablet. Who needs sleep when you're blessed with the miracle of the modern pharmacy? Not this little drummer boy.

23.

IN SPITE OF EVERYTHING else Christine was still doing her folk thing, Tuesday night was still her night at the Riverboat. She played a pretty decent bass by now and was even taking some simple solos on the mandolin, but whether it's boyfriends or girlfriends or musical genres, your first love is always your first.

The Riverboat was small, seating only about a hundred people, so it felt like you were sitting in somebody's living room who happened to know Gordon Lightfoot and Simon and Garfunkel and Joni Mitchell. By this point folk music wasn't the only game in town any more, but it was still Yorkville's heart and soul. Go to the history books if you want the entire who's who, but trust me, the Riverboat was the place to be if one guitar and one voice were what you were looking for.

At the moment, though, I was looking for the hands on the clock on the wall. Because whenever it was showtime at the Riverboat it was dark. Very dark. Which was great for digging whoever was up there on stage, but Christine's set was over at midnight and after that we could split and get started on our usual late-night Tuesday practice. We'd arrived at the club around nine and she'd gone on at nine-thirty and it seemed like she'd been playing now for at least a couple of hours and . . . ah, shit. Truth time: I was bored.

We were *all* bored. Not the audience, not the thirty or forty purists who sat there sipping their java and politely applauding after every capably performed song. But me, Thomas, Heather, we were bored. Hell, even Christine was bored.

We just had to sit there and listen to the same old songs being played the same old way, but Christine was the one who actually had to be up on stage and sing them. I recognized from my seat at the back of the club the identical spaced-out gaze she was prone to these days when, yeah, we were screwing, but I could tell that what she was really thinking was how long practice had run and how late it was and how little sleep she was going to get before going to work the next day.

"How much longer do you think, Buckskin?" Thomas whispered. Folk crowds took their music very seriously, especially at the Riverboat. You kept your hands folded on your lap when the music was playing, you clapped your hands enthusiastically after every song, and if you had something to say to the person sitting next to you that couldn't be said between sets, you said it the same way you were taught to talk in church. *Quietly*.

"CHRISTINE! HOW MUCH LONGER?"

Every bowed head lifted and turned to squint through the darkness in the direction of the back row. Even Thomas looked embarrassed, and that wasn't easy to pull off. Heather, though, hurler of the query, calmly lit her cigarette, crossed her black-stockinged legs, and leaned back in her seat waiting to know how much longer. Because Thomas—her old man, Thomas—he wanted to practise.

Okay. Heather.

Like her boyfriend, it seemed as if she'd dropped in out of nowhere. She was Canadian, though, from northern Ontario, from a tiny place called Geraldton. She was eighteen years old and came to Toronto because she was eighteen years old and from Geraldton. One day no one had ever heard of her or even seen her around Yorkville before, and the next she was at the studio with Thomas and every night after.

Sometimes she'd fool around with a set of Tarot cards at the corner table beside scribbling Scotty while we practised. Or maybe she'd work on a sweater or scarf for Thomas that he never ended up wearing with a pair of blue knitting needles and a big ball of yarn. But mostly Heather adored Thomas.

He'd play his guitar and sing and she'd look up from her cards and gaze at him and smile. He'd walk us through a particularly pesky set of chord changes to one of his new songs for half an hour and the entire tedious time she'd gaze at him and smile. He'd ask her if she'd be a sweetheart and run down to the Grab Bag and get us all Cokes and she'd take his dollar and gaze at him and smile. He'd take a minute to himself and smoke one of her cigarettes out on the balcony and she'd stare out the half-fogged door pane and gaze at him and smile.

"Darlin', darlin', it's all right," Thomas whispered, hand on her knee. "Miss Christine is just going to finish up here and then we're going to go and practise."

It was all the explanation Heather needed to hear. "Okay," she said. And that was that.

But—order restored, all eyes back on the bristly-headed singer up front in the granny dress and combat boots resuming her set by racing through Dylan's "Only a Pawn in Their Game"—Christine, it appeared, wasn't okay with it. What lyrics she didn't mess up or flat-out forget she mumbled. Where she was supposed to sound coolly ironic she sounded like she couldn't be more sincere. And maybe Bob could get away with not being able to hit the right note every time, but Christine sounded like she was strumming and singing two entirely different songs. She finally put the thing out of its misery no more than halfway through with an angry whack of some chords I'm positive Dylan had never even dreamed of.

Christine put a hand over her eyes and peered into the audience. Thomas and I stared down at the floor under our table looking for somewhere convenient to crawl into. Heather noticed a run in her tights and patiently tried to stop it with some black nail polish retrieved from her bag.

"Bill? Thomas?" Christine said. "Are you guys still here?"

Sliding down in my seat, Why pick on us? I thought. Heather's the one who said it.

"Yeah, hey, there you are. Hey, it looks like you two are falling asleep out there."

Each of us slowly straightened back up and waved pathetic little half-waves Christine's way. The audience seemed to get a real kick out of this and smiled a nice big folk club smile before returning its attention to Christine.

"What do you guys say we give these folks some Duckhead to take home with them tonight?" she said.

She shielded her eyes with both hands this time and blinked out into the stage light. "Thomas? Bill? Guys?"

There was no way the audience could have been as confused as I was. True, they didn't know what the hell taking home some Duckhead meant—Complimentary wild game delicacy? Just-out opiates gratis for the masses? A hip new sexual position?—but, worse, I actually did. But how and why? And when? Now? *Right* now? We weren't ready. We weren't near enough ready. I wasn't ready. But Thomas was.

Thomas stepped—Stepped? More like leapt—right over me, slapped me on the shoulder, and was halfway up to the stage before turning around and, walking backward, said, "C'mon, Buckskin, let's have some fun."

Probably seeing how plainly terrified I was, Heather kissed me softly on the cheek and pressed my hand and whispered into my ear not to worry because Thomas wouldn't let anything bad happen to me. Seeing that I still wasn't going anywhere, she gave my hand another encouraging squeeze and turned over one of her Tarot cards.

"See," she said. "The Ace of Pentacles—I told you nothing bad was going to happen."

Not quite sharing her unshakable faith in the divine providence of her boyfriend or the destiny-describing powers of the Tarot, the realization that there weren't any drums up there and the fact that every eye in the Riverboat was on me pushed me out of my seat toward the stage. No death-row inmate ever walked a lonelier last walk.

Thomas grabbed me by the arm and yanked me up onto the stage and I took the hint from my rumbling stomach and kept my eyes off the crowd by gluing them to a heating vent in the middle of the ceiling. Then somebody stuck a tambourine in my hand and somebody else handed Thomas an acoustic guitar and then Christine said, "Well?" and Thomas answered, "It's your show, Miss Christine," and she said, "How about 'Dream of Pines'?" and when she asked if that was all right with me I heard myself say, "Sure."

Dream of pines
Dream of pines
Never what you find
A home I'll never know.

Where to now?
Where to now?
Where and how
A home I'll never go.

We murdered them. We murdered the audience, we murdered the waitresses, we murdered the kitchen staff, we even murdered us.

Before the applause was even over, still looking up at the roof duct, "'That's for a Stranger'?" I shouted out.

"Let's go," Christine answered.

Thomas counted off.

"One . . . Two . . . Three . . . Four . . ."

And then we murdered them all over again.

24.

"HEY, BUCKSKIN, you ever heard of Slippery Bannister?"

"What's a slippery bannister?"

"Not a *what*—a *who*."

"Okay, who? Who's Slippery Bannister?"

"Slippery Bannister is all that we're missing."

"All that we're missing from what?"

"From the Duckhead Secret Society."

I washed down the uppers he'd handed me with a swig from my bottle of Coke.

"Steel guitar?"

"And slide. The man plays a positively wicked slide guitar. Can sing a spell, too."

"He's good?"

"He's the best."

I could already feel the little white pills beginning to do their thing.

"What are we waiting for?" I said. "Let's get him up here."

Raising his own bottle of pop, swallowing some of his own self-prescribed medicine, "Buckskin," he said, "you read my mind."

25.

SLIPPERY BANNISTER was the real deal. And that isn't necessarily always such a good thing.

Thomas and I went to meet his 3:25 a.m. bus arriving from

Detroit and were standing around the nearly deserted Greyhound terminal drinking bad slot-machine coffee to keep us warm even though it was already early April. We'd finished up practising a couple of hours before and had walked Christine and then Heather home before hiking over to Bay Street and the depot.

"I thought you said this guy"—I wasn't quite ready to call anybody Slippery yet—"was from the South," I said.

"Blytheville, Arkansas," Thomas answered. "Right in the heart of Dixie."

"So what's he doing in Detroit?"

"I believe Slippery said something about Thunderbirds."

"If this guy is as good as you say he is, what's he doing working an assembly line?"

Thomas forced down a long drink from his paper cup of coffee.

"Slippery Bannister is an aesthetic rebel, Buckskin. Much like ourselves, he believes that the guts have been ripped out of contemporary country by those soulless piss-ants down on Music Row. And in spite of repeated lucrative offers from the Nashville establishment, he refuses—he absolutely refuses—to compromise his artistic principles just to make a few quick bucks whoring around as a session man. And frankly, he couldn't have been more excited when I explained to him what we're trying to accomplish up here and how we envision his considerable musical talents meshing with our own. He said it sounded like we're just the kind of fresh breeze everybody's been waiting for down there. Dying for, in fact."

"You got all this from him in one phone call?"

"Not in so many words, no, but—Hey, that must be Slippery."

A bus pulled into the station, but it was from Montreal, not Motor City. We sipped our coffee in silence and watched a string of stunned-looking travellers stumble down the steps of the bus and onto the platform.

When the last passenger was off, the driver started hauling bags out from the berth underneath the bus and everyone began to wake up to where they were and the fact that their luggage was being tossed into one great big growing pile of black and brown and tan. The only other person inside the station, a plain-looking young woman with her hair hidden underneath a blue kerchief standing a few feet down from us with a sleeping baby in her arms, rapped at the glass a few excited times to attract someone's attention. She didn't get it, so she knocked again, harder, and this time the entire crowd turned around to see who was the lucky person being welcomed to town.

Only one of them was, though, a guy about our age but with short hair and wearing a crisp checked sports jacket in spite of his seven-hour trip, and everyone else lowered their eyes and returned to the job of separating their stuff from everyone else's.

"One of you boys Graham?"

Thomas and I turned around. And there he was, Slippery Bannister, aesthetic rebel, in the flesh. Neither of us had noticed the simultaneous arrival of his bus at the other end of the platform.

He looked like a middle-aged 1930s dust-bowl sharecropper who'd come into town to argue with the bank manager about his delinquent mortgage, the moth-nibbled brown suit and tie hanging off his skeletal frame testament to the years of futile struggle to keep the failing farm in the family. The only thing that indicated that he really had cut out for the city years before was the pound or so of gleaming Vaseline he used to slick back his thinning black hair. He shook a cigarette free right from his pack to his lips and lit it with a silver lighter that shot up a flame a good six inches, expertly avoiding setting his eyebrows on fire. He took a long drag and immediately filled up the entire terminal with the stink of what a Canadian nose knows can only be one thing, American cigarettes. I noticed that his hand shook slightly as he lit his Marlboro. The smell of whisky competed with the stench from his smoke.

"Mr. Bannister, sir," Thomas said, going right for the old man's free hand and shaking it vigorously, "Thomas Graham. Welcome to Toronto, Canada. I'd like to introduce you to Bill Hansen, our drummer. Buckskin, Mr. Slippery Bannister. Everybody up here calls Bill 'Buckskin.'"

If Thomas ever decided to let go of his hand, I was prepared to shake it—although whether to address him as Mr. Bannister or simply Slippery I hadn't decided yet—but I didn't have to worry. He let go of Thomas's grip and dismissed me with a quick nod.

"There's a matter of bus money," he said. He looked at Thomas. He looked at me. I looked at Thomas. Thomas looked back at him and nodded his head several times in rapid agreement.

"Of course, of course," Thomas said. "Your transportation costs, just as we'd discussed. But you've got to be tired after your trip. Let's go and get you bedded down first and—"

"Nobody's going anywhere until I get my money." The old man crushed his fresh cigarette dead underneath the sharp tip of his pointy black cowboy boot and folded his arms across his chest. I was almost ready to start counting the change in my jeans when Thomas laughed and pulled out his wallet.

Turning to me, "You see, where Mr. Bannister and I come from, Buckskin, you know a man by his word." He handed over the money. "There you are, sir."

There were only four bills, but the old man took his time, slowly moving his lips as he counted each one. "This here's too much," he said. "I can't make no change for you right now."

Thomas laughed again and patted him on the shoulder. Turning to me, "I think we can trust Mr. Bannister, don't you, Buckskin?"

I laughed an imbecile's laugh right along with Thomas and he picked up the old man's bag and we were off for a short cab ride over to Heather's place, which Thomas had decided the final piece of the puzzle that was the Duckhead Secret Society was going to call home for the next little while. Thomas and I stepped into the dark street to see if a taxi was coming. Back on the curb, fresh Marlboro ignited and assaulting the fresh night air, "Two things," the old man said.

"First off, this here's a round-trip ticket I got in my pocket. I don't like what I see up here, I'm gone, you understand? Gone. And with that $100 bonus we already discussed. In cash. In full."

"Absolutely," Thomas said, "we're in complete understanding. But really, I really think you're going to—"

"Second off," he said, smoke pouring out of both nostrils, "either of you boys know where a man can get some *barbecue* in this town?"

26.

STARTING UP A BAND or plotting a revolution is always so much easier in the planning stages over a tableful of beer. Little things like your steel-guitar player staying drunk his entire first week in town and no one wanting to book you into their club because country and western music isn't real popular with the counterculture these days tend not to get discussed over those first few ecstatic brews, only the really important stuff, like whether the group's first record should be a single or double album and who you're going to acknowledge on the jacket sleeve.

"But it's none of our business," I said. "And if Heather's cool with it, why are you getting so worked up?"

"Don't insult my intelligence," Christine said. "Either that or don't be so naïve. How could she possibly be cool with it? This guy, this Bannister guy, he sleeps until noon every day, only leaves her place long enough to walk to the liquor store and go out looking for *barbecue*, whatever that is, and then spends the rest of the day and half the night sitting at her kitchen table in his long underwear spitting chewing tobacco into a plastic cup and drinking whisky until he passes out on the floor."

"At least he's not loud."

"I hope that's you trying to be funny."

I was leaning up against the cash counter at Sam's waiting for Christine to finish her shift. "But if Heather says it's all right with her, then—"

"Oh, *come on*, Bill. I like Heather, you know that, I think she's sweet. But if Thomas told her to jump into Lake Ontario the only question she'd ask would be what time."

A short, skinny, acned, black horn-rimmed kid no more than fifteen—the entire dripping ball of teenage angst wax—slouched up to the counter and tentatively nudged across a copy of *Rubber Soul*. The way he couldn't meet Christine's eyes when he handed over his cash and the sweaty palm he stuck out to collect his change screamed out his heart-fluttering infatuation a thousand times louder than any words ever could. He cleared his throat for the umpteenth time and managed a surprisingly deep, if under-his-breath "Thanks" before practically running out the door. Christine went back to sticking price labels on a fat stack of albums, oblivious to the act of trembling worship she'd just inspired.

And how come my hands never got sweaty any more when I looked at Christine? I wondered. How was it that sometimes I could look right into her eyes but all I'd see was Christine, Christine Jones, you know, Christine, my girlfriend? How come once in a while we'd be walking around Yorkville together and I'd spot some girl I knew wasn't even half as attractive as her—I mean, I *knew* she wasn't—but who would get my motor running harder and hotter than Christine had done in ages? How was it that they were talking about putting a man on the moon but nobody had made a pill yet that allowed a guy to look at his girlfriend's ass the same way he looked at it the very first time? For some reason I didn't feel so sorry for the kid any more.

"Look, it's real simple, Bill," Christine said. "It was wrong of Thomas to put Heather up to what he's putting her through, and it's wrong for her friends to sit around and let him get away with it." With every word she spoke the stickers got slapped down that much harder. "I mean, if Thomas wants this guy in the band so badly, why doesn't he let him drink all day at his place?"

"Because Thomas's place is—"

"—too small, yeah, so I've heard. Smaller than that broom closet Heather lives in? Smaller than yours?"

"He says it is."

She looked up. "You mean to tell me you've never been to Thomas'?"

"He lives in Cabbagetown. Why would I want to go all the way out there if I didn't have to?"

"No reason, I guess. Still, it's a little weird, don't you think?"

"Not really. He's always hanging around Yorkville. And like I said, what do I want to be doing in the east end?"

"I guess."

Christine stuck a few more labels on a few more records. Man, how many Sonny & Cher albums did the world really need?

"So basically we don't even know if Thomas's place *is* too small for him to bunk down with Stinky."

"Slippery," I said. "The guy's name is Slippery, Slippery Bannister."

"Whatever. For all we know, Thomas could be living in a penthouse while poor Heather is getting chased out of her own kitchen."

"Yeah, right. Now Thomas is some eccentric millionaire who's decided to slum it in Yorkville for a while and who's keeping a butler and maid in his mansion in Cabbagetown."

"He is always flush," Christine said, "you've got to admit that. Look at all the instruments he's bought, the studio he's rented, the new recording equipment."

"But that's all from the patron."

"Oh, Bill, *please.*"

She didn't need to elaborate. The story of Thomas's golden handshake with the mysterious Mississippi benefactor in the beautiful white suit just wasn't something Christine and I talked about. Hadn't from that first night Thomas told us about him.

As eager to change the subject as I was, "I still don't know why we need this guy playing with us, anyway," Christine said.

"Thomas says he hears a steel guitar in our songs and supposedly Slippery is one of the best."

"Supposedly's the right word," she said.

It probably was. The first night of rehearsal he fell asleep at his instrument, hands still on the strings, head straight back, openmouthed and snoring. Another time he tumbled off his stool while playing a solo. Most of the time, though, he spent unsuccessfully trying to get the beautiful Sho-Bud pedal-steel guitar Thomas had got for him in tune, taking fifteen-minute cigarette breaks out on the balcony, and bumming shots of scotch from Scotty's flask. Scotty eventually packed up his poetry and quit coming to our practices. Thomas asked us to be patient and give our newest fellow Duckhead time to adjust to his surroundings and assured us that we hadn't heard the real Slippery Bannister yet. Christine and I weren't so sure we wanted to.

"Let's wait and see what happens," I said. "Thomas is getting nowhere with any of the clubs once they find out we've got a steel guitar in the band. Maybe he'll send Slippery packing and it'll just be us three again. If it were just us three we could get gigs. We were great that night at the Riverboat." I looked down at the pile of records. "Weren't we?"

Christine smiled. "Yeah."

"Yeah?"

"Yeah," she said.

"Really? I mean . . ."

"Yeah. We were. We were great."

Instantly, heavy duty lovey-dovey eyeing of each other for a good long while.

"But in the meantime, what about Heather?" Christine said.

My palms were almost moist for the first time in a long time, so out of my mouth the first thing that was all peaches-and-cream appeasement. "Slippery can stay at my place," I said.

"But your place is even smaller than Heather's."

"Between work and practice I'm hardly ever there."

"But what about us? I mean—"

"We can always crash in your bedroom when we feel like it," I said.

"But the cats." Christine shared an old house just outside Yorkville with two cats, four full-time anarchists, and various couch-crashing friends of the Movement. The house's number-one rule of iron-clad communalism didn't bother me all that much, but the cats did manage to mess around with my allergies some.

"That's what antihistamines are for. And co-op life hasn't extended as far as your bedroom yet, has it?"

Christine smiled. Goddamn, I thought, how could I have ever forgotten what a great smile she has?

"It's good of you to do this, Bill," she said. "Although Thomas should be the one making the offer, not you."

"Thomas is Thomas. Besides, I want to do it. No woman should have to share her kitchen with a man named Slippery."

More and more and then still some more of that brand new beautiful old smile of hers.

"Sometimes I forget how lucky I am to have gotten a guy like you, you know that?"

I leaned across the counter and gently wrapped my hand around the back of her head, pulled her lips to mine.

"Not half as lucky that I've got you, babe."

27.

TECHNICALLY SPEAKING, we were a quartet. But by the end of Slippery's second week in town what we really were were a guitar player, a bass player, a drummer, and a guy who occasionally honoured us with his presence at practice, always managed to show up mute drunk when he did make it, and who found rehearsal as good a time as any to grab a few winks before resuming his solitary whisky-drinking back at my place. To his credit, as his former roommate I can verify that he wasn't going out of his way to make trouble just for the band.

I lasted forty-eight hours with him on my floor and me in bed with a pillow over my head before packing up and moving in with the anarchists over at Christine's place. Having to share my jar of peanut butter thirteen ways was a small price to pay for not having to try to fall asleep to a man in his filthy long underwear slumped over the nook of my economy kitchen drunkenly humming Roy Acuff tunes to himself until five o'clock in the morning. Or having to wake up to the stomach-curdling sight of a sink full of Marlboro butts and spat-out Red Man, and Slippery trying to get the last stubborn ball of mucus out of the bottom of his lungs. That, and having to watch him nostalgically fondle the little Aspirin bottle of genuine Arkansas homemade barbecue sauce he carried with him everywhere he went and be subjected to his daily tirade about "What kind of place is this Canada, anyway? If I don't get me some real barbecue soon, I'm on the next Greyhound outta here. Even Detroit had barbecue."

But he wasn't going anywhere. At least not until Thomas cut off the weekly allowance he was laying on him to sleepwalk through rehearsals. Slippery wasn't much of a talker, but he wasn't shy, at least not with me, about why he'd been manning a rivet gun at a Ford plant in Detroit and not a steel guitar in Nashville when Thomas had lured him even further north.

"They fired Hank Williams from the Opry for liking his whisky," he said. "And I ain't no Hank Williams."

There was one thing Thomas wasn't fibbing about, though. Slippery Bannister did have a pretty impressive list of session credits to his name, had guested on records by Acuff, Lefty Frizzell, Patsy Cline, and the young George Jones, among others. Thomas loaned me a few of them and, contrary to what we were hearing at the studio, the guy really could play, had a way of making his instrument run the gamut from funereal sad to downright joyous without ever sounding sentimental or cheesy like a lot of steel players.

Near sun-up on the last night we'd played at being roommates, after I'd faked being asleep for as long as I could and finally asked him if he wouldn't mind smoking his last cigarette and drinking his last drink, he'd just silently nodded, flicked his Marlboro into the sink, made sure it was dead with a blast of water from the tap, and swallowed the final inch of booze left in his glass. He lay right down on the floor and took a long, deep breath. When, the night before, I'd offered him a blanket to go along with the tiny pillow he'd produced from his suitcase, he'd said, "Floor's fine as it is. I'm used to it this way."

Now that his smoke was out, the only light was what managed to make it down the alley from the street lamp on Huron and into my room. I doubled-checked to make sure he wasn't thinking about sparking up a fresh cigarette and saw that his eyes were wide open and he was staring straight up at the ceiling.

"If I didn't get a chance to mention it already, I do appreciate you opening up your home to me like you done. Same as with that Heather woman. Although sooner or later that girl's gonna have to get it through her head that it's the devil's work to be messing around with them cards of hers like she does.

"But I don't plan to be in this Canada for too much longer. Like I told your buddy Graham when he telephoned me up, soon as I put the bottle down for good I'm on the first bus back to Nashville. So many folks cutting records down there these days, a man can earn his fortune just making union scale. Mind you, the music's not much. But if I play my cards right, two, three years, I'll have enough to get my hands on a little piece of land back home I've had my eye on now for a while. My brother Tom, he's watching it for me, making sure nobody else gets to it first."

It was the most I'd heard him say in the entire two weeks I'd known him.

"I'm no boy any more," he said. "This here ain't no way for a grown man to be carrying on."

I struggled to think of something to say. He was asleep and snoring before I could come up with anything.

28.

THE POWERS-THAT-BE decided that if Christine and the seven others at the protest each paid a token fine and promised never to do anything naughty again like hold up traffic they could run along and play and hopefully someday soon see the light and get on with the serious business of understanding their responsibilities as citizens of a democratic community that expects—nay, assembled young sirs and madams, *demands*—that each member respect and uphold such basic community standards as blah blah blah. Our trust in the wisdom of the judicial system renewed, Christine only fifteen dollars poorer and immediately ready to resume wreaking havoc on the business interests preying upon poor little innocent lamb Yorkville, we ducked into a stall in the woman's washroom on the second floor of city hall fresh from the acquittal for half a shared joint and one quickie, doggie style. Take that, your Honour.

So, no, I wasn't going to have to bake Christine any chocolate-chip convict cakes with files and hacksaws buried in them. I also decided that I wasn't going to lose any sleep over Slippery's pledge to clean up his act and get out of Toronto ASAP. I let Thomas in on all that Slippery had told me and left it at that. If Thomas wanted him in the band so badly, let him worry about it, I thought. I had other things on my mind. Or, rather, in my blood.

Like all the shops, clubs, and apartments in the village with all their doors and windows bursting off their hinges wide, wide open once again, me greedily gulping in great big long-overdue spring-time-fresh air breaths, all the lovely swirling sensations of music and happy café chatter and incense filling the streets and pushing out of mind if not out of sight the one too many cops on the beat frowning the happily derelict hippy-dippy smile of the neighbour-hood. Even Scotty was in what for him passed for a good mood these days, had returned with the birds and bees and the warmer weather to his usual roosting spot at the corner card table, for a nice change doing a lot more silent reading than cutting-up of the poem in front of him.

Sitting right across from him, Heather serenely flipped Tarot cards on the tabletop. And with the first fresh gust of spring Christine kicked aside her black combat boots and socks to bet-ter explore the sole-thumping, soul-soothing effect every *plunk*

plunk plunk vibration of her bass guitar sent through the studio's hardwood floor. It was a permanent experiment. I couldn't really tell what this meant for her playing, but it did wonders for me. Women's exposed toes, no matter what the occasion, always were one of my favourite things.

And who ever heard of a musical revolution or any other for that matter on such a galloping green gorgeous day as this, anyway? I felt like having a picnic and drinking a gallon of Kool-Aid and playing Frisbee with somebody's dog all afternoon long.

But instead we were in the studio, waiting as usual for Slippery to show up so we could practise around him. On Sundays, when Christine and I weren't working, we rehearsed in the afternoon. The idea was that a change was as good as a rest, but today nothing short of joining the laughter in the street down below and getting some of that good sunshine on my winter-white face and inhaling as many springtime scents as I could was going to do the trick. My nose was twitching like a nervous rabbit's in the direction of the open balcony doors.

"Want to try 'Dundas West' again?" Christine said to Thomas, strapping on her bass. "I think I've got an idea of what you're trying to do in the middle part now, that part that drops out."

Christine didn't want to be stuck inside any more than I did, but, unlike me, was always for sensibly getting down to whatever had to get done. The well-organized political agitator in her, I guess.

Thomas was casually tuning his unplugged electric. "Slippery's not here yet," he said.

Christine looked at me behind my kit. I rat-tatted the snare and tightened its head.

"Do you think anybody'll notice?" she said.

Thomas looked up from his Gretch and gave a little smile. "Hey, now, that's not nice. That's no way to talk about your fellow band member."

"Band members practise with the other members of their band," Christine said. "All this guy does is occupy space for two hours."

She turned on her amp and immediately began plucking out the jaunty opening notes of our instrumental, "Dundas West." I joined in, clod-hopping along on high hat and wood. After a couple minutes of waiting for Thomas's guitar to come in, we stopped. The room went silent and we both looked at him. He was still happily tuning away.

"Care to join us, Thomas?" Christine said.

Thomas looked up from his guitar again, gave a cursory glance around the room. "Slippery's not here yet."

Christine shook her head. "And?"

Thomas smiled, then went back to his guitar.

Christine looked at me again. I shrugged.

"Tell me something, Thomas," she said. "What's the big fascination with this guy, anyway? I really want to know."

"I hear a steel guitar, Miss Christine."

"Great, you hear a steel guitar. Fantastic. But why does it have to be this guy's steel guitar?"

"Slippery's got something we're looking for. His sound and our sound belong together."

"And when exactly do we get to hear this sound of his?"

Thomas stood up, strummed some chord changes, but didn't turn on his amp. "Soon."

"Soon," Christine said.

"Soon."

Christine fired me a don't-just-sit-there-say-something-why-don't-you? glare, but I pretended there was something wrong with my foot pedal and slid down behind the kit to check things out. The official philosophy of Bill Hansen: When in doubt, turtle.

"Okay," Christine said. "Let's say that this guy eventually does rise from the dead and dazzle us all with his playing. What then? What's the point? Nobody around here is going to book a band with a steel guitar in it. Maybe that's not right, maybe that's prejudiced, but if we want to get a gig we've got to face facts."

"We've already got a gig," Thomas said. "One week from Saturday night. Mark it in on your calendars, y'all."

I peeked out from behind the bass drum. Christine looked at me, then back at Thomas. But before either of us could ask how he'd done it and where we were playing, all of us turned in the direction of the creaking steps at the top of the stairs.

Slippery paused at the studio door and stomped out his cigarette, the only time he'd ever done so to my knowledge without Thomas's having to ask him to three times. He nodded at Thomas, ignored Christine and me, and sat down behind his pedal steel. He flipped on the power switch underneath and asked what we were working on.

No one said anything, just looked at him like we didn't have a clue who this obviously sober, clean-shaven guy was. Sober, but by the snarly, slightly anemic look on his face, not all that happy about it. Clean-shaven, but with about half a dozen tiny pieces of blood-blotted white toilet paper plastered to his chin and neck. He ran a shaky hand through his Vaselined hair and reasserted the freshly combed part; wiped his hand on his suit pants and picked up the silver tension bar and put it to the strings of his instrument. Addressing Thomas, "Are we gonna play or aren't we?"

Thomas smiled and plugged in.

"Sweet baby Jesus! Yes! Yes!"

And just like that we knew that Scotty had finally finished the poem he'd been wrestling with all winter. He dropped his pen to the table and drew Heather to her feet and waltzed her around the room, wee man him expertly leading tall woman her. When

Scotty dipped her over by my drum kit, she threw back her head and laughed like she knew everything had been in the cards all along.

To Christine and me, "'Dundas West'?" Thomas said.

"Dundas West" it was.

Thomas tapped his cowboy boot to the steady beat we were laying down for a few closed-eyed seconds before ripping into the song's opening notes, something between a tart twang and a full metallic roar charging out of his amp. And when Slippery found his way into our groove, answering the fat slabs of Thomas's guitar with run after run of mean little twists and turns of sharp pedal steel, something happened.

We blasted away, all four of us, until the inching shadows of evening swallowed up the room's natural light and the red glow of the amplifiers was all that was left to guide us.

29.

"HOW DID YOU KNOW he'd end up doing what you wanted?" I asked.

Thomas and I were mopping up the remains of our breakfast and slurping down refills of coffee at Webster's because we had a 10 a.m. appointment to look at a couple of new microphones we needed for our inaugural show that night.

"Who's that?" Thomas said, managing to mop and slurp at the same time, fork-speared sausage link and coffee cup both suspended in the air.

"Slippery."

"Afraid I don't follow you, Buckskin. Hey, you gonna finish those potatoes?"

"Go ahead," I said, pushing my plate across the table.

I was down about five pounds from all the speed I was taking, but the food on my plate and not in my stomach this particular morning was due more to the tumbly-tummy thought of that night's gig.

"I mean," I said, "you must have known this guy was a wreck right from the first time you talked to him on the phone. What made you so sure you could turn him around?"

The deal was that Thomas would pay Slippery twice what he was previously giving him for every week he managed to stay sober. One Slippery slip-up, though, just one performance compromised by a sloppy Bannister, one practice with even the faintest hint of hooch detected on his breath, and he got nothing, zilch, nada. Slippery's only other choice was to collect the hundred-dollar bonus Thomas had promised him and ship off back to Detroit the same way he'd arrived, an alcoholic ex–auto worker with about as much chance of earning the money he needed to make the down payment on his Arkansas dream house as I did of staging a miraculous comeback and cracking the Leafs' starting lineup.

Thomas speared the last home fry off my plate, twirled it around in a glob of ketchup and popped it into his mouth. Waiting until he was done chewing and had swallowed, "You gotta have faith, Buckskin."

"Sure," I said. "But I get the feeling you knew right from the start that you could get Slippery under your thumb as soon as you got him up here."

"I still don't get where you're coming from, buddy."

"Where I'm coming from is that within two weeks you managed to blackmail a quart-of-whisky-a-day alcoholic hillbilly into quitting drinking cold turkey and committing to playing in a long-haired rock and roll band."

Thomas leaned back in the booth, picked at a piece of something stuck between his teeth with the forefinger of his strumming hand. "'Blackmail,'" he repeated. "Hey, that's a little heavy, don't you think?"

"What would you call it, then?"

Picking up his napkin, wiping his lips clean, "Sometimes the Good Lord, Buckskin, sometimes He works in very mysterious ways."

"And let me guess. The Good Lord, He also helps those who help themselves."

"You said it, not me," he answered, balling up his napkin and dropping it onto his empty plate. "Wouldn't catch me disagreeing with you, though. No, sir, that you would not."

30.

"GEEZ, THOMAS."

"Where did you . . . ?"

"Geez," Christine repeated.

"Yeah, I mean, how did you . . . ?"

"Isn't it great, y'all?" Thomas said. "Got it from a guy at the Cellar. Overheard him telling the fellow he was playing chess with that he wanted to unload it and I made him an offer right on the spot. I got a great deal."

"This here's a hearse," Slippery said.

"Yes, sir, that it is, a '58 Buick hearse, in fact. And from what I understand, a vintage year and make, too." We were on the sidewalk in front of our studio. Thomas spotted a freshly plopped blotch of bird shit on the vehicle's black trunk and used a fallen leaf to wipe it off.

"But why?" I said.

"Take a peek inside," Thomas answered.

I looked at Christine.

"Go on," Thomas said, sliding open the side door. "Nothing in there's going to get up from the dead and bite you."

I stuck my head in and looked around.

"I don't see anything but a whole lot of nothing," I said.

"Exactly," Thomas said. "Which means a whole lot of room for all our equipment."

Getting it now, "For gigs," I said.

All four of us looked at the long black hearse anew now, the occasional hippie type even slowing down to stare from the other side of the street. It took a lot to get somebody to stop and stare in Yorkville.

Slippery fired up a fresh Marlboro. "I ain't ridin' around in no hearse," he said.

"Don't you worry, Mr. Bannister," Thomas said, "there's plenty of room for all of us as well as our stuff. And depending on how Buckskin and Miss Christine feel, I was thinking it was only fair—musically, seniority-wise—for you to ride up front with me." Thomas looked at us.

"I've got no problem with that," I said.

"Sure," Christine said.

"Got nothin' to do with not having enough room for ridin'," Slippery said. "It just ain't proper to be blaspheming the Lord in such a way. Funerals is serious business."

"Mr. Bannister, you misunderstand my intentions," Thomas said. "It wasn't only for pragmatic purposes that I procured for us this fine specimen of an automobile."

"One more time?" Slippery said.

"Hear me out, sir. Just as Mr. Johnny Cash has taken to wearing black garments during his recent performances to illustrate his sympathy with all the earth's distressed and downtrodden, so, I hope, will the Duckhead Secret Society be able to pay their respects to all those who share in the sorrow that is manifest in the necessary leave-taking of family and friends to that other shore each and every time we're out on the road."

Slippery sucked on his cigarette and squinted at the hearse. "You're sayin' this"—he pointed with his Marlboro—"ain't no sacrilege?"

"The farthest thing from it," Thomas answered, sitting on the hood now. "I call her Saint Chrome Christopher, Christopher, for short." Gesturing from back bumper to front tire, "A ton and a half of Christian metaphor everywhere we go is no inconsiderable fact to be denied, sir."

Slippery took a last long drag and tossed his butt into the gutter. "As long as it ain't no heresy."

"C'mon, now, Mr. Bannister," Thomas said, sliding off the car. "I'm from Mississippi. I was brought up *right*."

Cracking what for him passed as a smile, "I suppose," Slippery said.

"All right, then," Thomas said, looking at his watch. "Almost two o'clock. That gives us six hours until sound check. Everybody meet back here at six-thirty to help pack up and we're off for the club by seven."

"Any club in particular?" I said. "Or are we just going to drive around until we find one that'll take us in?"

"Yeah, c'mon, Thomas," Christine chimed in. "Cut the suspense already."

Thomas got inside Christopher and turned over the engine.

"Six-thirty, right here," he said. "And let me remind everyone that six-thirty does not mean six-thirty-one."

31.

"MAYBE I'LL HANG around here until you get off," I said. I'd walked Christine to work and we'd already kissed and said goodbye about ten times. Five hours to kill so as not to think about five hours later and no one willing to help me play assassin.

"Everything's going to be fine," she said. "Once we start playing you won't have a chance to think of anything but music."

"Easy for you to say. This isn't your first time on stage."

"It's not yours either. Remember how good the three of us were that night at my show?"

"The Riverboat doesn't count. I was too shocked to be properly terrified. Now I've got all afternoon to get good and ready."

"Go back to my place and smoke a joint and try to relax. Lay down for a while."

Since I'd started carrying around my own bottle of uppers, naps weren't much of an option any more. "I know what would make me relax," I said, running my hand down her back, cupping a handful of blue-jeaned flesh.

She laughed and twisted around to see if anyone inside was looking and kissed me one final time. "It's a drag, I know, but unfortunately Sam's doesn't pay me to get groped by my boyfriend." Opening up the door, "Pick me up at five-thirty," she said. "And try to stay out of trouble, okay?"

I said I'd do my best and let the Yonge Street tide roll me away.

Where, after taking half of Christine's advice, the part about smoking a joint, I passed the afternoon sticking my head into nearly every club along the strip until somebody would invariably ask me what I wanted or who I was looking for or where my ID was. Blinding dark as only badass bars on afternoons of absolute sunshine can be, none of these places had ever played host to Pete Seeger or Joni Mitchell and definitely did not cater to the peace-and-love set. The bars that ran along Yonge from Gerrard to Queen like the Steele's Tavern, the Colonial Tavern, and especially Le Coq d'Or, were the anti-Yorkville in every way, urban-burning neon bright on the outside, hot and heavy by way of the ballsy R&B sounds pounding against their walls within. I drifted down the street like some turned-on tourist and let the music play a bump and grind soundtrack to the same sexy flick I kept seeing everywhere I went.

Because even in their tight white sweaters and high black heels and blowing perfect rings of smoke with those candy-apple red lipsticked lips, what really got me were all those breasts. Actually, all those bras. Miles and miles of silky white cloth and thousands and thousands of shining silver hooks and eyelets aching to be undone. Brassieres, in other words. Lingerie. Bras.

No self-respecting woman of the revolution ever wore a bra in Yorkville. And politically, not to mention aesthetically, I couldn't have agreed more. Nine times out of ten. But this was that one other time, when every Sears catalogue I ever pored over behind my parents' locked bathroom door while ogling the lady's underwear section burned back to mind just below my belt buckle, when every dumb male fantasy of garter belts and spiked heels that had owned my mind as a monkey-spanking preteen growing up in the fifties once again possessed it. Not an excuse, but the best explanation I could come up with for the few times I'd persuaded Christine to use her mother's For Emergencies Only credit card to bring home with us for the night an expensive pair of strapped evening pumps or plain white five-inch heels before returning them the next day with receipt in hand and lowered eyes.

By the time I'd drifted clear down to King Street it was nearly five. Christine was waiting for me outside Sam's when I got back.

"Am I late?" I said.

"You're right on time," she answered, kissing me on the cheek. "I actually finished about half an hour ago. Things were slow so I asked if I could split early."

We started walking toward Bloor, toward Yorkville. "What's in the bag?" I said.

"I decided to do a little shopping."

Christine liked shopping about as much as she did hairspray. "What for?" I said. "For tonight?"

Still walking, she pulled a cardboard box from inside the large brown plastic bag. Opening its lid and watching my face for a reaction, she got the one she wanted. I took one last look, replaced the top, and put the shoebox under my arm. I grabbed her hand.

"What time did Thomas say we had to be at the studio?" I said.

"Six-thirty."

I began to walk faster. "That doesn't give us much time."

Squeezing my hand, "How much time do you really think we'll need?" she said.

32.

WE ALL PITCHED in and loaded up Christopher. And even with all our equipment and Heather and Scotty along for the ride, no one was seriously put out, Thomas and Slippery with lots of leg room riding together up front. Besides, we were only going down the street. Christine and I even had a bet going. I said the Boris', she said the Purple Onion. The loser had to return the stilettos.

Across Yorkville, south on Bay to Bloor, thirty miles an hour east.

I crawled to the front and stuck my head between Thomas's and Slippery's. "This club, it's not in Yorkville?" I said.

"It's a little outside Yorkville," Thomas answered, flipping on the turn signal. Slippery spit some chaw into a paper Dixie cup resting on his thigh. I crawled back to the others.

Down some side street to Carlton, down to Dundas, and then to Queen.

On my hands and knees, I made it through the maze of musical instruments to the front one more time. "Did you forget something?" I said. Thomas lived in the east end and by now we were only a few minutes away.

"Everything I need to conquer the world I got right here in this Buick, Buckskin," he said, stopping for a red light.

"Then where are we going?" I said. I felt like some back-seat-banished ten-year-old desperate to be let in on the action, begging his parents to let him know when they'll get there. A cymbal crashed on its side and Christine pushed her head in beside mine.

"Where are we?" she said.

"Nowhere," I answered. We were idling in that part of Queen Street East where the pawnshops and Salvation Armys took over. I looked out the window and recognized the bar on the corner, the Canada Tavern, from my earliest Interstellar edification lesson with Thomas.

"We're playing down here?" she said, looking at me.

"We're not playing down here," I said.

The light turned green and Thomas pulled left onto Sherbourne and then right into a parking place on the street beside the bar. We all sat there for a moment listening to the sound of the engine rattle and ping to a stop.

I squeezed forward even further. "What is this, Thomas?" I said.

Thomas slowly turned his head toward mine. "This," he said, "is where it all begins."

That look in his eyes. Goddammit. I knew there wasn't anything left to do but unpack.

33.

THE CANADA TAVERN was the kind of place that didn't have any windows. Spilt beer, urine, and the sound of a deep-fryer bubbling away in the tiny kitchen beside the bar informed all available senses that we weren't in Yorkville any more.

No one played the jukebox. When, in between trips out to Christopher to unload our equipment, Thomas fished out a dime and punched in a few tunes, no one appeared to notice. Even the few scattered drinkers who weren't actually old still managed to somehow seem it, on every face that hard, used-up look that only poverty, loneliness, and anger working together can carve. They watched us cart in our stuff with a distrust that went way beyond our long hair and goofy clothes. We didn't have to be here but they did, and they wanted us to know they knew it.

While Thomas stayed behind to talk to Leone, the Canada Tavern's owner, a balding behemoth in a grease-stained apron with a lip-dangling toothpick, Christine and I followed Slippery's lead and started to set up. Whether because her Tarot cards told her to or because she knew we'd all have a much better chance of not getting knifed if we stayed huddled together, Heather sat close by on the edge of the stage waiting for Thomas's return while working on her third nervous cigarette since we'd walked in the door.

The five or six solo drinkers scattered across the cavernous room seemed more interested in nursing their first early-evening beers than in us putting our instruments in order, but I kept an alert eye anyway for any stage-rushing rowdies. Not that I would know what to do if any trouble did break out—my last fist fight being a grade-nine rumble with Pete Elson over a broken road-hockey stick and who was going to pay for it (I like to remember it as a well-earned draw)—but I blew the hair out of my eyes with purpose as I assembled my crash cymbal so that everyone could get a better look at my drop-dead sneer. That'll keep them in their seats, I thought.

Much more effective at making us all feel a little bit safer was Scotty playing his usual skid-row regal role, lording over his own private table topped off with his usual glass of beer, today's *Daily Star*, and the ink-smeared sheets of his newest poem. I took his calming cue and gradually set to work in earnest putting my kit together. Even if I'd never played in public before, everybody knew that the drummer was always stuck way at the back of the stage, protected behind everyone else. I got on my knees and screwed in my bass pedal and counted my blessings.

Except for saying where to put that and let me carry those, none of us had spoken a word yet about what our odds were of surviving past the first set. Slippery, I'm sure, didn't even notice. Thirty-plus years on and off the road from Salinas to Cincinnati, he'd probably seen a lot worse. Christine, though, had even more reason to keep her shoulder to the wheel of the job at hand than me.

A couple of the bar's relatively younger patrons in red flannel lumberjack shirts managed to look up from their beers long enough to discover that, hey, that bald hippie girl up there on stage with no shoes or socks on and wearing no bra is real easy on the eyes, isn't she? It was like watching some new Olympic event, synchronized leering. Ogle for ogle, every one of Christine's even slightest body movements was matched exactly by the two pairs of eyes. Because of where they were sitting, the spirited run of commentary the two were carrying on was thankfully out of earshot. I caught Christine's eye as she plugged her bass into the amp beside my drums.

"How's it going?" I said.

"Fine."

I nodded, tested my bass pedal.

"I think it looks worse than it actually is," I said.

Christine heaved a deep, bothered breath and shook her head. "What? What looks worse?"

"You know, the really dangerous dog is the one that doesn't look it. Same thing as here, only the opposite."

She stopped fiddling around with the dials on the amplifier long enough to say, "If you've got something on your mind, Bill, spit it out, okay? I haven't got time for riddles right now." She stared at the amp like if she looked at it long and hard enough the answer to why she was here and not somewhere else might suddenly appear. The thing wasn't even turned on.

I took off her bass, set it down, and grabbed her hand. "C'mon," I said.

Heather shot up from her spot on stage. "Where are you two going?" she said, pulling down her long purple peasant skirt on all sides.

"Just outside for a minute," I said.

"Can I come?" she said, stamping out her cigarette, coughing, waving away the heavy cloud of smoke encircling her head. Having already emptied her own pack of Player's while waiting for Thomas's return, she was smoking Slippery's Marlboros, but without having quite gotten the hang yet of the extra nicotine punch.

"We'll be right back," I answered, pulling Christine toward the side door.

Hurriedly gathering up her fringed cloth bag, "I'm coming with you."

"Don't worry," I said, "Thomas'll be back any minute now."

She tugged down her skirt over and over again, like if she didn't the thing would fly up over her head. Hugging herself tight with a gently freckled arm, "Why is it taking him so long then?" she said. "What's he doing up there? What's going on? Why is he leaving me alone like this? He *knows* I don't like being left alone like this, Bill."

Christ, I thought. Haven't I already got one petrified woman on my hands as it is?

From the other side of the stage, "You and Christine go on and get yourselves some fresh air," Slippery piped in from behind his pedal steel. "Heather, if you ain't too busy, I'd appreciate your help over here."

Heather turned around and faced him but didn't say anything, still clutched the handful of cigarettes he'd given her so hard that several had snapped in two, tobacco slowly spilling onto the stage.

"This here's what you might call a spiritual matter," Slippery said. "I think I might be in need of a dose of them foreseeing cards of yours."

Heather looked once again in the direction of the bar in the other room. Thomas was laughing at something Leone had said, Leone smiling and pouring Thomas and himself drinks from a bottle of Crown Royal. Heather turned back to Slippery and loosened her grip on herself a little. She licked her lips as if to speak, but nothing came out.

Slippery pulled out his red-and-white pack of Marlboros from the top pocket of his shirt, tapped out two, and stuck one in his mouth. "Like I say," he said, holding out the other cigarette, "I'd be much obliged if you could help me out."

Her arms gradually relaxed, fell to her sides. Slippery produced his blowtorch of a silver lighter and lit first her smoke, then his.

Heather sucked deeply, exhaled. "What month were you born?" she asked.

"November."

"I knew it," she said. "I knew you were a Scorpio."

"We'll be back in five minutes," I said.

In spite of the warm night and the fairly heavy foot traffic of unshaven, unsteady men, no one asked Christine or me for any spare change. It took me a while to realize that the hard-up don't panhandle the hard-up. Poor people might not usually have much education, but they're not stupid. They can't afford to be.

The occasional old man's long lecherous stare in passing at Christine kept us a little unsettled, though, so we hung close to the side door I'd jammed open a crack with one of my drumsticks. I put my arms around her waist and pulled her close. "Are you going to be all right with this?" I said.

She wouldn't look at me, kept her eyes on the sizzling red sign over the shop across the street. *Bud's Bond Office* was now *ud's Bo ice*.

"All right with what?"

She said it, I heard her, but she didn't mean it, I heard that, too. Right then and there I was ready to tell Thomas we were packing up and heading back to the village and if he didn't like it he could find himself a new drummer. Period. All Christine had to do was say that she hadn't finally found in Yorkville a place where nobody cared if you decided to shave your head or got arrested for civil disobedience or slapped a bass guitar in your bare feet if you felt like it only to end up playing Playboy centrefold to a bunch of dirty old men. All she had to do was say it.

But Christine had been the only one the cops had had to literally drag away during the Yorkville bust, forcing two of them to carry all 125 protesting pounds of her to their waiting paddy wagon. Christine didn't know what a white flag was.

We hugged. Then Christine told the next greybeard who lingered a little too long in his lusting, "Get a good look, grandpa, it's the closest you'll ever get to getting any in this life," and we hugged again, this time topped off with a long, hard kiss and a beautiful bare foot snaking up my leg. Then there was Thomas.

"Sound check, y'all," he said.

This time Christine took me by the hand and we went back inside. I pulled out my drumstick and the door shut tight all on its own.

34.

SUCKED WOULD BE too strong a word.

I mean, no one walked out on us. But, then, there weren't that many there to begin with, maybe double the half-dozen or so who'd watched us set up. True, no one covered their ears or booed or hissed or hurled cold French fries in the direction of the stage, but no one appeared to be actually listening, either. The end of each song was received with the exact same echoing silence, Thomas's occasional between-song banter ignored as much as our music.

The second set went about the same as the first except that at one point a man with a spaghetti-thin moustache that he must have gotten the idea for from an old gangster film on late night TV and decked out in a brown pin-striped suit that was too tight in the jacket and too short in the legs got up to dance with a woman who was either his girlfriend or wife. The song was a slow one, the Everly's "Take a Message to Mary," Thomas and Christine trying out their close high harmonies for the first time in public.

Before they made it to the chorus, though, the woman for some reason pulled back a balled fist, punched the man square in the face, and stomped off to the washroom. The man managed to find his seat, sit back down, and order another round. Periodically he'd dab at his bloody nose with a white handkerchief. By the time the next song was over the woman had returned to their table and was sipping the fresh rum and Coke that had been placed in front of her and wiping the man's nose, shaking her head in slight disgust the entire time. The bleeding eventually stopped and no one else decided to crack the boards for the remainder of the evening.

I saw the entire thing from behind my kit. Whether he wants it or not, a drummer, I found out, always has the best seat in the house.

35.

LEONE, IT TURNED OUT, either didn't mind or didn't much care what our Duckheaded take on bar-band C&W sounded like, and wasn't even all that concerned about the meagre crowd or the less-than-rabid audience response. Leone had a cardboard sign in the window that said LIVE ENTERTAINMENT FIVE NIGHTS A WEEK, and if we were willing to work for the pittance he was paying and capable of keeping the hippie shenanigans to a minimum ("No whacky-tobaccy breaks in the bathroom"), the job of being the Canada Tavern's official house band was ours if we wanted it. Thomas told us we did. Christine and I weren't so sure.

The afternoon after our first show was Slippery's one-more-week-sober payday, and he neatly folded the wad of bills Thomas handed him into his silver money clip and let us three worry over the band's immediate future. The day was a dazzling duplicate of the one before, but no matter what the blue sky outside the opened studio doors said, just the idea of putting our collective nostrils through the ordeal of another long night of backed-up toilets, mildewy rugs, and cheap cologne was enough to make it feel like the middle of gloomy February all over again. I'd brushed my teeth twice and taken three scouring showers but still couldn't get the smell of stale cigarette smoke out of my pores.

Christine walked over to the balcony and breathed in a good, long noseful of fresh air like she was storing up for what she knew was ahead. Still apparently stuck on not being the party-pooper to say that this particular cut-off to the Interstellar North American Musical expressway was a tad bit rougher than she'd imagined, she was putting me in the rare position of being the one to go toe-to-toe with Thomas. I gave it my best shot. I didn't have a chance.

"There were twelve people there last night," I said. "Believe me, I counted. But the way those zombies were paying attention, there might as well have been none."

"But that's the beauty of it," Thomas said, "that's the best part. That's just what we need right now."

"An audience full of drunks?"

"Elbow room, Buckskin. All the time and space we need to stretch out and get ourselves ready to get to the next level. Five nights a week, two sets a night of uninterrupted elbow room."

"Five nights a week after working five days a week," I said. "Where does sleep fit into this equation? Twenty bucks a week isn't going to pay anybody's rent and groceries." Or anybody's student loan, either, I could have added, but didn't. Thomas looked down at the mandolin in his hands. Slippery looked away. They both knew I wasn't talking about either of them.

Standing right in front of me now, plucking away at the thread of a melody I'd never heard before, "There was a reason I didn't want anybody we know there last night," Thomas said.

"We were all right," I said.

"We were just where we should be right now. The question is, are we prepared to go where we need to be?" He turned his attention back to the mandolin and closed his eyes, concentrated on coaxing out the emerging tune.

The sounds he was making weren't like anything I'd ever heard before. The dozen or so songs of his he'd taught us so far were definitely out in left field, but this thing, now we weren't even in the ballpark any more. 1883 Old West yellow. Psychedelic cum-shot purple. Infinite snowstorm white-noise white. And orange. The setting sun a flaming tangerine ready to burst juicy burning bits of fiery pulp all over the parched earth's scurvy-scarred face.

For nearly five minutes the melody arched and looped and curled through the air like lunatic smoke, repeating bits and pieces of chord progressions along the way, at times even seeming to pull itself apart as if looking around inside before finally drifting back to catch the next melodic wave. And all of this on a mandolin. Even Slippery was paying attention now, tilting his head to one side like a puzzled dog.

Song finally finished, its harmonic hum still alive and hanging in the air, "What is it?" I said.

Thomas looked up from the instrument, the slightest smile on his exhausted face. His brow was wet. "Something I've been working on," he said. "One of a whole bunch. Something new."

The first time—the only time—was when Thomas was eleven and Selma got the new vacuum cleaner his father had been promising her for months and everyone was standing around the parlour watching her haul the huge machine around behind her. The thing looked like a small silver tank and made almost as much noise. So much so that Thomas's mother only stayed around long enough to smile politely in response to her husband's raised eyebrows in the direction of his kind-hearted purchase. One by one all of the Grahams eventually quit the room and left Selma to her work. All except for Thomas.

Thomas stood glued to the same spot listening to the sound the vacuum cleaner made until Selma poked at his white bucks with the end of her nozzle for him to move out of the way. He sat on the couch until she was finished and had shut off the machine and unplugged the cord from the wall and asked him what he was doing just sitting there.

"Nothing," he said.

"Well, you can do that just as well outside in the fresh air."

Thomas nodded but followed her up the stairs and from bedroom to bedroom anyway. Every room, same thing. He'd just stand there until she needed to get where he was with the cleaner, then be startled awake with a nudge from her nozzle and go and sit on the bed until she was done and ready to move down the hall. After a while Selma got tired of asking him what he thought he was up to sitting there like that and him mumbling "nothing" every time she did. Besides, it was nice to have the company.

When there weren't any more floors to clean, when all of her work was done, Selma stepped on a silver foot pedal and the long white cord slithered back inside the machine, its loud plastic-to-metal snap waking Thomas up for good. Selma asked her little helper if he wanted to come downstairs with her and have a piece of Chess pie and a glass of milk, but Thomas said no thank you and went to his room and locked the door and lay down on the bed and tried not to forget.

But what he heard in his head was like the sound the chugging Mississippi Southern made at night coming in his window so loud and so clear and then, three minutes later, so faint and so gone, just like the picture on the TV screen when Daddy turned it off for the evening, sucking down in seconds to a dying silver dot. Notes, chords, and even entire fully formed melodies floated fat and bright before his eyes, but not the whole thing, not the one long remarkable song of before. He tried so hard to remember what he'd heard that he got an upset stomach and a pounding headache and had to stop trying. He fell asleep exhausted, thinking this must be what Momma felt like when she didn't come out of her room for sometimes two days at a time and he and Becky weren't allowed to talk above a whisper and Daddy seemed mad about everything.

The next time, the next week, Thomas was right there and ready when Selma lugged the machine out of the closet and set to work. But it was just the racket from a vacuum cleaner and not the most perfect music he'd ever heard. This time, before she was even halfway done with the parlour, he did go outside, and without her asking.

He climbed to the top of his favourite Dream of Pines pine and stayed there until dark. By the time he came back down, he knew who he was.

36.

YOU KNOW YOU'RE a regular when the bartender starts taking phone messages for you.

"Your boss, Kelorn Something, called," Leone said, refilling my glass of Coke from a black nozzle behind the bar. "She said to tell you you left the lights on again."

"Shit."

"And that she had a couple complaints about the store not being open."

"Shit."

Leone spotted an empty draft glass and lumbered off to replace it with a swiftly poured other. With only one drink legally allowed per person per table at a time back then, one thing I'd learned for sure over the month and some we'd been playing at the Canada Tavern was that the number-one requirement for a good bartender was excellent long-range vision.

I sucked the brown glob of foam off the top of my glass, nose involuntarily wrinkling at the Coke's tickling fizz. It was incredible I wasn't immune to the stuff yet. Alcohol we had to pay for the same as everybody else, but Leone gave the band free refills on coffee and pop. Twenty-five cents down and I was set for the night, by the time we were all packed up and ready to go home was more jingle-jangle wired than Mr. Tambourine Man himself.

Which meant that even after putting in eight hours at Making Waves and nearly another five at the Canada Tavern, between the pep pills and the gallon or so of Coca-Cola I guzzled every evening, I was lucky to conk out before sun-up. I'd lie awake for what felt like hours staring at the ceiling of Christine's room, trying not to fidget around too much so at least she could get some sleep. Having to be up by nine in order to open up the bookstore by ten, I began to live in dread of the sound of the birds in her backyard beginning their first-light twittering, their nauseatingly cheerful announcement of another way-too-soon morning.

But every show was better than the one before. Every *set* was better than the one before. No one actually said anything, of course. Christine and I locking eyes in a shared moment of deep, clean rhythm, Slippery and Thomas slashing back and forth competing but complimentary electric and steel-guitar runs, all three of them stacking their voices on top of each other in the soulfully raggedy country-gospel style Thomas had taught them, no one had to.

I heard the electric crackling of Thomas's guitar coming from the stage and emptied my pop. Break was over. Leone was back behind the bar and put the nozzle to the lip of my glass and blasted it to the brim.

37.

HERE'S A RECIPE you shouldn't try at home: take one couple and one blossoming amphetamine habit, mix in a generous portion of mostly sleepless, mostly screwless nights, and then let not-so-gently simmer over a steadily smoldering early morning melee that begins with something really important, like:

"That's not what I said."

"What did you say, then?"

"I don't remember my exact words, but—"

"You can't remember what you said, but you know you didn't say it. Huh."

"I *know* what I said."

"So I'm a liar, then? Is that what you're saying?"

"I'm not saying you're a liar. Don't put words in my mouth."

"I'm not putting words in your mouth, I'm just repeating what you said."

"No, you're not, you're putting words in my mouth."

"No, I'm not, I'm just repeating what you said. That I'm a liar."

"I didn't say . . . Jesus Christ, I wish I had a tape recorder every time—"

"I wish *I* had a tape recorder every time—"

And when any argument gets to the I-wish-I-had-a-tape-recorder stage, it's probably just best to declare a ceasefire and aim to move on as peacefully as possible.

So, bursting through the front door of Christine's place, still sticking arms through shirt sleeves and plucking sleep crust from our eyes, we scurried together in silence down the street looking like a couple of those exercise nuts who aren't actually jogging but are doing something more than mere walking, like they've pulled the hamstrings in both legs but are in too much of a hurry to stop. Hitting Bay Street, all the shops busily peopled and every newspaper box already half empty, we didn't need the alarm clock back in her room to tell us that it was nearly eleven.

Kelorn wouldn't be real pleased to find out that I'd been an hour late in opening up the shop, but at worst she'd be disappointed in me, meaning I'd probably end up feeling worse about the whole thing than she did. Christine's boss was an entirely different kettle of capitalist fish. Just a month before, he'd canned one of her anarchist roommates, Kent, who'd gotten his job solely on her recommendation, because of chronic lateness. Unlike Kent, who not long after getting sacked inherited a couple of thousand bucks from a wealthy aunt and simultaneously came to the powerfully philosophical conclusion that "Working is, like, for fools, man," Christine didn't expect to become an heiress any time soon.

At the corner of Bay and Cumberland, where I was supposed to go one way and she another, "Keep walking," I said, "I'll be right back," and raced off ahead of her.

"Bill, I don't have time for . . ."

I ducked inside the first store I thought might sell something edible, a pharmacy, grabbed a Kit Kat bar from the shelf, and got in line behind an elderly woman buying a clear plastic bag of cotton balls, a *Happy Birthday to a Wonderful Grandson!* birthday card, and a bar of soap. Christine could get by without a lot of things—sleep, sex, her boyfriend's less-than-perfect memory— but got woozy and weird when her blood sugar level fell too far below normal. The ten cents' worth of glucose and fat weren't a fully balanced breakfast, but they'd get her through until lunch. And, incidentally, demonstrate what a selfless, considerate sweetheart I was after all.

"I'm sorry, Mr. Smith, how much was that again?" the woman asked the man behind the cash, an only slightly less-antique-looking guy in a blue cardigan with black reading glasses hanging around his neck on a thin silver chain. The store radio played CHFI, the same station my parents listened to at home, Frank Sinatra's "Summer Wind" serenely blowing through the room.

The man carefully rested his glasses on the edge of his nose and stooped forward to peer at the till. "I believe I said two dollars and ninety-six cents, Mrs. Peters."

"That's what I thought you said, but I wanted to be sure." The old woman took out a small change purse from inside her regular purse and placed two crisp dollar bills on the countertop. Then poured out a clattering pile of change and began to count.

"Ten. Fifteen. Thirty. Thirty-five. Thirty-six, thirty-seven . . ."

"Can I just pay for this?" I said, holding up the candy bar.

The old man looked up and the old lady tilted around like I'd just asked if I could camp out for a few days in my sleeping bag in the middle of the store.

"I'm sorry, *sir*," the old man said, "you're going to have to wait your turn. Just like everyone else." They both returned to the mound of coins.

"Now, where were we?" he said. "Ah, yes, let's see." He picked up where the old lady had left off. "Thirty-eight. Forty-three. Fifty-three, fifty-four . . ."

Christine rapped twice on the store window and pointed to an imaginary watch on her wrist. I plunked down the Kit Kat and my quarter.

"If that's all just going in your till," I said, pushing across my own coin into the pile of theirs, "I'll just take back my change and—"

The old man brought his glasses down to his chest.

"Look, I don't want any trouble," I said. "It's just that I'm running a little late this morning and my girlfriend—"

"I don't believe I want the business of such a rude young man as yourself," he said, sliding my quarter back toward me. I watched it skid off the counter, bounce to the floor, and roll on its edge underneath a greeting card display case. Even then I wasn't really angry; more curious, actually, at how many coins over the years had been lost forever in that wasteland of dirt and dust and human hair particles. Then he snatched the Kit Kat out of my hand and things went white.

From that point on all I really remember is screaming at him about how if I had short hair he'd be singing a different tune and how now he owed me two Kit Kats and something I remembered one of Christine's roommates saying about how when the revolution came there wouldn't be enough room in the streets for all the blood that was going to get spilt. Then Mrs. Smith put her wrinkled hand to her mouth and screamed and the old man reached for something underneath the cash register and I snatched the nearest chocolate bar and tore for the door.

"Bill, what—"

I grabbed Christine by the hand and almost wrenched her arm from its socket.

"Run!" I said.

"Bill—"

"Run, goddammit, run!"

I dragged her behind me down Bay for a couple of full-tilt minutes until we hit a red light. We slammed on our brakes as traffic slowly rumbled by and tried to catch our breath. I finally let go of her hand.

"What's going on?" she said, rubbing her freed fingers.

I could still feel the adrenalin pumping through my veins. My arms and legs felt like rubber, my head like I was faintly high.

"Here," I said, handing over the Crispy Crunch. The red wrapping paper was torn in a couple places and damp from my still-soaking palm. It looked like it'd barely survived ten minutes in the spin cycle of a washing machine.

"What's this?" she said.

"It'll hold you over until lunch. You've got to be careful about not eating."

She looked down at the battered chocolate bar again; looked up at me.

"*This* is what that was all about?" she said.

"What do you mean *this* is what that was all about?"

"Do you have any idea how late I am for work?" Christine said.

"That's all you have to say? How late you are for work? I was trying to do you a favour, you know."

"Don't twist this around, this isn't about you."

"Yeah, it is, Christine. This is about me trying to be nice to you and you pissing all over me in thanks."

"Oh, get a grip," she said.

The same blizzard of fury I saw at the pharmacy came blowing in at a hundred miles an hour, and before I could grab my snow goggles I snatched the candy bar from her hand and slammed it to the ground and jumped up and down on it until it was an even-sorrier mess of chocolate and wrapper than before. I crossed my arms like I'd really proven something. For a second or three, actually felt like I had.

Christine stared at me for a moment. In an even voice, "You should lay off the speed, Bill," she said. Then she walked away.

I waited for her to turn around and let me have it, to give me her best parting shot, but she just kept moving away from me down Bay, eventually disapearing in the late-morning bustle. I kept thinking, Any minute now she's going to storm back here and really lay into me. But I was ready. I could feel my toes clenched tight like hooves inside my boots, my fists involuntarily tensed into hard balls at my sides.

She didn't turn around, though. I kept waiting, but she didn't.

38.

MAYBE I'VE BEEN fibbing a little. Not lying, just exaggerating. Going by the dictionary, doesn't lying a little equal out to exaggeration? Which stinks a bit of a rationalization, I know, but it's not. Oh, hell, maybe it is. All right, it is. It is.

I liked the drugs.

Sure, between work and the band and everything else there were times when anybody could have used a pick-me-up. But I was twenty years old and still at that age when a good-night and good-morning rumble-tumble within the same 24-hour period wasn't the stuff of pure male fantasy. And besides, Christine didn't pop pills and she got by all right. Slippery, too, and he was double my age and then some.

I *liked* the drugs.

They say opposites attract, and it's as true for pharmaceuticals as it is for matters of the heart. I always had a vague suspicion that I'd been sleeping through my own life, and on speed I found out just how right I was. Yeah, every time a car horn would send me up a tree or I'd lie awake at night twisting in my sheets or wonder why Christine and I never banged around the village or Kensington Market any more like we used to just holding hands and happy to be doing nothing and having nowhere to go, I'd tell myself I really had to cut down and get back to normal. But normal never had a chance.

As kids, when we'd be walking home from school and it would start to rain, without fail somebody would say that if you ran fast enough you'd never get wet. I never believed them, but I always wanted to. And I always ended up running.

39.

THOMAS WASN'T GETTING much shut-eye, either. I'd figured that while the rest of us paid our real-world dues he'd be smart enough to sleep in late or lie around in the sun all day or make love with Heather until showtime. I should have known better. That's what I would have done.

Dropping by the studio one day during my lunch break to pick up the bottle of uppers I was hoping I'd forgotten there, I found him busy rewinding the tape machine he used to record all our shows and making notes in the spiral notepad he'd recently taken to scribbling in during breaks at the Canada Tavern.

"Buckskin," he said. He looked surprised, but not unhappy I was there.

"How do we sound?" I said, nodding at the whipping wheels of the reel-to-reel. I was relieved to right away see what I'd come for and picked up the bottle from the table.

"You tell me," he said, tape clicking to a stop. "Have a seat." He removed a rumpled brown paper grocery bag from a chair to the floor and motioned for me to sit down. The bag made a rattling sound like there were ten maracas inside.

"I've got to get back to work," I said. "Besides, you're in charge of quality control. I trust you."

He hit a black button on the machine and the two huge reels slowly started moving again.

"Hey, I was there last night, remember?" I said. "Whatever it is, let's talk about it tonight, okay? I was late opening up again and don't want to be too long."

But it wasn't the previous night's gig; it wasn't even us.

A single electric guitar—not loud, not soft—chopped along in regular eighth notes right on top of an insistent backbeat kept with the heel of somebody's boot and the floor. In musical terms, instead of the guitar syncopating to the drums like it normally would, it doubled up the beat. *Bump-bump-bump-bump-bump-bump-bump.* It was like putting an amplified stethoscope to the chest of somebody who'd drunk way too much coffee. It made me nervous.

"I don't get it," I said. I screwed the lid off my pill bottle and looked around for something to wash a couple down with.

"Hold on there," Thomas said. He picked up the grease-stained grocery sack and pulled out his own bottle. He tapped out a single black capsule into the palm of his hand. "Try one of these."

"What are they?"

"Desbutols."

"Yeah, but what are they?" I said.

"What they are is what you get when you take the training wheels off and ditch those diet pills you're stringing yourself out with. These new pills are tools, Buckskin. They're precise, scientific. You want to work, you take one. You want to crash, you don't. I can barely keep my eyes open. I'm going home to bed right now."

I briefly considered the cautionary tale of his slightly dilated pupils but took the offered capsule anyway. I think I was thinking that if just one of the Desbutols could take the place of everything else I swallowed and sipped over the course of twenty-four hours, maybe by the end of the day I could get a decent night's sleep. The logic of a burgeoning pillhead. You had to be there.

I swished around a Coke bottle sitting on the table. It was warm, more syrupy sweet than usual, but it did the job. The tape machine was still rolling, the guitar still grunting away. I still didn't get it.

"It sounds kind of . . . nervous," I said.

Thomas smiled. "Good."

"That's good?"

"Sure. It's supposed to make you feel nervous."

"It is?"

"Of course."

I turned my ear back toward the machine's tiny built-in speaker. Maybe it was his partial explanation, maybe it was the Desbutol-induced concentration. Either way, no definite colours yet, but not just noise now, either.

"What's it called?" I said.

He sat down at the table and palmed out another two Desbutols, swallowing them both without bothering with the Coke. He rested his elbows on his knees and rubbed his eyes very slowly and very hard. Even with the music playing I could hear the crunch of his eyeballs.

"Like I said before, these new songs I'm working on, they're different," he said.

I couldn't stifle a laugh. "That's for sure."

"Not just the way they sound. These past few weeks, it's like all I've got to do is stay awake and get in the right state of mind and there they are, everywhere I look, waiting for me to pluck them out of the air and get them down on tape." He grabbed at one that just happened to be drifting by at that very instant; caught it in his clenched fist and kept it captive for a couple of long seconds before opening his hand and letting it float away.

"But none of the words I write for them seem to fit," he said. "Even the titles don't work. It's like . . . I guess I don't know what it's like."

"The colours don't match," I said.

He looked up. "That's it," he said. "That's exactly it."

I felt wonderful. And it wasn't only the *mot juste* ego-stroke, either. Already I could feel the powerful difference between the pep pills and the Desbutols. Instead of merely jittery not asleep, every pore of my body seemed to ooze wide-awake calm.

Picking up the bottle of Desbutols, "Freddy?" I said. Freddy was Thomas's shadowy pill connection.

Back from his colour-coded epiphany, "You haven't met Chris T. yet?"

"The biker?" I said.

Chris T. was Chris Toulese, leader of the Vagabond biker gang that had squealed into Yorkville earlier that summer and rapidly established itself as the village's number-one source for all things illegally ingested. You couldn't miss them. They'd taken over the Upper Crust and parked their huge hogs outside in one long shining row of polished silver to let everyone know it. Some people thought they were just another version of our own countercultural middle-finger salute aimed squarely at the straight world; others— quietly, and definitely not within earshot of the Vagabonds— started to worry about rumours of back-alley ass-kickings and gang initiation rapes. As usual, I didn't have any firm opinion on the matter. Kelorn hated them.

"A great guy," Thomas said, "I'll introduce you." He nodded at the bottle in my hand. "You can keep those."

I stuffed the pills in my jeans pocket and said I'd better get back to Making Waves. Thomas walked me downstairs to the street. We stood there for a sun-soaked moment watching the hippie parade drift by before he said he'd better get back to work.

"I thought you were going home to bed," I said.

"The wrong colours. You said it yourself, Buckskin. You've inspired me."

He slapped me on the back and headed back up the dark hallway.

40.

NO LONGER MAROONED together at Christine's after she'd convinced penny-pinching Slippery that now that he was bringing in some steady dough it was only fair that he vacate my apartment for a tiny room in the basement of the building where our studio was, usually I crashed at my place and she at hers. Incredibly, both her bed and mine had shrunken somehow in the time since we'd started going out, had gotten narrower, shorter, less capable of accommodating two comfortably. Strange, strange science.

After our gigs Thomas would usually drop Christine off first. Leone let us leave most of our gear behind on stage under a few thin sheets of long black tarp, so at least we didn't have to finish up the evening unloading Christopher any more. I'd kiss her good night and through the hearse's back window watch her vanish behind her front door, which out of firm anarchist principles was never locked. The June streets of Yorkville would be still very much alive and shaking at one o'clock in the morning, and everywhere I looked there'd be summer-browned, half-naked bodies all tangled up together in lip-locking twos lusting to become ones, everybody but me falling in love for the very first time.

Once, after I'd gotten home and was already undressed and under the sheets, I stubbed out the joint I was smoking, threw my jeans back on, and barefooted it down to the payphone at the corner a couple of minutes away. I slid in my dime, blinked at the numbers for a few seconds, then slowly rested the receiver back in its place.

I played with Christine on stage almost every night. I saw her practically every day. Had, for the last year. Sometimes I'd look at her face and it was like I wasn't even looking at somebody else, just the female version of me. And here I couldn't remember her fucking phone number. I stared up at the full moon through the smudged glass of the phone booth and tried to concentrate. But the harder I tried to remember, the more it felt like I'd never known what it was in the first place. It was a warm night, the trees in the backyards at the end of the street swaying in summer fullness in the soft breeze, but my toes started to feel cold standing on the cement slab lining the bottom of the booth.

I walked back to my room and kneeled down by the window. I looked and looked, but the moon never showed up. I told myself I really had seen it, and not ten minutes before. I dragged the pillows and blankets from the bed to the floor and fell asleep with my jeans on.

41.

THERE WAS NO WAY either of us could have turned back, even if we'd wanted to. At best, all we could have done was pretend. But Thomas came out of the front door of the Park Plaza Hotel at the very instant I walked by. There wasn't enough time to lie.

He stared at the sidewalk while I watched the traffic stop and start along Bloor. "You going to the show?" he said.

Local boys made good, the Ugly Ducklings, were riding "Nothin'," currently number eight on the CHUM Chart Top Ten, into a spot opening for the Rolling Stones that night at Maple Leaf Gardens. I was meeting Christine and Kelorn and we were all walking over together. And Heather. I was supposed to meet up with Heather, too.

"Maybe," I said. "You?"

"Think I'll head over to the studio," he said. "Still trying to put those colours you were talking about into some kind of order."

He served over one of his all-is-well-in-the-universe smiles but I didn't return the volley, let the pathetic little effort dribble right past me. I'd been looking forward to tonight for weeks, had kept it quietly circled in my mind as the one day I could kick back with several thousand long-haired friends and not think about anything Duckhead-related. And now I'd have to spend the entire time with some sham smile pasted to my face every time I looked at Thomas's freshly cuckolded girlfriend.

"Anything you want me to say to Heather when I see her?" I said. Fuck it. Why did everything have to be about Thomas?

"Buckskin," he said, "it's like this—"

I raised a hand to deflect the flurry of bullshit I knew was bound my way. "I don't want to hear it, man," I said. "This is between you and Heather, it's got nothing to do with me." Then why did I feel so guilty? I thought.

He nodded without looking up.

"Just make sure Heather doesn't find out, all right?" I said. "I don't want to think what'd happen if she knew." Thomas nodded his head a couple more times. There wasn't anything left for either of us to do but go our own way.

As soon as I crossed the lights onto Avenue Road I cut over to Victoria College, where we'd said we'd meet up. And sure enough, there they were, Christine, Kelorn, and Heather, all three of them sitting side by side on the steps of the college, big grins on their sunshined faces, each of them holding a red plastic bubble-blower in her hand. They saw me coming and waved but kept pumping out their lazy, soapy circles. So many bubbles filled up the air around them, for a second or two it seemed like the sky wasn't there.

42.

BY THE END OF SEPTEMBER Christine decided it was high time that everybody we knew from Yorkville finally get a chance to hear what we'd been up to. Not even Kelorn had checked us out yet. From the beginning, Thomas had been adamant that Heather (of course) and Scotty (whenever he felt like it) be the only people from the village allowed to make the scene, claiming that the band was like a picture that wasn't finished yet and that there'd be plenty of time later for everybody to see us once the paint had dried properly and the thing got hung at precisely the right angle.

This time, though, Thomas had no problem at all with the idea, didn't even think twice.

"Why, that's just fine, Miss Christine," he said, driving us all home.

"What about next Saturday?" Christine said. "That'll give us time to spread the word and maybe even put up some signs."

"Think of all the extra foot traffic," I added, trying to help her clinch the deal. "Leone'll be ecstatic."

"Sure, sure," Thomas said. "Whatever y'all say. Sounds great."

Christine arched a puzzled eyebrow my way but was soon lost in Yorkville-postering plans with Heather. I watched Thomas pull the bottle of Desbutols from his shirt pocket, gobble down a handful right from the jar, cap it, and put it back, all without once taking his eyes off the road. I wasn't surprised he was suddenly so agreeable about letting whoever wanted to listen to us come on out, and neither should Christine or anybody else have been. But, then, not everybody had the benefit of the observatory of my drum kit.

At the end of every set I'd watch him put down his guitar before the last note had barely faded away and scoot off to take his pick from one of several empty tables. There, he'd whip out his drugstore notepad from his back pocket, equal parts humming to himself and gnawing away at the end of his Bic pen while running his fingers through his hair over and over until break was finished, oblivious to Heather, the draft beer she'd dutifully placed before him, and everything else going on in the room. Something was on his mind these days, and it sure wasn't all the new ways he planned to bowl them over at the Canada Tavern.

As usual, by the end of the night there was only Thomas and me left in the hearse. I'd slide into Slippery's spot up front and Thomas would let the engine idle for a couple of minutes in front of my place and we'd yak a bit about that night's gig. Lately we'd just sit and listen to the motor run and the sounds of two o'clock in the morning up and down Huron Street. Tonight, two dogs wouldn't stop their back-and-forth backyard jawing, neither one willing to let the other get in the last bark. I thought about Snowball and how at this very instant he'd be a ball of white fur fast asleep on the tattered old couch downstairs in my parents' rec room. I yawned and thought I might get some decent Zs myself for a change.

Hand on the door handle, "Okay, I'll see you tomorrow night," I said.

Thomas clicked off the ignition. Somebody yelled at one of the dogs to shut up but the animal still had things to say, kept right on howling.

"Be patient," he said. "I just need a little more time."

In the street light, the hard frown he wore these days seemed even more pronounced, not like he was angry about something, but more like he was busting his brain trying to wrap it around some monster algebra problem. Behind his back Christine had taken to referring to the thick ridge of furrowed flesh between his eyebrows as "Thomas's devil horns," as a kind of gentle warning when she'd found out I was sharing his dealer. But I knew it wasn't about the drugs. The drugs were the chicken. Or the egg. Anyway, the part that doesn't come first.

"Don't sweat it," I said. "The new songs'll come when they come. In the meantime, it's not like we're hurting for material. And it's not like the old songs are old songs. I mean, we've only been playing them for how many months now? Three? Four?"

He turned the key, the hearse's engine roaring back to life.

"Get some sleep, Buckskin."

43.

FRONT TO BACK, shoulder-to-shoulder packed; with tie-dye, with ponytails, with Indian love beads, with army-surplus jackets, with purple headbands, and, in spite of Leone's fiat, the pungent smell of freshly rolled marijuana. Christine had done her usual wonderful job of rallying the troops, and my initial fears about the Canada Tavern locals not taking well to the annexing of their homeland were put to rest by the time we hit the stage at a little after nine. Normal is always what the majority wears and says and does, and tonight that meant lots and lots of long hair, "Hey, man"s, and hugs.

Leone quickly discovered he wasn't going to make a fortune on drinks—hippies don't drink; they sip and space and munch—and jacked up the price of potato chips, pretzels, and french fries. Leone ignored the trail of sweet smoke that crept out of the bathroom every time somebody opened the door, and none of our friends said anything but thanks when the price of a bag of chips made its way from a dime, to fifteen cents, all the way up to a quarter by the end of the night. The Americans and the Russians threatening to Cold War us all to death should have gotten along half as well.

Even Thomas seemed renewed by the full house. After he counted off the start to our usual opener, "Dundas West," the enormous roar that leapt up to embrace my boom-chick-a-boom drumming intro was definitely out of the ordinary, stunning Thomas enough that he flubbed the tune's opening chords. After the song was over and the room didn't go completely nose-blowing-in-the-back-row-painfully-audible quiet as usual, Thomas swivelled around and grinned first at me and then at Christine like he wanted to thank us for reminding him of something. He turned back to the audience.

"Hey, Yorkville," he said, "nice of y'all to drop in." Wild applause. Thomas scanned the room.

"The last time I saw this many hippies together in one place, I was in jail." Loud laughter, more ecstatic cheering. Up until tonight Thomas had been pretty much all business between tunes, quietly thanking the audience for their imaginary applause or announcing the break with the same, "Thank you, we'll be back in a few minutes."

"This next one's called 'Walk with Your Feet,'" he said. "And if y'all feel like dancing a spell, I don't think Leone'll mind too much." Thomas strummed his guitar. Mouth tight to the microphone, in a soft, clear voice, "One, two, three, four . . ."

"Walk with Your Feet," indeed, and a pounding thunderstorm full of a whole lot more. And boy, oh boy, did it ever come down.

During Slippery's already smoking solo on "One O'clock in the Morning" Thomas crouched low and stuck his nose so close to the neck of the steel guitar and the old man's string-bending fingers that it was as if Slippery didn't have any say in the matter any more, his hands simply had to find a way to move that chrome bar faster. Slippery'd played more gigs than every musician in the room combined, but the whoops and whistles he received for each searing run he ripped out of his instrument and tossed into the crowd made him play even harder. I watched him bear down on the steel like I'd only seen him do before over a bottle of whisky. When a strand of black hair fell free from its carefully Vaselined place and he didn't push it back once the song at hand was over, I knew we were now officially somewhere I, at least, had never been before.

The set list was history by now, Thomas calling out for one table-thumping scorcher after another. But he and Christine, with a little help from Slippery on the low parts, still weaved their voices in, around, and on top of each other like a funky back-woods church choir intent on keeping the melody to an out-of-control jackhammer. Unbelievable. Thomas had the hippist of Toronto's hippies bopping up and down on the dance floor like a bunch of Coca-Cola–buzzed teenagers at a sock hop.

Thomas exchanged his Fender for an acoustic.

"We'd like to do one for you now about a place that's a long, long way away and a long time back. I know everybody's been there, though." Strum, strum. "Maybe this'll help take you back there for a spell."

Thomas had his own microphone in front of him and Christine hers in front of her, but he walked over to where she was, looked into her eyes, and without a word they launched a cappella into "Dream of Pines," Thomas's bittersweet ode to his birthplace. We'd never performed it like this before, but somehow Slippery and I knew what to do anyway. Waiting until the first verse was over, Slippery with soft puffs of smoky pedal steel and me with quiet brush accompaniment joined in with Thomas's guitar and Christine's softly throbbing bass. I must have heard the song a hundred times before—the thing was practically part of my DNA by now—and I'd never once been to Jackson, Mississippi, but tonight the only way I could get rid of the ache in my throat and make sure I didn't screw up the beat was to try to remember all the teams in the NHL's newly created Western conference.

The applause for "Dream of Pines" started at the back of the room—hesitant, scattered at first, then steady, and finally roaring—eventually pouring over all of us up on stage. Walking back to the other side, "That one's for my Uncle Pen," Thomas said into his own microphone. "Although I can hear him saying to me just as sure as I'm looking at y'all, 'Why, that's right nice, boy, but do you know any Merle Haggard songs?'"

Well, *I* laughed. And so did Christine and Heather. And I thought I saw Slippery smile. Of course, it helped that we actually knew who Merle Haggard was.

"Well, we're gonna do a Merle Haggard song for you now. Just in case Uncle Pen's listening."

And we did. And an electrified Leadbelly country blues, a George Jones weeper, and two of Thomas's most dirge-like ballads after that. With betrayal on his lips and a guitar in his hands, he could make a broken heart seem like an attractive option. The Age of Aquarius never knew what hit it.

And neither did I when I happened to notice a girl in red hip-hugging pants with long, straw-yellow hair parted in the middle and an exposed midriff slowly dancing by herself by the left side of the stage and looking at me every time I glanced up and over at her long enough to feel guilty. Because this girl wanted to fuck me. Not because she'd found out I was funny and sweet and easy to talk to and that once she got to know me I was sort of cute in my own way and— No. This girl wanted to fuck me.

Of course, it wasn't really me she wanted to fuck; it was the drummer. She wanted to fuck the guy up there on stage all lit up in the hot white light laying down the beat that was keeping her body swaying back and forth all night long. She wanted to fuck me because I was in THE BAND. And because I was in THE BAND, I could do anything I wanted with her and to her and that would be exactly what she wanted me to do, too. And, you know, I never got much of that sort of thing growing up in Etobicoke. Never got much of that sort of thing at all.

Finishing up the first set with a killer country-waltz version of an old gospel tune, "Farther Along" (Christine turning a few heads with her tasty mandolin work), Thomas called us together and said he wanted to try "Barney, No," a tune we'd rehearsed only maybe a half-dozen times during sound checks. Of all the new songs he'd been working on since we'd begun our residency at the Canada Tavern, "Barney, No" was the only one Thomas had apparently found words for and let us actually hear. To this day I have no idea what it's about, although a dog getting into things he shouldn't is as good a guess as any.

Thomas turned the acoustic guitar duties over to Slippery and took the lead on a Chet Atkins Country Gentleman which, by monkeying around with the volume pedal and tone bar, ended up sounding something like a cross between a reverb-laden steel guitar and a naked woman two-stepping out of her black lace panties.

"Don't anybody go anywhere," Thomas said. "It isn't a party until somebody gets their heart broken."

O. . .kay. I could hear the collective crunch of Christine's roommates knitting their eyebrows over that one. Leone plugged the jukebox back in and "Paperback Writer" blasted throughout the room. Half the audience got up for their first refill of the night while the other half looked for a safe place to light up.

After our seven-thirty sound check the band normally headed out to Christopher and passed around a single joint behind the black curtains as a sort of pre-gig cerebrum-calming calisthenic.

During break, though, we all pretty much went our own way, Thomas with Heather across the table from him scratching away at his notebook in lyricless frustration, Slippery smoking a couple of cigarettes by himself by the back door, staring up at the moon, me and Christine going for a walk around the block. But not tonight. Kelorn was the first one to greet us as we stepped off the stage. The others drifting off into other congratulatory embraces, Kelorn took me by the hand to have all to herself.

A cheer went up at one of the middle tables and we both turned to see Thomas, Christine, and Heather knocking back shots of liquor to the loud delight of the crowd surrounding them, a handful of old men puffing on hand-rolled cigarettes and a couple of old women wearing too much makeup included. Slippery, with a Marlboro hanging out the side of his smirking mouth, looked on approvingly. A burly guy in biker duds, obviously a Vagabond—dark shades, beard, leathers, the whole deal—ho-ho-hoed like a very drunken Santa Claus and stuck a five-dollar bill in Leone's hand.

"Who would have guessed you had such big fans among the leather jacket and chain set?" Kelorn said. We were sitting side by side on the edge of the stage.

"They're friends of Thomas's," I said. "They can't all be bad guys. It looks like one of them just bought the band a round of drinks."

"Yes, well . . ."

Pretty much everyone in the village was concerned about the same things Kelorn was regarding the Vagabonds, but we were willing to let them prove themselves unworthy of our trust. Kelorn said that's what Chamberlain and England did with Hitler and the Nazis. But we'd had this conversation before and I didn't feel like repeating it now, even if, as usual, I knew if I listened to her long enough she'd start to make sense. But not now. Not tonight.

"Well?" I said. "What'd you think? Was it worth the wait?"

Kelorn smiled. For real. She didn't have to say anything after that. You never do with the real stuff.

"Really?" I said.

She nodded. "It looks like you're having fun."

I frowned. "It looks like we're having fun? What's that got to do with anything?"

"Isn't that enough?"

Of course that wasn't enough. But how does the believer convince the non-believer that the old rules no longer apply, that *fun* doesn't even enter into the equation? He can't. So he doesn't. Instead, he changes the subject.

"C'mon, there must have been some songs you liked."

Kelorn laughed and rested four heavily-jewelled fingers on my arm. "My goodness, Bill, you *have* become so serious, haven't you? There were lots of songs I liked, dear. I wouldn't know where to start."

"Try."

She hesitated, studied my stone-serious face.

"Okay. Well, you know I'm no expert when it comes to this kind of music, but I guess I'm a little surprised at how different it sounds from the sort of thing I've heard you play around the store. I suppose I'd expected something a little more old-fashioned, if that's the right word. And it is like that, to a degree, but also new, too, if that makes any sense."

The smile I lit up with told her that it did. "What else?" I asked.

"What else. Well, I thought the first slow song, the one about the place in the pines, was quite moving. And another slow one, the second to last song before the break."

"'Farther Along,'" I jumped in. "You know, that song's so old nobody even knows who wrote it, that's how long it's been around. It's so beautiful people just keep wanting to play it."

"It *is* beautiful," Kelorn said. "Although you should be thankful you're not Thomas and don't have to sing those lines about 'when Jesus comes' and all the rest of it." She shook her head.

"Just think of it as a symbol," I counselled. "Jesus Christ, Muhammad, Love, the Life Force—whatever. Something like Jung's Collective Unconscious."

"So you have been actually managing to stay awake at Making Waves these last couple of months after all."

I looked down at the floor, didn't hear the blaring jukebox or the noisy room any more.

"Look, I know I haven't been there for you and the store like I should be, but I want you to know that I appreciate your putting up with me and how cool you've been about—"

"Oh, Bill," she said, throwing an arm around me, "it hasn't been *that* bad. So you've been prone to making a lousy pot of tea and leaving the door unlocked now and then. To be perfectly honest, dear, you never did learn to steep the tea bags long enough anyway. And anyone who decides they want a book of poetry so bad they're willing to steal it obviously needs it more than we do, now, don't they?"

I planted a wet one on her warm jowl and wondered what we were going to open up the second set with and whether I had time to grab a Coke and pop a pill.

"There is one thing about the store I do need to talk to you about, though," she said.

Just then Christine passed by, filing out the back door behind a line of her anarchist friends obviously intent on finding somewhere nightime-secluded to blow a joint. She walked right by Kelorn and me without even noticing us. She looked like she was having the time of her life at a high-school reunion hanging out with some old buddies she hadn't seen in years.

"Is Thomas here in Canada because of the draft?" Kelorn said.

"What?"

"A Mountie came by the shop today asking if I knew where he could locate Thomas and when you would be working next."

"Me? What'd he want with me?"

"When I told him I'd never heard of anyone by the name of Thomas Graham, he said he was interested in talking to one of my employees, a Bill Hansen, because he'd heard that you and Thomas were friends."

I ran my hand through my hair. "Jesus, why didn't you tell him you'd never heard of me either?"

"Bill, you don't have anything to worry about from an RCMP officer; Thomas does. The FBI sometimes asks Mounties to enquire after dodgers, and obviously this person knows you work at Making Waves or he wouldn't have asked, so telling him you didn't would have meant zero chance of him believing me about not knowing Thomas. Not that I think he did."

I looked to the opened doorway Christine and all the rest of them had just paraded through in search of a safe place in the night; smelled the cooling damp of late evening drifting into the steamy room.

"Thomas is a draft dodger?" I said.

"I don't know. When I asked the Mountie if I could help him with anything he just thanked me for my time and said he'd be back tomorrow to talk to you."

Running both hands though my hair now, "What are we going to do?"

"The first thing you're going to do is ask Thomas what's going on. If he's just a dodger, as long as he stays in Canada the worst thing that can happen to him is being classed an international fugitive and that will be that because our government doesn't send deserters back. But we need to know the truth. The complete truth."

"But what about tomorrow?" I said. "This guy, this RCMP guy, he's coming to Making Waves tomorrow. What am I supposed to tell him? If he knows that I work at the store then he knows for sure that I know Thomas. Maybe I shouldn't go in. Maybe you can tell him I quit, that I split and you don't know where I live or where I was headed." I felt like the first rat to hit the water as the ship goes down but that didn't stop my furry little feet from paddling just as fast they could go.

"Listen to me, Bill," Kelorn said. "This is very serious business and Thomas is going to need all the help he can get from his friends. Which means that, as his friend, he needs you to show up at work tomorrow with a big smile on your face and tell Mr. Mountie that, yes, you knew Thomas, you'd hung around Yorkville with him, but that you haven't seen him for a long, long time and that you have no idea where he is."

"But—"

"No buts, Bill," Kelorn said, pushing herself up from the stage. "That's how it has to be." Words like *but* didn't exist in Kelorn's vocabulary.

"I've got to get going," she said. "I promised Gretchen I'd help her with her German grammar tonight. Silly girl, a midterm tomorrow morning at nine and now she decides to let me know she's having problems conjugating her verbs."

She hugged me again, whispered "I'm proud of you" in my ear, and squeezed my hand goodbye. "And talk to Thomas tonight, Bill. *Tonight*."

Dying isn't the problem. That's the part nobody gets. It's not about not dying.

What makes Thomas go thirteen days straight without a shower and makes sure he shows up at the downtown L.A. Induction Center in the same reeking, rotting rags he's been wearing around town for a week while gobbling down so much Methedrine he's got the metabolism of a lab rat and the sunken cheeks and bulging eyes of a death-camp survivor isn't about being afraid of simply not existing. If it was, how come sometimes, out of his gourd out in the middle of the desert, a bird flies high over the San Andreas Fault and Thomas turns to this weekend's special friend and says, "That's me, darlin'. Way up there, over there, there, that's me. That's what I want to be."

Any way you perform the mystical math, dying's not the problem, that's not the scary part.

The scary part also isn't some doctor in white plastic gloves up to his elbows telling you to drop your drawers and cough as he yawns and covers his mouth with one hand while squeezing his ten-thousandth pair of testicles of the day with the other; isn't some bozo in a brush cut you haven't known for thirty seconds screaming at you to get your head out of your ass and keep that line moving, mister, and have your medical records out and ready for inspection by Corporal Smith; isn't telling the shrink "no" when he asks you if you want to serve your country and seeing him check the YES box anyway, saying, as he shuts your file, "That's all right, son, I'm sure you'll feel different once you have a chance to fit in."

None of that and more isn't the scary part.

The scary part—the really, really scary part—is being lactose intolerant and getting killed in a head-on collision with a milk truck. Is having an orange-lacquered transmission fall on your head on your honeymoon. Is blocking the other team's last-second field goal attempt to win the game and picking up the ball and running faster than you've ever run before right into your own end zone.

The scary part is not being allowed to die for what you're living for. That's the problem. That's always been the problem.

So, tell you what, Sam. You fight your war, I'll fight mine. You can contact me c/o the Great White North and I'll see you in heaven sometime. And let's just see who gets there first.

44.

THE SECOND HALF went just as well as the first, Thomas one minute pedal-to-the-metal driving us into whipping the crowd into a frothy frenzy, the next slowing everything down until the entire room was a soft, breathy hush, Thomas and Christine once again sharing the same microphone and hitting all the high notes and pushing all the right buttons, her voice getting where it was supposed to be every time, his cracking and breaking occasionally but always at the just-right emotional moment.

Then all the lights blazed on and Leone, brown plastic tray in hand, was racing around the room clearing away any unfinished drinks while people spilled out the doors and shouted out good-byes, and before my knuckles could unclench from around my drumsticks it was all over. I looked over at Christine, bass still slung low around her neck, and she looked the same way she used to after we'd first started making love: all at once joyful, sad, and relieved. Thomas had his back to me, was still standing at attention in front of his microphone, but I knew he must have felt just as bone-marrow empty as we did. Ever the professional, Slippery was wiping down his tone bar with the white towel he kept underneath his seat while whistling the chorus to "Lilies by the Side of the Highway." It was the first time I'd ever felt like I actually needed a drink. If there was a God, I reasoned, this must have been how He felt on the seventh day. What an all-powerful bummer of a comedown those twenty-four hours must have been, I thought. Maybe that's why Sundays are always so depressing.

Eventually we unfroze, slowly started moving again like those marionettes you see encased in glass machines at spring fairs that for twenty-five cents come to life for three or four minutes to bang time on their drums and saw away at their fiddles and prance in place until the quarter runs out and the power gets cut off. Except we weren't dancing or performing any more, just mopping down our faces and peeling off our equipment and getting ready to go home. Out of the clatter of stoned bodies shuffling off into the night, a guy who looked like us, but didn't, stepped up to the edge of the stage.

"I just wanted to tell you guys I really dug your stuff tonight a lot," he said. "A lot."

His hair was chopped sharply at the shoulder, longish rather than long, his clothes more funky conservative (paisley suit jacket and goofy, oversized tie) than all-out hippie cool, the cuffs of his trousers neatly tailored rather than rolled.

"Thanks," Thomas said, reaching down, extending a weary hand. "We appreciate it." Christine and I smiled and offered over our own tired thanks. Too pooped to be any politer, we all went back to turning off amps and wrapping up cords and packing away our instruments. By now Heather had joined us on stage and was carefully laying away Thomas's several guitars into their respective cases.

"You aren't all Canadian, are you?" the guy said. I double-taked on his tie and half-assed hippie haircut and did the logic. I jumped up from behind my kit and planted myself between him and Thomas.

"Yeah, all of us are," I said. "All four of us are T.O. born and bred. And look, man, I'm glad you dug the show and everything, but the guy who owns this place doesn't like anybody hanging around after closing time and I wouldn't want him pissed off at me if I were you. He's not one of us, if you get my drift."

"That's cool," he said. "I've got to get back to my hotel to take a phone call from the coast anyway. If I'm not in my room when my old lady calls there'll be hell to pay."

Continuing to wrap a black guitar cord around his elbow and fist, Thomas peered around me. "Y'all are from California?" he said.

"San Francisco. Marin County, actually. But I'm working in L.A. now."

"How is old Lost Angels?" Thomas said. "Everybody still tripping out on the carbon monoxide down there?"

"You never told me you've been to Los Angeles, Thomas," I said.

"I did some time down that way," Thomas said, addressing his answer to the pig in sheep's clothing instead.

Christ, don't say that, I thought.

"I know you did," the suit said.

"You do?" Thomas replied.

He went to move by me but I wasn't having any of it, executed that little stutter-step thing where you try to get around somebody on the street but every time you go your way, they go yours. We danced like this for a few rounds before Thomas finally gave up and looked over my shoulder to get a better a look at the guy, trying to place the face.

"Colin Fielder," he said, sticking out his hand again. "We've never actually met, but if you talk to the right people around L.A., they all know who Thomas Graham is."

Thomas ran a hand through his wet hair. "I'll be right honest with you, Colin, the name doesn't ring a bell."

"It wouldn't," he said, reaching inside his suit jacket. He handed Thomas a business card. Here we go, I thought, this is it.

"But people still talk about you down at Snoopy's Opera House and The Steer."

Thomas finished reading the card and handed it to me.

"What's an L.A. label rep doing down in the San Fernando Valley and Orange County?" Thomas said.

The card read Colin Fielder, ELECTRIC RECORDS, Los Angeles, California, and listed the company's address and phone number.

"We're a young label that's small enough that I've got the ear of the guy who runs things, and he digs that I'm more interested in artists who are doing something a little bit different." Christine and Heather and even Slippery gathered around me, taking turns reading the card.

Thomas began unscrewing his microphone. "So you think Dick Clark's ready for longhairs playing country music, do you?"

"We're not the kind of label that particularly cares what Dick Clark thinks."

"So you're not interested in selling records, then? Huh, record companies sure must have changed a lot since I was last down there."

"Sure we want to sell records. But there are lots of other ways to get our bands the exposure they deserve other than the Top Forty. Like I said, we're a pretty new label with lots of fresh, new ideas. Underground radio, for example. We think it'll make the idea of releasing singles obsolete within two years."

"Even country singles?"

"I love pure country, I grew up on it, but if I had to describe what the Duckhead Secret Society was all about to somebody, well, I couldn't—and that's what I love so much about your sound. You can't pigeonhole it. But if I had to, if somebody held a gun to my head, I guess it would be country-rock, a little on the heavier side of maybe what Hearts and Flowers or the Beau Brummels are up to these days."

"Bubble-gum music," Thomas said, folding up the mike in a towel.

"Fair enough," Colin said.

The jukebox unplugged and darkened dead, the room was empty now but for us and Leone, the clink of him gathering together the last of the empty glasses its only sound.

"How does a guy growing up in Marin County get turned

onto *pure country?*" Thomas said. "That's 'I-Ain't-Marchin'-No-More' land."

"My dad was—actually, still is—a history prof at SFU. He did his thesis on the depression in California. The labour camps, the unions, the radical left, that sort of thing. Anyway, Woody Guthrie, Hank Williams, you name it, you heard it around my house as a kid."

Thomas folded up the second mike and placed it on stage beside the other; stayed down on one knee and began wiping down the wooden body of the mandolin. And kept wiping.

"How did you know Thomas was playing with us here tonight?" I asked.

"I didn't," Colin said. "I'm actually in town to check out the Paupers and a couple other bands. I just happened to be hanging out in Yorkville this afternoon talking to the fellow who runs the Riverboat when this elderly gentleman who must have gotten wind of who I was shoved one of the fliers for your gig in my face and said, 'Do yourself a favour and listen to something besides noise for a change.'"

So Scotty had been with us tonight after all. When we'd asked him to come for about the tenth time the night before, he'd said that the muse had him by the balls and that a hot overcrowded room full of hippies wasn't what the doctor ordered to pry her loose.

Leone shouted, "Those lights are going off in five minutes," and everyone looked to Thomas. He snapped shut the mandolin case and took back Colin's business card from me and read it again. Stood up and dropped the card in the pocket of his red sequined shirt.

"I'm writing some new songs now," he said. "They're better than the ones you heard tonight."

"I'd love to hear them," Colin said.

"They're not finished yet. But they will be. Soon."

"Whenever you're ready. But I'd like to talk to you"—he paused; made a point of looking at each of us—"I'd like to talk to all of you right now about the music you played tonight. I mean, you must be tired and I've got to wait for my call, but how about lunch tomorrow? Any place in particular you feel like spending some of Electric Records' money?"

"Café El Patio," Christine said. "It's supposed to be beautiful tomorrow and we can sit outside. You've got to see Yorkville at street level in the day to really appreciate it."

"Sounds great," Colin said. "Around noon at Café El Patio then?" Looking only at Thomas now, "Is it a date?" He might have burned a few more brain cells than your average American businessman, but this guy knew what he was doing, he knew who really made the Duckhead Secret Society fly.

"One question," Thomas said.

Colin waited. Us too.

"Who wrote 'That's All Right Mama'?"

"Arthur Cradup," Colin answered.

"See you at noon," Thomas said.

45.

SO WE WERE going to be rock-and-roll stars.

Colin wined us and dined us underneath a cloudless blue noonday sky on as many macrobiotic munchies as we wanted with all the wheat germ–supplemented fresh fruit smoothies we could drink to wash it all down. Occasionally making his point with the aid of an expensive-looking silver pen and a hardbacked small black notepad, Colin reiterated to us all (Slippery, begging off and sleeping in, excluded) how special he thought the Duckhead Secret Society was, why Electric Records was the right record company for what we were trying to do with our music, and all the many things he and Electric could do for us and our career.

Career. Yeah. You start out liking what you hear on some records and say to yourself, "That's cool, I'd like to do that, too," and the next thing you know somebody's encouraging you to have a side order of stewed okra and tomatoes with cilantro and your second Very Berry Cantaloupe Shake on their nickel and talking about recording studios and touring schedules and advance money. Advance money, that's right. "Hello money," Colin called it. Five thousand dollars, half now, half when our album came out. Actual dollars and cents for what you'd be doing with your friends for free anyway.

Because all at once the counterculture was big business and American record companies were sniffing around under every rock-and-roll rock looking for new product to meet the day-glo demand and make those cash registers go ching-ching. Over the course of the afternoon Colin did his job, won over even doubting Thomas regarding his honest appreciation for his tunes and our sound. But even he thought it was important that Electric's publicity department have a "hook" to hang the band's music on if we wanted to start a "buzz" going in "the industry" and "get people talking."

Thomas let it be known he wasn't real fond of hooks.

"Country-rock," he spat, tilting back in his chair, arms locked across his chest. "So what you're saying is that you think we could be your very own back-home Herman's Hermits."

Colin took a bite of his granola.

"Maybe you'd like us to do a honky-tonk version of 'Mrs. Brown You've Got a Lovely Daughter,'" Thomas said. "Maybe call it 'Mrs. Brown I Reckon You've Got a Lovely Daughter, Ma'am.' Get yourself a crossover novelty hit on the pop *and* country charts."

Colin smiled politely. "It's only a label, Thomas," he said. "Just a way for people to get a handle on what you're trying to do. You can only accomplish so much by touring. We need to do all we can on the publicity end as well."

"How much touring?" Christine said.

We were holding hands and playing footsies underneath the table. Although completely straight, we both giggled like brain-bruised stoners every time one of us ordered up something else to eat or drink courtesy of Electric Records. And the sun was shining and somebody wanted to sign us to a record contract.

"To begin with, not much, a couple of months, just long enough to get your name out there and get you used to being on the road. But don't worry. After the album comes out and we start working the media, we'll have you busier than you've ever been."

Christine let go of my hand and lit a cigarette.

Thomas leaned forward, the front two legs of his chair smacking flat on the cement patio. He peeled off his shades. "You want a label?" he said. "All right. How about Good Music? How about Honest Music? How about Music with Integrity? How about those for labels?"

"Every one of them would be true," Colin said. "Unfortunately, we're still going to need something to act as a point of departure for people not as musically sophisticated as you. Something to capture their imagination and make them want to try to understand what at first might seem a bit out of the ordinary."

"Interstellar North American Music," I piped in, sucking up the last of my shake.

Colin spooned some more granola and considered, repeated the phrase aloud.

"Is that yours, Bill?" he said. "Did you come up with that on your own?"

I shook my head and continued noisily slurping, thumbed at Thomas getting a light from Heather.

"I like it," Colin said. "Edgy new attitude meets rootsy music to make something exciting but traditional at the same time. I like it."

I licked my strawberry-coated straw clean.

"Another shake, Bill?" Colin said.

"Don't mind if I do, Colin."

Thomas looked at Heather.

"Darlin'," he said, "I do believe we've created a monster."

46.

"I THOUGHT YOU'D like them," I said.

"I do like them," Christine said. "It's just that I think you bought them more for you than for me."

"I bought them for us. So we'd have our own pair when we're on the road."

"For when we're on the road."

"Yeah. What if we end up in Bumfuck, Idaho, on a Sunday night and feel like, you know? This way we're prepared."

We both looked down at the pair of fire-engine red stilettos still wrapped in white tissue paper, the opened shoebox on Christine's lap. Foreplaying around, suave guy that I was, I'd leaned over the edge of my bed and pulled them out from underneath, hoping to surprise Christine with the $49.99 gift. It was the first time in months that we'd had time just to lie in the sack all afternoon and smoke some grass and listen to records and fool around. Only the fooling around part wasn't going so well, even before the red-light stilettos had slowed things down to a complete stop.

Just before the appearance of the heels, after what'd seemed like hours of me trying to kiss and caress a limp-bodied mannequin to life, Christine'd softly stroked my damp hair as I lip-walked my way down her belly and said, "I'm having my period. Come here and lie with me for a while." I'd just smiled my seductive best and decided to concentrate my attention on every other part of her that wasn't off limits. It wasn't difficult. The only good thing about not seeing your girlfriend naked for weeks and weeks was finding out all over again what she looked like. And now we had all the time we needed to do all the rediscovering we wanted.

Because contracts had been signed. A mini-American tour culminating in an L.A. showcase at the Whisky A Go Go was in the planning as we spoke. Studio time was being reserved for us two months in advance so that by the time we got to California after as many months on the road we'd be tighter than an ill-strung banjo and ready to lay down twelve of our best tunes. And Colin had cut us the first half of our advance and told us to go out and spend some money and put our affairs in order before we left Canada. Because our first show was in Flint, Michigan, in five days.

Christine put the lid back on the shoebox and set it down on the floor beside the bed, pulled all the blankets up to her neck. Although it was already the last week of September, the fan was going back and forth full blast and it was still warm enough to not even need a single sheet, let alone the duvet. But she sank down low under the bunch of them anyway.

"Tell me again what Kelorn said when you told her about not being back until December," she said.

I was naked and lying on top of the covers on principle. If she was going to interrupt our long-postponed lovemaking to gab about my boss, I was going to make damn sure she knew I wasn't in any mood for cuddling. I tried to ignore the itch of the wool blanket on my ass.

"Like I said before, nothing, she's cool about it. She understands what we're trying to do."

"And you'll have your job when you get back?"

"If I'll want it back, sure. But who knows? By then our album will be ready to come out and Colin says if everything goes as planned we'll be back on the road again by the end of January."

Christine stood up, stepped into her black panties, tugged on my flung white T-shirt, and got back into bed. She snuggled herself on top of the blankets next to me with her head resting on my chest. I kept my hands at my sides and didn't put my arm around her; licked my lips, cramped from all my fruitless kissing, dry from too much speed.

"Mariposa's in two weeks," she said.

"Yeah, well, I think we'll manage to get by without seeing Judy Collins live and in the flesh."

"And the Diggers are helping to put together a new round of protests. I think awareness is high enough now to really make it work this time."

"Can't you let somebody else save the planet for a change? You're allowed to have a life, too, you know."

Christine slid off me and onto her side. "Meaning you don't think I have a life now?"

"That's not what I said."

"Meaning that trying to stop the exploitation of the village isn't as worthy a life goal as riding across America in a cramped hearse?"

"Take it easy, all I said was—"

"Bill, I'm not even sure I *want* to go on tour."

I sat up, grabbed a pillow, and placed it between my legs.

"What do you mean you're not sure you want to go on tour?" I said. "We've already told Colin we're ready to go. We've already signed the contract. You've already cashed your part of the cheque."

"I've read the contract over three times," she said, "and technically, all it says I have to do is be a part of the album we're supposed to make. And I haven't cashed the cheque yet." She leaned over and pulled a folded piece of paper from the back pocket of her jeans on the floor.

I registered the unfurled, uncashed cheque. "I don't get it," I said. "For months we have to play that shit hole the Canada Tavern every night for nobody but Leone and six drunks. And then along comes the kind of deal any young band would die for and you're talking about throwing it all away."

"Maybe I'm not as excited as you are because being one of Thomas's musical puppets isn't exactly how I see my life unfolding."

"Is that how you see me? As one of Thomas's puppets?"

She didn't say anything, just folded the cheque in two and put it back in her jeans. I looked out the window at the brick wall across the alley gleaming red in the bright afternoon sun. The same album we'd been listening to all day at Christine's insistence, Dylan's first, played on.

"This is kind of sudden, isn't it?" I said.

"Not really, no. I suppose if I really think about it, it's kind of been in the back of my mind for a while now. I mean, I don't even know what's going on in Yorkville any more, Bill, I don't talk to anyone but you guys. Did you know they're thinking about instituting a 10 p.m curfew?"

In spite of myself, "Jesus Christ," I said.

"Yeah. Neither did I. I had to read it about it in the *Telegram*. I mean, how pathetic is that?"

Side two was finished and Christine got up to flip over the album. She cued up the second to last song on the side, her favourite, "Song to Woody."

"But I understand how these things happen," she said. "You get started on something and you want to see it through and you want to do it right and then one thing leads to another and before you know it those bastards down at city hall have decided they've got the right to decide what time your bedtime is." She grabbed her cigarettes and lighter from her bag and climbed back into bed.

"The more I think about it, the more I think that's why I wanted to have everybody down the other night to hear us play. Let's face it, we're not going to get any better than we are right now, we're as tight as we're ever going to be, no amount of touring is going to make that happen. So maybe my organizing the other night was my way of fading things out in style."

She flicked her ash into an empty Coke bottle.

"But then Colin came along and there was all this excitement and everything got sort of crazy for a while and I guess I kind of got caught up in it, too. But now that the smoke's cleared a bit it's forced me to be honest with myself. Which is good, I guess."

We were both leaning up against the wall now, each of us staring straight ahead at the wall opposite, blank but for a small black-and-white picture of a fuzzy-cheeked Dylan Christine had pinned up around the time we'd met. I'd wanted her to feel as comfortable crashing over as I could and had told her to consider my place hers. One night after one of her Riverboat gigs she took the picture and a tack out of her bag and stuck the thing up. "Bob Dylan," she'd said. "Patron Saint of No Bullshit. This'll help keep us honest. Let us pay our respects." We'd tumbled onto the unmade bed and worshipped in our fashion, just like He would have wanted.

"Don't get me wrong," she said. "I've had fun. I've had fun playing with you three creeps." She smiled, put her hand on my bare thigh.

Fun. There was that word again.

"We're going to make an album of Thomas's songs, Chris. An album. Think about that. Imagine how many people we can reach once we have our own LP. Pretty soon everybody'll be in the studio full-time because everybody will be able to get their message across in crystal-clear sound in a million bedrooms and living rooms and basements all across the world every time a needle drops onto a record. Colin says we need to tour now to get our name around and build up word of mouth and plug the first record, but maybe in a couple of years—"

"A couple of years! Bill . . ."

She took a final drag on her half-smoked cigarette before crushing it out on the inside lip of the bottle. Looked at me through her last exhale of smoke.

"It's funny, you know?" she said. "I always thought it would be me."

"No, I don't know. What are you talking about?"

"That I'd be the one who knew."

"For Chrissake, Chris, c'mon, this is important, talk sense. Knew what?"

"Knew, knew. Just . . . *knew*."

I tossed off my pillow, pulled on my underwear, and rifled through the layer of dirty clothes on the floor for a T-shirt. "Remind me never to smoke pot with you when we're talking about our relationship, okay?" I found a reasonably clean dirty shirt and pulled it on over my head.

"I guess maybe I'm even a little jealous," she said.

I took a deep breath and sat down on the bed beside her, took both her hands in mine.

"Chris, I really don't know what you're talking about, I really don't. And honestly, I don't care. All I know is I want us to do this."

"I'm not saying you shouldn't go," she said, squeezing my hands. "I'd never want to stand in the way of someone doing what they feel they have to do. Never."

"But I want *us* to do it. I can't even imagine doing it without you."

She placed her hand on the back of my neck, scratched me there gently. "You will," she said.

"But I don't want to."

She pulled my head toward hers and kissed me, softly. "You're sweet," she said. Then she kissed me again, through my underwear rubbed my only-now finally deflated cock. *Now* she wants to screw, I thought. Against the better judgement of the lower half of my body I took back my lips and stopped her roaming hand.

"Two months," I said. "Let's just give it two months. I mean, two months—that's sixty days! That's nothing! Think of it as a chance to check out how some other communities are dealing with all the stuff that's starting to go down in Yorkville. Think of it as research! And we'll be back in plenty of time for Christmas. And by then, if you decide what we're doing isn't for you, that you've got better things to do with your time, then fine, that's it, we'll both pack it in. I'll tell Thomas myself, I swear. He'll understand. He'll have to. He knows how much you mean to me."

The record scudded to its end again, but neither of us made a move to change it. Christine took my head in her hands and kissed both my eyelids. "You really are sweet," she said. She tugged her T-shirt over her head. "Lift up," she said, taking hold of mine at the bottom. "I want to feel you next to me."

Then she pushed me back onto the bed and her skin was my skin and we finished what we'd started.

47.

"—NO, WAIT. I mean Flint, Ann Arbor, Dayton, and then Cincinnati."

"Just a second, dear, I've almost . . ."

Tip-toeing on the top step of the ladder, Kelorn stretched for the bookstore's sole copy of Robert Burns. Scotty stood beside me

frowning impatiently, waiting for his book. Open-collared and
tie-less, his only fashion concession to the humidity and heat,
Scotty'd burst through the door that afternoon, cane first as usual,
challenging us with "Let's see what kind of commune you're running here anyway. Robbie Burns. Eighteenth century. Anything
you've got. *My Love Is Like a Red Red Rose* preferably. Go."

Lowland Scot poetry erring a little on the sentimental side
wasn't a big mover at Making Waves, and so relegated with a few
Elizabethan dramatists and the *Selected Essays of Charles Lamb* to a
topmost cubbyhole built for some long-forgotten reason right into
one of the walls. And because ladder-climbing really wasn't among
Kelorn's many strengths, I'd told her, twice, not to worry, that I'd
go up and grab the book myself. But somehow, somewhere
between good intentions and actually getting my ass up the ladder,
the intricacies of our tour itinerary kept me earthbound. Hey,
sixty-eight hours away and counting. And did I mention that we
were booked into forty-two clubs in sixty-one days?

Kelorn stopped her straining long enough to stare up at the
stubborn book and then, for a moment more, down at us. "Mr.
Robinson?" she said, reaching down with one hand. "May I?"
Scotty got the idea right away and handed her his cane. One carefully placed poke later, the Burns came fluttering down. I caught
it in mid-air, smoothed its slightly dog-eared cover, and handed it
over to Scotty, all without once having to interrupt myself.

"And Colin is paying for a complete tune-up for the hearse. I
mean, complete. Lube job, new filter, new spark plugs, even new
tires—everything."

Kelorn slowly climbed down from the ladder, one careful step
at a time, and stood in place holding on to it for a few seconds
when she eventually reached the bottom.

"Isn't that great?" I said.

"I'm a little dizzy, Bill, just give me a moment."

Scotty finished flipping through the paperback and put it into the pocket of his suit jacket. "I'll have this back by Monday," he said. Making Waves wasn't normally a lending library, but, then, Scotty wasn't a normal customer.

"I won't be here Monday, Scotty, remember?" I said. "By this time Monday we'll be pulling into Flint. The club we're playing in isn't actually in downtown Flint but a bit on the—"

"I'll have this back on Monday," he said, and shuffled out the door.

Kelorn had recovered from her climb long enough to plug in the kettle. Blazing sun or blinding snow, Kelorn needed her cup of tea.

"Shouldn't you be getting ready for your trip, dear? Don't you have things you need to do?"

"Nope," I said, "I'm all set. I've already packed, I got my passport yesterday, and I've already paid my landlord two months' rent in advance. I've even said goodbye to my parents. I'm all ready to go."

One thing I was always aware of whenever I went back home was how I smelled. Not bad, necessarily—I mean, I didn't stink, I was definitely a raised-right, wash-behind-your-ears hippie—but within the first few whiffs of sitting down on the lint-free living room couch or washing my hands in my parents' sparkling bathroom sink I couldn't help but notice a certain funky odour that couldn't be coming from anyone or anything but me, scented confirmation that I didn't fit in any more with the wall-to-wall carpeting and the perfumed toilet paper. This trip out I also noticed that I couldn't sit still for more than two minutes straight without rapping out a beat on whatever flat surface happened to be handy and couldn't understand why my parents both talked so incredibly s l o w.

Later, ducking into the washroom after dinner to pop an upper before taking Snowball for a walk with my dad, sideways slurping from the faucet to wash down the pill, I got a good look at myself in the mirror. For a second or two I considered that it might be me who was going too fast. But Snowball hated closed doors like every dog does and scratched and whimpered to let me know he already had his leash on and was way past ready to go. I turned off the tap and opened up the door and we were off.

"And Christine?" Kelorn said. "I take it she's as excited as you are? I'm afraid I haven't spoken to her since the night of your performance."

"Oh, yeah, she's excited. She's just been busy helping out with making posters and writing letters and making phone calls and stuff. For the next round of protests. For after we're gone. But she told me to tell you she's going to drop by and see you before we split."

Before *we* split. Like all really important decisions, nobody said anything, nothing got put down on paper, no clear consensus was reached. The only thing for sure was that we were going. We were both going.

"And has Thomas determined how he's going to negotiate customs?" she asked.

"Thomas doesn't need a passport," I said. "Only Christine and Heather and I do, and even then nobody'll probably ask to see them."

"Yes, dear," she said, filling up the teapot with boiling water, "but if they're interested enough in Thomas to look for him all the way up here, they're most certainly going to have their eyes open for him at the border. That's why I think it's so foolish for him to attempt to go back." She put a single cup on the counter and dropped a tea bag in the white porcelain pot. "You did talk to Thomas about this. You did speak to him."

I wandered off to the Ancient History section at the back of the shop and wished it wasn't just a subject heading. "God, it's hot in here," I said. I wrapped my fingers around the bottom of one of the room's two already-opened windows and yanked it upwards for all I was worth, which wasn't much.

"My goodness, Bill, you did . . ."

Kelorn didn't finish her sentence and I didn't turn around, just kept staring straight ahead at the wall of the house next door. Granted, it wasn't much of a view, but it did remind me of the one back in my room. Strange what you'll get all nostalgic about sometimes.

"But you knew how serious this all is," Kelorn said. "What could you possibly have been thinking?"

Well, nothing, I wanted to say, I wasn't thinking of anything. And just because it *was* all so serious. But Kelorn was a doer, just like Christine, and would never have understood what made a person like me who's never worn a watch in his life tick.

"But that guy," I said, turning around, "the RCMP guy, he never showed up the day you said he would. Has he been back?"

"No, but that's not the point. You simply must tell Thomas what's going on, Bill. And today, this afternoon, right now. And this Colin fellow, too, the one who's in charge of your affairs."

Then the door handle jiggled and the chimes tinkled and a platoon of badge-flashing Mounties didn't rush the room. Actually, the door stayed shut. I was all set to jump out the window anyway, but Kelorn calmly came from behind the counter and opened the door.

Thomas kissed Kelorn on the cheek and handed her a bunch of yellow daisies, long, dirt-dripping roots and all, somebody's nearby garden obviously the poorer. Through his ripped jeans, both knees were covered in fresh blood mixed up with small pebbles and black earth. He joined us in looking at the clump of dirt and flowers. The whites of his eyes were barbed-wire red.

"Yellow, yeah, that's a colour," he said. "It's just one, though. There are lots of other colours you can really get your head around if you . . . but yellow, yeah." He looked at Kelorn. "Buckskin—he knows where I'm coming from. Buckskin, he's the original Technicolor man himself. Buckskin, he's my main man."

Kelorn stepped out onto the porch to see if any irate neighbour with his lawn shears was on the warpath, then gently guided Thomas inside and shut the door.

"I'm going to get some hydrogen peroxide from upstairs and clean out those cuts," she said. "Then I think you and Thomas should sit down somewhere nice and quiet and have a talk, Bill. Somewhere indoors, preferably. Somewhere private."

I nodded.

"C'mon, Thomas," I said. "Let's go hang out for a while." I put an arm around his shoulder but he instantly stiffened.

"Sorry, brother. The time for talking's over. We've got work to do. But don't you worry. Now I know what I didn't know before. Now I understand what has to happen."

"Sure, that's cool," I said. "Let's go to the studio and talk. And work, I mean. Let's go there and work."

48.

"SHHHHHHHHHH."

"Yeah, because Kelorn, she's . . . I mean, we don't . . ."

"Shhhhhhhhhhhhhhhhhhhhh."

"Right."

As usual, Thomas was right. We did need to be quiet. Because, being a little after four in the a.m., Kelorn would be asleep upstairs. And even if she wasn't, likely wouldn't be too thrilled with the idea of Thomas and me ripped out of our gourds on acid and bumping into the walls of the bookstore on the look-out for songwriting inspiration.

Let me explain.

I prefer the slow mellow of good bourbon and long dog walks with Monty over nervous insights these days, and this stuff is old, mostly twigs and seeds and dry as powdered bone. But let me light up, inhale, get in tune to the tale. Because sometimes sacrifices have to be made if the song is going to get sung.

49.

I'D DONE WHAT Kelorn had told me to. Well, most of it. I'd walked Thomas from the bookstore to our rehearsal space as coolly as possible—slight glitch only when Thomas loudly insisted that we stop in at the Grab Bag and purchase the store's entire stock of cheap sunglasses and a can of whipped cream—and basically played watchdog until he gradually came down from his trip. I didn't tell him about the RCMP, though. I decided to wait until he was together enough to understand what I was saying.

It was my first experience with an acid case face to face, and, to be honest, I was a little disappointed. Thomas sat across from me wordlessly plucking away at his guitar like I wasn't even there and unsuccessfully attempting to get through the same song, a sort of a cross between "Green Sleeves" and "Bo Diddly" (believe it), always tripping up on the same intricate middle section. Aside from trying on and discarding every one of the twelve pairs of black shades before he began playing, I realized that with a song running through his head Thomas zonked wasn't all that different from Thomas straight and that he probably wasn't going to start flapping his arms like a chicken and jump out the window any time soon. After a solid hour of this I began pacing the room, occasionally stepping out on the balcony, hoping to see Christine down below tacking up some posters. She never showed.

On the card table I spotted Scotty's borrowed copy of Robert Burns. I flipped and skimmed until the rhymes on the page and Thomas's repetitive chord changes worked together to put me under. I dreamed of an undisturbed and endless coal-black river and woke to the sound of a chair scraping across the floor.

Except for the green volume levels of the reel-to-reel, the room was completely dark. I must have slept while the sun set and fell. Thomas flipped a switch on the tape machine, returned to his chair, and played the tune he'd been working on all the way through— flawlessly this time—then stood up and clicked the thing off.

"Sorry about the delay," he said, as if he'd just popped back from a quick trip next door. "But I had to take care of that before we could get started."

"No problem." He seemed like he was all right now, eyes not pinwheeling in their sockets any more and speaking in full sentences. "How do you feel?"

"Fine, fine," he said. He put a hand in his pocket and pulled out a white tab. "You ready to get going?"

"What are you talking about?"

"I'm talking about getting down to business, Buckskin. About getting down to work. You're the Colour Man, no question about that, but everybody can use a little inspiration from time to time." He jiggled the tab in his palm.

"I think you've worked enough for today," I said. "And if you think I'm going to volunteer for the same deal I just babysat you through, you're still more spaced out than I thought."

He didn't protest, didn't say a word; just nodded like he'd expected to hear what I'd said and returned the acid to his pocket. Then promptly announced that what he really wanted was a cup of fresh, hot coffee and a roast beef sandwich with mayonnaise and onions and tomatoes and salt but no pepper. He checked his pocket for his wallet and started for the door.

"Hold on," I said.

He looked and sounded like himself again, but I didn't want to run the risk of having to deal with the fallout from any flashback freakout in the street, not with him holding another dose and who knew what else. Plus, it was probably safe to lay the story of his fugitive status on him now, and I wasn't in any hurry.

"Give me some cash and I'll go," I said.

He shrugged, pulled a ten out of his wallet, and repeated his order. Sitting down at the table to wait, picking up the Robert Burns, "Hey, pick yourself up something to sustain you for a spell, too."

Which I did. An egg salad sandwich and my own cup of coffee to go. I handed Thomas his change and sat down at the studio table. He excused himself to go to the washroom down the hall and took his own brown bag with him. I slowly peeled the waxed paper from my sandwich.

The Mynah Bird had great takeout, but, of late, also a guy outfitted in only a white chef's hat, Yorkville's first and only nude cook. I tried not to think of him buttering my bread or laying on my lettuce.

Back, "What y'all got there, egg salad?" Thomas said.

"Yeah," I said.

"Damn."

"What?"

"Nothing."

I set down my sandwich. "What?"

"Nothing. It's just that if I would've known that what you were getting was going to smell so darn good I guess I would've . . ."

"Here," I said, pushing mine over. I took his still-bagged roast beef.

I figured Thomas needed food in his stomach more than I needed to maintain my if-you-can-pet-it-you-shouldn't-eat-it line of thinking. And Christine, after all, wasn't there to help keep me in line. I took a big bite of flesh and bread.

"Over here," I said.

"Shhhhhhhhhh."

"Here it is."

"Shhhhhhhhhhhhhhhhhhhh."

"Right."

I dragged Making Waves' hardback edition of *The Collected Works of William Shakespeare* off the shelf. Thankfully, one of the lower shelves. If it was on one of the higher ones I might have had to levitate up there. Not that I wasn't pretty sure I could make it, but I'd only realized I was capable of flight less than six hours before when the acid had kicked in. The acid stuck inside Thomas's sandwich. The acid he'd spiked me with.

Because I hadn't known I'd been dosed until I felt the first gentle loosening of the screws to the top of my head, my brain eventually agreeably spread like thick globs of peanut butter all over the walls of the studio, I hadn't had a chance to be justifiably enraged. If I'd felt compelled to say anything to Thomas at that point it probably would have been thanks. But I hadn't felt obliged to say a word. Or do or think anything. It was almost the entire opposite of what I'd always heard about LSD. You know: visions, epiphanies, twelve-hour full-body workouts of the soul, that sort of thing. Not me. Uh uh. I'd just wanted to stare at my foot. In particular, my right foot. A lot of people in Yorkville were starting to mess around with meditation and talking Zen and aspiring toward the sweet serenity of nothingness, and here I'd found nirvana in the middle of a roast beef sandwich.

"Come on, back here," I said, guiding Thomas toward the rear of the shop.

We sat down side by side on the springless couch. "Where do we start?"

"At the beginning," Thomas answered, leaning forward, plugging in a recent addition to our arsenal of equipment, a small, portable tape machine.

"Right."

He switched a couple of buttons to the ON position, adjusted a few knobs, and softly but clearly out came the first of the fourteen tunes he'd performed for me back at the studio.

Even though the acid was bona fide Owsley, it turned out he'd only given me half a hit, cut the dosage in two. After generously allowing me an hour or so for uninterrupted foot absorption, Thomas decided I was sufficiently turned on to listen to what he'd been busy with for the last several months.

Acoustic guitar, electric guitar, banjo, organ; carefully selecting the instrument each number required, Thomas played every one of his new songs for me from start to finish, all the tunes he hadn't let anybody listen to up to now. Some were as screaming anxious as the single one I'd heard before, the nervous-sounding thing I'd walked in on a few weeks back; some were mashed-potato cloudy, willowy white gentle; others were just kaleidoscope freaky (here more deep-bruise purple, there more snot-green olive). After every one he'd get up, stop the tape machine, sit back down in the metal chair across from me with his notebook and pen at the ready, and say, "Okay, what do you see?" And I'd tell him what I saw. And he'd write it down.

At around three in the morning he played me his last song, the one he'd been struggling with before, the "Green Sleeves" ditty with the shave-and-a-haircut-two-bits beat. But I didn't say anything this time, only sat there with that brain-itchy funny feeling you get sometimes when you know there's something you want to remember but have no idea what. Then my eye caught on the Robert Burns on the table.

"Hold on a second," I said. I flipped until I found what I wanted. "Flow Gently, Sweet Afton."

Thomas put pen to paper but looked right back up. "Come again?"

"But that's not it. That's not my dream."

"Steady now, Buckskin, we're almost there, just one more song to go. What dream?"

"While you were playing this same song this afternoon I was reading this book and fell asleep. And dreamt about this river."

"What river?"

"The river in the song."

"Buckskin—"

"The same river that's in the poem," I said, holding up the Burns.

Catching on now, "Let me see those lyrics," he said.

"No. The lyrics aren't our song."

"How do you know?" he said, reaching for the book.

"Because they're not," I said, closing it shut.

He sat back down in his chair.

"But 'Flow Gently,'" I said.

"Yeah?"

"That's our title."

"Are you sure?"

"Play the song again."

A quarter of the way through he stopped.

"I'll be damned," he said.

"Yeah."

"Goddamn, Buckskin."

"Yeah."

But man cannot live by Robert Burns alone. And how handy is it at nearly four o'clock in the morning to have the key to the front door of your very own bookstore? Load up the tape deck and don't forget the whipped cream and Desbutols.

The first song twisted itself around my brain as I sunk down deep in the old couch and started reading where the Shakespeare fell open, *The Winter's Tale*.

Nothing.

Rewind the tape, play the song again, move on to *Romeo and Juliet*.

Nothing. Next tune, please.

When we hadn't come up with even one more colour-coded tune title yet and Thomas saw I wasn't just slumping in my seat but was as good as horizontal, he taught me how to swallow Desbys dry. And hello there. So that's what fresh as a daisy means. *Antony and Cleopatra*, yeah, and just let the tape run, let's give this sucker a whirl.

A couple of hours later, just after sunrise, after several fruitless times through the same fourteen tunes, we still hadn't added to "Flow Gently" and our song catalogue, but we popped another Desby anyway, turned up the tape machine as loud as it would go, and kept walking around the room in tight circles, punching our fists into our hands and taking turns filling each other's mouths with whipped cream right from the nozzle. Because by dawn we had something better. We had the name of the album. Everything that Thomas's new songs were and would be, we'd gotten it, we had it, we'd *nailed* that motherfucker.

"Bill."

Kelorn stood at the bottom of the stairs in her white terry-cloth housecoat with Gretchen, in one of Kelorn's tie-dyed T-shirts hanging down past her knees, peering around from behind her. Gretchen stifled a yawn, covered her mouth. Kelorn took in the bibliophilic massacre of about a hundred books scattered around Thomas and me, streaks of melting whipped cream smeared across the floor.

"Moody Food," I said.

"I beg your pardon," Kelorn said.

Thomas began packing up our stuff. Thin slits of sunlight razored through the blinds into the room, dust particles like a million meteors careening through each beam.

"Moody Food," I said. "The name of our album is going to be *Moody Food*."

Kelorn crossed her arms.

"I think it's time you two got started for wherever it is you're going," she said.

three

50.

EVERY WINDOW AND vent was cranked open as wide as it would go; you could smell the hot asphalt underneath our tires as Thomas decelerated and pulled over to the side of the 401. I'd slapped out every tune I knew on my leg with my drumsticks to distract me until my thigh became sore, but I knew if I didn't say something soon my head was surely going to explode. So I said it: What should have been said days before, as soon as Kelorn had told me to. What none of us, least of all Thomas, wanted to hear.

Everyone sat quietly for a couple of minutes as the cars and trucks whizzed past, but it felt like the whole hearse-load of them were an inch from my face and giving it to me as loud as they could. But there was only the tick-tocking sound of the hazard lights to let everybody else on the highway know we weren't going anywhere. I picked up one of Christine's books and slouched down against the interior panel. At Thomas's insistence I hadn't said a word, not even to Christine, about what we'd been up to with *Moody Food* because, he explained, there was always the danger of talking a big project right out of existence. But this was a different kind of silence altogether.

"Hand me the map out of the glove compartment, will you, Mr. Bannister?" Thomas finally said.

Slippery unfolded the map and Heather lit Thomas a smoke without him asking for it. Thomas pulled deeply on the cigarette and considered the map carefully, traced a finger up and then back down a section of it.

"What time is it, sir?" he said to Slippery.

"Eleven."

"Straight up?"

Slippery looked at his watch again. "Straight up."

Thomas nodded and fingered the map again. Took another drag from his smoke.

"What's going on, Thomas?" Christine said. She and Heather were on their knees with their chins resting on their hands on the back of the front seat.

"Planning our alternate route, Miss Christine."

"There's another border crossing?"

"Yes, ma'am, there is."

I looked up from my book. "A safer one, you mean?"

"By all accounts, a much safer one."

"How do you know?"

"Some fellows I'm acquainted with in international sales back in Yorkville tell me that the authorities at this particular crossing are a fair bit more lenient than at any other point along the shared border of our two great nations."

Heather kissed Thomas on the cheek and sat back down, picked up her needles and yarn.

"Cool," Christine said. "Where is it?"

"Sault Ste. Marie."

"Sault Ste. Marie? That's the other way. We'd have to go back to Toronto and start all over again. It'll take forever."

"If we keep our rest breaks to a minimum, twelve hours, I figure. Which would mean we'd pull into customs around midnight. Which would stack things in our favour even more, I'd say."

"Isn't there any other way?" Christine said. "What about Buffalo?"

"Buffalo is not an option."

"But we'll miss our first gig," I said.

Everybody turned around.

"Yeah, we are going to have to miss our first gig," Thomas said.

I looked at Heather happily crocheting away and wondered what happened to all those sweaters and scarves and mittens she was always making for Thomas. I lifted Christine's book in front of my face. For about the tenth time I read about how 175 years ago sixty million bison covered the Canadian plains and how now there were none. When would we ever learn?

Thomas clicked off the hazards and turned the key in the ignition.

"Next rest stop," he said, "everyone go to the washroom and get something to eat and something for later, too. I'll call Colin and see if he can get them to reschedule tonight. But we're not going to miss tomorrow night. Or any other dates after that. Any questions?"

Christine sighed and removed the bookmark from her paperback. Slippery lit up another Marlboro. Heather carried on with the scarf she was making, softly humming away. And I slapped out the beat to what was going to be the opening track to *Moody Food,* "Flow Gently," on my other thigh, the one that wasn't sore yet.

51.

IT WAS A LITTLE AFTER midnight and foggy and cool, the windows having slowly inched their way up over the last couple hundred miles. Ours was the only car parked at the white line that a large yellow sign instructed us to stop behind. A tiny red brick building entirely nondescript except for a huge Government of the United States Customs logo stencilled on its side, it was like a little piece of *1984* in the middle of an untouched hinterland. It was also, according to the Vagabonds, the most lax border crossing in the entire country, ideal for both drug smugglers and draft dodgers. Thomas slowly pulled up beside the glass booth.

It was empty. Thomas clicked off the ignition and it was so silent it was loud, like my ears were a pair of those shells you hold up to hear the sound of the ocean. Finally Thomas hit the horn—once—and we waited. The hearse's honk echoed through the mist and trees.

A few seconds later a short, balding, fat man struggling with his loosened tie emerged from somewhere in the back. He seemed apologetic for not being there when we'd showed up and asked us what our nationalities were and what the purpose of our trip was as if he didn't want to bother us but this was something he had to do so please bear with him. We told him a surprisingly close facsimile of the truth, that three of us were Canadians and two of us weren't, and that we were playing a week's worth of gigs in Detroit.

"What's the name of your band, folks?" he said.

Before anyone else could speak up, "The Schizophrenic Farm Boys," Thomas answered.

The man smiled. "The Schizophrenic Farm Boys. Hey, that's a great name. Well, you folks have a safe trip and knock 'em dead, you hear?"

We promised him we would.

A few hundred feet past the checkpoint we parked for a minute to get our bearings and go over the map. It was still several hours until Detroit. Although the pines and the fog and the moon sure looked the same, apparently we were now in a different country. I was a little disappointed it didn't feel like it.

"Why didn't you tell him our real name?" I said.

The tidal wave of silence had ebbed, crickets and hoot owls dotting the thick quiet. Christine was already back to sleep. She dozed with her head on my lap and I waited in the darkness for Thomas to come up with an answer as to why he'd lied when he didn't have to. Heather leaned forward and put her cigarette to Thomas's lips.

Thomas leaned back in his seat, exhaled a billow of smoke. "I don't know," he said.

52.

THE NORTH WAS THE north and the south was the south, each in its own 100-proof USA way like nothing else at least one rubber-necking Canuck percussionist had ever seen before. First Michigan, then Ohio, then the Midwest, then Texas, then, finally, California. But first things first.

First, Michigan, a three-night opening-act gig at the student union on the University of Michigan's Ann Arbor campus, the country-rock stylings of the Duckhead Secret Society all the way down from Toronto, Canada, to get everybody good-and-rowdy ready for local favourites the Stooges, the latter headed up by nineteen-year-old hometown wild child Iggy Stooge. And notwithstanding the peanut butter and raw steaks he smeared all over his scrawny white chest and the pieces of broken glass he gouged into his arms during their encore performance of "No Fun," Iggy wasn't even the most alarming item on that first day's itinerary.

Because none of us had had a clue that Ann Arbor wasn't in Detroit, was actually about a half-hour ride away, we'd checked into the first place that agreed to put us up for the night. In spite of getting only four hours of sleep on the musty blue shag rug of the motel room—Thomas and I at 4 a.m. flipping a coin and he correctly calling heads, so he and Heather getting the single bed, Slippery saying he'd be happy outside in Christopher in the parking lot by himself—I woke up with a sore back from the thinly disguised concrete floor and with a five-year-old's Christmas-morning excitement that simply wouldn't allow my body any more nighttime nourishment.

I kissed still-asleep Christine on the cheek, silently stepped into my jeans and boots in the dark, took the room key off the desk, and cracked open the door as little as possible so I wouldn't wake anyone up. Heather was on Thomas's side of the bed with her arms wrapped around his waist, her face buried in his back. He was facing the other way with his arms dangling over the side of the mattress. I gently shut the door behind me and slipped on my sunglasses and hit the sidewalk.

It was early morning, early fall, but the street wasn't dappled in fresh daybreak dew and the only discernible new-day scent was car exhaust mixed up with the sharp stench of urine coming from the alleys and boarded-up storefronts. In more than a few of these, huge, refrigerator-sized cardboard boxes pushed onto their sides with human knees and feet sticking out of them. Black metal cages protected the shops still in business but not yet open for the day, like the stores had been busted and sentenced to a night of house arrest. Along the entire street it seemed like every third parked car had been abandoned by its owner and left to rot, tire-less axles, cracked windshields, and stripped interiors typifying this year's model.

I almost turned right back around to let the others in on the war zone we'd walked into and enlist their help in pushing all the furniture up against the motel room door, but it was like not being able to stop yourself from gawking at a three-car smash-up on the interstate. I kept moving down Brush Street.

Where, at eight-thirty in the morning, every corner store flashed neon red advertising what brands of beer they sold, and a teenage girl with dead eyes and a tight mouth in a pink housecoat and dirty pink fuzzy slippers and a crumpled five-dollar bill in her fist screamed at her three small swarming children to get away from the chocolate bars if they didn't want to *get it* and grabbed her change off the counter then her package of Pall Malls out of her paper sack and tore off the cellophane wrapper and tossed it to the ground before she was out of the store.

Where a sign in the window of the liquor store down the avenue declared THIS STORE INSURED BY SMITH AND WESSON, and who the hell needs a pint of Old Crow before breakfast? Someone, apparently, a COME IN WE'RE OPEN sign hanging in the door shining red-and-black bright in the sunlight, a guy in a camouflage jacket and hunting cap and smoking a pipe sitting behind the cash register armed and loaded and ready for business. Empty bourbon bottles and vodka bottles and whisky bottles squatted on top of overflowing garbage pails or lay smashed on the sidewalk.

Unless you walked far enough east.

Where the liquor bottles turned into either crushed cans of Colt 45 or broken wine bottles, Thunderbird wine bottles mostly, and the black men in camel-hair coats and feathered fedoras hanging out on the sidewalk in front of the pool halls and bars and rib joints already pumping out the delicious burning message of hot barbecued beef made you think how you only see black people with black people here. Which, come to think of it, means that before you only saw white people with white people. But if you're white you didn't notice that you didn't notice that. But the eyes of the black people with black people in front of the pool halls and bars and rib joints sure notice you. And even if nobody says it with actual words, it's time to go west, white boy, back to your own part of town. *Now.*

Waiting for the light to change on the other side of the crosswalk from the motel a couple of hours after I'd started out, I paused in front of a White Castle restaurant. It looked part Anne of Green Gables cottage and part drive-in hamburger joint. I'd never seen anything like it. My light turned green but I didn't walk. I pushed open the glass door of the White Castle and went inside.

The first thing I saw was a fat man and his fat wife and their fat son and fat daughter sitting on the edges of their white plastic chairs, gorging themselves at a white plastic table. It was hard to see what they were eating—their hands moved so fast and their mouths never stopped chewing—but every few seconds one of them would tear the white paper wrapping off one of what must have been fifty of the world's tiniest hamburgers and stick it in their mouth whole. I walked up to the shiny white counter.

"Those people," I said, pointing at the family, "what are they eating?" The woman wore a white polyester uniform and cap but was elderly and black, the only instance I'd seen all morning of the two races mixing together. She smiled, a little embarrassed at my ignorance.

"Hamburgers, sir," she said.

"But they're so small."

The woman smiled again. "Those are White Castle hamburgers, sir." She pointed to the price list on the wall behind her. "Just ten cents each or ten for a dollar."

"Ten cents each?"

"That's right, ten cents each."

I put my hand in my pocket.

"Do you take Canadian?" I said.

"Sure we do," she said. "We get Canadians in here all the time. I thought you sounded different."

"I think I'll have ten," I said. "It's ten for a dollar, right?"

"It sure is," she said, taking my money and ringing it in, handing me back the difference. "Now let me get your order for you, sir."

I scooped up my American change and waited for my ten hamburgers. On our nickel there was a picture of a beaver. On theirs was the profile of a guy I didn't recognize. In God We Trust, it said.

53.

BECAUSE IT WAS our first out-of-town gig and we were too excited to be otherwise, the student population of U of M's general indifference to our opening efforts on behalf of Iggy and the boys barely registered. We used the opportunity of hardly anyone showing up until the Stooges came on—and those that did drinking beer and talking throughout the show—to get our shortened set list in order and adjust to playing through some-one else's sound system. We all hung around backstage the first night to watch the Stooges do their thing. Almost as much as Iggy's psychotic performance—we never got to know the band well enough to call him Jim like everyone else—the band's ridiculously short forty-minute set startled me. Even as out-of-town under-studies we'd been instructed by the promoter to play for an hour.

After we'd come off stage the second night and the head-liners were milling around getting ready to go on, I watched the Stooges' shirtless main man wash back a dose of LSD with a can of Pepsi. I'd been rapping with the band's drummer. He looked like he'd been shooting smack at the bottom of an aban-doned swimming pool for a few months before deciding on his life's real vocation as an acne-scarred human mole. He played his instrument with the same black towel draped over his head night after night and wore it now as we talked. If you buried a large chunk of Gorgonzola cheese inside an old tennis shoe underneath a chicken coop you might come close to imagining what he smelled like. Was one hell of a drummer, though. Just punished those skins.

"Is that guy nuts?" I said, motioning toward the Iggster. "He won't last past your first tune."

"Jim? Fuck, no. Jim knows what he's doing. He trips before every show."

"My God," I said. "You must have to cancel a lot of gigs."

"Nah, he's okay for a good solid half-hour before we've got to drag him off stage."

Whackety whackety whack.

The drummer pounded his sticks on the back of an exposed wooden beam. It sounded like a suicidal woodpecker trying to beat its brains out.

"Besides," he said, "we haven't found an audience yet who could handle us for more than forty-five minutes."

Whackety whackety whack.

The Duckhead Secret Society survived Iggy's acid-assisted ravings and the proto-metal onslaught of the Stooges in Michigan, persevered through two nights of open-mouthed teenybopper staring opening up for fading British folk duo Chad & Jeremy in Toledo, was sandwiched between two Cleveland garage bands, the Tyrants and Buck and the Decoders, endured repeated requests for "Last Train to Clarksville" by prefabricated Fab Four heartthrobs the Monkees while playing a high-school dance in suburban Akron, and headlined for the first time on U.S. soil in Cleveland at a place called the Paddock that sounded like a country and western club and the promise of something like a musically sympathetic ear, but was actually an illegal betting operation that advertised live music and cold beer to help keep its cover.

After the first set, during which not one person came in— I mean not one single person; our only audience the bored, blonde waitress idly filing her fingernails and holding up the untended bar—and we were ten minutes late for the second, Slippery off somewhere smoking and the rest of us sitting on Christopher's hood watching the orange and yellow flames from the chimney of a factory in the distance mix with the smoggy downtown skyline to create the prettiest poisoned sunset you've ever seen, the guy in the black suit and open white collar we'd talked to when we'd first showed up stepped outside, cleared his throat, crushed out his cigarette on the brick wall of the bar, and motioned Thomas over with a single forefinger. He put his arm around Thomas's shoulder and they went for a short walk around back.

Thomas refused to talk about what the two of them had discussed, but we weren't late starting another set again. Thomas made sure of that. We ended up playing five minutes into every break and starting back up five minutes early every time. At the end of the night Thomas was in such a hurry to pack up and get us out of there he forgot to collect our money and we literally had to push him out of the hearse to go back in and get it. A minute later he tossed me a paper sack with our fifty dollars in it, jumped behind the wheel, and peeled out of the parking lot. We drove through the night all the way to Pittsburgh.

And then to Clarksburg and Columbus and Dayton and Cincinnati and lots and lots of other towns and cities I've long since forgotten. And then to St. Louis, Missouri, gateway to the West, for us the doorway to Dixie, where we began our slow descent into the mouth of the South.

54.

THE SCHEDULE WAS SIMPLE. After the gig, when everybody but Thomas and me was asleep, when for the only time all day we didn't have to worry about reading the road map right and getting to the next club in time for a proper sound check or figuring out where we were going to stop and eat or where we were going to crash for the night—when we could finally forget about everything that didn't have anything to do with *Moody Food*—we wrote.

We wrote by moonlight on torn deck chairs out by deserted motel pools. We wrote in parking lots sitting on the bumper of whatever car was furthest away from our room and Christopher so that no one would be woken up, the high beams of the transport trucks rolling past on the dark highway momentarily illuminating Thomas's guitar and the notebook and pen in my hands. Whenever Christine or Heather would wake up and not find us there, we'd just say we couldn't sleep and felt like getting some air or having a smoke. They were both so exhausted most of the time we didn't have to lie that often.

For some reason I'd gotten into the habit of being the one to check in and pay for our motel room. But whenever the forecast turned gloomy, Thomas would jump out of his driver's side seat and accompany me inside the motel lobby, me signing in and paying for the band's room and him paying for another—our own private writing room located as far away from the first as possible—with a shiny white credit card with his name on it. He never offered to explain. I never asked.

55.

COLIN HAD SET UP THE entire tour in advance, and at times it seemed as if his sole criterion had been booking us into any place that would have us, no backwoods bar too out of the way or its musical policy too Duckhead-inappropriate, no double bill too bizarre for us to share. But even when we were scheduled to be the headliner and it turned out we were the main attraction at the Polar Bluff, Missouri Critters and Crafts Annual Fall Festival and Tractor Pull and our opening act the Polar Bluff Auxiliary Firemen's Barbershop Quartet, no one hijacked Christopher and demanded we head home, not even Christine.

Everything was in a hurry, and it wasn't only the effect of the ration kit full of Desbys Thomas had taped to the bottom of Christopher in case a flashing red light showed up in the rear-view mirror. Getting up in the morning was in a hurry, our wake-up call of choice being the maid pounding on the motel room door and screaming that it was fifteen minutes past checkout time and that she had to clean the room, us scrambling to pry open our eyes and throw our stuff together and get to the nearest coffee shop so we could get started on the day's required amounts of sugar, fat, tobacco, and caffeine, the four essential food groups of a musician's life on the road. Getting to the next gig in time was in a hurry, everybody taking their expert turn misreading the map and contributing to the babble of contradictory directions that usually meant missed turnpikes and dead ends and going the wrong way down one-way streets.

Most of all, America was in a hurry, so unlike our home and unhurried native land so many different faces and places and cars with different-coloured licence plates speeding off on their who-knows-what-where-why way. And Walter Cronkite delivered his nightly Vietnam body count to the nation, you could buy a six pack of beer from a corner store from an old lady with a cross hanging around her neck, and look at that, Chris, what the hell's that? We don't have Burger King McDonalds Kentucky Fried Chicken Dairy Queen Pizza Hut Baskin-Robbins Dunkin' Donuts 7 Eleven back home do we?

Christine might have started off every step of the trip with something like *The Letters of Sacco and Vanzetti* in front of her face, but it's amazing how a ten-foot-high red-and-yellow concrete clown by the name of Ronald can make even the most committed anti-capitalist turn her head and stare. Thomas drove and Slippery dozed most of the time, but the Maple Leaf contingent of the band had their noses firmly pressed to the windows of the hearse and their eyeballs glued to the American Dream giving Mother Nature the shiny facelift I'm sure she never asked for.

Everything was in a hurry except Christopher at night.

We didn't always spend the evening in the place where we played. Sometimes, if the next show was close enough and the weather was okay, we'd drive the two or three or four hours to the next town so as not to have to worry about showing up late the following day and scrambling around looking for Big John's Hanging Tavern out on I-17 and not getting a chance to at least try to civilize the more than likely primitive PA system. Thomas and I didn't mind; a night off from writing once in a while had its advantages, gave us a fresh set of legs when we sat down again the next night ready to run.

We'd load up the equipment, grab something to eat on the way out of town, and talk about the show a little. Then Slippery would start snoring and somebody would start laughing and then everybody else would start laughing too which would wake up Slippey with a loud snort and cause everybody to laugh even louder and him to mutter something under his breath and turn on his side in his seat and go back to sleep for good. And before too long Heather would put down her needles and Christine her book and Thomas would click off the inside light and he and I would be the only ones awake at three o'clock in the morning as we rolled down Highway 70 on the lookout for something called Terre Haute, Indiana.

You don't stop using speed just because you don't need it; the body still demands that rush it's grown accustomed to even if you don't have any particular place you feel like rushing. Because Thomas insisted on doing all the driving, on the nights we weren't writing he still found something to do. I'd pull my knees up to my chest and look out the window at America rolling by behind us with my hand resting on sleeping Christine and let the gentle hissing of our tires on the blacktop and the sigh of passing cars and trucks lullaby me for hours.

The odometer turning over, the miles adding up, somebody else might have let their mind wander to wonder just exactly where they were going and why. Christine, for instance. But not me. And I was the one wide awake.

56.

"I'M SENDING KELORN a postcard. Do you want me to say anything?"

Christine was taking advantage of the rare rush-free day doing her best Scotty imitation, turning the desk at the Home Away from Home Inn or something just like it somewhere in Ohio or Indiana or Illinois or Missouri into her very own private work-station. Her little collection of paperbacks was stacked neatly at one end, the last three days' worth of the local newspaper had been fished out of the motel office garbage pail and reassembled to be pored over later, and she'd already mapped out on hotel stationery the quickest way for us to get to our gig that night. She even had her own version of an in box and out box going, a pile of postcards yet to be written on her left, those already done on the right. I'd forgotten what she was capable of given a decent night's sleep and a couple of hours to herself.

"Kelorn," I said. "Sure. Tell her . . . yeah, tell her . . ."

"I'll just tell her you send your love."

"Great," I said. "Thanks. That's great."

It'd been a long night. Our ration kit was running danger-ously low, and for the last couple of days Thomas and I had been halving our normal dosage of uppers and doing a lousy job of writ-ing. The connection Thomas had been given the name of the last city back had been busted the week before we got to town. Thomas had finally gotten a hold of a Vagabond back in T.O. who'd made some calls, but it would be noon before we could go over and score. After spending most of the night in the hearse sweating through my T-shirt (and telling concerned Christine not to worry, that I must have been coming down with something), Thomas had doled out some Diazepam for us both when we'd hit the motel before dawn. I'd finally slept, but downers, I discovered, definitely weren't my thing. My brain felt like it'd been pickled, and every time I went to speak it seemed like I needed five min-utes to plan out what I was going to say. Thomas seemed all right, though. He and Slippery were waiting for me in Christopher. I could see them from the opened motel room door, Heather leaning into the driver's side window talking to Thomas, Slippery calmly blowing smoke rings out of the passenger side.

"You should send your parents one, too," Christine said, head down, still scribbling.

"That's a good idea. I will. As soon as we get back."

"Where are you guys going again?"

"A cousin of Thomas's lives across town and he wants to go by and say hello."

"A cousin? Here?"

"Yeah. Pretty weird, huh?"

I didn't get off on lying to Christine, but was all for painting the best possible deception I could. Browse through the history books and they all say the same thing: Every lasting society is founded on shared illusions. No nation lasts ten minutes without them.

"Plus, Slippery wants to go to the Red Cross," I said.

Well, that part wasn't a lie, at least. Slippery got paid five dollars for each pint he let them drain from his arm, every blood-red cent he received going directly into his growing Arkansas retirement fund.

"Is that safe?" she said. "He gave blood just a couple of days ago, didn't he?"

"It must be, he's going to give again."

She looked up from her postcard. "How are you feeling?"

"Fine. Better. It must have been one of those 24-hour things."

"Good."

"Yeah. Hey, I should get a move on," I said.

"Okay."

"We won't be long. Before two, anyway."

"All right."

I was already out the door when Christine called my name. I ducked my head back inside.

"What's up?"

She looked at me like she was waiting for me to say some-thing, like I'd been the one who'd wanted to talk to her.

"Chris?" I could feel a line of sweat gathering above my lip. I licked it away. "What is it?" I said. "I've got to get going."

Christine lowered her eyes and shuffled her finished post-cards, rapped them four-square even on the desktop.

"Will you get me some stamps while you're out?" she said. She shuffled the other pile. "Ten should do it."

"Ten stamps, sure." I shut the door.

As soon as Thomas saw me coming down the sidewalk he started up the engine. I slid open the side door and climbed inside.

"Now, if you decide to sit out in the sun, I want you wearing sunscreen and your new hat, darlin'," he said to Heather. "We don't want that fair skin of yours burning up on us now, do we?"

Heather smiled and held up the enormous floppy yellow sun hat Thomas had picked out for her at some truckstop. She leaned through the window even further to give him a kiss and then watched us pull away.

We were down the street when I realized I hadn't kissed Christine goodbye. I flipped on the radio. "Be My Baby" by the Ronettes poured out of the speakers and I clicked it back off. Only when your heart hurts does AM radio finally make sense.

Thomas handed me a map.

"See if you can find Violet Street somewhere on there, Buckskin. What we're looking for is 265 Violet. Rick says it's a yellow house with a bunch of old mattresses out front. And a '52 Chevy. On blocks."

57.

SHACKS, LITERAL fucking shacks, with a white beat-up Cadillac parked out front and three black kids in bare feet stand-ing out on the front porch sucking on Mr. Freezies and all that suspicion and hate and fear already there searing in their eyes as they watched us cruise by and me hanging my head out the window watching them watch me. Twenty-five minutes later and lost, actual white picket fences and flapping American flags and the suburban perfume of freshly cut lawns and fathers and sons tossing footballs back and forth in the autumn air. Back on track and fifteen minutes east, the first sad scene all over again, but this time the dirty faces and skinny bodies on the front porches white although the hard stares and stench of human hopelessness hanging in my nostrils the same.

"It's an odd number so it's got to be on your side," Thomas said. We'd already dropped Slippery off at the Red Cross building not far from our motel.

"Two-forty-one, 243—slow down," I said, "it's coming up."

Just as promised, a square cinder block house painted violent canary yellow with a couple of stained mattresses with the stuffing spilling out of them like they'd been stabbed to death shared the front yard with a stripped Chevy up on wooden blocks. Thomas pulled up the steep gravel driveway, killed the engine, and put it in park; you could feel Christopher roll backward before the brakes locked and we jerked to a standstill.

We shut our doors with a careful, gentle click, but I was too busy watching a woman in hair curlers, housecoat, and white running shoes beating the hell out of a carpet with a baseball bat to see the Rottweiler tearing toward us down the sloping lawn. Even when I did get him in my sight it was Thomas's scream and not the gleaming fangs and bucket of saliva pouring from the dog's mouth that first registered. But before either of us could unfreeze and scramble back inside Christopher, the dog came to the end of his silver chain and snapped backward a good couple of feet in the air, without missing a bark landing right back on his four feet, just as intent as before on ripping our faces off.

"Who are you, man?"

The guy standing in the front door of the house had hair down to his ass and a stringy, knotted goatee and was in bare feet and blue jeans, but wore mirrored sunglasses and had a can of Budweiser in one hand and a shotgun hanging from the other. I didn't know whether to flash a peace sign or give a Klansman salute. The Rottweiler, seeing his master not giving him some kind of doggy sign that we were okay, went into full-out watchdog alert, eyes rolling back in their sockets and foam cascading down his chin.

"I said, 'Who *are* you, man?'"

The guy pumped the shotgun and took a sip of his beer at the same time. I turned to Thomas, but he kept staring at the dog like if he stopped watching him for an instant all those white teeth would be at his throat.

"Thomas?" I said.

Sorry, no one home.

"Thomas, say something." By now he and the dog were locked in some kind of weird trance, the animal's loud snarling replaced by a spooky low motor roar.

Giving up, "A friend of yours said to come by," I yelled out.

"Everybody's your friend when you're on the good side of a gun, man. You're gonna have to do better than that."

"A friend from Toronto, a biker, a Vagabond."

An instant of concentration flickered in the guy's eyes. He ran his fingers through his goatee with his Bud-holding hand. I kept my eye on the shotgun.

"Toronto, huh? Got a few brothers up that way."

Loud enough for the guy with the gun to hear, "Thomas, what's your friend's name again? Our friend."

Thomas appeared as if he'd completely fallen under the

dog's spell, his eyes almost as glazed over as its were. I punched him in the arm, hard.

"Rick," he blurted out.

"Rick," I echoed.

"Rick from Toronto?" the guy said.

"Rick, right," I said.

"Vagabond Rick?"

"Right."

"Vagabond Rick from Toronto?"

"That's right."

He lowered his chin and peered at us over his shades.

"Shit, you must be the guys Rick said would be coming over today."

"That's us," I said, "we're them."

"But he said you'd be driving a hearse."

I wasn't sure what to do. I turned around and gestured at the big black thing on four wheels parked in the driveway.

"And hey, there it is," the guy said. "A hearse. Hard to mistake one of those things, isn't it?"

"Yeah, well—"

"Lyndon!" he screamed. The frothing dog didn't seem to hear him. "Goddamn it, Lyndon, it's all right, these are friends, it's all right." In an even louder, but clear, calm voice, "Lyndon. It's all right. Lyndon. It's alllll righttttt."

Something finally clicked inside the dog's brain and his steel muscles melted, uncoiled, his growling gradually ceased. He lay down on the grass and tried to catch his breath, his pink lollipop tongue hanging down to the ground.

"Come on inside and have a beer, man," he said. "You guys hungry? Nancy'll fix you up something if you're hungry."

Thomas and I kept staring at the dog.

"Shit, don't worry about Lyndon, man, he knows you're all

right now. I let him know you're part of the pack. See, I'm the alpha male and he listens to what I say. It's totally cool, man. It's scientific. I've got a book all about it."

Scientific proof to the contrary, Thomas and I didn't move an inch.

The guy laughed, pulled from his beer. "Where's your baby, Lyndon? Go get your baby and bring it to momma. Go get your baby, boy. Bring it to momma."

The dog jumped up on the cement porch and picked up a dirty stuffed doll. The guy unhooked the dog's chain and patted him on the head. We all watched Lyndon trot inside with his baby.

"Come on, man," he said, waving us inside with the shotgun. "You guys are a long way from home. Take a load off. Any friend of, uh . . ."

"Rick's," I said.

"Rick's, right. Any friend of Rick's is a friend of mine."

Inside was like a hippie bomb shelter. Every window was covered with aluminum foil and sealed tight with black masking tape, the tens of candles burning throughout every room supplying the only light in the house. Having nowhere else to go, the smoke from the sticks of incense poking out of a bunch of empty Budweiser cans hung in the air like a thick fog, slightly watering one's eyes. "Eleanor Rigby" played from a record player on the floor. Everything was on the floor. An overflowing ashtray, a black telephone, a couple of dirty dishes, several paperback books. The walls were covered with half-finished, wildly surreal murals, each sporting a mad swirl of different designs and bright colours, giving the impression that the artist had either gotten bored, tired, or went insane. The guy, Fred, offered us each a dirty cushion covered in dog hair to sit on and went to get us some beer.

I leaned over to Thomas. "I don't like this. Let's get the speed and go. I don't like this."

Thomas didn't have a chance to answer. Lyndon ambled into the living room with his doll hanging from his mouth, ready to greet two of his newest fellow pack members. He dropped the thing at Thomas's feet. Sat and wagged his tail.

Careful not to look at me, only the dog, "That beast is fixing to jump me, Buckskin."

I almost had to laugh. Almost. The girl who came in the room with our beers did.

"Lyndon, you leave those boys alone. They don't want to play with you, they're tired." She handed each of us a beer and introduced herself.

"If he's bothering you fellas, just give him a smack on the behind and tell him to shoo. I swear, that dog will play with that thing with you until one of you drops dead."

Fred came into the room carrying a fresh can of Bud and a joint the size of a small cigar on a roach clip. He winked at us.

"Now, don't you be bad-mouthing my little buddy, Nance, I know you're just jealous." He joined us on the floor, sucked from the joint, and passed it on to his girlfriend. He saw Thomas staring at the dog.

"I don't have to tell you that these are some strange times we're living in, brothers. There are forces at work out there"—he pointed at one of the tin-foiled windows—"that the average man on the street not tuned into the proper channels of consciousness isn't aware of, doesn't even know exist. Those not as cosmically advanced as we are are in danger of being psychic victims of these enemy forces and don't even know it. These are days when a man needs to take care of his family by whatever means necessary." He leaned over and scratched the dog, who was still intent on getting something going with Thomas, between the ears.

"I call him Lyndon because when I got him I was trying to come up with the meanest name I could think of, the name of the nastiest SOB alive. But then I figured, who was a badder ass than LBJ fire-bombing an entire country and killing all them babies? Of course, strictly speaking, LBJ, he takes his orders from his old lady. It's all scientific, man. See, the female aura, that's what runs the universe. It's a fact, you can read up on it yourself."

I inhaled and nodded, couldn't help coughing. It was impossible, but I felt instantly, absolutely spaced.

"What is this stuff?" I asked, passing the roach clip to Thomas. He took it without taking his eyes off the dog.

Fred and Nancy looked at each other and smiled.

"It's my own very special brand, man," Fred said. "I call it Wheelchair Weed."

"Why do you call it that?"

"Because if you smoke enough of this shit, you're going need a fucking wheelchair, that's why."

He exchanged another smile with his girlfriend and got up to turn over the record. I told myself I couldn't possibly be as high as I felt and, because I was, stared without embarrassment at Nancy. Her eyes were green and her hair long and blonde, her body thin but girly-curvy. She was also black-soled barefoot just like her boyfriend and wore the hippie chick uniform of the day, a bright tie-dyed skirt that looked like it'd been made out of an old flour sack and a white blouse tied above her belly button, no bra underneath. She took a long pull from the joint. With lips sealed tight to keep in the smoke, she smiled a long smile at me that said her half-exposed breast was all right and that my being mesmerized by it was all right and that everything— everything, everywhere, for all time everything—was forever and ever all right.

Fred sat back down. I thought he'd gotten up to turn over the record. Instead, he'd put the needle back at the beginning of "Eleanor Rigby."

Having grown tired waiting for Thomas to make the first move, Lyndon grabbed his baby and flopped it down at Fred's feet. He picked it up, shook it in the dog's face, and the tug-of-war was on. The dog resumed growling through toy-clenching teeth, but with a fiercely wagging friendly tail. Thomas managed to shake himself loose from himself, took a long chug from his beer and set the can down in front of him with a clank.

"You know, it's really fine of y'all to open up your home to us like you've done, but we should start thinking about getting to the club and setting up for tonight. Any chance we could talk some business?"

Fred was standing up on bent knees, see-sawing back and forth with Lyndon. It was hard to tell who was having a better time. "Talk away, brother," he said.

"Well, I think 150 Desbutols should hold us okay until we get back home. Or maybe 200. Yeah, let's make it 200."

Now Fred had both hands wrapped around the stuffed baby's plastic head and was swinging Lyndon by the mouth around him in a circle, the dog pumping its legs in the air, trying to get earthbound. "Like to help you boys out," he said, "but I'm afraid no can do."

"But Rick said—"

Fred let go of the doll and Lyndon flew halfway across the room, bouncing off one of the walls with a sharp yelp and scrambling to a frantic, clawing stop on the cracked linoleum floor.

"Rick who?" Fred said, standing straight up.

"Rick, you know—Rick," Thomas said.

"Rick *who*?"

"Rick from Toronto."

"Rick from Toronto?

"Rick from the Toronto Vagabonds."

"Rick from the Toronto Vagabonds?"

"Right."

"Oh, yeah. Rick. Hey, how's old Rick doing these days?"

"Great," Thomas answered, "he's doing great. But what about the Desbys? I thought—"

Recovered, Lyndon shook his head a couple of times, picked up his baby, and trotted back across the room, ready for one more round. He and Fred picked up where they left off.

"Sorry to say you missed out by about twelve hours, boys. Guy who does some business out at the truckstop bought every one of my uppers last night."

"What about Bennys?" Thomas asked. "Do you—"

"Desbutols, Bennys, meth—everything, man. Got to keep those big wheels of capitalism rolling, right?" He got down on his knees and began growling in tune with the dog. Thomas took the joint from Nancy and proceeded to smoke the rest of it like a cigarette without offering it to anyone else. "Eleanor Rigby" came to an end and Fred got up and restarted it.

"Hey, don't worry, brother," he said. "I've got something better than speed. You guys are musicians, right? I've got what all the bands are using now. You just hold on a second." He disappeared inside one of the candlelit rooms, Lyndon trailing right behind him. Thomas took a last toke and dropped the dead joint into his can of beer. When it hit the bottom it made a soft hiss.

"Thomas?" I said.

He looked up at me as if in slow motion, his eyes beet red, his skin chalky white.

"What are we going to do?" I said.

Thomas licked his lips. I ran my hands through my hair and scratched my scalp and decided that if I heard "Eleanor Rigby" one more time I'd have no choice but to snap the record in two.

Fred returned with an old wooden shoeshine box and placed it on the floor between us. He pulled out a small plastic pouch of white powder from inside, closed the lid, and poured a tiny pile on its top. With a razor blade he inched out two lines.

"What's this?" I said.

"Vitamin C, brother," Fred said.

"What?"

"White Lightning from the coca, man, all the way from the beautiful fields of some of our South American brothers."

"Cocaine?"

"Cocaine," Nancy said, smiling.

"We don't want it," Thomas said.

I was shocked. Thomas's chemical consumption policy was pretty simple: When in doubt, do it.

"No problem," Fred said. "I just thought you and your partner here looked like you might need a little pick-me-up." He lowered his face to the box, inhaled a line, and rubbed his nose. Nancy leaned over and did the same.

The change was immediate and incredible. Their eyes shone like lit windows on a freezing dark night, their faces pulsed with an electric healthy glow.

"Can I try some?" I said.

"Be my guest, man. No charge to sample the merchandise."

Thomas put four fingers on my chest. "This isn't what we came for."

"It may not be what you came for," Fred said, "but it's all you're going to get in the way of the stimulant family. Now, if you're looking for downers, that's a whole other story. I've got—"

"For the work we're doing we don't need any fucking downers," Thomas snapped.

"Then I suggest that if this here work of yours is so fucking important you'll fucking take what you can fucking get." I noticed Fred's shotgun leaning against the wall by the door. I wondered if it was still cocked.

"Of course," he said, "you're free to look around elsewhere. But this isn't San Francisco, brother. And the suits and ties down at city hall haven't got around to putting together a hippie yellow pages yet."

The record player's needle edged into the next song. A wash of sitars flooded the room.

"We've got a lot of work to do before we get to L.A., Thomas," I said. "We've got to have something."

Lyndon had rejoined us and was lying on the floor beside Fred with his head between his paws. Thomas looked over at the animal without visible fear for the first time.

"If we do this," he said, "it's just for work. It's just for *Moody Food*."

"Sure," I said.

"For only when we're working, Buckskin."

"All right, all right."

He paused for a moment and then wet his finger, dabbed up some coke and ran it along his upper gums. He cut a long line with the razor and snorted it up; closed his eyes and tilted back his head. What sounded like a cat whining to get in a back door could be heard from somewhere in the house. Nancy got up to let it in.

Thomas opened his eyes. "How much for a gram?" he said.

"Depends on how much you're looking to buy. I can give you a good deal if you're not looking to score again soon."

"We're not. I'm going to have to come back, though. I haven't got that kind of cash with me."

"We're not going anywhere, brother."

I took the opportunity of the deal going down to get my own taste of inner radiance. Which I got, but with an unexpected bonus. I felt like ditching Christopher and jogging the twenty miles back to the motel and fucking Christine for a few hours or at least until she'd orgasmed seventeen times. Just for starters.

Nancy came back into the room cradling something in a wrapped blanket. And there was that whining again. I expected to see the cat all gussied up in a bonnet and baby clothes.

Except that it wasn't a cat but a baby, an actual buck-naked bona fide baby boy with the tinniest little pink willie hanging right out there for all the world to see.

"There's my little man," Fred said, getting up and going to the kid.

"Yellow Submarine" filled the room and Fred and Nancy took turns coochy-cooing and making funny faces at the gurgling infant. The music was kid's music, bright and colourful, and the baby had Fred's brown eyes and Nancy's blonde hair, and Thomas and I weren't going to suffer the shakes any more, and with the help of the coke *Moody Food* was going to get done. I felt so happy I thought I was going to cry. I asked if I could hold the baby.

"Sure, brother," Fred said, and Nancy handed him over.

"Brother, meet Leonard. That's short for Leonardo. You know, like the artist, the Renaissance Man."

I held the baby like my aunt Lori had shown me how with her kid, under the butt and supporting the head. He looked like a little angry old man wondering what the hell he was doing here. He looked perfect. The kid caught a load of one of his toes way down there at the other end of his body and moved all ten as best he could and watched the show with mesmerized eyes.

"Hey, brother, watch this," Fred said.

After he'd handed me Leonard, he must have sparked up another joint. He took a deep toke, came in close like he was going to kiss his son, and then gently blew a cloud of smoke in the baby's face, some of it lingering in white curls around Leonard's nose and mouth, some of it slowly lifting above his head like a dirty halo. The baby blinked a few times, sneezed once, then stared expressionless at his now no-longer-moving toes. His face looked as frozen as the plastic head on Lyndon's doll.

"Eleven months old and he's stoned, man," Fred said, taking his own deep toke. "Isn't that beautiful?" Nancy caressed the baby's cheek and wiped a line of spittle from the corner of his mouth.

I looked to Thomas. He tapped out another line of coke and snorted the top of the shoeshine box clean.

I stood there holding the baby in my arms.

Because when Thomas was nine his father took him to Shiloh and he cried on the walking tour of the battlefield just like his daddy had done when his own father had taken him there thirty years before, Thomas was allowed to choose from the dusty shelves of the gift shop one expensive hardcover book on the Civil War. His father offered to buy him a T-shirt and mug commemorating the bravery of the doomed Confederate troops as well, but Thomas politely declined.

The book was thick and heavy and full of footnotes and complicated maps and wasn't intended for children, so mostly Thomas looked at the pictures—artists' recreations of battlefield scenes and burning cities and grainy photographs of cocksure, bearded generals and the proud, grey-clad soldiers. Somehow the actual pictures never looked as real as the drawings and paintings.

But there was one short section Thomas read all the way through and eventually didn't need to read any more because he knew it by heart. It was the story of Stonewall Jackson and his last battle.

Jackson got his nickname, "Stonewall," at the First Battle at Bull Run when, early on in the war, a courageous defensive run by his undermatched Confederate troops allowed the South to route the Federals and send them in retreat all the way back to Washington. But that wasn't the part Thomas liked. Thomas liked to read about Jackson's final fight.

The book said that when Stonewall Jackson was a young man and took his first taste of whisky, he ever after refused to allow another drop of alcohol to pass his lips because, it was rumoured, he realized he liked it too much. During the battle at Chancellorsville on April 27, 1863, Jackson led an unexpected and crushing movement against an exposed Union flank and sucked on a fresh lemon all day long. Throughout the afternoon of April 27, as Jackson's boys pounded the Yankees' 11th Corps, Jackson sat on his horse and sucked at his piece of bitter fruit. When one lemon was sucked dry he'd drop it to the ground and bite into another. The bright flash and dull roar of battle, and Jackson biting and sucking.

After the collapse of the 11th Corps Jackson got greedy and continued the advance. Later that same day he was accidentally killed by the fire of his own men, an untouched lemon on the ground not far from his fallen body.

As a boy lying on his bedroom floor Thomas would wonder what it meant to like something so much you couldn't allow yourself to have it. Later on, as a young man riding off into important battles of his own, he no longer wondered about the answer to that question. Now he wondered about the best way to surprise the enemy and attack its exposed flank. About getting greedy and pushing on through the trees. About the risk of friendly fire. About Stonewall Jackson sucking on that lemon.

58.

"YOU BOYS been to a cathouse?"

Slippery toed out a Marlboro on the sidewalk and took my spot in the front seat while I climbed in the back. He'd been waiting for us out front of the Red Cross just like he'd said he would, even if we'd shown up nearly an hour late. His shirt sleeves were rolled up and there was a clean white bandage taped to one of his forearms.

"What are you talking about?" I said.

"None of my business, but it don't take no rocket scientist to figure out that one way or another you two been fucked somehow."

"I think you might want to slow down on the blood drive," I said. "Remember to save some for your brain."

Slippery lit a fresh cigarette. "Like I said, none of my business."

"Hey, pull in here," I said. We were getting close to the motel.

Thomas steered Christopher into a White Castle parking lot. Suddenly I was hungry. Very hungry. For meat. For red meat, the bloodier the better. Seagulls circled the grey steel trash bin out back of the restaurant.

"You guys want anything?" I said.

"This is a hamburger place, Buckskin," Thomas said, keeping the engine running.

"So?" I said, sliding open the door.

"Since when do you and Miss Christine eat hamburgers?"

"If you don't want anything, just say so," I said.

A brown Chevy cruised by on its way out of the parking lot, but not before its driver could toss a couple of White Castle paper sacks out the window. The seagulls were on them in a second. They screamed and squawked and tore open the bags and pecked at each other over the ketchup-bleeding French fries and bits of leftover hamburger bun scattered over the blacktop.

It was my first time since the very first time in Detroit. I had my money ready and devoured the ten tiny hamburgers in the rear of Christopher by the time we got back to the motel. I didn't even offer Thomas or Slippery any. When we were almost there I made Thomas drive around the block while I smoked one of Slippery's Marlboros to get rid of the smell of meat on my breath.

Heather, lying by herself out by the pool, waved at us from underneath her yellow sun hat as we drove up.

I walked back to the room. Christine was asleep on the bed with something called *The Social and Economic Basis of Anarchism* on her lap. It was still hours until we had to be at the club and we didn't usually have a free afternoon to ourselves, so I thought about maybe going for a long walk together or the two of us taking off somewhere close by for coffee. Then I saw the pile of completed postcards on the end of the desk and realized I'd forgotten to get her stamps. I shut the motel room door as quietly as possible behind me.

I joined everybody else out by the pool.

Although Heather said it was too cold, I stripped down to my underwear and swam laps while everyone watched until my lungs hurt and my arms felt like they were tied down by invisible ropes attached to weights at the bottom of the pool. When I finally climbed out of the deep end everyone applauded and said how impressed they were. I rubbed myself dry with the rough white motel towel Heather handed me and thought about how it had been years, since early on in high school, that being happy had been as simple as going as fast as you could.

59.

LACKING CEREMONY, it isn't a vision, it's a scheme. We had more than just some plan. We had a ritual.

I would close the curtains to the already-darkened room, Thomas would lock the motel room door, I'd light the candles, and he'd lay out one line of coke each to start with. The rest of the band was long gone beddy-bye by the time we got going—usually no earlier than two or three in the morning—and that suited us fine. We didn't want to be disturbed. We had *Moody Food* to make.

Two whiffs, a little preliminary warm-up playing on Thomas's part, and the race was on. To wed melody and word. To fuse music to script. In particular tonight: a downright nasty piece of metallic-tasting, grating electric guitar work that Thomas heard a creepy organ line running through on the breaks and that I saw as copper and rust with dark brownish-red sneers every time I heard it. Thomas started banging out the tune on his unplugged electric and I closed my eyes to better see the song and let fate play its part in helping to select from the pile of library books on the bed.

Library books, yes. Every time we'd hit a new city Thomas and I would use the excuse of dropping Slippery off at the Red Cross to head straight for the local public library. Thomas would hand over his Mississippi driver's licence and get a brand new lending card all inky fresh and neatly typed up and walk beside me up and down the aisles while I filled up his arms with as many volumes as we were allowed. Sometimes it was impossible to get the books back to the library before we had to split for the next gig, and I'm not proud of the fact that the name Thomas Graham must still strike fear into the hearts of certain elderly librarians.

Of course, we could have just told everybody what we were up to. Once upon a time the idea was simply not to piss away our vision in chit-chat. Then at some point along the line Thomas and I became Masons worshipping at the altar of *Moody Food* and it was treason to talk about all matters Moody above a whisper. Cocaine is great for nurturing obsessions. And the best part is that all you really need to become obsessed is an obsession. Having something to actually be obsessed about is just an added bonus.

I could tell tonight's first choice had real potential right from the moment I scanned the book's table of contents. Sometimes Thomas had to keep playing the same tune over and over again, literally for hours, until I happened upon one sentence that even hinted at in words what I was seeing in colours. Sometimes there wasn't even that. Sometimes the sun would come sliding underneath the door like a dawn-delivered early edition and the only thing we'd have to show for an entire night's work would be blisters on Thomas's fingers, a floor covered in discarded library books, and two snoutfuls of toot that, in my case, necessitated doing laps in the motel pool to calm me down enough to be able to steal a couple of hours of sleep. But I felt lucky about *The Collected Poems of Wallace Stevens.*

"You ever heard of this guy before?" Thomas said.

"I don't know. Maybe. Maybe in school."

Thomas fished out a new pick from his guitar case.

"Get this," I said. "'The only emperor is the emperor of ice cream.'"

"That's all right."

"Yeah," I said, not looking up from the book. "It is."

"It's not this song, though."

"No. It's not."

I turned the page.

"Okay?" he said.

"Let's go."

Thomas would play and I would read, skim, recite aloud, and test out lines by scribbling them down in Thomas's red notebook. Occasionally we'd take a break and do another line of coke so Thomas could keep playing and I could keep reading, skimming, reciting aloud, and testing out lines by scribbling them down in Thomas's red notebook. The key was for Thomas to never stop strumming and for me to never stop seeing colours. With enough persistence, patience, and cocaine, eventually, we knew, the job would get done.

Every decision had to be unanimous. Song title and tune only ended up getting hitched when we'd discovered a perfect match. You vote with your body and everything else is just blah blah blah. The shiver up the spine, goosebumps on both arms, the tingle of recognition in all ten toes. And when Thomas's eyes and mine would meet and both our bodies would light up like drunken Christmas trees, it was like the words we ended up using so completely captured what Thomas heard and I saw that until we hacked them free from the dead trunk of whatever poem or story or novel they'd been shackled to they hadn't really existed, were only incubating in the musty pages of some book waiting for us to set them free.

Around five in the morning, forty-two poems, two broken guitar strings, and a gram of coke later, "You Like It Under the Trees in Autumn (Because Everything Is Half Dead)," I said.

Thomas stopped playing. He closed his eyes. I could hear the sound of a passing transport truck on the highway a few hundred feet from our door. It was still too early for birds.

"One more time," he said.

I repeated it. "From 'Because' on should be in parentheses," I said.

He spoke the line aloud himself, then slowly nodded and set his guitar down on his knees. I closed the book and put it on top of the others.

We both sat there trying to get used to the sudden quiet. That was always the hardest part. Shivers and goosebumps and tingling toes are a wonderful barometer of aesthetic purity, but they aren't the kind of nightcap you want to take with you to bed. My ears pounded with the room's silence.

I stood up. "I'm going for a swim," I said.

Thomas picked his guitar back up. "I think Thomas is going to work for a while," he said.

"Try to get some sleep."

"I will," he said. "Thomas just wants to get started on this."

I closed the door and headed out to the pool.

Once we had the title of a song in place, Thomas took over. He'd reclaim his notebook and use what I'd come up with as a sort of lyrical compass to set him in the right writing direction. Usually by the next week the tune would be done. I'd read over what he'd written to make sure the lyrics were the right colour. They always were.

60.

"YOU CAN'T JUST HAVE PIE, BILL," Christine said.

The young waitress kept snapping her gum in tight little pops and pressing her pen to her notepad, but couldn't stop staring at the stubble on the back of Christine's head. After some kind fellows in yellow hard hats enjoying a few cold beverages at a truck stop in Ohio a couple weeks back offered to show us what they "did to muff-divers around here" and help Christine understand what it felt to be made love to by a real man, she'd reluctantly agreed to join Thomas and me in donning a baseball cap whenever we decided to break bread in public, he and I tucking our shoulder-length hair up and under.

Christine ran her finger down the grease-smudged paper menu.

"He'll have the grilled cheese," she said. "On brown. And instead of french fries, make it a side salad, plain. Thanks." She picked up her paperback. To Heather, sitting across the table, "What some of these places pass off as salad dressing is worse for you than red meat."

Heather smiled and proceeded to order up the goriest item on the menu, the Fatburger Deluxe, a quarter-pound of charred ground beef saddled with a fried egg, one slice of processed cheese, and three thick strips of fat-bubbling bacon, all the major slaughterhouse food groups in one. Every day she ate the same thing: the biggest hamburger she could get her hands on, french fries, and a vanilla milkshake. Slippery, who always found a way to get to a grocery store and cook up something sufficiently greasy on the hot plate he'd brought with him, was snoozing out in the hearse.

The waitress managed to scribble down Christine's order and continue to blow bubbles without breaking her stare. Christine attempted to disappear behind *The Murder of Mother Nature: Healthy Eating for a Healthy Planet* for as long as she could before finally taking off her hat and slapping it in my lap. Shaved scalp right out there for all of northeast Missouri to see, "If we need anything else we'll be sure to let you know," she said. The girl kept her eyes lowered to the floor all the way back to the kitchen.

"C'mon, Chris, put it back on," I pleaded, rubbernecking around the room, trying to gauge the fallout. It was after two and most of the lunchtime crowd had thankfully returned to work, but I didn't like the vibes I was getting from the old couple in the corner sharing a basket of barbecued chicken wings. You don't have to be working on a coke habit to be paranoid, but it doesn't hurt.

"Don't do this, Chris," I said, her hat in my hand.

Christine set down her paperback. "Do what? Not wear a baseball hat? Yeah, right, how dare I."

You learn how to fight in front of other people when you go on the road with a band. Heather began laying out her Tarot cards between the water glasses, cutlery, and ketchup bottle. Thomas picked up Christine's book.

"This time tomorrow we're going to be in the South," I said. "The South, Chris."

"So what you're saying is that I should get ready to be even more embarrassed of how I look and who I am."

I set the cap down between us on the seat. I emptied another packet of sugar in my coffee and scoped the room for the nearest exit.

"Miss Christine, what's a kg?" Thomas said. He had her book opened up on the table in front of him.

It took Christine a couple of seconds to figure out what he was talking about. "It's a kilogram—a way of weighing things," she said. "It's about two pounds."

"Did y'all know it takes seven kilograms of feed grain, which takes about seven thousand kilograms of water, just to produce one kilogram of beef?"

Christine looked at me, then back at Thomas. Heather kept carefully laying down cards with one hand while happily squeezing Thomas's non-book-holding hand with her other. She'd said she wanted to do a reading for our trip south.

"And that one hamburger takes about as much water as you'd use in fifty showers?"

"Yeah, well, that's . . . it's not good," Christine said.

"You're damn right it's not good. It says here that as more and more water is being used to raise animals instead of for crops, millions of wells are going dry all over the world. Millions."

Our waitress appeared beside the table juggling four steaming plates and trying her best not to look directly at Christine's bristly head. To Thomas, "You had the hot beef sandwich, right?" She set down his meal of beef and gravy over white bread first and then everyone else's. I never understood why he even bothered. He rarely did more than shove the food around on his plate for a few minutes before settling down to his real meal of a couple of cigarettes and coffee. Tonight he didn't even do that.

"Yes, ma'am, that's what I *was* having," he said. "Before I got the facts. Before I got the *Word*." He pushed his plate as far away from himself as possible.

"You mean you don't want your hot beef sandwich any more?"

"Indeed I do not."

Heather flipped a final card before managing to get both hands around her dribbling, bulging burger. I had no idea what a Tarot card with a tower getting zapped by a lightning bolt meant and didn't want to find out. Heather was on the point of first-bite bliss when Thomas slowly pushed her burger plateward with two insistent fingers.

"Darlin'," he said, "I have only one question for you. Answer me truly once and for all and I will not ask you again. In my home state of Mississippi—the poorest state in the union—there still exist children in this day and age of jets and spaceships whose families go without running water. Now, listen closely to me, darlin'. With the rapid population growth, the increasing urbanization of invaluable wetlands, and the boom in destructive factory farms, ask yourself this: Are those fifty showers you're holding in your hands right now worth all the pain and suffering you are surely causing for this and future generations of under-privileged children?"

Heather's fingers were still wrapped tightly around the burger. She looked up at Thomas. "No?"

"That's my girl," he said. He put her Fatburger back on the plate and nudged it off to the side of the table alongside his own rejected meal.

"We'll both have what Buckskin is having," he said, pointing at my plate.

The waitress scratched the topmost floor of her beehive hair-do. "I'm gonna have to charge you for the burger and the roast beef sandwich," she said.

Thomas grabbed his wallet and peeled out a fifty. He placed it on the edge of the table and stood up.

"A small price to pay for doing our part to help heal Mother Earth, aren't I right, Miss Christine?"

Christine smiled weakly and pulled on her baseball cap. Smoothed down the peak and back until it was tight on her head.

Thomas went off to the bathroom.

When he came back to the table five minutes later with his shades on and his own hat stuffed in his back pocket, I knew he'd had a snort. When his and Heather's second meal arrived she couldn't hide her disappointment, picked up and sniffed a piece of lettuce before putting it back down and nibbling suspiciously at her grilled cheese. Thomas looked on approvingly. He ate the dill pickle speared into his coleslaw with a toothpick and lit up a fresh cigarette.

"Ma'am?" he called out to the waitress, holding up his coffee cup. "Could Thomas trouble you for a refill?"

61.

"BILL?"

"It's just me, go back to sleep."

"What time is it?"

"Around five."

"What's that smell?"

"Shhh, you're going to wake up Heather."

"Where's Thomas?"

"He couldn't sleep either. He's having a smoke."

"What's that smell?"

"Shhh, go back to sleep."

"Is that chlorine?"

"What?"

"You smell like chlorine."

"You're crazy."

"Why do you smell like chlorine at five o'clock in the morning?"

"Go back to sleep, Chris."

"Bill . . ."

"Go back to sleep."

"Bill . . ."

62.

EVEN A BROKEN WHEEL can keep turning for a little while. But then Thomas got bored. To his credit, he tried not to be. But Thomas wasn't the kind of person to tell himself what to do. Thomas did what he was. And by the time we hit San Antonio what he wasn't was interested in our live shows any more. Truth was, I wasn't much either. But, then, I didn't have to stand up there in front of an audience for two hours and pretend to be. I only had to keep the beat. But he tried. You couldn't say he didn't try.

In Memphis, during our first-ever Deep South musical date, all at once his voice was all southern-honeyed charm. You always could tell he was from around down there, but now he sounded like he'd never left. It was a little ramshackle joint out by the airport full of white people who worked at the factories outside the city, but it was still Memphis, Tennessee. There was an organ on stage and we played every Stax-styled tune Thomas had taught us with him at the keyboard and Slippery taking over the low-tone vocal parts. Most of the songs we hadn't performed since we left Yorkville, but by the time we got to Sam and Dave's "You Got Me Hummin'" we really were, dishing out big fat chunks of greasy

Duckhead soul, steel guitar oddly accenting every beautifully filthy vocal chop-chop, Thomas's tripped-out rhythm changes turning around and around the R&B beat.

But every time the audience thought they knew what they were getting—basically, twang-tinged rhythm and blues pulled apart and pumped right back out by three skinny white hippies and an old man in an old suit—Thomas would avoid the tackle and outfox the defence and do a musical end run: a fuzz-drenched number like our own "Early Morning Overcast"; a plain-old hard-core country number like "She Thinks I Still Care"; a straight-ahead rock and roll chestnut like "Lucille" done up in high wah-wah style that anybody who could hear the beat and had two feet knew wasn't black or white but only a good old boogying time. The jammed dance floor never stopped moving long enough to wonder what it was sweating to. Thomas finished things up with, "Y'all been as fine an audience as we've been lucky enough to play for as long as I can recall, and remember that even the itty-bittiest little animal has got rights too, you know, and peace in your city and have a good night."

In Dallas it wasn't the audience but us that Thomas ended up working to win over. The Lone Star Saloon was a phony country and western place with brass railings and glass coffee tables and mirrors everywhere you looked with the country-shmoltz stylings of Jim Reeves and Eddy Arnold pumped over the club's sound system. The pot-bellied men all wore big white cowboy hats and the women expensive dangling earrings in the shape of the state of Texas, but I had more country soul in the tip of one of my split ends. Thomas tried to make friends with the crowd by instructing Slippery to cool it with his Evil Kineval steel-guitar licks and guiding us through nearly an entire set's worth of traditional country tunes played as straight as we could manage, but the audience looked almost as listless as we felt.

When Thomas tried to get something going with a steel-guitar-warped version of Chuck Berry's "Roll and Roll Music," they went from apathetic to irate, the women staring out at the empty dance floor through slit-eyes, the men repeatedly taking off their hats and putting them back on like they couldn't decide whether to leave them on or not while they lynched us.

Thomas announced we'd be back in fifteen minutes and shut off his mike. "Everybody inside Christopher," he said. "We're going for a ride." Forty minutes later we were back for our second set with a couple of notable differences.

For starters, everybody but Slippery was righteously messed up on half a bottle of very expensive Sauzo Tres Generaciones bought at a nearby liquor store and consumed at Thomas's insistence while we drove around looking for a store that Thomas said he'd recognize when he saw it.

Second, when we finally stepped out onto the stage in front of about half the audience that'd originally been there when we'd started, each of us—Heather in her usual spot off stage included—was wearing not only a shit-faced grin but a silver silk turban. Thomas had left Christopher running and us guessing and bought the things at some sleazy backstreet boutique. Five minutes later, in between gulps from the bottle of tequila, he passed around the turbans and explained that they were something the old R&B groups in the fifties used to wear so they'd look more East Indian than Negro and get more bookings, and that if those ignorant crackers back at the bar wanted to treat us like spades then, by God, we were going to give them what they wanted. He'd made sure that each person's turban had his or her very own different-coloured fake jewel stuck right in the middle. By the time we got back to the club and the bottle was half empty it all made sense.

We ramshackled right in with a sloppy version of Ray Charles' "What'd I Say," a tune we'd never even practised that Thomas walked us through out in the parking lot, and things only got funkier from there. Even when we finally played something the ten or fifteen couples left in the place recognized—one of Patsy Cline's sugary ballads, "I Fall to Pieces"—the stinging electric guitar runs Thomas choked off every time the tune's title was sung by everybody (off-key me included) in our highest, loudest falsettos made it sound nothing like a gentle lament to a long-lost love and everything like an unrequited psychotic's suicide note set to molar-rattling music.

When the bar's owner, another little man in a big hat, said he was only going to pay us half of what he was supposed to, take it or leave it, Slippery handed Heather his turban and grabbed the man by his wide collars and threw him back across the bar. "I've got an Arkansas mortgage to pay, Hoss," he said. "And nobody's taking money out of my pocket."

We got paid, in full, and stopped at the nearest motel to continue the party, the baddest rock and rolling, country and westerning, motherfucking music-making outlaws anybody'd ever seen. At least that's what we kept telling ourselves as we finished off a couple of six-packs of Pearl and skinny-dipped in the motel pool, the full autumn moon illuminating our silver turbans as we waterbugged around and around, careful to keep our jewelled heads aloft in the warm Texas night. Slippery, still in his suit, smoked in a recliner and kept an eye on the front desk.

Later, Christine and I even made it while everyone else waited for us at the 24-hour coffee shop next door, the first time since a brief spell of near-constant randiness on my part right after I'd started in on the coke.

In Austin, at the Broken Spoke, we played to what was just about our ideal audience. The brush-cut and big-haired two-stepping crowd was already there waiting for us, and we brought in the bizarro element ourselves by way of an interview we'd done the afternoon of the gig on a local college radio station. Colin had told us that as we got closer to our recording rendezvous with him in L.A. and our coming-out party at the Whisky A Go Go, the Electric Records people would start setting up publicity spots for us in the more knowledgeable markets.

I was taking a leak in the radio station washroom before we were supposed to go on the air when Thomas came in and dragged me into one of the stalls and practically stuffed a line up my nose. I didn't put up any protest. The day's inaugural snort wasn't coming around early enough for me either. We giggled all the way down the hall like a couple of school kids sneaking a smoke in the can.

In the cramped studio the guy who interviewed us knew what he was talking about, Electric had done its homework. He wore a green headband and a STOP THE BOMBING! button on his jean jacket, but asked Thomas all about what he meant by Interstellar North American Music and how he was influenced as much by Little Richard as Hank Williams and everything else the Electric Records press release he'd received said. The interview was supposed to be with all of us, but Thomas ended up doing most of the talking. The sound of him crunching on a carrot from the plastic bag he'd taken to carrying around sent the sound meters into the red, but he came across loud and clear.

"It's all the same song. Louis Armstrong, Hank Williams, Chuck Berry, Doc Watson. It's all God's breath sung back to Him in syncopated celebration."

"Braces and a broken recorder. Twelve years old and glasses and patches on both knees and even the chess club doesn't want you. Hey, that's a blues song, too. You know Paul Revere and the Raiders aren't going to write it, so I guess it has to be us."

"Rule number one: Unless you have something to say, don't pick up the instrument. Thomas has always believed that deeply."

"The kind of person who listens to our music doesn't want to live a bit and die a little and find a friend. The kind of person who listens to our music wants to live forever and die a lot and fall in love."

"I can't speak for anybody else in the band, but personally, I've always felt like a stranger in my own house looking for a back door I haven't gotten around to building yet. Does that answer your question?"

It probably didn't, but it did make for damn good radio. When the interviewer concluded by asking what people who weren't all that familiar with country music could expect from our show and Thomas answered, "Heartaches, sore feet, and fleshless Satori. And please remember to tip your waitress. They're working girls just like the rest of us," a few people must have decided to come on down just to see what this freak show was all about.

We never played better. Thomas got so into his "Dream of Pines" duet with Christine that he closed his eyes and waltzed around with an imaginary partner during her mandolin solo and fell off the stage and into the crowd, which thought it was all a part of the act. And the people standing at the edge—shorthairs and longhairs, truckers and tokers standing a little uneasily there side by side—caught him in their outstretched arms and pushed him back up just in time for him to sing the next verse and he didn't miss a word.

63.

AUSTIN TO SAN ANTONIO is only about an hour and a half, A to B blacktop, straight down I-35. But time doesn't mean anything. It might take half a second, it could take years, but once the bow has been drawn, eventually the arrow will fly. Call it hippie bullshit or common cosmic sense. Either way, by the time we were two songs into our first set at Bar l'America in San Antonio it was obvious there wasn't going to be any inspired repeat of the Memphis or Austin or even Dallas shows before we split for L.A. Because Thomas didn't care any more. What's more, he didn't care who knew that he didn't care any more.

He wasn't unprofessional. He just couldn't be bothered to sing with any emotion or play his instrument with any inventiveness or put any thought into the song selection. After a while, Christine got tired of waiting around for him to signal what was next and took over counting off the next tune. Thomas didn't mind. He was happy to play sideman. That's the thing. He wasn't spaced out or pissed off or surly with anyone. He just didn't care.

It was as if the last few days had been nothing more than him running into a long-ago ex and deciding to go for a week's worth of auld lang syne lovemaking. It wasn't until later that I realized he was saying goodbye for the last time, too.

His father was good about it. He gave Thomas his mother's third-generation family Bible, a $25,000 per year trust fund contingent upon him never setting foot in the state of Mississippi again, and a firm handshake. His father would make sure that Becky, away at school in Louisiana, got his letter. When Thomas came downstairs that morning with his bag, Selma had a big cry in the kitchen and gave him the silver cross from around her neck and told him to hurry along because he knew how much his father hated to be kept waiting.

Thomas shook his father's hand and climbed aboard his Harley and terrified the birds nesting in the treetops of Dream of Pines one last time.

His father watched the dust from the dirt road and the exhaust from the bike rise and whirl and become the same thing. He called out to Lee, his mongrel hunting dog who let only him come close without grrring, and the two of them walked off together back to the house.

Later, hitting the open road along the coast near Biloxi, finally going fast enough to slow down his mind, Thomas came to the conclusion what it wasn't.

It wasn't about refusing to get a haircut or playing guitar in his room all day or the girls at all hours. It wasn't about getting expelled from Harvard for missing an entire semester's worth of classes. It wasn't about being presented at his daddy's doorstep more than once at four in the morning after being picked up at Charlie's Place or the

Chicken Shack or Franklin's, the only white face in the entire joint ("And you from a good family, too, boy," the officer in the squad car would say. "What would your momma think knowing her son was hanging around Niggertown?"). It wasn't about his father threatening him that if he was going to throw away an opportunity at an Ivy League education then he was damn well going to take the job that was waiting for him down at the front office if he didn't want to be looking at this house from the outside. It wasn't about the one time his father's name and money hadn't mattered—midnight downtown alleyway Jackson and a gram of coke in his pocket and Thomas too messed up to talk his way out of it for once. It wasn't about the article about the bust in the Jackson Daily News *that mentioned not only Thomas's father by name but also every one of his business affiliations. It wasn't even about the emergency meeting of the company's stockholders in Memphis and the not-so-subtle suggestion that Mr. Graham learn to control his nigger-loving, dope-taking, long-haired hippie son or . . . or, well, Mr. Graham damn well better.*

Thomas knew what it was about. It was about "Money Honey." "Money Honey" by Jesse Stone as recorded by Elvis Presley on his self-titled first album.

The coffin was in the ground and the Reverend Wilson had said his thing and someone put a single red rose in Thomas's hand and nudged him toward his mother's grave. He walked to the edge of the hole and looked down inside at the polished mahogany and shiny silver latches and looked and looked and kept on looking. And when Selma came forward and placed an arm around his shoulder and clasped his rose-holding hand and gently attempted to help him let go, Thomas tightened his fingers around the flower's stem until the thorns burst through his flesh and the blood began to flow and his brain was on fire and he finally felt awake again.

Because he was not yet as strong as his father Thomas went right to the song's last verse, the one about money, love, and which way the wind really blows, alternately singing as loud as he could and biting down hard on the hand trying to stop him, every bowed, embarrassed, graveside head hearing every single word he sang, a trail of dripping red on the cemetery green all the way to the back seat of the Cadillac.

Thomas popped the clutch on his bike and pulled in front of a lagging transport. With any luck, he'd be in L.A. by Tuesday.

64.

"IS THIS SOME KIND of guy thing, Thomas?"

"I'd just as soon finish what I start is all, Miss Christine."

"This isn't a contest, you know. This isn't about you. This is about somebody fresh taking over for a while so we end up getting to Los Angeles in one piece."

"Oh, don't you worry about that, Miss Christine, Thomas is going to get us all there nice and safe and sound. And before you know it, too. You just go on back to your book there and relax a spell. Here, have a carrot."

Thomas kept one hand on the steering wheel and with the other offered his bag of carrots to the rear of the hearse; there were no immediate takers so he stuck it back between his legs with a shrug. "Y'all don't know what you're missing," he said, crunching into a fresh carrot. "Plenty of beta carotene in just one of these little beauties to help your natural detoxifiers do their job."

Christine slid her bookmark into her paperback and rolled over onto her side into a tight ball, placing her pillow squarely over her head. The disappearing act with the pillow was a recent development.

"Mind you, now, parsley, kale, and spinach are also good sources of beta carotene. Just because Thomas is partial to carrots doesn't mean everybody's got to like what he likes."

Thanks to the coke, Thomas had plenty of time to memorize lots of interesting tidbits from Christine's *The Murder of Mother Nature* to generously share with us. At the moment, though, he was busy single-handedly pushing Christopher harder than was probably wise across Texas, New Mexico, Arizona, and California so we could score two whole bonus days worth of work in the studio. Except for filling up and the infrequent do-it-and-dash pit stops Christine had to practically petition him for, the speedometer rarely dipped below seventy-five, not the coolest road plan in the world considering we were transporting several grams of cocaine across four state lines in a black hearse. The entire trip, the whole twenty-four hours, all twelve hundred miles, I never saw him once get out of his seat. I slept for a few hours here and there, so maybe I missed it. I must have. He had to go to the bathroom. And he had to blow his nose. We both had to.

I spotted a sign for an upcoming service station and poked my head into the front of the hearse. "We should probably stop here," I said. "We've got less than a quarter-tank left and the sign says it's the last Esso for forty miles." It was sometime in the afternoon, twelve or more hours since we'd left Texas and my last snort, and I'd been bugging Thomas to pull over ever since I'd started getting a little fidgety just outside El Paso. He seemed put out even to slow down long enough to get gas, but could see the nearly horizontal needle just as well as I could. He hit the blinker and pulled over into the right lane.

"Anybody wants anything, tell Buckskin what you need and he'll scoot in and get it. Everybody else, go to the can if you've got to and then come right on back. Thomas wants to make Phoenix by supper."

The opportunity to stretch our legs was usually cause for hearse-wide celebration, but Heather and I were the only ones to hit the parking lot pavement. Christine had apparently succeeded in joining Slippery in turning the middle of the day into the middle of the night, head still buried underneath her pillow. I almost touched her on the shoulder to see if she really was sleeping, then decided that if she was, she was lucky to grab the winks and needed them, and that if she wasn't, if she was only pretending to be unconscious, well, maybe she needed that, too.

"No dilly-dallying, you two," Thomas called out after Heather and me. Heather turned around and blew him a kiss and we went inside the restaurant.

"Medium black, cream and two sugars, right?" I said, hand on the door of the men's washroom. Heather smiled and nodded. "And no dilly-dallying," I added in my best Thomas Graham. The smile dropped from her face.

"I wouldn't," she said. "I told Thomas I wouldn't."

"I know, I was just . . . See you in a bit."

I found an empty stall with another empty stall on either side of it and snorted a line off the back of my hand and felt so much better when I stood up that I forgot to take a leak. An old man washing his hands looked at me funny in the mirror when I came out so I coughed and sniffled a couple of times to cover my tracks.

I got in line to get the coffee, and the smell of a hamburger sizzling in sautéed onions for the guy ahead of me gave me a hard-on, I mean an honest-to-goodness pokaroo stiffy. Before I had time to feel guilty about even thinking about it, I was asking for extra onions and cheese please on my burger and wondering if I had time to order and inhale a second one before Thomas started to get antsy.

I decided not to push my luck and got Heather's coffee and my single burger and skipped out a back exit to a small grassy rest area. I sat down on top of a picnic table and was on the verge of tearing off the burger's yellow tin-foil wrapper when Heather came out the same door and took a seat at the same table and peeled the lid off her coffee and blew on it without saying a word, just as if we'd agreed to meet there all along. Caught red-meat-handed, I couldn't deny the steaming flesh and bun in my possession so I decided to play it cool, set it down casually on my knee like I was watching over it for a friend. I didn't have to worry. I don't think she even saw it.

"Why is Thomas calling himself Thomas and talking about himself like he's somebody else?" Heather said. She kept her head down and her eyes on her coffee, on the swirls of steam rising above it and disappearing into the air. The camera Thomas had bought her to give her something to do when she wasn't knitting or reading Tarot cards or running errands hung from a thin black plastic strap around her wrist.

"Is he? I hadn't noticed," I said.

"And he makes me eat things I don't like. My mother used to make us all eat pickled beets nearly every night for supper and it feels like that now. It feels like I'm eating pickled beets every night. I hate pickled beets."

"You know Thomas," I said. "When he gets into something, he really gets into it. And he just wants you to eat healthier and feel better because he cares about you. All those hamburgers you were eating, you were going to have a heart attack on us before we got back home." I gave a hearty laugh that sounded sickeningly false even to my ears and that jiggled the hamburger on my knee. I readjusted it and ran my hand through my hair.

"What do you two do at night?" she said.

I picked up the burger and set it down on my other knee.

"Nothing. Thomas and I just haven't gotten used to sleeping in motels like you and Christine."

Heather turned around on the seat. "Please don't lie to me, Bill. I can't stand it when people lie to me."

I couldn't help but be back on Bloor Street catching Thomas coming out of the Park Plaza fresh from fucking somebody other than the one person he should have been fucking. I was angry at him, pitied Heather, and felt sorry for myself all over again.

"Christine says you're doing drugs you don't do with the rest of us. She says it's your right to do what you want to do and it's none of anybody's business if that's what you want."

It was hard to decide what unnerved me more: that Christine knew, or that I hadn't known that she knew.

"I want to do what you and Thomas are doing."

"We're not doing anything," I said, pulling down the brim of my baseball cap.

"At night. I want to do what you two are doing at night."

I felt the heat of the hamburger still on my knee. I unwrapped the tin foil and carefully tore the thing in two, right down the middle. I handed Heather half.

"Hurry," I said.

65.

IT NEVER RAINS in California, my ass.

And it's not a good rain, either, the kind that pours down clear and hard and cold and sweeps the gutters clean and bleeds the heavy air and gives the earth the vigorous nose wipe it so desperately needs. L.A. rain is sideways-drizzly and stings the flesh warm and filthy; and when it finally fizzles out, the sky is still mucus yellow and the stale air maybe even more noxious mucky. We ran from Christopher to the front door of the Chateau Marmont with the pages from that day's *L.A. Times* held low over our heads.

The Chateau Marmont looked like a twelfth-century Danish castle on a small wood-covered hilltop right in the middle of downtown L.A., but with one- and two-bedroom bungalows and 24-hour room service. Hip movie stars and rock royalty made a point of staying there, and it definitely wasn't in our price range. Once we hit town and got our bearings, Christine kept saying we couldn't possibly afford it and that since Electric was picking up the bill at the Continental we'd be crazy not to take advantage. Thomas listened patiently to what she had to say then simply announced that this was the way it had to be as he double-parked Christopher out front of the hotel.

In front of the entire group he paid in advance for three one-bedrooms for an entire month with his own credit card. When he tossed the plastic across the front desk Christine looked at me out of the corner of her eye like we used to do when there was Us and Them and we didn't need ESP. I pretended like I didn't notice. Thomas told the guy behind the counter to please make sure we got the quietest rooms they had because we were going to be working very hard recording our first album and needed our rest and that there were strict vegetarians in our party and would he be kind enough to ask the chef to prepare some appropriate dishes. He scrawled his name across a receipt and handed us our room keys.

"Everyone get a good night's sleep," he said. "Tomorrow we start recording and I want everybody fresh as daisies." He winked at me. "And don't be surprised if Buckskin and Thomas have got a surprise or two for y'all."

66.

WE'D ARRIVED SO far ahead of schedule Colin wasn't even in town. We showed up at Electric Records' small, storefront office and a guy with mutton-chop sideburns in a SEEDS T-shirt shuffled around some papers on his desk and told us Colin wasn't expecting us for two more days, was somewhere in San Francisco at the moment scouting new talent. Thomas was polite but couldn't have cared less; all he wanted to know was where the recording studio was located and if we were clear to start laying down tracks. The guy rustled through some more paper, said he couldn't give us the okay until he spoke with Colin since it was usually Electric Records policy that bands be accompanied by a member of Electric management when recording on company time, and asked if we had a phone number where he could reach us. Thomas gave him a number and thanked him for his time.

"Now what?" Christine said as we piled back into Christopher.

Thomas flipped down his sunglasses and turned the key in the ignition. "You heard the man. 1567 Sunset, right at the corner of Sunset and Highland. We're fifteen minutes away."

"But he said we need someone from Electric with us," she said.

Thomas eased us into traffic. We'd been in town less than twenty-four hours but it seemed like all you ever did in L.A. was ease into traffic.

"Fifteen minutes," he repeated. "Twenty-five if we stop off at the supermarket and stock up on supplies."

Realizing he needed to be in the right lane to make the turn he wanted, Thomas hit the gas and cut off a shiny red Jaguar, narrowly avoiding whacking its front end with our rear. Thomas didn't appear to notice the car's insistent honking or its owner's raised middle finger.

"And I just can't emphasize enough," he said, "how fresh fruits and vegetables are the best get-up-and-go you can give yourself. Absolutely natural, too. I'm telling y'all, it's the only way to go."

67.

WELL, not the *only* way.

Once Thomas bluffed us through the door—hauling out our Electric Records contract and dropping Colin's name several times to the receptionist on duty at the front desk—we went back out to Christopher and unloaded all our equipment, two brown paper bags full of oranges and apples and carrots, and a gram of coke. The engineer, a guy our age named Paul with short hair who'd just gotten out of jail on a marijuana bust, said he didn't have anyone booked for several hours in Studio B and if we didn't mind sharing him with the other band who'd also be recording that afternoon he'd just chalk up our time to Electric's account and try to help us out as best he could. He said he knew Colin and was sure it would be cool. "He digs motivated people," he said.

While Slippery and Christine and Heather got started setting up, Thomas and I split for the washroom. Normally we would have headed off one at a time to quash any sniffing suspicion, but by now, especially after what Heather had told me at the picnic stop, neither of us was too concerned with keeping up appearances. Probably the only reason we didn't take our whiffs right then and there in the studio was because Paul was on probation and he'd asked us not to smoke any pot in the building because if he got caught even talking to somebody with dope on them he was looking at five years of hard time. Thomas and I climbed the single flight of stairs to the upstairs john.

"Maybe we should go outside to Christopher," I said.

"I don't know about you, Buckskin, but that's one saint I could definitely use a holiday from."

"But Paul. He asked us not to do any dope inside."

"Inside, outside, outside, inside—we don't have time for that kind of running around." Thomas pushed open the door to the washroom and stooped to look for any shoes underneath the stalls. The coast clear, he cut off two fat lines directly on the sink counter.

"Besides," he said, bending over and snorting, "if you recall, I believe what he said was that he'd prefer if we didn't smoke any marijuana on the premises."

He stood up straight, rubbed his nose, then did the other line.

"And this," he said, "surely is not marijuana."

I razored off my own line and snorted. I couldn't disagree.

68.

"WHAT WE WANT HERE, y'all, is a little more yellow, I think. Wouldn't you say, Buckskin?"

"More like flaxen, actually, but sure, yeah, yellow, let's go with that."

"All right, then, everybody, the tape's rolling, let's try one more time. One, two, three—"

"Hold on, hold on. Flaxen?"

"You know, that's the third time I've started counting off and you've interrupted me, Miss Christine."

"And that's the tenth time in the last forty-five minutes no one but you two has known what you're talking about."

"I don't believe I know what you mean."

"Oh, I don't know, how about these lyrics you expect me to sing?"

"What's wrong with these lyrics?"

"Nothing, I'm sure. If I could understand them."

"Exactly what part don't you understand? Maybe I can assist."

"How about where I come in and sing 'Under and under / Star-spangled tapioca fish eyes / Complete' with you four times until—let me check my sheet here—oh, yeah, until on the next break we sing the same thing all over again except this time we substitute 'Over' for 'Under' and in every other line change 'Complete' to 'Incomplete.'"

"Every new song sets its own rules, Miss Christine. Don't worry, you'll come around."

"This thing isn't a song, Thomas, it's . . ."

"It's what?"

"Look, I'm sorry, but no one has satisfactorily explained to me yet why we're not working on the songs Colin signed us to record. What about 'Dundas West' or 'Lilies by the Side of the Highway'? What about 'Dream of Pines'?"

"If Colin liked what we were doing before, then he's going to love what Buckskin and Thomas have been working so hard on."

"I think what you and Buckskin here have been working so hard on every night might just be the reason no one but you two understands these new songs."

"I'm afraid I don't follow you, Miss Christine."

"I'm going outside for a cigarette."

Door opens, closes.

"Heather, darlin', maybe you should go and keep an eye on Miss Christine. I could be wrong, but I do believe it might be that time of month when she might be experiencing some woman problems, if you understand what I'm getting at."

Door opens, closes.

"You know, fellas, too often we take for granted the great burdens God has given the fairer sex to endure. That's why it is so important to remember that it's not enough for men to simply love their women—they've got to learn to *understand* them, too."

Someone clears his throat.

"Hey, Buckskin."

"Yeah?"

"'Bout time for a washroom break, wouldn't you say?"

69.

IT WAS A GOOD THING PAUL didn't have much time to spare. He might have turned himself into the cops just to get away from us.

He'd miked all the instruments and brought everybody into the control booth to let us help decide how much treble and bass and echo we wanted to add to our sound, and within half an hour Thomas was twirling knobs on the recording board and running the show. He'd known all along the noises in his head he wanted to end up hearing on record, so it was just a matter of figuring out how to work the technology well enough to get them. It didn't take long.

Not that we had any business being in a recording studio. Not recording *Moody Food*, anyway. Thomas and I were the only ones who'd even heard the songs before the tape started turning, and all we had were song titles, lyrics, and a skeleton to the music as worked out by Thomas on his guitar in a million motel rooms.

The rest of us might have been able to plead ignorant, but he and Slippery knew that you went into the studio after—and not before—you've pretty much perfected the songs you're attempting to lay down. But it wasn't his money we were wasting so Slippery didn't care. And Thomas insisted that it was important that we get absolutely everything down on tape because, unlike our old stuff, these new songs were in 3-D and needed to be built up note by note, layer by layer, and you never knew when you might need to go back and pull out something from the archives to fit in with where you're at now. It's the way everybody records today, with 64-track studios and computer-generated mixing, but we were working with only eight tracks and a very limited budget. Actually, we weren't working with any budget at all, at least not until Colin got back.

And until then the tunes got taught and fleshed out on Electric's nickel, the reel-to-reel rolled, and Christine took a lot of cigarette breaks.

70.

THE WHISKY A GO GO. Whew. It made the Mynah Bird seem like the Etobicoke Legion Hall where my dad drank draft beer on Saturday afternoons. The first time I walked though the door, with Christine, the night before we were supposed to take over centre stage ourselves, and saw the gyrating go-go dancers in the elevated steel cages, I thought, These people don't *need* drugs—they're freaks enough as it is. Actually, that's what the Whisky's star patrons were called, Vito and his Freaks.

Headed up by Vito himself, a fifty-something seasoned scene-maker with a long, pointy black beard, every night about twenty of L.A.'s most beautiful young hippie girls got decked out in white face paint, boa feathers, and antique see-through nighties and danced in wild, free-form fashion to whomever they deemed the most happening band in L.A. Management never charged them a cover. If Vito and his Freaks started coming to your shows, you and the club you were playing at had it made, the word immediately went out and you were undeniably *it*.

The guy at the door of the Whisky had no problem taking our money even though there weren't any tables left and we had to stand wherever we could find a few inches of free floor space. It was between sets, but by the buzz in the crowd and the way people kept watching the empty stage waiting for the band to come back, you just knew something special had been going on up there. The Doors hadn't even released their first record yet but were already local legends. They were recording their debut album at the same studio we were, and Paul was sure it was going to break big time. Christine had jumped at the idea of seeing L.A.'s newest hottest thing. She also said it'd be a good idea for us to get a sense of what kind of club it was we'd be playing. I suspected that her real motive was simply to get away from Thomas for a while. I was still a little overwhelmed that we'd be scuffing up the same stage less than twenty-four hours later.

Ordinarily, unknowns like us never would have even gotten an audition to play the Whisky. But the guy who owned the place had loved every other band Colin had sold him on so far, so we got a guaranteed week's worth of gigs at $495.50, plus a house option for one more. No one in town might have heard of us yet, but we were recording our first album by day and playing the Whisky A Go Go by night.

We didn't even try to get to the bar and have a drink, the place was so packed. Holding hands so we wouldn't lose each other in the crowd, we wormed our way as close as we could get to the front, thirty or so feet away from the stage along the left wall. Christine started talking to a couple of girls standing beside us and I watched the three musicians who'd come out on stage tinker around with their instruments. When the blond one with rimless glasses in a suit jacket and tie lit several coloured candles on top of his Vox organ I prepared myself for the worse. Maybe it wasn't so hard to be the biggest deal in Los Angeles after all, I thought. As they inched their way into the blues number "Back Door Man" I was relieved but also surprised, having a hard time imagining how any one of these three dweebs was going to pull off a Willie Dixon tune about being, well, just what the song says.

In spite of the thumping, building rhythm, Christine tugged on my shirt and introduced me to Lee and Emily. By the time I shouted hello and turned around, a pale figure in tight black leather pants and a loose white Mexican shirt with a face out of a book of Greek mythology was slumped over the mike as if he'd been crucified. He looked up once long enough to open his eyes as if he was about to sing or say something, then shut them again and clutched the microphone stand to his body even tighter. The entire bar strained to get closer, even the girls in the front row with their faces already practically pushed into his leather crotch, everyone waiting for him to rise from the dead.

When he did, the entire Strip knew it. Strip, shit. The entire city. The entire country. The world.

At first, I thought he'd been shot, then that he'd blown his load right there on stage. A scream, a screech, a certified back-of-your-neck-and-down-your-arms, goosebump-raising wail of suffering or deliverance, I couldn't tell which. He ground his cock into the microphone stand and repeatedly slammed the heel of one of his black boots into the wooden stage to the pulse of the pounding beat.

The music itself was ancient and electric, wicked and sacred. The organist kept his face pressed low to the keys and nodded his head from side to side as he played, as if he couldn't quite believe the noises he was raising from his instrument. The guitarist stared off into space and carved burning lines of fluid guitar into the air. And the sideburned drummer, so different from my pedestrian plodding, snapped and popped jazzy beats every time he struck stick to skin, making sure the band never once sounded rock-and-roll predictable. But Morrison was the one. He was the one everyone in the audience watched and listened to and waited to see what would happen next.

Somehow I ended up with my head pressed right next to the large speaker just off stage left. I knew I'd pay for it the next day with throbbing eardrums but I didn't care. Once, I turned around to share with Christine my stare of disbelief over the blind swan dive Morrison took into the audience during the long organ solo on "Light My Fire," but she wasn't there. I searched the sea of bodies until I saw her still standing exactly where we'd docked when the show had begun. Even more incredibly, she wasn't even watching the band, was blabbing away with her two new girlfriends over top of the blaring music.

Except for a couple of blues covers, I didn't know any of the songs. It seemed like everybody else in the place did, though, especially Vito's girls hurling their nearly naked bodies around the dance floor like insane ballerinas while lip-synching along with Morrison's every bark, grunt, and shout. An hour, two hours, ten hours later—I'd lost all track of time—the first tentative tingle of "The End" fluttered through the room. Everyone stopped moving, and I mean everyone.

The music was everything what had come before hadn't been: sorrowful, meditative, with a mildly Eastern-tinged note of lilting menace. Vito and his harem just stood there in the middle of the room with their hands at their sides and their mouths hanging open like a broken circle of lost children. Nobody moved. It was group hypnosis time. The bartender stopped serving drinks.

When the song was over the organ player blew out his candles and the guitarist set down his guitar and the drummer his drumsticks and Morrison his microphone and they all walked off stage one after the other. The audience's stunned silence was the loudest applause it could have delivered.

The lights came on and people started moving again and talking. But gingerly, softly, like they were slowly waking up from a trance. Everybody except Christine and her pals. She saw me standing by the speaker and came skipping over with the other two in tow.

"You're not going to believe this," she said, "but Lee and Emily know a place close by called Tiny Naylors where you can get vegetarian burritos and hummus sandwiches and pecan burgers and all kinds of good stuff that we can actually eat. They're vegetarians, too, can you believe it?" Lee and Emily grinned and nodded together in testimony. "I'm starving just thinking about it. It's on La Brea, wherever that is, but Lee's got a car. And guess what? They're both helping organize a protest against the closing of some club called Pandora's Box that the city wants to tear down to make room for a bigger road and a three-way turn signal. I'm going to help them make signs tomorrow after our show so we can get every hippie in California down here. Isn't that great? God, I'm starving. Are you ready to go?"

I wanted to hit her. Not hard, but hard enough that I could knock some sense into her, enough so that she'd quit talking about food for a minute and pay the proper amount of respect to what we'd just witnessed. No, I didn't want a fucking pecan burger, I wanted to shout. What I want is to inhale a mountain of coke and round up Thomas and Slippery and Heather and tell them all about what they'd missed and for the five of us to break into the recording studio tonight and try to make *Moody Food* so perfectly perfect that one day someone will catch *our* act and hear *our* music and want to shout out loud themselves.

"Great, sure," I said. "Just let me take a leak first. I'll meet you outside."

I shut the stall door and snorted what was left in my plastic baggie; wet my finger and stuck it inside and rubbed the remaining coke dust across my gums like I'd seen Thomas do.

I hit the street and there was Christine waving me over from the back seat of a brand new '66 red Mustang convertible with AM/FM radio, power windows, and full leather interior. I knew it, I thought, waving back and climbing in beside her. Rich-kid revolutionaries trying to be cool slumming it.

Lee turned on the radio and she and Emily kept gently bumping each other shoulder to shoulder and slapping each other's hands play-fighting over who got to pick the station. I looked at Christine leaning forward and grinning at their goofy touchy-feely game. I rubbed my nose and wrapped an arm around her and pulled her back and as close to me as I could.

71.

MOODY FOOD WAS STILL the thing. Even after Colin showed up unannounced at the studio one day and heard us working on "A Quality of Loss" and wondered aloud over the talkback about the weird way we were warming up and Thomas fast-tracked us into our first afternoon's worth of automatic-pilot old stuff. Colin said he loved the raw sound we were putting down and was soon insisting that we do all our vocals live to match.

But that day and every day after, before Colin got to the studio and long after he left, Thomas held up the burning hoops of *Moody Food* and we all jumped and leapt as best we could. The couple of hours Colin sat in the booth in the producer's seat working with us on what he wanted to call *Dream of Pines* were, to Thomas, just a necessary distraction. But there was no way I was going to let him take a two-set-a-night holiday at the Whisky. Not after what I'd seen the Doors do.

My excitement about getting Thomas and Morrison in the same room together and then standing back and watching the sparks fly fizzled out to pretty much nothing. They met all right—once—but it was the big snowstorm the weather forecasts have been predicting for days that never manages to show up. Because of our Whisky commitment we were strictly afternoon visitors to the studio, while the Doors didn't start rolling in until after dark. But one day, just as we were pulling into the parking lot, Paul and the entire band were filing out the front door, having been up all night recording and only now packing it in. Paul introduced us and everybody said hey and Morrison mumbled that he dug our hearse and kept checking out Christine over the top of his shades. I kept trying to get Thomas and Morrison talking about music, but they only exchanged pleasant banalities about the tight fit in the vocal booth and what a great engineer Paul was like a couple of friendly but naturally wary dogs, tails definitely wagging but ready with a raised leg to leave his mark if he had to.

I was disappointed but not about to forget the impression Morrison had left from the Whisky A Go Go stage. My plan was to get Thomas to do a couple of lines of coke right before we hit the boards to get him up and into it, and even during break if necessary. I didn't expect much of a fight and I was right. With enough blow at the Marmont beforehand I even convinced him to dig his Nudie jacket out of mothballs and wash his hair. Christine and everybody else were just relieved there wasn't any talk of playing any of the new songs.

The first night was nice. Vito and his Freaks weren't there, of course, and the place was maybe only half full, but Electric had commandeered several tables right up front and lured out as many of L.A.'s hip set as possible with the promise of free drinks. Besides Lee and Emily, I even recognized a few faces from the Doors show. Regulars, I guessed.

Between the drugs I fed him and the fact that he had to get some kind of kick over landing back in his old L.A. stomping grounds feet first and front and centre stage at the Whisky, Thomas dusted off "Dundas West" and "Lilies by the Side of the Highway" and all the rest of yesterday's musical news and helped us deliver them in fine fashion. Colin and his friends applauded longest and loudest, but by the end of the first set I could tell by the nodding heads that a few people had started to get it, Slippery's alternately wailing and weeping steel guitar— undoubtedly the first to ever grace the Whisky A Go Go's stage—included.

We closed up the first half of the night with a smoking medley of the Chuck Berry rocker "30 Days," Buck Owens' country hit "Act Naturally," and the old blues tune "Love in Vain" and definitely got people wondering what we were up to, not to mention dancing. It was a good place to stop. Thomas told the crowd not to go anywhere because there was a whole lot more where that came from, and we crowded around Colin's table and said hello to everybody from the label. Christine gave me a quick peck and skipped off to where Lee and Emily were sitting.

"Thomas, Slippery, guys," Colin said, "I want you to meet Rod Crawley of *Open Wound*. Rod writes a music column for the paper."

Open Wound, it turned out, was the alternative bible in town, and the kid did look a lot like a music writer for an underground newspaper—all the hippie accoutrements were firmly in place—but with what looked to be the same black plastic-framed glasses and string-bean arms and sunken chest that probably stopped him from getting laid back in high school and kept him locked up in his room on Saturday nights listening to his treasured collection of 45s.

Everybody shook hands and Colin stood up. "Hey, what can I get you guys?" he said. Heather and I settled on beers, Slippery a Coke, and Thomas nothing.

"Not even a soda?" Colin said. "C'mon, you've earned it."

"Especially not a soda," Thomas answered. He looked at Rod across the table. "Thanks to publications like yours, sir, we now know exactly to what extent the government has been lying to us over the years about just how poisonous that stuff is. Right from your lips to your brain cells and—" He cocked his head sideways, rolled his eyes back in their sockets, stuck out his tongue.

All of a sudden Colin didn't look so sure about abandoning the table. But then he saw the amused smile on Rod's face and decided to risk it. He leaned over and whispered something into the ear of the guy who'd greeted us at the Electric office that I could only imagine was of the *keep your eye on this guy* variety and split for the drinks.

Rod pushed his glasses up his nose. "Chuck Berry, Buck Owens, Robert Johnson—that's quite a mix you guys threw together there at the end. What do you call that kind of eclecticism?"

Thomas leaned forward across the table. "We call it goose-bump music," he said. "If it's good, it's *all* goosebump music."

The kid's glasses kept sliding down his face but he kept pushing them right back up.

"You really think country music and the blues are the same thing?"

"The spades have had their way of getting through and the white man has had his. But we're all singing about the same pain. It's about time we got together and did a little inbreeding."

"Inbreeding," Rod repeated. "As in . . ."

"As in plucking out our eyes and opening up our ears and getting down to what really matters."

Rod pulled a pad and pen out of his back pocket. "Do you mind if I write some of this down?"

Thomas leaned back in his seat and absently ran his hand through Heather's hair, eyes scanning the dark room.

"Somebody's going to have to eventually," he said.

And Rod wrote that one down, too.

72.

UNTIL L.A. I was pretty sure God didn't exist.

But sometimes it seems like there just has to be some kind of Supreme Master of Irony working away behind the scenes and laughing His almighty ass off while pulling all the strings. How else was I supposed to make sense of never once getting asked to the Sadie Hawkins dance during high school and now being encouraged by the soft smiles and long stares and lusty what-not of this or that California girl to take what I wanted from the carnal candy store although, since I'd met Christine, my sweet-sampling days were officially over? The Lord giveth and the Lord taketh away. And ain't that a bitch.

There was one girl more than the rest. Upstairs from the recording studios, right next door to the bathroom, there was a small lounge where she and a couple of her friends would hang out making coffee for whoever wanted it or running errands if anybody needed anything or just giving somebody a neck massage if that was what was called for. Groupies, I guess, if you had to put a name to them. Not for any band in particular, but for all the different groups that passed through the studio, for anyone who sang or strummed or made soft or loud sounds. They all looked to be in their late teens and one was a blonde, one was a brunette, and one was a redhead. Paul had dubbed them the Three Graces, and that's what we called them, too.

No one knew any of the Three Graces' real names, and nobody ever bothered to find out. The one that was more than the rest called herself Dew, and that was good enough for me. She was summer sweetness and first morning light and smelled of patchouli sunsets and midnight walks along warm ocean sand. She was short, quiet, boyishly thin, blushed easily, and had long blonde hair. Everything, in total, that Christine wasn't. Not everything that I'd always looked for in a woman, understand; just everything the opposite of what the woman I'd ended up with was. Which, if you've been with the same person long enough, begins to seem like the same thing.

One afternoon on break, while Thomas was on the phone arguing with our dealer and Christine and everybody else were outside having a smoke, I wandered into the lounge, one part of me hoping Dew would be there, another part of me wishing I would quit hoping for things I knew I had absolutely no business hoping for. She wasn't alone—Magnolia was sitting beside her using the shirt on the table between them to make some point of sewing etiquette—but by the time I turned around from the sink with my glass of water there was just me and Dew and the cowboy shirt she was holding up in front of her. It was brown, with white swirling stitching around the collar and over the pockets and shiny silver buttons down the front and at the wrists.

"What do you think?" she asked.

"It's great," I answered. She kept looking at the floor, and I wouldn't take my eyes off the shirt.

"You really like it?"

"Yeah, it's . . . it's great."

She nodded her lowered head a couple of times and blushed; raised her eyes and caught mine and kept them.

"Why don't you try it on, then?" she said.

"Me? Why?"

"Because it's for you, silly," she said, getting up and coming over. Still leaning against the sink, I shifted the water glass from one hand to another and crossed and uncrossed and recrossed my boots. No wonder no one ever asked me to a Sadie Hawkins dance.

"You made this for me?" I said.

"Of course."

She said the two words softly, slowly, stretching out the two syllables forever, so that by the time she was done there was only the shirt between us.

"It didn't seem fair that Thomas gets to wear all kinds of great clothes on stage and you're the best looking one up there and no one's ever made you anything special to show off."

She placed both of her small feet on top of my size-ten cowboy boots. As far back as high school I'd always gotten off on lanky girls who were at least as tall as me or even bigger, but now all I wanted to do was take Dew's tiny blonde head in my hands and lean down and kiss her little red lips. At least until Thomas stuck his head into the room.

"Hey, Buckskin, let's go. Early supper break. You and me have got a road trip to take over to Watts."

Dew blushed and stepped down. She folded the shirt in four, kissed me on the cheek, and handed it to me.

"Wear it for me," she said. "I'm going to watch and see if you do."

I let her float out of the room, then went downstairs. I stuck the shirt inside the bass drum of my studio kit. I jammed it in just as deep as it would go.

73.

IT WAS ABOUT an hour before we usually left for the Whisky and I was lying in bed trying to decide whether, if I was a castaway like Gilligan, I'd make a play for Ginger or Mary-Ann. Long tall Ginger was definitely more my type, but Mary-Ann looked like the kind of girl who'd stand beside you no matter what, no small virtue whether you were living on a deserted island or not. There was no one else in the room to disturb my contemplation. When I'd woken up that morning, Christine had already left. Something about silk-screening anti-something T-shirts and see you later at the studio. There was a note scribbled on Marmont stationery lying around somewhere.

Gilligan dropped a coconut on the Skipper's foot and the Skipper yelled at Gilligan and the phone exploded and I picked up the receiver on the first ring with a trembling hand. And I'd only done two lines that afternoon. What I heard on the other end didn't settle me down.

"Bill. Please. Come down here."

"Heather?"

Between the low whisper and panic in her throat, I honestly couldn't tell.

"Bill. *Please.* He's . . ."

"Thomas? Thomas is what? Christ, speak up."

"I can't, he's in the kitchen and . . ."

And then the dial tone droned in my ear and I tore off down the hall to Thomas and Heather's room. It was too short a sprint, just six suites down, to imagine what the worst scenario might be, but even if I'd had the time, what I saw when I banged on their door and Thomas shouted "Come on in" wouldn't have been it.

"Afternoon, Buckskin. Excuse our mess here, but we're kind of in the middle of something." To Heather, "Would you bring me the rest of the tomatoes, darlin'?"

Heather was sitting on the bed by the phone. She looked relieved that I'd come but unsure what to do now that I was there. I saw her put a hand to her freshly purpled eye but warned myself not to jump to conclusions. I nodded toward the little kitchenette and winked and she got up and left Thomas and me alone.

"Thank you, sweetheart," Thomas said. "And don't forget to wash them good, now."

He was naked except for his jeans and sunglasses and was sitting on the floor with his bony feet sticking out from underneath the coffee table like it was a miniature desk. Except that instead of books and papers, the table was covered in carrot peelings, the unused ends of tomatoes, loose lettuce leaves, a package of paper plates, and a roll of Saran Wrap. In his hand was the biggest knife I'd ever seen outside of Tarzan movies. He hadn't looked up since I'd come through the door.

"What are you up to, Thomas?"

He whacked the last tomato on the table into six pieces like he was hammering a row of nails. A cigarette with a two-inch ash hung from his lips.

"I'm making salads, Buckskin," he said. He shook his head like I was either stupid or putting him on and butchered the six slices into six more. I was amazed he still had all ten fingers.

I looked around the room and he sure had been making salads. The unmade bed and both end tables, the couch and easy chair and the desk and its chair, even the top of the TV—every available surface in the room—was covered with what my ballpark figure put at around a hundred of the most pathetic-looking salads in the history of haute cuisine. Seeing as there wasn't anywhere else to put them, the decision had obviously been made long ago to start stacking the damp, limp paper plates loaded with a couple hunks of iceberg lettuce topped off with a few maimed tomatoes and carrots and wrapped tightly underneath a

Saran Wrap lid two and now three deep throughout the suite. Heather was peeking around the entrance to the living room, Thomas's requested tomatoes filling up her hands. I signalled for her to go back inside.

"What's going on?" I said, motioning around the room.

He ripped a clump out of a head of lettuce.

"Thomas, what's going on?"

He didn't look up but did stop tearing at the lettuce; stared out the window at the exclusive Marmont view of everything green and growing that downtown L.A. wasn't.

"All people are good," he said. "But some people act bad. They act bad not because they are bad but because they're ignorant. And it's the job of those who aren't ignorant to help those who are so they can learn how not to be so they can be good. I'm making as many salads as I can so Heather and I can give them away at tonight's show. At the door. Free of charge." He looked over at me. "People need to *understand*, Buckskin."

I saw a good inch of the white ash from his cigarette fall into the salad he'd been working on, but just nodded along with what he said. He nodded too and then packaged up his newest creation with the see-through wrap, ash and all, and stacked it on top of three teetering others. He finally crushed out his cigarette in an overflowing ashtray and bulldozed away the vegetable debris in front of him with the dull end of his knife. Underneath the mess, the table was covered in a thousand tiny scars. He called out to the kitchen.

"Heather, I said I was out of tomatoes, darlin'. Now, I can't make a proper salad if I don't have the proper ingredients, can I?"

I wanted her to stay where she was, but as soon as she heard Thomas's voice out she shot, weighed down with the goods. She carefully unloaded the tomatoes on the tabletop and he started right in chopping away.

"Juan said the kitchen would have those boxes for us any time after five. Would you be a sweetheart and go down and get them?" he said. Heather grabbed the room key and was out the door before I could shoot her an approving look. You don't need to tell a trapped animal to run.

"You won't mind giving us a hand carrying these down to Christopher will you, Buckskin?"

"No. No, no problem."

"I think I've got enough tomatoes for about ten more salads but that's going to be about it. Can't say I like the idea of showing up down there with not enough to go around for everybody, but we can only do what we can do." He picked up a carrot and hacked off a quarter-inch on each end.

"How's Heather doing?" I said.

Thomas finished up doing his best imitation of peeling a carrot and carefully laid the end result down on the table; picked up another orange victim, then set it right back down.

"What are you asking me, Buckskin? I don't think I understand exactly what it is you're asking me."

"I don't know. I guess I'm just thinking that it must be kind of hard on her to have to keep the crazy hours we do and deal with all the stuff we've had to go through. I suppose it must be sort of tough on her, that's all."

He lifted his sunglasses up on his head and looked at me straight on. His pupils were so dilated his eyes looked too big for his face.

"Heather understands, Buckskin. She might not hear what we hear or see what we see but . . . she understands. She understands and is patient. Oh, she is patient. She is so, so patient."

And I was so, so glad Heather came through the door with the cardboard boxes when she did. Because even if there were tears rolling down Thomas's cheeks, I wasn't going to be the one to coax him into setting down his knife long enough so I could give him a great big hug. Heather dropped the boxes to the floor, got down on her knees beside him, and did.

Then she started to cry, too, and Thomas began to cry harder and they pulled at each other tighter and tighter and Thomas kissed her hair and her forehead and her wet cheeks and finally her lips. I let myself out and went back to my room.

Where the Skipper was still yelling and Gilligan was still in trouble. And Ginger was nowhere in sight.

74.

IT WAS CHRISTINE'S FAULT.

If she hadn't been so busy trying to save the world she would have tuned in to what was going on in her own backyard and supplied Heather with enough books on the dynamics of abusive relationships and the necessity of positive female self-esteem so that if Thomas ever pulled that kind of crap again he'd get his heart broken as well as his testicles. As it was, she complimented Heather on her brand new makeup job. Heather touched her pancaked eye and said thanks.

It was Thomas's fault.

No one knows what goes on between a man and a woman when the door gets shut, but boys don't hit girls. Sandbox Commandment Number One: Boys don't hit girls. It doesn't matter what she said or even what she did when you weren't around. Curse, yell, bust up her record collection if you must, only don't touch the girl. It's just one of the rules. Thomas broke the rules.

It was Heather's fault.

What do you expect when, whenever your master's voice calls, you're there before the words are out of his mouth? Don't you know that need feeds need? Maybe next time you come running as usual but not quite quickly enough. Maybe next time you don't love him enough or read his mind well enough or forgive him enough.

It wasn't my fault.

Like the bumper sticker says, Don't Blame Me, I Didn't Vote for What's-His-Name. I didn't actually make it to the voting booth myself, but I wanted the other guy to win. You know who I mean. What's-His-Name.

75.

SATURDAY NIGHT SO SOON, and everyone but Colin and me not anywhere near as tickled as they were supposed to be about the Whisky asking us back for seven more nights. Between Rod's rave in *Open Wound* and general groovy word of mouth, by the end of the week people were starting to talk and the club was always busy if never quite full. Colin let us know the good news right after what was supposed to be our final sound check. He joined us up on stage balancing a bottle of Dom Perignon, five glasses, and a bottle of Coke for Slippery.

"And we've already got two more print interviews lined up for next week and are real close to getting you a local TV slot on a fundraiser for the free clinic the night of your last gig. Some of the best bands from around here are dying to get on. It'll be incredible exposure."

"I'm not missing the sit-down on the eleventh," Christine said. "I haven't gone without sleep for four days just so I can stand around smiling for some cameraman."

After every night's show Lee and Emily would whisk Christine off to do whatever it was they did to get ready for the protest. Although they were never anything but smiley-smile nice to me for the few minutes I saw them post-gig, I'd begun to periodically and without any warning whatsoever feel furious hot flashes of intensely physical rage toward them for trying to slowly turn Christine against me and, at the same time, convert her into a lesbian like them. I had no proof, not a scrap of evidence, and absolutely no reason for believing any of this. Not that that made me feel any better when I'd swim my laps and imagine with every stroke bludgeoning each of them to a chlorinated death. To my credit, though, I did notice that I tended to get most worked up when I was most coked up, so I never said anything.

"The eleventh is not a problem," Colin said, working on the champagne bottle's cork. "The sit-down is in the afternoon and the fundraiser is an all-day and all-night deal. They're talking about you guys playing the 3 a.m. spot. We'll all drive over right after your show here. And I think it's just great the way you guys have become such a part of the community so quickly."

Slippery stood up behind his instrument. He took out a Marlboro and stuck it in the side of his mouth.

"One more week," he said, "that's it. Then we start north." It was supposed to be a question, I think, but that's not how it came out.

"Theoretically, yes," Colin said. "The way we're going gangbusters in the studio, we should have the album wrapped up by Monday, Tuesday at the latest. Then we start mixing. But you never know what's going to happen."

"Meaning?" Christine said.

"Meaning, I didn't want to say anything until we knew more about it, but . . ." He popped the cork and a brief slosh of champagne splashed onto the stage. Mine was the only outstretched glass. He filled it first.

"C'mon," I said. "But what?"

"I didn't want to spook you guys at the time, but I know the guy who manages the Byrds pretty well and he tipped me off that McGuinn and Hillman were coming down to catch your act on

Wednesday night. And it turns out that they really dug it, Hillman especially."

Colin looked over at Thomas, who still had his guitar around his neck and was slumped over with his back to us sitting on top of his amplifier near the rear of the stage. He hadn't had his pre-show snorts yet and, what was more, judging by the way he'd mumbled his way through the sound check, I was pretty sure he'd snuck down a Nembutal on the way over. I should have known something was up when he asked Christine to drive.

"Hillman played mandolin in a bluegrass band for a couple of years before he even picked up an electric bass, you know," Colin called out.

It hadn't taken him long to get over the sight of Thomas and Heather greeting amused but confused Whisky-goers of a couple nights before with freshly made salads and the repeated boost that "Vegetarians taste better," even if Colin and his guest for the evening, Fillmore East mover and shaker Bill Graham, were among the slightly stunned recipients. Afterward, Graham told Colin he'd loved our act and would be in touch. Colin had been ecstatic.

"I think the name of their band was the Hillmen," Colin said. "You ever heard of them?" Thomas didn't move or speak. Colin turned back to us.

"Anyway, it turns out that the Byrds are heading out on a mini-tour of the east coast at the beginning of January, and the Springfield, who were supposed to open up for them, have decided that since their own album is coming out they're not going to do anything but headline any more, so the opportunity is there and I've made a few calls and . . ." He raised his eyebrows and with one hand crossed his fingers and with the other motioned with the end of the champagne bottle for Christine and Heather to get with the program and raise their glasses.

I didn't need any encouragement and took a long gulp from mine. It was my first drink of alcohol that was intended to be actually tasted before carrying out its brain-buzzing duty. It was as if I hadn't even swallowed anything liquid at all, as if the champagne had vaporized on the back of my tongue before it'd had a chance to go down. And the Byrds had heard of us and saw us and liked us, and these were the actual Byrds, the same guys whose albums I'd bought back in Toronto, the *Mr. Tambourine Man* and *Turn! Turn! Turn!* Byrds. I took another, much smaller sip of the champagne and damn if it didn't lift right off my tongue just like the first time.

"You're saying we ain't going north next week," Slippery said. He hadn't touched his unopened bottle of Coke.

"Let's not get ahead of ourselves," Colin said, filling up one last flute, Thomas's. "And for God's sake, don't say anything to anybody, especially anyone from the media. But let's just say I think L.A. is starting to take to you guys as much as you are to it." He saw my half-filled glass and topped it off; handed Heather Thomas's glass and raised his own.

"To a great beginning for a great new band. To the Duckhead Secret Society."

Colin's and my clink forced Christine and Slippery to chime in with a reluctant ting of their own. Both Heather and Thomas were over by the amp now, Thomas still sitting on top of it and facing away from us, Heather with her hand on his knee, looking up at him.

"Come on, you two," Colin said, holding up two fingers so the rest of us wouldn't drink yet. "This is a group toast."

Heather stared over at us and then up at Thomas and then back at us. She looked like she did the time at the truck stop when she asked me why Thomas kept talking about himself in the third person.

"What is it?" Christine said.

Heather peeked around to get another good look at Thomas,

then over our way again.

"Hurry up, you two," Colin said. "Our bubbles are starting to pop over here."

Christine handed me her glass and walked over.

"What's wrong?" Colin asked. "Dom Perignon not good enough for Thomas?" He said it as if it were a joke, but you could tell he was a little miffed. Maybe he was thinking that if it wasn't for Thomas's salad giveaway scheme we'd already be booked at the Fillmore. "I guess I should have got Cristal instead."

"I don't think it would have mattered," Christine said, an arm around Heather now and slowly leading her away.

"Why?" he said.

"Take a look for yourself."

And it is awfully difficult to enjoy even the finest champagne when you've passed out sitting upright on an amplifier with an unopened bag of fresh carrots cradled in your hands. Downright impossible, some people would say.

It's always his momma and not anybody else who always wakes up when Thomas starts his rocking.

Almost nine now, Thomas doesn't ride the horse any more. Not when he's awake, anyway. Everyone, even Thomas, knows he's outgrown it. But that rocking horse was the best Christmas gift he ever got. The best any kind of gift. There's a photograph his father took with his new colour Kodak of five-year-old Thomas in his white Doctor Denton one-piece cotton sleeper sitting astride his Toddler Wild Rider. The horse is painted sky blue with a white tail and mane and snout and each eye dabbed a hurried blob of splashed black. Brown wooden foot supports and handles sticking out of the animal's hard plastic legs and head make sure the rider stays in the saddle, four coiled springs underpinning each rippling thigh keep the horse moving. In the picture, Thomas is looking right into the camera, pajama-clad feet jammed deep into the tiny stirrups, ten little fingers clenched tight around the ribbed handles. It's hard to tell which is bigger, his all-teeth smile or enormous blue eyes.

Thomas rode that horse. Up in his bedroom, he rode it all day long during his last year at home alone with Selma and his momma. After he started kindergarten he rode it before and after Selma walked him to and from school every day. He even rode it after he'd turned seven and weighed more than the cardboard box the thing came in said he should.

Even his father had to admit that it was kind of cute the way the boy had so taken to the thing. One day he brought him home a cowboy hat and silver-plated gun and holster set from Memphis to complete the getup. Thomas put them both on so his father could take a picture—miniature white Stetson tilted back on his head with both guns raised and blazing—but once his father got the shot he never wore them again. What Thomas liked to do was ride. To get that rhythm going. To make that horse rock and roll until not even him and it any more, just that long slow ride.

But now he's nearly nine and the horse has been put out to pasture for some time. Every day that Thomas comes home from school and opens up the door to his room he sees it frozen stiff by his bedroom window but it rarely ever registers. Lollipops and training wheels and rocking horses. Thomas isn't a kid any more. Next spring he's going to be starting quarterback in Pop Warner if he practises taking snaps and throwing spirals to Fat Man Jones long and hard enough. Coach Slaughter says he's got all the natural ability in the world. All he has to do is apply himself, he says.

But sometimes, usually just after midnight when everyone's bedroom door is shut tight for the night, Thomas's mother will open her eyes and lie there in the dark and listen to her son riding his horse.

The first time she heard it, she'd been so terrified there was a prowler loose in the house she'd decided it was worth risking her husband's wrath by waking him up to get his shotgun and go look. But on her way down the hallway to his bedroom she passed by Thomas's and realized that the sound she'd been hearing was the noise of her son's rocking horse. More frightened of what his father would do to him if Thomas woke him up than she had been of the imaginary trespasser, Thomas's mother opened up his door all set to give him his marching orders right back to bed.

She called out his name in a loud whisper but knew instantly that he was sound asleep. The light of the moon coming through the third-storey window was all she had to go by, but his bare feet were where they were supposed to be and both hands gripped the wooden handles and his eyes were definitely wide open. Open but sightless. Full-speed rocking, his pyjamaed bottom raised an inch or two off the saddle, Thomas leaned into his horse like a desperate jockey at the finish line. Except this rider never got to the end, just kept riding and riding.

His mother quietly shut the door. After looking in on her husband and being reassured by his thankfully oblivious snoring, she went back to her own room, took off her housecoat and slippers, and slipped back underneath the sheets. It was March and the window was open halfway. Lying there listening to Thomas's rocking, to the pure, perfect motion of his blind midnight race, she noticed the wind chimes on the veranda tinkling in the night's soft wind.

Later, as spring turned into summer and everyone else in the house could only fall asleep to the loud whir of an electric fan, Thomas's mother would go to bed aided only by a wide-open window so that when she awoke when Thomas would start his rocking, the sound of it and the wind chimes together would keep her company throughout the long, hot night.

76.

THOMAS STARTED TO TURN GREEN. Thomas started to turn orange. And the scariest part of all was that none of us said anything. Not to him or to each other. Heather might have taken him aside and said something on her own about him morphing into a human bruise, but I doubt it. And maybe that's the worst thing about coke. No one talks.

Cocaine is like any other drug—is like any other anything—what you gain one way, you lose in another. Coked-up people get done yesterday what needs to get done today, but coked-up people don't have time for small talk. Even people not coked-up themselves but who hang around people who are coked-up end up catching the same silent drug bug. And tunnel vision is a wonderful thing for taking you places, just don't expect to remember much of what the scenery looked like along the way once you get there.

77.

IT WAS COLIN'S JOB to be together enough to always have enough time, though, and he did say something to Thomas. He also handed him a slip of paper and told him to go see a doctor he knew who was experienced in dealing with people in the entertainment industry. When Thomas predictably replied that he felt fine and, besides, was too busy right now, Colin threatened to shut down recording until he got himself looked after by a professional. This wasn't about selling records, he said, this was about making sure a friend took care of his health. Plus, he pointed out, we started back up at the Whisky in two days and it just wouldn't do to have Thomas, unintentionally or not, radically reconfiguring his image. It might confuse our core audience.

The only time the doctor could work Thomas in was eleven o'clock the next day. Naturally, Heather went along for the ride and Slippery hung the DO NOT DISTURB sign outside his door, leaving Christine and me on our own. It was our first free day since we'd landed in town.

I woke up in a tangle of cool blue sheets with a naked girl lying beside me on her stomach, raised chin in her hand, with one bare leg lifted in the air and a look in her eye that said she knew what she wanted and was used to getting it. Then I woke up. I woke up in a tangle of cool blue sheets with Christine still in her clothes from the night before, still asleep flat on her back on top of her half of the blankets, mouth wide open and a most audible snore rattling from her nose.

I looked over my shoulder at the alarm clock and saw it was just after eleven-thirty. I felt like a kid sleeping in late because school was cancelled. I shimmied over closer to Christine and kissed her softly at the base of her neck. She smelled like stale cigarettes and cold sweat but I didn't care. Stolen days always seem more alive.

I felt her body stir and slightly stiffen upon waking up, then relax and move into mine once consciousness kicked in and she realized where she was and what was happening.

"This is a nice wake-up call," she said.

I let my hands go where they wanted and moved my lips to her ear. A couple of minutes later I felt her breathing turn into a steady, heavy rise and fall and she turned over onto her side and pushed her lips into mine and dug her fingers into the flesh of my ass, pulling my groin into hers.

Somehow—when it's good, it's always somehow—she was as naked as I was and I was on top and we were doing what I'd almost forgotten we used to be so good at doing.

My God, I thought, why the hell aren't we doing this every day?

"I was just thinking the same thing," Christine said, hand around my neck, pulling me to her, biting my upper lip.

Well, I thought I'd thought it. Whatever, it was the first time we'd been in agreement about anything important in what felt like forever. Christine put her hands on my chest and gently pushed me over, wordlessly so careful both of us that I stayed inside as she got on top.

Upright and rooted, she closed her eyes and moved her hips and made both of us happy. When the phone rang once, twice, ten times, neither of us even bothered to say not to get it. I lay back with my head on the pillow and watched Christine momentarily flutter her eyes half-open and register the alarm clock on the side table. And then shut them again and go back to pleasantly grinding away. And then flash them wide and double-check the time on the clock and leap off my hard-on like a rodeo rider with the world's biggest burr in her saddle.

"Jesus Christ, what's wrong?" I said.

"The alarm must not have gone off," she said, hopping into her panties, then sitting down on the side of the bed to pull on her jeans.

"It didn't go off because we're not recording today, remember?"

"You mean you didn't set the alarm? Bill, I told you I had to meet Lee and Emily at eleven to . . . Shit, that must have been them calling. I knew I should have answered."

Now that, I admit, hurt. And I didn't care how good she looked sitting there naked except for her faded jeans.

"You didn't say anything about having to meet them," I said. "And I didn't set the alarm because I thought we were going to spend some time together today. I guess I should have known better."

Christine stood up from the bed and looked down at me still lying there in all my manly glory. I pulled the sheet up to my waist.

"You know," she said, "even if I wasn't an hour late for a very important meeting, I don't think I'd want to go near that. And I really don't think you should either."

"Go near what? The fact that hanging out with your *girlfriends* is more important than keeping your word to me."

"Bill, we didn't have any plans for today. None. We didn't have any plans for today, yesterday, tomorrow, or for the last year, for that matter."

"Yeah, well, maybe we should have."

"Maybe we should have. But that's kind of beside the point right now, don't you think?"

"So what you're basically saying is that your dyke friends are more important to you than us."

She raised her right hand like she was going to either make some pivotal point or hit me with a karate chop, then dropped it to her side and walked away.

"So it's true, then, right?"

She still didn't say a word, kept stalking around the room kicking away dirty clothes on the floor while looking for the KEEP THE STRIP OURS T-shirt she'd helped design.

"Are you fucking one of them? Is that it?"

She covered her breasts with two cupped hands and kept searching.

"Both of them? Are you fucking both of them?"

Christine finally found her T-shirt underneath the kicked-off bedspread and tugged it on and turned around and pointed right at me with a shaking finger. "I will not talk to you when you're like this."

"Like what? On to you? On to you and your dyke friends?"

"You know I haven't said anything before because if that's what you want to do with your life then go ahead, do it, but I'm not going to stand here and be subjected to—"

"You realize I don't have a clue what you're talking about."

"Oh, c'mon, Bill. Just because you're destroying your brain with that shit doesn't mean everyone else is, too."

She jammed on her combat boots and did them up in what must have been record time, military or civilian. She slammed the door shut and didn't leave a number where she could be reached.

I probably could have made the elevator with her, but the stare I got from the Spanish maid pushing her cart down the hall made me realize I was only wearing a sheet. I raced back inside our room and threw on my jeans and took the stairs.

All those laps I'd been doing in half of America's hotel swimming pools paid off because I hit the sidewalk in my bare feet not ten yards behind her. When she saw me coming she caught the tail end of a green light and bolted for the other side of the street. I stood there for a minute waiting for a break in the noon-hour L.A. traffic, but could see that Christine was getting away and had her hand in the air to hail a cab. I made my move and was nearly across when a white van slammed on its brakes so as not to hit me, putting its driver halfway up the dashboard with his face smudged right to the windshield. The guy behind the wheel craned his neck out the window.

"Jerk!" he yelled.

"Fuck you!" I said, head somewhat aware that I should be apologizing but body already one full step ahead.

"Fuck *you*!" he hurled back.

"No, fuck *you*!" I answered.

Traffic snarled behind the stopped van. But before he could get out or I could make a move closer, Christine was in the middle of it all and grabbed me by my arm and hauled me off to the other side of the street. Traffic began to move again, the guy in the van predictably shot me the finger, and one more "fuck you" was exchanged on both sides.

"Man, what a clown," I said.

Christine looked at me as if partly in disbelief that this half-naked fool could be the same man she'd shared her bed with for the last eighteen months and partly doubting whether she had done the right thing by saving me from doing battle in the middle of the intersection with the van man.

Sensing this, "He almost ran me over!" I said.

"You were running across the road against a red light, Bill. In your bare feet."

"Only because I was trying to talk to you."

"Well, I don't want to talk to you."

"Yeah? Then how come you came and got me then?"

I folded my arms across my chest like I'd just made the eleventh-hour point that would set my client free when all hope had seemed lost. Might have even smirked a little, too.

"Bill, don't you think that the fact that you and Thomas are the only ones who believe that that stuff we waste our time on every day in the studio is anything even close to music is proof enough that you need help? That you both need help?"

"Waste our time? You're kidding, right? You heard Colin last night. We're talking about the Byrds, Chris, the fucking Byrds. Colin thinks—"

"Colin! Bill, just think about this for a second, okay? Slow down and really think. Why do you think we have to sneak behind Colin's back and wait for him to go home every night to record Thomas's new songs? Because Thomas thinks he'll like them?"

"So it's going to take time," I said. "Colin's not ready yet. A lot of people aren't ready yet."

"But you and Thomas are."

"Yeah, we are."

"And isn't that a coincidence."

"What? What's a coincidence?"

"That you two are also the only ones coked out of your minds half the time."

Christine put up her hand, a cab stopped, she got in, and then she was gone. The window was tinted and rolled all the way up so I couldn't be sure, but I thought I saw her wave goodbye.

78.

IT'S NOT LIKE THE idea had never crossed my mind. Towelling off poolside at the Marmont at dawn, sitting on the toilet staring up at the same two lines of graffiti on the bathroom stall wall at the recording studio, lying in bed waiting for the Nebutols to kick in and cloud my brain and cut my body's ignition and allow me a few hours rest, sure, the notion flickered there in front of my eyes once or twice. That Thomas and I were on the same musical wavelength only because we were both plugged into the same white-powder power source was possible, I supposed.

But no. Ultimately, no. Because the music was good. *Moody Food* was good. It was great. I knew it was great—even in the piecemeal bits and chunks we were slowly laying down—because I kept seeing colours. Granted, these particular colours tended to flash on and off and, even when they were in focus, were mostly strange blends of hues and tints I didn't have any name for. And sometimes, if Thomas was being more than usually exacting and things were going especially slowly—Christine gritting her teeth to keep from saying anything, Slippery staring at his bored reflection in the glass of the sound booth—they weren't even colours at all, just grainy images like in an old black-and-white movie where you can tell the colour of the heroine's hair although you can't say you actually see it. But they were there. Underneath the band-saw scream of the distortion pedal Thomas had rigged up to Slippery's pedal-steel guitar and the forty-seven takes it took to get a ten-second harmony part done, they were there.

Good doesn't grow old. Bach isn't passé and neither are California redwoods and neither is *Moody Food.* And if anybody thinks I'm just an old hippie who's sucked too many peace pipes and has delusions of moody glory, come on down and visit me and Monty in Tilbury sometime and lend a hand mailing off the sixty or seventy orders a month I get for the *Moody Food* CD I sell out of my house. Mostly they come from the U.S. and Canada, but I've had requests from as far away as England, Australia, and Germany, and there's even a steady trickle of interest in Amsterdam. Look me up at www.duckheadsecret.com and see what all the fuss is about for yourself.

Because that's right, yeah, I'm all grown up now and have joined the other side and got my own Web site. Where you can sample a few tunes and download the lyrics to "Some Good Destruction" written in Thomas's own hand and see some pictures of Thomas all done up in his white Nudie jacket and shades sitting on the hood of Christopher and of all of us playing on stage together at the Whisky. I'm the first and last disciple of Thomas Graham and I take Visa, MasterCard, and American Express.

But I'm getting ahead of myself.

There were only two stalls in the studio john and I always took the second one. Human nature, I guess, to call somewhere home even if it's the same seat in a classroom or a bathroom. Anyway, sitting there with my pants wrapped around my ankles was one of the few times a day when I'd be alone long enough to wonder whether Christine and the rest of the world weren't right and Thomas and I weren't just a drugged-out Don Quixote and his equally spaced but faithful percussionist Sancho Panza. Then my eye would fall on the couple of lines of blue ink neatly penned on the wall.

THE LIZARD KING

CAN DO ANYTHING

Of course, now everybody knows all about the Doors' resident poet's reptile fixation, but at the time I couldn't tell whether it was Morrison's or Thomas's doing. Sitting there listening to the toilet next door gurgle and run, I figured both of them were up to it. Either way, it did the job. I'd wipe and flush and wash my hands and return to the studio, ready to get back down to work.

79.

FIRST IT WAS THE cloud shadows drifting across the Joshua Tree hills; they floated along the sides of the mountains like enormous hand puppets, like Ma Nature making funny with silhouette and light. Then it got dark and it was the stars that kept my eyes on the sky. I'd never seen anything on earth so hard or so bright. Thomas handed me the binoculars.

"Keep an eye over there, Buckskin, near the Big Dipper. I think something's cooking over that way." He slowly made his way down the huge boulder we were camped on. When he hit the desert earth the crunch of his carrot seemed like the only sound for miles.

Even if our intention had been to trip out on some low-grade acid and hunt the sky for flying saucers—because Thomas felt we were getting a little too linear in our musical manoeuvring and needed to "stretch out our cerebral cortexes some and get back off track"—he still had to have his veggies. The doctor he'd seen that morning had counselled him to cool it with the carrots for a while in deference to his slowly oranging flesh, but Thomas knew what was good for him.

What the doctor had to say about the creepy green pallor of his face didn't make much of an impact either. "Check this out," he'd said, tossing me a blue plastic pill bottle across Christopher's front seat.

As soon as he'd gotten back to the Marmont from his appointment downtown he'd knocked on my door and flung the idea of the trip to the desert at my feet like a stir-crazy dog with his leash and favourite ball. With Christine long gone for the day and probably half the night, I didn't have anything to do or wait around for, so we'd struck out for Joshua Tree just after two o'clock in order to beat the traffic. It turned out that rush hour in L.A. is every hour, so we spent most of the afternoon squinting through our sunglasses at the sun lasering off the chrome bumper of the car ahead of us and crawling a couple of inches forward every five minutes.

"They couldn't hurt, I guess," I said, handing back the container of vitamins.

"Oh, yeah, well how about these?" he said.

I took the bottle and read the white label with Thomas's name and some neatly typed instructions on it. "Valium?"

"Sonofabitch's got the nerve to tell me to cut back on the nose candy and to try taking these instead." Snatching back the drugs and rattling them in front of my face, "You know what this shit is, Buckskin? Lobotomy in a bottle. Ten milligrams four times a day of instant brain fuck. Another sonofabitch with a degree on his wall filled my momma up with this poison once . . ." He leaned into the horn and stared hard at the snake of metal and glass stretching out in front of us.

He seemed pissed off enough as it was that I didn't bother asking how, if he was an orphan from birth, he knew about something like his mother having been given Valium. Instead, "Why bother getting the prescription filled then?" I said.

"Because Colin would have cried like a stuck pig if I didn't and Thomas doesn't need that kind of aggravation right now." There was a break in the log jam and we finally got up over twenty miles an hour. Thomas tossed the prescription bottle and the vitamins out the window.

I heard him finish his piss down below and start the climb back up. I set the binoculars down beside his notebook and pen, acoustic guitar, and the carton of orange juice we were taking turns swigging from and wished we had Heather's camera to take some shots of the sky. I'd actually thought of it before we left, but the sight of her standing by herself in the Marmont parking lot waving goodbye kept me from asking for any favours. When Thomas had knocked on my door and I'd asked him if we were going to invite her along, he'd just said, "This is a working holiday, Buckskin. Heather doesn't understand our work any more than your woman does." I felt a rise of something in my gut and the need to jump to Christine's defence, then realized I couldn't.

"Any luck?" he said, sitting back down.

"I thought I saw a shooting star but . . ."

"Yeah."

"Yeah."

Enough but not too much acid is a pretty comfortable place to be; enough reason and logic, but not too much. Enough that you could spot a UFO if there really was one out there, but not so much that until then you don't spend your time asking yourself what you're doing sitting on a boulder in the desert at midnight looking for UFOs. I lifted my eyes to the sky and resumed work on my moonbeam tan. Thomas picked up his guitar and strummed something. It took me a couple of minutes before I recognized it as a radically reworked version of "Faith is a Fine Invention."

This was actually starting to be one of the biggest sources of tension in the studio. Just when Christine and Slippery thought they knew what they were doing—what kind of crazy shit it was Thomas wanted them to play—he and I would return from the bathroom and he'd decide to move Slippery over from steel guitar to slide and totally change the song's time signature and drop the bass part and in its place have me dig my tuba-playing skills from high school out of mothballs while instructing Christine on how to provide proper percussion by beating off-notes on the bottom of an empty plastic water cooler bottle. One more time, please, from the top.

"I like it," I said.

Thomas smiled, kept playing.

Somewhere near or far away, I had no idea which, a coyote howled a consummate coyote howl and Thomas stopped strumming and we listened together until the animal's long final notes were swallowed up by the star-pocked black night. The desert was a tomb again and I wasn't sure I'd heard what I heard until Thomas said, "Some people say that's a lonely sound. But it's not nearly as lonesome as when he stops."

I thought about this for a moment, then gave up. Just enough reason and logic, but not too much.

"How'd you find this place?" I said.

"It found me."

"Yeah, but—"

He started playing again. I shut my eyes and listened until he stopped in mid-strum.

"Don't let them bury me anywhere but here, Buckskin."

I knew I should have said something like "Bury you?" or "Why would anybody be burying you anywhere?" or even "Who's *them*?" But all I said was, "Why?"

"Promise me you'll take care of it," he said.

He took hold of my sleeve. His sleeve, really. I hadn't counted on the desert night being so cold and he'd loaned me his Nudie jacket.

"Promise me."

I did what he asked and he came as close to me as he could without his face touching mine. Satisfied that I'd meant what I'd said, he thanked me, just said thank you, and let go of my arm.

Then, impossible but true, another variation on the very same song, this one even more painfully beautiful than the last. I closed my eyes again and wondered when it would be the last time.

80.

"MOO"

"Didn't you hear what Paul just said, Thomas? Colin called and will be here any minute."

"Miss Christine, I believe it's apparent I'm a little too busy right now to be worrying over when Colin is or isn't arriving."

"Yeah, well, you might change your tune when he finds out you brought a—"

Over the talkback: "Hey, guys. What's all this 'Colin could be here any minute?' stuff? Since when did I become the big bad wolf?"

Studio door opening, two bare feet padding, door closing.

"MOOOO"

"Where's Christine going? And what's that noise? It sounds like you've got half the L.A. Philharmonic horn section hidden back there."

Thumpthumpthump thump.

"Oh . . . ."

"Goddamn."

Studio door opening, four more feet running, door closing.

"MOOOOOO"

"That can't be what I think it is."

"MOOOOOOOO"

"Thomas, tell me what I think just happened out there didn't just happen."

"MOOOOOOOOOO"

"Thomas!"

"Well, that's news to me, Buckskin."

"What's that?"

"Thomas!"

"I would have sworn cows liked carrots."

81.

WHAT A DAY FOR the heat, more than a thousand hippies in the street, Christine Jones included.

But not me. I was blotto in the studio helping put the final vocal touches on "Lenny's Last Waltz #302" with Thomas, Heather, and Paul. And Dew. Because we needed another female voice to round out the mix and she was hanging around as usual and was always glad to pitch in in any way she could and Christine was busy waving around her sign and getting chased by the cops and we really did need another female voice. Really.

The cow in the studio wasn't the straw that broke Colin's back—Thomas was still his boy, the genius goose who was going to lay the country-rock golden egg—but from that point on Colin made sure to have a telltale bell tied firmly around his prize heifer's neck. Even if Thomas usually showed up late and tended to nod off from time to time, Colin made sure he was right there beside him in the studio from noon onward every day helping to mix what he was now officially calling *Dream of Pines*, each of us being brought in to do an overdub here and there as needed.

The original idea for "Lenny's Last Waltz #302" was to get a bunch of winos off skid row to sing "Amazing Grace" at the song's end in their best blitzed-out worst, after I'd finished narrating an old-timey talking country song done up typically Moody Foody cryptic. The song was about a miserable, obese drunkard—"As mean as cat piss / As wrong as right as rain"—who ran a roadside honky-tonk and terrified everyone in the joint but also, when the place was empty at the end of the night and he was done cleaning up, danced around the bar with his mop for a partner to Patti Page's "Tennessee Waltz" on the jukebox until one morning he was found dead of a heart attack face-first on the dance floor. Before we'd laid down the instrumental cut a couple of days previous, Thomas had explained to us that it was a parable for the delicate indestructibility of that most disastrous of human miracles, the broken heart. Christine asked if he could be a little more specific. Thomas answered that he wished he could, he really did, but no, he could not.

Thomas insisted that I drink as much of a fifth of scotch as I could get down and narrate the tune in my everyday normal voice just like, he said, I was reading a letter to a blind friend. It was critically important, he maintained, that I be good and liquored up while I recited the words, so much so that when I stooped to take my sniffing turn in the washroom before the start of the session Thomas stepped in my way. "Uh uh, no snow for you, Buckskin. Think about what poor old Lenny would think." We went downstairs and he poured me my first double.

After the line on the bottle went down about halfway and we got a sufficiently slurry but mistake-free take of me reading the ballad of Lenny and his mop, Thomas herded everybody upstairs to the kitchen and kicked back like in the old days with his cowboy boots up on the kitchen table and entertained us all with some honky-tonk numbers from the fifties and we killed the rest of the bottle, Dew included. She was happy to join the party but admitted she wasn't much of a drinker. While Paul called out one more obscure request after another, hoping to stump Thomas, and Heather nursed her drink and looked happy for the first time since we hit L.A., I volunteered to show Dew how to drink scotch. If watching my old man sip the single Dewars he allowed himself every night after supper didn't make me an expert, the half a bottle or so sloshing around in my stomach did.

She coughed and put her little hand to her rosebud mouth. "You actually like this stuff?" she rasped, but smiling.

"You get used to it," I said. "Give it a chance."

"I trust you," she said, lifting the glass to her lips with both hands, eyes wide and on me while she sipped.

Feeling my crotch tingle slightly, I gulped from my coffee cup full of booze.

Dew set down her glass and picked up the shirt she'd been working on. "It's not finished yet, but be honest."

"I love it," I said.

She pressed it against me. "Looks like a good fit to me."

"It's not for me."

Faking a little girl pout, "You don't like it," she said, snatching it back. I wanted to reach out and touch her button nose. I took another swallow instead.

"I do, I do," I said, "but . . ."

"But what?"

Paul poured himself and Thomas another. "'The Wild Side of Life,'" he said. It was the first time any of us had gotten a glimpse of how our mild-mannered engineer might have ended up in jail.

Thomas picked up his glass, took a sip, smacked his lips. "Imagine that, darlin'," he said, turning to Heather. "A city boy who knows his Hank Thompson."

Paul, gracious in defeat, clinked Thomas's water glass. Heather leaned over and kissed Thomas on the cheek. Thomas began playing.

"But you've already made me one shirt," I said. "I can't ask you to—"

"You didn't ask me to do anything," Dew answered. "I made that first one for you because I wanted to. So you'd feel good on stage. Do you feel good when you wear my shirt?" She put her hand on my thigh and I didn't give a little embarrassed laugh and move my leg or send her a friendly but firm look and take away her hand.

"All right, man," Paul said, "this is my last chance." He held the bottle suspended over his empty glass but didn't pour. "'Just Can't Live That Fast Any More.'"

Thomas squinted into space and strummed his guitar for a few thoughtful seconds; stopped, and adjusted his E string. Still tuning, "You know, Paul," he said, "you're right, you're absolutely right. Lefty Frizell *was* one fine singer, wasn't he?"

Paul shook his head and poured the last of the scotch into Thomas's glass.

Heather kissed him again.

"He never misses," she said.

82.

IT'S NOT ALWAYS CALM before the storm. Sometimes the sky roars and the air crackles and the people in the audience stomping their feet and pounding on the tabletops know. Just like you know. Plug your ears and duck and cover all you want, but what's coming is coming, just like it always has. Always will.

Our final show at the Whisky was toe-jammed crammed and sold-out steaming hot. There were rumours Dylan was in town, had heard what we were up to and was intrigued enough to maybe make an appearance. Brian Jones of the Stones and a colourful coterie of acid-head toadies definitely were in attendance, skulking around a large table at the back sipping champagne and ignoring the hippie star-struck. Colin's buddy, the guy who managed the Byrds, was also out there somewhere, apparently wanting to give us a final going-over before making a decision about us joining his boys on the road. And after the gig we were heading straight for the TV benefit and a possible full band interview with *San Francisco Chronicle* big-shot columnist Ralph Gleason. And we were half an hour late going on stage. Out of boredom or anticipation or both, the audience was making lots of noise to let us know it, too. But we didn't need the crowd. We had Colin.

"Is she done with him now? She's got to be done with him by now. Bill, go see again if she's done with him now." He had to yell to be heard over the crowd. "I know he's doing this just to piss me off."

Colin, Slippery, Dew, and I were standing in the corridor that led to the stage. I walked back to the bathroom.

Sometime after we'd left the studio for the gig Colin got a hold of the *Moody Food* tapes. When he finally roused Paul, passed out on the couch upstairs and still drunk, he got the whole story. Confronted with the tapes in our dressing room, Thomas seemed almost pleased. He placed a long staying forefinger on Heather's helpful hand gently dusting his face with a powder puff and turned in his chair toward Colin. Ever since Thomas's unfortunate turn toward the resplendent, Colin had insisted that Heather apply a thin but concealing foundation to his face and the backs of his hands before every show.

"Well, what do you think?" Thomas said, leaning back in his chair.

"I think you've lost your fucking mind." None of us had ever heard Colin swear before, let alone raise his voice.

Thomas's face sank. Quiet for a second, "If you're worried about the cost of the sessions, I—"

"Fuck the cost of the sessions. *This* shit is why you couldn't be bothered to stay awake while we mixed *Dream of Pines*? Running around behind my back for *this* is the thanks I get for rescuing you from freezing your ass off in Canada fronting a fucking bar band?" He was only looking at Thomas, knew only he could have been responsible for the music he'd heard. He waved one of the tapes in front of Thomas's nose.

"*This* is why you're so screwed up half the time I have to force you to go and see a doctor?" Colin pulled a bottle of pills from inside his suit jacket adorned, I noticed for the first time, with a shiny new black-and-white DUCKHEAD SECRET SOCIETY button. "Which reminds me," he said. "Doctor Stevens called me. He said you hadn't picked up your refill yet. I'm sure it just slipped your mind." He tossed the tape on the counter in front of Thomas as if he were topping off his trash can at home; dropped the bottle of Valium in his lap.

Thomas slowly got up from his chair and just as slowly walked right past Colin. I stuck my head out the door and saw him head for the crowded dance floor.

An hour later I was pounding on the bathroom door at Colin's request for the third time that night.

"One more minute," Heather called out.

I walked back down the hall.

"Well?" Colin said.

"She says one more minute."

"What?"

"One more minute!" I shouted.

"One more minute, shit. They've been in there for forty-five minutes. Thomas needs makeup, not a facelift. And why does Thomas still need makeup? I'll tell you why. Because he's not doing what the doctor I sent him to told him to do, that's why. Well, I know one thing. If I was turning orange and green I'd do what the doctor told me to do."

I sat down backward on a metal folding chair and rat-tatted my sticks against its edge, regretted giving Colin a line of coke. To counteract the scotch, I'd snorted twice as much as I usually did before a gig and ended up feeling like such a dope pig I offered everybody else in the dressing room some, too. I don't think Colin usually did hard drugs, but was pissed off enough that he didn't hesitate when I cut him a line. Dew, wearing a backstage visitor's pass around her neck, channelled her buzz into massaging my shoulders through the blue satin of my brand new shirt.

"One minute or ten minutes, it don't matter none," Slippery said to no one in particular. "Can't go on without our bass player." He took a long drag on his cigarette, pulled aside a thin curtain covering the end of the hallway, and stared out at the crowd.

"I told you, her friend called," Colin said. "She'll be here."

The call had come from the police station. We'd spent all day and the early part of the night recording, but everybody in the club was talking about traffic being backed up for miles on the Strip and people overturning cars and the cops cracking skulls and hauling away hippies. Christine had used her one phone call to get a hold of me at the studio, but Paul was with us upstairs finishing off the bottle of scotch and there was no one there to pick up. Emily or Lee ended up calling Colin at Electric to let us know that they and Christine had been busted but not to worry, no one was hurt, and that Christine would be at the Whisky in time for the show. That had been more than an hour ago.

"You tell that to those folks out there," Slippery said, stamping out his Marlboro. He let the curtain drop.

"Look, traffic is still pretty messed up out on the Strip. She's probably—"

Probably wondering why some groupie had her hands all over her boyfriend, I thought, standing up and breaking free of Dew's magic fingers when I saw Christine and Emily and Lee being hurriedly escorted down the hallway by a security guy. Colin had assured me as soon as he'd finished bawling out Thomas that

Christine was fine, so I was surprised at how relieved I was when I saw her. And how relieved I was that I was so relieved. I hugged her tight and kissed her head and put my mouth to her ear. "Are you all right?" I said.

"What?" She hadn't gotten used to the thunder of the audience yet.

"Are you all right?" I yelled.

She covered her ear and pulled away from me. "It's bad enough I almost got maced today, Bill, don't make me deaf, too."

I sat back down on the chair. Christine and the other two began jabbering at Colin and Dew and Slippery at the top of their lungs about what had happened, and after a while I ducked into the dressing room and did another line. When I came back out, nobody had noticed I'd been gone. Christine was still talking, but somehow Colin had gotten her bass around her neck. He gave her a big hug and said he wanted to hear more about it later, but that right now we owed it to that audience out there to give them a great show. "People need music at a time like this," he said.

Christine's two partners in crime nodded reflectively.

"Where's Thomas?" Christine shouted.

From the other end of the hall, "Here he is!" Heather yelled back. "Thomas is right here!"

She led him out of the dressing room by the hand like that scene in the black-and-white Frankenstein movie where the good doctor encourages his creation along in his first clumsy baby steps. Thomas's face was caked thick with what must have been a triple or even quadruple dose of makeup, his head so thoroughly soaked with what looked to be Slippery's entire jar of Vaseline that his long hair glistened like a universe of stars under the florescent lights of the hallway. He sleepwalked to a stop directly in front of Colin.

Slowly, barely above the noise of the crowd, "Hey, boss man," he said. "No time to jaw. Time to give the people what they want."

He walked up the steps and right out on stage, the explosion of the audience our only cue to follow. Colin threw up his hands and split for his table out front. Lee and Emily gave Christine good-luck hugs and followed Colin's path, Christine and Slippery right after joining Thomas on stage. I grabbed Heather by the arm.

"He fixed, didn't he?"

She closed her eyes and shook her head.

"He scored some smack, didn't he?"

She kept shaking her head, so I shook her arm harder.

"Didn't he?" I yelled.

She threw her arms around my neck and cried so hard I could feel her entire body convulsing with every sob.

He made her watch him, I thought. That sonofabitch, he made her watch him fix.

"People don't understand him," Heather managed. She lifted her head off my shoulder. "We understand him, though. You and I are the only ones."

I felt a tug on my shirt and let go of Heather and turned around. Dew was holding open the curtain that led to the stairs and then the stage.

"It's time, Bill," she said.

I heard Thomas's voice booming over every speaker in the club, and it was.

83.

ANYONE WHO KNOWS L.A. music history knows what happened. That we made the *L.A. Times* but Colin wished we hadn't is all anybody needs to know.

Two songs into our set Thomas began to melt. After ten minutes under the heat of the stage lights, thick globs of white make-up began dripping down his face. When he turned around and locked eyes with me during Slippery's solo he looked like he was crying wax. I closed my eyes and leaned into the beat.

Thomas decided to sit out the next number. Stand it out, actually, directly behind the stack of speakers to the left of my drum kit. The three of us struggled to fill in for his unannounced missing guitar and vocal parts—Slippery taking two long solos and Christine picking up the words after the surprise of the first silent verse—but I looked up long enough to see Thomas running his hand over his head over and over again and thought he was trying to wipe his hair free of Vaseline. When the tune was over he took centre stage again. Christine, with her microphone up front near his, was the first one in the band to see what was going on. She shot first me, and then Slippery, alarmed glances, but we couldn't see what she could.

"Hey, L.A.," Thomas mumbled. His hands were wrapped around the microphone stand as if for support, his lips so tight to the mike it looked like he might swallow it. "Hear we had some, uh, action down on the Strip today."

The audience exploded. This was more like it. Somebody started what must have been one of the protesters' cheers—CLOSE DOWN THE STRIP! CLOSE DOWN THE STRIP!—and soon the entire place was yelling in unison. I kept time to the chant with my bass drum. Thomas put a hand in the air. The crowd quieted down.

"That's great, that's great. Because some people . . . you know, some people are afraid of change. Get stuck in the past. Are afraid of the future."

A few scattered "That's right, man"s and "Fuck them"s, then quiet again. Then quieter still when everyone, Slippery and me stuck near the rear of the stage included, got a grip on what was going on.

During Thomas's moment off stage he'd evidently stuck as many of the pills from the bottle of Valium as he could into his Vaselined hair, each individual capsule sticking out of his scalp like he was harvesting an Rx bumper crop. Once under the heat of the lights again, every few seconds one more Valium would slide down his face before dropping to the ground, greasy hair-gel snail goo trailing right behind.

"But we're not, uh, we're not going to let that happen to us. No, sir. Anybody who can't keep up with us is going to get left behind. Because when a hurt animal can't keep up with the pack any more, it gets left alone to die. But don't feel sorry for the dead. If they were supposed to be here, they would be."

Somebody shouted out "Right on"; someone else "Shut up and play." A couple nervous coughs throughout the room.

"But Thomas isn't going to let that happen to us. Thomas knows how to stay alive. Anybody that wants to stay alive, y'all better stick close to Thomas. And everybody else . . ." He strummed his guitar. "Everybody else can go off and die right now. Because if the buzzards don't get you, believe me, motherfuckers, we will."

He stumbled around, barked, "'Exit Pursued By Bear,'" then turned to face the audience again.

But "Exit Pursued By Bear" was a new song. A *Moody Food* song. We hadn't even finished recording it, let alone ever performed it in public. And how could we even if we'd wanted to? So far, Thomas had overdubbed twelve-string acoustic, electric, and steel-guitar parts, added an accordion effect processed through a clavinette, and for percussion had taped the sound of my high hat and played it backward, giving the track a soft, sucking, swooshing pulse. Christine and Slippery and I just looked at each other. Slippery picked up his silver tone bar.

"Whatever that sawbones told that boy to do, somebody oughta make sure he does it," he said.

"One, two, three, four . . ."

We tried. We tried to follow him. But he heard what the song was supposed to be, us only what it was. It sounded like the

"Louie, Louie" version of a 200-year-old English nursery rhyme as composed by a screamingly mad bishop with a clever way with words. We struggled through to the end, though, all of us ending up in more or less the same place four minutes later, and the song was over. And so was our set, the shortest in the history of the Whisky A Go Go. Colin hopped on stage. Standing in a pool of makeup and pills, he grabbed the mike from the stand.

"Hey, man, let's take a break and let everybody cool out, all right? The band is obviously still dealing with what went down today, so let's all take a few minutes to get ourselves together." He shot the crowd a peace sign before giving the soundman a throat-slashing gesture just in case Thomas had any ideas about making any more speeches or sabotaging our musical reputation any further.

He didn't have to worry. Thomas let himself be led off stage and into the dressing room by Heather before promptly nodding out with her holding his hand and keeping him vertical in his chair. The attack Colin had planned to launch on Thomas he aimed at Heather instead. The small room was noisy and bursting with the band, Lee and Emily, Dew, and a couple of Electric Records flunkies desperately attempting damage control by busily handing out DUCKHEAD SECRET SOCIETY buttons, but soon Colin's was the only voice in the room.

"You're supposed to be his old lady. Didn't you see what was going on? Didn't you think it might have been a good idea to let the rest of us know that your boyfriend had decided to single-hand-edly destroy everything we've worked so hard for?"

Heather squeezed Thomas's limp hand harder and buried her head in his shoulder.

"Hello?" Colin said. "I'm sorry, I'm not done talking about this."

"Yes, you are," Christine said. She kneeled down and put an arm around Heather, who was softly crying into Thomas's shirt. "Leave her alone. Thomas is the one who screwed up, not her."

"Thomas is the one who screwed up? Just Thomas?" Colin crossed his arms. "Then who was that pickup band I heard him embarrassing himself out there with?"

"You think it was any more fun playing that garbage than listening to it?"

"Well, that's the right word, anyway."

"You haven't heard the studio version we're working on," I said.

During the commotion of our arrival I'd snuck off to the john and fired up another couple lines of coke. Enter zealot Bill with a head full of blow and no place to rest his accelerated heart rate.

"I thought you believed in what Thomas was trying to do, man," I said. "When did you go over to the other side?"

"What other side? Sanity?"

I looked at Thomas, at Heather cocooned around his prostrate body. The slightest grin was painted on his passed-out face.

"What did you sign us up for if you weren't going to let us grow?" I said. "Is this what makes you so different from Columbia and Warner Brothers and all the rest?"

"Grow? Bill, c'mon. This stuff"—he poked at the pile of tapes on the counter—"is an abortion."

The first syllable of the first word of a full-throated counterattack was almost out of my mouth when I saw what I thought I saw. In that instant's flash, I saw it.

Heather was still quietly crying. Christine still had her arm around her shoulder, softly shhhing her to stop. Lee was kneeling down beside Christine. One of the kids with Colin pinned a button to my new cowboy shirt. This much everyone could agree on. Only I saw what happened next.

"What did you just do?" I said. I'd spoken maybe eight words to Lee and Emily combined since we'd first met, but Lee knew I was talking to her.

"What?"

"What the fuck did you just do?"

Lee pointed to herself. "Me?"

Christine slowly stood up. "Bill, what's wrong?" She knew a cocaine cyclone when she saw one by now.

"Don't protect her, don't lie to me."

"Bill—"

"Fuckingdykebitchfeelingupmyfuckinggirlfriendrightin-frontofmyfuckingfaceyoufuckingdykebitch."

Unlike me, Christine didn't need drugs to be enraged. She jabbed a hard finger into my chest. "Do you have any idea how pathetic you look right now?"

"Why? Because I see through your dyke friends?"

Emily and Lee were at the door. "Christine, we're going," one of them said.

Colin put a hand on my shoulder. "Bill, c'mon, calm down."

"Get your hand off me, man."

"Hey—"

"Who do you think—"

"I was just—"

"Don't—"

"I'm not going to—"

"Fuck you, you—"

"Fuck *you*, you—"

Louder and louder and more and more, until undoubtedly some rule of feuding physics took over and the room simply couldn't contain us all. I felt as if I was vibrating, I was shaking so much. I closed my eyes and took a few deep breaths. When I opened them back up, Thomas and Heather in their little weeping world were the only ones left in the room.

"Have you got a place to stay?"

Dew, standing beside me, with her eyes lowered to the dressing room floor. All along she must have been there beside me.

"Because maybe you should let things cool off for a while. Between you and Christine, I mean."

Maybe I nodded. Maybe I said yes or yeah or maybe that might be a good idea. Maybe I didn't say anything.

"Let's go out the back," she said, webbing five little fingers through mine. "I live just a couple of blocks away. It's a nice night. We can walk."

four

84.

HER LIPS WERE SLIGHTLY chapped and she wasn't a very good kisser. Too loose, too spongy, like her mouth was just lying there waiting to be worshipped, like kissing was a one-way thing. She wasn't a very good kisser but neither was I until Christine taught me not to get stuck in long samey rhythms and how to make your lips firm but soft. Now it was my turn to pass on what I knew to Dew.

The details are the same for anyone who's ever done what they shouldn't have. Of the making of breaking of promises there is no end. Steaming dandelion tea, Donovan's *Sunshine Superman* on the record player, a quilt her grandmother made for her, and, eventually, inevitably, magnetized lips and you can't fight science, all the songs say so.

The aerobics end of it was fine. The thrill of the unknown other, the delightful difference from what you're used to in height, weight, and smell; a new place to put your cock. But later—after—both cups of barely touched tea beside the mattress on the floor gone cold, the smoking candles burned nearly all the way down to white waxy stubs, the same five songs on side A over and over and over, Dew gathered up the rumpled bedding and one by one spread them over top of me, from the first cool kiss of the white cotton sheet to the final heavy lump of the quilt. Then naked she climbed in beside naked me and shimmied up against me and put her head on my chest and fell straight asleep. I felt my stomach tighten. I felt like I was going to be sick.

I shut my eyes tight, then opened them back up, stretched my eyelids as hard and wide as I could, like you do when you're trying to wake yourself up from a bad dream. But when I opened them this time all I saw were fuzzy white stars. And this head—this head I didn't know—resting on my chest.

My God, I thought, who does this woman think I am?

85.

COLIN THOUGHT IT would be a good idea if we went home for the holidays, like we lived in Santa Cruz or just on the other side of the Golden Gate Bridge. Electric, he said, had everything it needed to put out and publicize the first single ("One O'clock in the Morning" b/w "Dream of Pines") and it would probably be in everyone's best interest if we spent Christmas not thinking about music and took some time off, particularly Thomas. It felt like we were being sent to our rooms two thousand miles away.

Colin had cancelled the remainder of our final Whisky show and that same night's TV gig, and, aided by a couple more lines of my coke, ricocheted around the room doing Duckhead damage control with as many of the who's who as possible. The next day, at the sourest photo shoot in the history of rock and roll, there wasn't any more talk of us sticking around and going on the road with the Byrds. When, later, somebody at Electric sent along a dummy of the album cover to Toronto for our okay, it looked exactly the way it had been: four strung-out people who didn't want to be where they were.

The idea—Colin's—had been to shoot us standing around in front of the grimy coffee shop across the street from the studio. Hanging out on one of L.A.'s mean streets with the urban down-and-out, the cover was supposed to say that this wasn't some Nebraskan cab driver's idea of country and western music, man, this was white soul music for right now, so open up your eyes and ears. It actually wasn't a half-bad plan, and it at least showed Colin hadn't given up on us.

In the shot they ended up using, Christine and I are wearing the clothes we'd had on the night before and are glaring hard into the camera as if it was responsible for making us so miserable. Slippery is standing right beside us, cupping his cigarette from the wind, squinting suspiciously over the towering flame of his lighter at the photographer. Slouching a couple of feet away, Thomas is wearing his sunglasses and Nudie jacket unbuttoned all the way down, oblivious to the December breeze and looking the other way down the street, his silver cross reflecting the rays of the sun. Somehow a white-whiskered old black man clutching a Styrofoam cup of coffee and wearing a stunned expression like he'd just undergone ten continous hours of electroshock therapy made his way into the frame, fuzzy but discernibly forlorn in the distance. He fit right in.

86.

WE SET CHRISTOPHER'S compass north and hit Highway 15 with Thomas at the wheel and a cardboard box full of 7 1/2 IPS copies of every *Moody Food* track we'd worked on sitting on his lap. Every time Thomas flipped on the turn signal his elbow would knock against the box, rattling the stack of tapes inside. Every fifteen minutes or so Heather would ask him if he'd like her to keep the box beside her in the back where there was more room. Every time, Thomas would answer, Thank you, no, and readjust the box. After a couple hundred miles Heather stopped asking.

Somewhere near the Arizona–Utah border a white Cadillac with Texas plates and a bumper sticker that read I HAVE A DREAM . . . THAT ONE DAY THE CONFEDERATE FLAG WILL FLY OVER WASHINGTON pulled ahead of us. Christine put her paperback down on her knee long enough to see what I saw and we locked eyes for the first time since the night before I didn't sleep at the Marmont. I took in the bumper sticker one more time then closed my eyes. It was time to go home.

He wasn't the fastest or the strongest or the most talented guy on the team, and he knew it. Just like he also knew that if it was fourth and goal, fourth quarter, and less than a minute to go and the good guys were down by six, there was only one play. The quarterback sneak. With the game on the line you can't trust anyone else to get the job done so you take it over yourself. Strap your chin strap on tight, keep your head down low, and push the bodies ahead of you forward toward even the slightest sliver of pay dirt daylight like moth to flame. And don't go down until you break that white line. For Chrissake, don't go down.

And if the coach calls for a play-action pass to the tight end, hoping to throw the other team off by unexpectedly putting the ball in the air, there's still only one play. Doesn't matter that the defence have pummelled the running back three straight times at the line of scrimmage. Doesn't matter that they're probably expecting another run. So much can go wrong when you float that ball up there. The blocking could collapse. The receivers could run the wrong routes. The tight end could drop the pass.

Even if everyone in the huddle, on the sidelines, in the crowd, thinks you're crazy. Even if they stick all eleven bodies right on the line. Straight up the middle, up and over that hill, on three.

87.

FIRST THOMAS GOT us a coke connection. Then he booked us time at the RCA recording studio near Church Street so we could get right back to work on *Moody Food*. It was nowhere near as high-tech as we were used to, but it was the best Toronto had to offer. Finding a satisfactory dealer was a whole lot easier. In the couple of months we'd been away it seemed as if the Vagabonds had tripled their leather-clad presence in the village. Suddenly you could score speed and coke anywhere you went, just the same as weed.

Two straight days and nights of white line fever and we were back in T.O. in less than forty-eight hours, aided by us crossing at Detroit this time and not the safer Sault Ste. Marie. When I saw we weren't taking the longer route and asked Thomas what was up, he just patted the cardboard box full of tapes still on his lap and said, "Got to strike while the iron's hot, Buckskin." Everybody else was asleep and he didn't seem worried, so I wasn't either. We stuffed what was left of the remaining coke up our noses in a truck-stop bathroom outside Toledo and weren't asked to pull over at the border for inspection. The guards probably reasoned that nobody could be stupid enough to try any funny business at an interna-tional border in a beat-up hearse at eight o'clock in the morning. Sometimes you need to be dumb to be lucky.

We pulled into Yorkville around noon on a freezing cold but sunny day. Christine and Slippery got dropped off first and lugged their stuff out of Christopher and retreated to their beds like a couple of Napoleon's most flaked-out almost-Muscovites. Every time I called Christine's place over the next two days one of her roommates would say she was sleeping.

They say infidelity is like potato chips—you can't have just one. Not me. A couple thousand miles of silence goes a long way toward visualizing in full nightmare Technicolor a lifetime of not having the only person you'd ever been able to really talk to not there to talk to any more. I'd had my ounce of forbidden flesh and knew I'd never need to eat again.

But I also knew that the *Moody Food* tapes Thomas brought back with us were still just iris-slashing brilliantly smashed diamonds that the master jeweller was still mulling over, still figuring out their worth and final placement amid all the glittering others. But he would. Drugs are great for looking on the bright side. The glass is half full, even when it's empty.

Thomas would do what he had to do and we'd help him do it, and when it happened, when the musical rainbow was complete and we all held hands and watched our work rise to the sky and bring everyone to their knees, Christine and I would once again sit at the Riverboat sipping espressos and laughing about nothing just like before.

All of which was exactly what I was going to tell Christine. As soon as she returned my calls.

88.

ONCE CHRISTINE and I did get around to talking there was one topic we weren't going to discuss. And not just because it fit my procrastinating profile perfectly not to. The thing was, I wanted to tell Christine about Dew, had been bursting to since the second I'd stood alone on the 6 a.m. sidewalk in front of Dew's house with the smell of her skin baked into mine. I'd stumbled down the street and felt my dumb groin tighten at the whiff of a stranger's scent on my wrist and thought that if I ran all the way to the Marmont and woke up Christine and vomited out everything I'd done the knot in my stomach would go away and in the future the sweet sound of dawn-bugling birds might not make me want to cry. But I was too hungover from all the scotch and the Marmont was too far away. By the time I pushed the elevator button for our floor I knew what I wasn't going to do.

Maybe it was coke-blown ego, maybe it was simple-minded simple vanity, but the more I walked off my hangover the more I became convinced that Christine wasn't going to leave me for doing what I'd done. She wouldn't be happy about it, but we had too much history behind us and too many things in our future to look forward to to tear the calendar from the wall just because I'd needed to find out what it felt like to be the cool guy for once. If I marched into our room and spewed out what had happened it would be for my benefit, not hers. Sparing her the pain and loading myself down with a lifetime of guilt was the first grown-up gold star I ever got.

Christine was asleep and still that way when I got out of the shower and into bed. I'd never been happier to be anywhere. I let go a deep, deep breath and rested my hand on her hip and she rolled over onto her side away from me. I deserved that, I thought. Just like I knew I'd earned the next day's silence and the one after that. The Bill Hansen she'd fallen in love with had gone missing in action and I was the only one who could bring him back alive. Fine. We'd go home and get *Moody Food* done and I'd slowly cut back on the coke and burn off whatever craziness was left over with extra laps and there he'd be again.

But there aren't any swimming pools in Canada in December. Or in January, February, March, or even April and May.

89.

WHEN WE WEREN'T eating up hours of tape at RCA, Thomas and I were at his suite at the Park Plaza working the kinks out of what we wanted to record when we got back in the studio the next day. I'd checked in with Kelorn as soon as we'd returned, but neither of us brought up the idea of me starting back at Making Waves. She did ask me if I was eating enough and why I insisted on wearing my sunglasses inside. I told her I wasn't used to life off the road yet and that I'd be sure to see her around.

And yeah, the Park Plaza. The same swank hotel I'd caught Thomas sneaking out of after doing Heather wrong. But there'd never been any other woman. There'd never been anybody else at all. It'd always been just Thomas. When he gave me his room number and told me to come over later to discuss the recording schedule he'd worked out, I didn't act surprised or ask if he'd been staying there all along while the rest of us had gotten by in under-heated and shoebox-sized rooms and his own girlfriend had had to open up her shabby door to Slippery at his slimiest because Thomas's place was, you know, too small.

Because for a long, long time you believe in Santa Claus, never even question how he gets an entire planet's worth of pres-ents delivered in just one twelve-hour shift. And then one year you don't. Nobody sits you down and tells you that Santa Claus doesn't exist. The bad news just rolls across the plains of the schoolyard like a mist you can only see in the distance, never when you're actually in it. And then you know just like you've always known, like everybody's always known, that the guy who knows who's naughty and nice was just something made up by the grownups to keep the little ones happy.

90.

THE DOCTOR WANTED to know if I'd recently had syphilis, tuberculosis, diphtheria, or typhoid fever. Any L.A. physician, like the one who'd given Thomas the Valium, wouldn't have had to ask. Once my nose had stopped bleeding I'd walked over to the emergency ward and the MD on duty started poking around inside with a cold steel instrument. When he started chipping out little pieces of bloody crust he couldn't hide his excitement and invited another doctor in the white-sheeted cubicle next door to take a look. Together the two of them scraped out the goriest trayful of desecrated hemoglobin this side of a Vietnam triage.

"It is," the other one said.

"It really is," my doctor agreed.

"It really is what?" I said. For the last half-hour I'd been sitting on the edge of an icy metal table naked except for a drafty hospital gown, trying to keep my nose stuck up in the air to provide the best possible point of nasal entry. And with watery eyes pinched tight from the pain of two strangers oohing and ahing over the world's most intense nose-picking ever. I felt like a prize-winning science experiment.

My doctor finally set down his tool on the goo-caked tray. "Mr. Hansen, you have a perforated septum."

"Meaning what?"

"Meaning you've got a hole inside your nose."

"Oh."

"It's not dangerous in and of itself, but it does indicate something's most definitely wrong. We're going to need to run some tests on you as soon as possible. In the meantime I want you to keep that nose elevated."

"Okay."

"Are you sure you've never had typhoid?"

"No."

"What about syphilis?" the other docter chirped in. "We're here to help you, not judge you."

Syphilis, I thought. I wish.

91.

ON THE RARE DAYS we couldn't book studio time we'd rehearse at our old space in the village. Christine emerged from her post-tour recuperative coma not much more chatty toward her boyfriend, but determined to make Thomas and me understand that once the new songs we'd started in L.A. were wrapped up she was taking a lengthy musical sabbatical. She said she'd learned a lot about successful political organizing out there and wanted to help put together a more successful Yorkville version. When she wasn't asking Thomas precisely what he meant by requesting that she play "an om-pah-pah sort of bass thing—you know, Barnum and Bailey meets 1930s Polish wedding hall music," that's what she usually talked about. I didn't mind. At least she was talking to me.

"I mean, enough is enough," she said.

We were taking a break from an hour and a half's worth of practise on the four-part background chant to "He Do the Police in Different Voices." Chanting was Thomas's new big thing. Combined with a strictly vegan diet, there was just no end to the amount of spiritual purity a person could achieve. Chanting came easier to Thomas and me. Long, repeated nonsense syllables feel pretty good on a charred nervous system. Oral downers for the brain. The om that refreshes.

"It's really important that we don't marginalize our efforts," she said. "We can't let the media portray what we're doing as just some kind of freak-out for potheads. That's why it's so essential that we educate everyone and not just preach to the converted."

After being reassured by Thomas for about the tenth time since we'd gotten back that the second half of our *Dream of Pines* advance money would be in his pocket soon, Slippery went downstairs to the hall payphone to make a call. Heather rubbed Thomas's shoulders while he sucked on a cigarette hanging out the side of his mouth and used both hands to rip tape after tape off the reel-to-reel, listening for whatever it was he was searching for in his headphones. Scotty sat absorbed in front of his latest opus at the card table like we'd never even left. I was the only one paying attention to Christine. If I ignored the fact that the last time we'd had a meaningful conversation I'd violently accused her of conducting not one but two lesbian affairs behind my back and then gone on later that same night to betray her with what turned out to be a seventeen-year-old groupie, it almost felt like old times. I nodded a little more empathetically.

"That's why I'm bringing a bunch of these home with me for Christmas," she said. She pulled several mimeographed pamphlets out of her of bag. "This isn't just our fight. What these developers and their political cronies represent is a threat to *all* generations, not just ours."

Christine and Thomas were the only two people I'd ever met who, when they got worked up about something, made certain words sound like they were underlined in the air. I needed to have that talk with her soon. The one about how I didn't want to go through life without her beside me underlining all the really important words.

"Do you want to take some back to Etobicoke?" she said. "You don't have to."

"Yeah, that'd be great," I said.

"Here we go!" Thomas yelled. He ripped off the headphones and stamped out his cigarette underfoot. Somehow smoking in the studio wasn't taboo any more and the floor was as good an ashtray as any. "Check this out, y'all," he said.

Tape hiss, and then the slowly escalating sound of human screams, incoherent yelling, car horns honking, and cop sirens wailing. Urban Armageddon with its very own soundtrack.

"What is that?" Christine said.

"Do you like it?" Thomas said.

Christine didn't answer, continued to listen.

"Buckskin?"

I scratched my head. "Yeah, but . . ."

He grinned and picked up his leanest, meanest Telecaster and ripped right into the opening discordant howlings of "Till My Wet Fur Froze." The chaos of the tape bubbled away in the background, every second threatening to boil over and scorch the song.

I got it, smiled. "We can splice them together tomorrow at RCA," I said.

"Exactly," he said.

Heather smiled because I'd smiled and because all was well in Duckheadville.

"What is this?" Christine said. "I know this."

"This?" I said.

"I *know* this," she said.

"I doubt it," I laughed. "For your sake, I seriously doubt it."

The tape ran down to how it'd hissingly begun. "Miss Christine does know this," Thomas said. He turned around and lit up a fresh smoke. "It's the riot on the Strip."

"The L.A. riot?" Christine said.

"The very same. I had a feeling things were going to get heavy so I gave the sound guy at the Whisky five bucks to tape some of it for us on his portable." Thomas took a long drag from his cigarette, flicked the ash on the floor.

Christine yanked her opened bag off the card table and all of the pamphlets inside fluttered to the floor like crippled white doves. I got down on my knees beside her and handed her what she didn't quickly manage to gather. She didn't say thanks and stomped out of the room.

"You've got to have a talk with that woman of yours about her mood swings, Buckskin."

I looked at the silent tape machine.

"I mean, how are we going to work on the middle section of the chant now that she's gone?"

92.

OUR SINGLE CAME out and died a quiet death, too rock and roll for country radio, too country-sounding for rock stations. But Colin wasn't surprised or even upset and reassured us over the phone that if ever there was an album group, it was us. The 45 was just for getting our name out there some more, he said. *Dream of Pines* the LP was where we were going to make our reputation. Only problem was, Electric Records didn't have it.

Thomas, it seemed, had taken the master tapes of the finished album along with our *Moody Food* material before we split town. Naturally, Colin understood the mix-up, but wanted the album back. Three weeks later he was a lot less understanding and still wanted the album back. Not so naturally, I was the one forced to deal with his growing long-distance frustration. Thomas didn't believe in telephones any more—something about electronic wire signals breeding brain cancer cells.

"Thomas says he's dropping it in the mail this week," I said. I was sitting at the desk in Thomas's room watching a sky full of nervous snow flurries white-out the tenth-floor view.

"Bill, that's what you said last week. And the week before that."

"We've been busy with the new stuff. Really busy."

"Look, I don't think you guys recognize the severity of the situation down here. The release date has already been pushed back a month. The people who can help make or break this thing are in danger of forgetting who we are. The media in this town have a very short attention span."

I tried to change the topic. As Thomas's new official mouthpiece to the outside world, it was something I was getting pretty good at.

"Thomas told me to tell you not to worry because *Moody Food* is going to make you forget all about *Dream of Pines*," I said. "Thomas says—"

"'Thomas says, Thomas says.' Why can't I talk to Thomas myself? He hasn't been messing around with you-know-what again, has he?"

You-know-what was heroin. When a single joint could net you five years in prison on either side of the border, there was no such thing as being too careful.

"Of course not," I said. "You just can't believe how incredibly hard he's been working on our new songs."

"Or how he won't talk on the phone."

"Right."

"Because he's afraid he might catch cancer."

"Um . . ."

"I want those tapes this week."

"Okay."

"*This* week, Bill. I haven't got time for this. This week or I'm coming out there and getting them myself. And taking the plane fare out of the rest of the group's advance."

I hung up the phone and looked out the window at what were now snowflakes the size of quarters slowly falling straight down. Gordon Lightfoot was playing at the Riverboat and I knew Christine would be there, had overheard her excitedly telling Heather that day at the studio. Since we'd returned to town she'd kept her promise to help see through *Moody Food*, but was also full speed ahead leading her own life once again: working part-time at Sam's, attending meetings that the Diggers were holding about what to do about Yorkville, and even picking up her acoustic guitar again and doing the occasional solo spot. I hadn't known about the latter until I saw a handmade poster in familiar handwriting advertising her and a bunch of others performing at the Bohemian

Embassy. I stood there in the frozen street looking at the flapping sign, hurt that I hadn't been told, guilty that I felt relieved I wouldn't have to try to talk myself out of going so I wouldn't miss a writing session with Thomas.

But tonight was going to be different. Tonight the plan was to calm down with a few Mandraxes and show up at the Lightfoot gig coke-free and cucumber cool and surprise Christine by sitting down beside her holding nothing stronger than a couple cups of coffee and with an ear sincerely tuned in to something other than *Moody Food* for a change. And maybe, finally, actually, really talk. About her. About me. About us.

A key clicked in the door and I felt the muscles in my butt and lower back instinctively tighten, although I knew it had to be Thomas coming back from dropping Heather off at her place and scoring. Nighttime at the Park Plaza was boy's night every night. I tried not to imagine Heather sitting down at her tiny kitchen table for a long night's worth of knitting Thomas another pair of mittens.

"Enjoying the view?" he said, dropping his leather coat to the floor.

The guy who'd designed the hotel would have had a hard time connecting the original room with this one. Several room-service plates full of slowly moulding steamed vegetables along with a couple of silver coffee urns and anything you could imagine being used as an ashtray—half-finished Coke bottles, the soap dish from the bathroom, even an old cowboy boot—surrounded Thomas's king-sized bed like a junkyard fort. Several guitars and the portable tape recorder were all within horizontal grasp so that whenever inspiration visited he wouldn't have to get up.

"Colin called again," I said.

Thomas went straight for the bed. When we weren't at the studio, that's where he usually was. He grabbed the rectangular piece of wood he kept beside the bed and laid it across his knees, stuck his hand down the front of his jeans and pulled out a baggy of coke.

"I think he means it this time," I said. "He said that unless you send him the tapes tomorrow he's going to come up here and get them himself."

I didn't know why Thomas refused to hand over *Dream of Pines* any more than Colin did. Thomas's official version was that he wanted *Moody Food* in the bag before the first album came out so we could follow it right up with a wicked one-two punch, but I didn't buy it. I just wished I didn't have to lie to Colin on the telephone every other day.

"He cannot have what he cannot find," Thomas said, cutting out four fat lines on the board. He leaned over and snorted two and laid the slat beside him on the bed and picked up his acoustic.

"He's serious, man," I said, staring at the coke.

"So am I."

I forced myself to look away from the two remaining white lines; watched Thomas's fingers dance all around his twelve-string; instead of telling him I was taking the night off to meet Christine, got lost in the churning sound of the guitar.

Today in the studio it seemed like we'd never get the rhythm to "Sabers Up!" right. Tonight, robin's egg blue with just the faintest glaze of an early May rain shower—perfect. I stopped thinking and just listened until he stopped playing. Thomas drew the now-empty board back onto his lap.

"Okay," he said, "just one more each. These new chords work, but the last line in every verse has got too many syllables now."

"Right," I said, rubbing my nose, bowing my head again. Just one more.

93.

ALL WINTER LONG you wait for it, know it's coming, never really believing that it will.

Sticking your head out the door every morning from the first week of March on—nothing. Just one more scarf and gloves and plenty of Chapstick day. Shut the door tight, pull on an extra pair of socks, and resign yourself to a lifetime of wet feet and cough drops.

Then it's here, it's really here, only when you've given up on it does it finally arrive, everywhere you look fellow spring-stoned zombies with their unzipped jackets flapping wide open in the warm afternoon breeze, sun-kissed perma-smiles on every stranger's happily stunned face.

And so what if the first day of spring makes a promise it can never keep?

94.

"DON'T TELL ME you're quitting on me too, Buckskin."

"Nobody's quitting on anybody, I'm just not sure what you want me to do."

"Don't tell me you're quitting on me too."

"Did you hear me? I'm not—"

"Don't tell me that, I don't want to hear that."

"Listen, if you want me to play the piano, fine, I'll play the piano. It's just—"

"Just what?"

"Well, I don't know how to play the piano. And you do. So . . ."

"Buckskin, we wrote 'Dance's Boat' *together*, remember? We *know* what this song is all about. The lone child in the empty sun-streaked room. The wooden building blocks lying all around him on the hardwood floor. The hours and hours he'll never not know again. Remember? *Remember?*"

"I remember."

"Good. Now, how can someone who knows how to play the piano play the keyboard part on a song like that?"

"They can't."

"No, they can't."

"No."

"So, here, put your fingers here. I'll get you started. After that, you just do whatever feels right."

95.

THOMAS TOLD ME to tell Colin he put *Dream of Pines* in the post, but *Dream of Pines* wasn't what he sent.

What Thomas mailed instead were the handful of *Moody Food* tracks he'd dubbed done and, as a special bonus—because the more I put Colin off about delivering the album, the more he started asking me to ask Thomas to consider recording a rocking Duckhead version of a classic country song to issue as another single after the album did come out—a very creepy deconstruction of the Kitty Wells song "It Wasn't God That Made Honky Tonk Angels" sung by Slippery in his foggy-throated most baritone. If it wasn't enough that Slippery was taking the lead on a tune made famous by a woman named Kitty that was about how girls weren't to blame for going bad because a two-timing man was probably lurking somewhere in the background, Thomas had us play it so slowly that I literally needed to leave the recording studio and go home and get my bottle of Mandraxes so I could hit the drums sluggishly enough. It came out sounding like the world's first and last country and western raga. Of course, I dug it. After four Mandys, I kept listening to it on the playback and seeing Neapolitan ice-cream swirls.

Colin didn't see anything. Except maybe proverbial pissed-off red when he opened up the package and hooked up the tapes and heard what we'd delivered. After seven messages from the front desk I snorted up the courage to return his call. I should have kept the stash beside me.

"Please tell me you're putting me on. Please tell me he's still mad at me. And please, please tell me the real album is going to be here tomorrow."

"You didn't like any of it?" I said.

"Bill . . . c'mon."

"Not even 'Till My Wet Fur Froze'? Thomas thought it was topical and might get some airplay. That crowd noise you hear in the song is actually taken from the riot on the Strip. Maybe the publicity people could let that get around and—"

"*Bill.*"

All right, so Thomas never said he thought it would get any airplay. Thomas never thought anything about a song other than whether or not it worked. And this one did, it did work. Was scary as hell then and still scares me now, long after that particular riot is over but a million more are just getting started.

"Are you going to come and get them, then?" I said.

I'd been hoping Colin would hop on a plane and come north almost right from the start, just take the damn tapes back and print up a few thousand copies of the album and that would be that. For one thing, whatever Thomas's reluctance at having our old songs see the light of day was, I was proud of them and it didn't feel right that they were gathering dust in a cardboard box on the floor of his hotel room closet. It was like an undiscovered Van Gogh rotting away in somebody's basement, like the thing didn't exist if people couldn't look at it. Plus, when I'd gone back to Etobicoke for Christmas the only way I could make my mother and father believe that I shouldn't be immediately hospitalized for exhaustion and maybe worse was that I really had been working overtime on an actual record album that they'd be holding in their worried hands sometime soon. That was four months ago.

"You know I can't, things are crazy right now with the festival."

"But it's two whole months away."

"Two whole months away just means there's that much more time for something to go wrong. Like everybody's agreed to play for free and now Ravi Shankar comes along and wants $3500 for some school he runs in India."

"Wow, what are you going to do?"

"Pay him, I guess."

I really was wowed. The Monterey Pop Festival was going to be the first hippie nation under the sun, three days in June of what turned out to be more than 300,000 freaks grooving on, among others, the Byrds, the Who, Jimi Hendrix, and even a couple of lesser-known bands under contract to Electric Records. But not the Duckhead Secret Society. Colin was on the festival's board of governors, but nepotism had its limits. Bands with one unknown single to their credit weren't allowed to play with the big boys and girls.

"So I guess I'll talk to Thomas again," I said. There was silence at the other end of the line for a couple of seconds, long enough that I said, "Colin?"

"You know I loved the music Thomas was making right from the start," he said. "That all of you were making. You know that, right?"

"Look, I'll talk to—"

"I mean, I wasn't stupid, I knew Thomas Graham wasn't going to be the next Jim Morrison, the next *Tiger Beat* pin-up boy. But the music was special enough and so was he that I thought there was a place for both of them, you know? That we'd *make* a place for both of them."

I didn't like the way the conversation was drifting into the past tense. "Hey, Thomas isn't dead," I said. "And neither is this band. Let me read him the riot act. He's due back here any minute and this time I'll make sure he gets the message loud and clear. This time I'll really talk to him. Really. You'll get the album. I promise."

There was another long silence.

"I thought getting him out of L.A. would be enough," Colin said. "I thought he'd straighten himself out on his own up there. I mean, if I wasn't so busy and we were bigger and had the resources I'd come up there myself and . . . Sometimes I think somebody should burn this fucking city to the ground. And not just the Sunset Strip."

I switched the phone to my other ear.

"The tapes go in the mail tomorrow," I said. "I give you my word."

I let the phone line hum.

"Sure. You send me the tapes whenever you can. We'll put them out then."

"Tomorrow," I said. "Not whenever—tomorrow."

"Sure."

I could hear someone calling him, something about another call on another line.

"I've got to go," he said. "Say hey to Christine and Slippery and Heather."

"Okay."

"Okay."

I heard the same voice as before calling Colin's name.

"Bill?"

"Yeah?"

"Be careful."

"What do you mean?"

"I don't know, man. Just be careful."

96.

I WAS ON MY KNEES in the closet when Thomas got back. The cardboard box was still there, but there wasn't anything in it. I kept feeling around anyway with both blind hands.

"My good suit's at the cleaner, Buckskin. Anything else I can get for you?"

I sat up on my knees, head still in the closet.

"People should hear that music," I said.

"We're going to give them something better."

"You know I believe that."

"Good."

He put his room key on the desk.

"Why can't they have both?" I said.

When he pulled a plastic baggy from his pants and then got the cigar box from underneath the bed and clicked on the bathroom light I knew we wouldn't be working tonight.

Just before he shut the bathroom door, "Didn't anyone ever tell you you can't serve two masters?" he said.

97.

"SO, BOTTOM LINE here, what you're saying is that we ain't getting paid."

"Well, no, not right away," I said. "But we will. As soon as the record comes out."

"Which you don't know when because nobody knows where the tapes is gone."

"We know where they are, Thomas has them."

"Yeah, and he ain't telling nobody where he put them."

"For now. For now he's not telling."

"Uh huh."

Slippery moved around the smoking skillet of pork chops on the hot-plate burner on the floor and stood up. We were in the hallway outside his room.

"Pardon me," he said, opening his door just wide enough to let him slide in sideways, then shutting it closed right after.

It was only a little after eight, but Thomas was passed out at the hotel and it was too nice an April night to be stuck inside nannying him. Besides, I'd rung up Heather and she'd been thrilled at the offer to come over and watch him sleep. Setting Slippery straight about what was going on with our final Electric Records payment wasn't my idea of celebrating the coming of spring, but at least it got me out of the room. I'd gone by Christine's place first, but there hadn't been anyone home.

Slippery came back out with a bottle of Tabasco sauce and a chipped white plate with a six-inch crack in it that looked like a long black hair and pulled the door tight. In all the months he'd lived downstairs from the studio I don't think I ever saw his door open longer than it took for him to duck in or out.

He kneeled down and uncapped the little red bottle and drenched the meat. "So I guess that's it, then," he said.

"Your food's done?"

He almost smiled. "That too." He forked over each fat slice of sizzling pork and bathed the other side.

"I suppose if this here record ever does come out you wouldn't mind mailing me my share," he said.

"It's not going to be that long. Thomas is going to come around to the realization that that music belongs to everybody sooner or later. By the time we finish *Moody Food* at the latest."

He turned off the burner and stacked the pork chops on the plate.

"You wait here," he said. "Let me put these inside and I'll get you my brother's address."

"Go ahead and eat," I said. "Just give it to me tomorrow at the studio."

He stood up with the plate in his hand; stood there in front of me with his eyes on the floor.

"You tell Graham and his woman and yours too it's been good working with them, all right? Tell them for a bunch of hippies we made some pretty good music there for a while."

"Why don't you tell them yourself?"

He lifted his eyes, but only as high as the meat on the plate. "Because as soon as I get my affairs straightened away I guess I'll be on a Greyhound south."

"We're recording tomorrow. Where are you going?"

He finally looked up.

"You think it would be a good idea do you if I stayed cooped up in that broom closet there just so I can piss away the rest of my God-given days listening to Graham and your woman scrapping over whether the fiftieth take of the middle section of the second verse of some song nobody is ever gonna hear anyway is good enough? That and watch you and him come back from the bathroom bouncing around the studio like a couple of long-tailed cats in a room full of rocking chairs? You think that's about the best I can do with the rest of my natural life?"

"What do you mean songs no one will ever hear?" It was probably the only thing he'd said that didn't matter right now, which was probably why I latched onto it.

"Wake up, Hoss, you hitched your wagon to a sick mule. That boy can write, I'll give you that, but he's gone wrong in the head, anybody can see that. Hell, even when Hank took to the bottle full-time and they booted him off the Opry he was still writin' good songs."

"So how come you hung around this long, then?" I said. "Just to see how wrong in the head Thomas was going to get?"

"Why do you think? The same reason I come up here in the first place. I was counting on the second part of that record company money to put me over what I need, but I'm close enough. I been talking to my brother back home. He's been dickering with the fellow that owns the place I'm after and all I got to do is let him know when any time now."

Now it was my turn to stare at the floor. "What am I going to tell Thomas?"

"Do him a favour and tell him you're all done, too. You and your woman."

Looking up, "How's that going to help *Moody Food* get finished?" I said.

Slippery rubbed his brow. "Christ, boy, do both yourselves a favour."

98.

HEROIN IS BAD. Once in a while the grownups are right.

I don't know if our last show in L.A. was the first time Thomas slid a spike into his arm, but I doubt it. Thomas knew more about drugs than most doctors will in a lifetime, and not because he was studying for his pharmacology degree on the sly. But from the day I met him until that night at the Whisky, only what made each moment more, not less. Uppers mostly, with the odd hallucinogenic added in when things got too ordinary and not odd enough. Stimulants of one kind or another, anyway, stuff to give life a little boost when it wasn't keeping up its end of the bargain.

Heroin doesn't do that. Heroin blocks out the sun. Heroin closes the windows and nails shut the shutters and unplugs the phone and doesn't answer the door.

When Thomas would show up at the Park Plaza and go for the cigar box before even taking off his coat, I knew that the white powder in the clear plastic bag in his hand wasn't coke. But I also knew that once he came out of the bathroom he'd be zonked out in no time and getting the R&R that staying up for two nights straight working on *Moody Food* demanded.

I guess now I sound like one of those women you hear about who lets her husband go on thinking she doesn't know about his mistress because he's happier around the house and more efficient at work. But try to understand that back then all I really knew was that the sonofabitch was finally getting some rest for a change and was always ready to go back to work the next day hungrier than the one before.

Try to understand that.

99.

THE DOWNSIDE WAS that Christine was as close to tears as she ever got. The nice part was that she'd phoned me to talk about why.

"Slow down," I said, "take your time." Thomas was passed out, curled up on the bed in the fetal position hugging his twelve-string. Heather sat on the desk chair pulled up beside the bed, contentedly knitting away.

"It's not the stuff," she said. "And except for what I was going to give to the people who run the Trailer, I don't even really care about the money." The Trailer was a way station set up on Avenue Road to help deal with the influx of new villagers struggling to cope with everything from VD to acid flashbacks. And now that Christine's house had been ransacked, it was one potential contribution poorer.

"I came by tonight around eight and couldn't believe there wasn't anybody home," I said. "There's usually always somebody hanging around there."

"We were all at the meeting."

"But the front door was unlocked."

"You know we never lock our doors."

"I guess it's time you started."

"If that's your way of trying to help . . ."

"No, no," I said, "all I meant was—"

"Forget it, just forget I called."

"Chris, calm down. You're worked up. Let me come over and we'll talk."

There was silence but no dial tone, so I held on.

"I don't feel like being here right now," she said. "It's creepy."

"So let's meet somewhere else."

"Aren't you under house arrest as usual?"

"C'mon."

"Why don't I come over there, then," she said.

"Here?"

"I don't know. Maybe the Park Plaza doesn't sound so bad right now. I don't suppose you have too many problems with break and enters there, anyway."

I was sitting on the edge of the desk and looked over at Thomas and Heather, him drooling onto the bedspread, her hooking and pearling.

"Meet me at my place in twenty minutes," I said. "Thomas and Heather are here and they're kind of talking some stuff out."

"I didn't think you'd kept your place."

"Where did you think I slept?"

"I wasn't sure you did."

"Be serious," I said.

"I am."

100.

UNHAPPINESS IS wonderful for breaking down language bar-
riers. That's a tune everybody knows. Although sometimes you need
a partner in song to help draw out how far gone you actually are.

"When I think of them having my mother's ring it feels like *I*
was there and they'd done something to *me*."

We were sitting with our knees pulled up to our chins
across from each other on the bed, mostly because it was the
only place to sit. I nodded and told Christine about how all the
really with-it guys in grade four had one of those nifty Crown
Royal purple flannel bags with the flaming yellow drawstrings
to put their marbles in and how my father was a second-gener-
ation Scottish-Canadian scotch man who would have rather
eaten raw peat than drink anything else. About how week after
week, one after-dinner drink per night at a time, I'd watch the
level fall on the bottle of Dewars he kept beside the bar fridge
downstairs and bug him to please, please get that stinky stuff he
drinks in the cool purple bag next time and not in the dumb
cardboard box. About how he didn't and didn't until one day he
did, calling me into the living room after dinner with a glass of
whisky in one hand and my very own Crown Royal bag hanging
from the other, making a face as he sipped his drink and tousling
my hair and telling me to go get my marbles and let him see
what all the bloody fuss was about. About how in the maelstrom
of a ten-year-old's mind marbles were now ancient history and
Topps hockey cards were now what made life worth living. How
I dug out my old marbles anyway and could have won an
Academy Award in the Best Appreciative Son category and how it
was the first time in my life I ever did anything for anyone else
besides me. How somebody stole the bag from me at the one and
only house party I ever threw during high school when my parents
were away for a week in Florida because of the nine bucks and

change I had in it from sidewalk snow shovelling and how I unsuccessfully tried to track the bastard that did the deed down because it was more than a purple flannel bag with a flaming yellow drawstring but was, I don't know, important, you know?

"I know," she said.

"Really?"

"Yeah. Especially after this."

"Yeah, I guess . . ."

"Yeah."

"Yeah."

I'd raced right over to my old place on Huron as soon as I'd gotten off the phone to bleed the radiators and light some candles and generally try to make it feel like I didn't just pay the rent there. I'd also fired up a couple of lines just before Christine arrived, which I knew were making me talk too much considering the idea was for me to listen to her but . . . Yeah. Yeah for hours and hours.

"I'm tired, Chris." I didn't know I wasn't just talking about tonight until I said it. I dabbed my nose with a bunch of balled tissues. It was only my second nosebleed since I'd checked in at the emergency ward, and neither had been as bad as the first one so I'd never bothered going back.

"You could have fooled me," she said, smiling.

"Really?"

Head down, "No."

Without thinking what I was doing, I slid my stockinged feet underneath hers. When she didn't move them away, I felt like there wasn't enough cocaine in the world to keep me awake for one more minute and how I wanted to peel back Christine's skin and snuggle down deep inside and not come out until I never wanted anything more complicated than a swell purple bag to put my marbles in.

"Stay the night," I said.

"There's not much of it left."

We both looked out my window; couldn't see it, but could smell dawn waking up and getting ready to step on stage.

"For what's left of it, then."

She looked down at her feet and mine together.

"I'm not sure that's such a good idea," she said.

"We don't have to do anything. I mean, we can just—"

She put her finger to my lips. "It's okay. I know what you meant. And I'm not saying it might not be nice. Even if we did do something."

"But what, then?"

"I just think we're in very different places right now and to mix those places up might make things more confusing than they already are."

"What are you confused about?"

"C'mon, Bill."

Now it was my turn to look at our feet.

Head up, "Well, maybe we could be confused together," I said.

She gave a little laugh and brushed some hair out of my face. When she looked into my eyes and kept on looking I thought she was going to kiss me.

"When we came back from the meeting tonight and found out what had happened, I was mad at you," she said.

"Me?"

"Yeah, you."

"Look, I know I said some things in L.A. I shouldn't have and—"

Christine shook her head, waved her hand.

"Haven't you noticed what's happened to the village?" she said. "You never heard of people getting their houses busted into before. And you never saw hard drugs on the street before either."

"So what's any of that got to do with me?"

She put a hand on her hip and shot me a come-off-it smirk.

"Okay, so what's your leaving your front door unlocked and getting robbed got to do with me?"

She pulled her feet from over top of mine.

"Can't you see that you and Thomas are helping keep the whole heavy drug scene in business?" she said. "You're part of the infrastructure that makes that element possible."

"Oh, come off it. Nobody makes anybody rip somebody else off. Least of all me and Thomas. We're too busy, believe me."

"Try to understand, Bill. If it wasn't for people like you, there wouldn't be people like them. Whatever you do has consequences that affect more than just you. Whether you can see those consequences right now or not."

I swung over the side of the bed and pulled on my cowboy boots, not really sure why but doing it like I was anyway.

"People like me? What does that mean? Since when was your boyfriend *people like me*. And please spare me this week's anarchist sermon from the mount about my personal role in the collapse of society."

She reached over and grabbed her combat boots off the floor and suddenly it was a race who could be shod first.

"You know," she said, "speaking to you on the phone and sitting here tonight, I started to ask myself why we never talk any more like we used to. Thanks for reminding me."

"Meaning what?"

I beat her by half a boot, but then I'd had a head start and didn't have any laces to do up.

"Meaning what?"

I followed five feet behind her the entire way to her house, asking the same question over and over. She never did answer. After slamming her front door in my face I heard the lock on the other side go click.

"About time!" I yelled.

On the way back to the Park Plaza I found an alleyway, squatted down in the dark behind a dumpster, and snorted one line and then one more off my forearm. When I hit the street again there was a bundle of bound *Toronto Telegram*s in front of a drugstore. I looked around and tore one out from the pile, stared at the date at the top of the front page.

How could it be tomorrow, I thought, when today's not even over yet?

101.

THOMAS WOKE UP from his most recent holiday out on the mainline, found out what was up with Slippery splitting town, and within twenty-four hours the old man had been bushwhacked in his sleep and all his money was gone and he was back on the bottle and feeding from Thomas's benevolent hand all over again with a black patch over his right eye covering up a scratched retina. His hands were fine, though; he could still work and record. They'd never touched his hands.

I put two and two together and told myself it was five. Told myself that Thomas was the motherfucker of all motherfuckers and told myself that two and two was five.

102.

"CAN YOU BELIEVE THIS?"

"C'mon, Thomas, let me out."

"Did you hear that? Did you just hear that?"

"Unlock the door, man."

"I'm asking you, Buckskin, can you believe this?"

"Unlock the fucking door, man."

He hadn't moved from his cross-legged vigil in front of the

record player's speakers since he'd plunked himself down there five hours before, when he'd blown through the hotel room door with the cellophane wrapper already torn off a brand new copy of the Beatles' latest, *Sgt. Pepper's Lonely Hearts Club Band.* He'd only gone out to score more coke, but had stopped off at the Grab Bag to get some smokes on the way back and somebody had been playing "Good Morning Good Morning," the album's second-to-last track. Bad move. When he heard those cats and dogs and chickens whooping it up in the background, he stormed around the corner to Record World to get his very own copy. The cow sounds on his own "Struggling for Purchase" were supposed to be rock and roll's first recorded livestock.

"What's wrong, Buckskin? If you've got to check in with anybody, why don't you use the phone in the room?"

The curtains were closed as usual, but it felt more like mid-afternoon than early evening. Because a single, final guitar overdub might be debuted, debated, and ultimately discarded over the course of two or three days' work at the hotel, we rarely left the room now, were only going into the studio about once a week. Thomas went to our dealer's three times that. Christine didn't care. That she only had to put up with Thomas for a couple of hours a week was good enough for her. Slippery was once again drunk most of the time, was beyond the point of caring.

"Who said I need to use the phone?" I answered. "It's just that I've heard this album six times in a row and I want to get some fresh air. Christ."

He stood up and picked up the receiver. "C'mon, use this phone. It'll save you a dime."

I shook the door handle. "Open the door, man."

He'd locked the deadbolt and pocketed the key when I'd said I was going out for a while after the fifth time the final crushing piano note to "A Day in the Life" signalled the end of the album. Was I overwhelmed by the potpourri of hard and soft rock, blues, psychedelia, show tunes, and even classical? No question. Was I coked-up enough myself to obsess over it in a hermetically sealed hotel room during the first brilliant week of May? You bet. But there's crazy and then there's crazy. And this was crazy.

"I wonder how they knew, hey, Buckskin."

I dropped my head and closed my eyes. It was obvious there was only one way out of the room, and that was by taking the same road Thomas was travelling. I buckled my seat belt and took a deep breath.

As calmly as I could, "Who are *they*, and you wonder how they know *what*?"

"Concentrate for a minute. I think if you do the answer might come to you."

I took another breath.

"Are you talking about the Beatles?" I said.

"Hey, very good."

I tried to think, but all I wanted to do was get outside on the street in the summer sun and start running until either I got somewhere or my heart exploded trying.

"Look, man," I said, "I really don't know what you're—"

He ripped the disk off the turntable and hurled it against the wall. It didn't break, though. Just sort of sailed into it edgewise like a thin black Frisbee and fell straight to the ground.

"Somehow somebody who knows what *Moody Food* is all about talked to somebody they shouldn't have talked to about something they shouldn't have talked about and that means you or me and I know it wasn't Thomas so who do you think that leaves, Buckskin, who do you think that leaves?"

"You think I called up John, Paul, George, and Ringo and told them we were putting crowd noise and animal sounds on our record and were layering on lots of different kinds of instruments and weren't using pauses between some of our songs. You think I discussed these things with the Beatles."

He was going to yell something else but noticed the album cover sitting on top of one of the speakers. He picked it up. Stood there staring at the catalogue of famous wax figurines on the front for a long time; eventually sat down on the floor and kept on staring. Buried there somewhere amid Karl Marx and Mae West and Dylan Thomas and all the others, I think he was looking for himself.

103.

WHEN THE LAST peace sign was flashed and the final joint passed, by the end of the day, May 22, nearly five thousand people, Christine among them, gathered in Queen's Park to listen to Buffy Sainte-Marie, Leonard Cohen, and several lesser-knowns officially inaugurate the Toronto Love-In and the Summer of '67 with an entire afternoon of music, open-air pot-smoking, barefoot dancing, and general out-and-out freak-power fun. The Summer of Love came too late for Thomas and me.

I'd left him hunched over his Gibson and gone out for a bottle of Coke. As soon as I stepped foot onto the street I felt the throb of the crowd in the nearby park pounding in my ears. I ended up making it half a block down Bloor before turning around and retreating to the hotel without the pop. It sounded like an army was coming. I hurried back upstairs to our room.

104.

THE NEW RULE was one at a time. There'd be Thomas and Heather and you in the recording studio putting down your part, and that would be it. RCA had pretty strict rules about always having an employee in the booth, but Thomas must have laid some cash on somebody because every time it was my turn to record a percussion part Thomas and Heather were the only ones there. Thomas never explained why, but I knew it was an attempt to keep Ringo and everyone else on the outside from stealing the secret recipe to *Moody Food*.

Thomas staggered our respective recording times so that none of us saw each other any more, but I was ten minutes early showing up one day and Slippery twenty minutes late leaving and I ran into him coming out of the front door of the studio. I was glad I knew him. If I hadn't, a clearly smashed, unshaven man with a black patch over one eye wearing a whisky-stained and cigarette-burned seersucker suit the first week of August might have given me pause. Heather was sitting on the top step in a tie-dyed halter top and blue-jean cut-offs alternately smoking and biting her nails. Unlike the Park Plaza, the studio was one place she was always welcome. When she saw me coming up the sidewalk she stood up.

"Thomas says that the trees where he's from are really different than from around here and where I'm from. If you want to know where I'm from just head for the northern tip of Lake Superior and before you get to Nipigon hang a right. There's one paved road and a Hudson's Bay Company and not much else, but the trees and lakes are nice. I love lakes and trees and animals and the sky and everything that's natural. There really aren't any trees or lakes or anything like that in Toronto. Thomas says that someday he's going to take me home with him to see the lakes and trees where he was born. After everything gets settled with his music. You know. The new music."

So now Heather really did know what we did at night. I didn't know what to say, so I used a couple of reassuring pats on her bare shoulder to sit her back down and nodded at Slippery fumbling for a smoke out of his pack. He gave me that gently baffled look wet-brained drunks do when you say their names and they can't quite place the face or voice but know that they should. I let him have a few seconds to make the connection.

"Bill." Pause. "Mornin'."

It was ten to four in the afternoon, but I wasn't real big on keeping regular hours at the moment either.

"How'd it go?" I said, nodding toward the studio.

Over the last two weeks Thomas and I had completely torn apart and put back together "Holiday Drive," the object of today's session, at least three times.

"I've got forty-eight dollars," he said. A cigarette dangled from his mouth, his lighter from one of his hands. "Fifty-two more and I'll have a hundred." The Marlboro and lighter stayed where they were. Slippery, too. His one exposed pink eye looked like a hungover rabbit's and kept blinking in hopeless defence against the gushing summer light.

I took off my Ray Bans and squinted against the sun. "Try these on," I said.

He lowered his head a couple of inches toward my hand, as if on a winch.

"I ain't in the market for no spectacles," he said.

"No charge," I said. "I've got an extra pair at home. A better pair."

He kept looking at the shades.

I slid the glasses over his ears. He slowly raised his head to meet the sun.

"That's . . . that's all right," he said.

Heather took her fingernails out of her mouth and popped back up.

"I want a pair, too," she said. "Thomas and you and now Slippery have got a pair and I want a pair, too."

I looked at her swollen pupils and the nail she'd chewed down to the flesh on her middle finger and wished I had another pair to give her. God, I wished I did. I put an arm around her shoulder.

"C'mon," I said, "let's get inside. Thomas is probably starting to wonder where we are."

105.

THE ROYAL CANADIAN MOUNTED POLICE managed to do what nothing else had been able to for weeks: get us all in the same room together. Fortunately, Thomas and I had been at the studio when they'd crashed his place at the Park Plaza. Unfortunately, we'd left enough drugs lying around to start our very own cartel. Thomas was now certifiably on the lam from two governments.

Everyone was gathered around the table in the practice studio trying to figure out the best strategy for getting him out of town. Thomas was smoking a cigarette and sitting on a chair pulled up to the opened balcony doors with his back to everyone, a rumpled paper sack resting on top of the white Fender on his lap. He could never go back to the hotel and get the rest of his things now. The *Moody Food* tapes were safe, though, had been rescued from RCA and were in the bag. Except for his guitar, they were all he had left.

"I talked to my friend Emily," Christine said, "and she says the L.A. scene is really well organized and would have no problem keeping him underground for as long as necessary."

"I liked L.A.," Heather said. "L.A. was nice. We could go back to L.A."

Somewhere along the line Heather had traded in her Tarot cards and knitting needles for her fingernails. She gnawed away at one of her thumbs as she followed the conversation ping-ponging back and forth between Christine and Kelorn, who'd insisted on coming over as soon as she'd heard there was trouble.

"Los Angeles would be fine, dear," Kelorn said, "except that crossing the border at this point is simply out of the question. The fact that you all made it across twice is two miracles too many already."

Christine nodded. Heather went back to her thumb.

Scotty was poring over the piece of paper in front of him on the table and Slippery was pouring himself another shot from his bottle of Old Crow, each apparently oblivious to the power pow-wow going on around them. But there was only room enough for five chairs around the table and I was standing behind Heather and watched Scotty slowly tracing over the same word again and again, at Slippery look over at Thomas before his every sip.

Looking up, "We could go home," Heather said. "I mean my home. Where I'm from. We could get on a bus and go north just like I came south. They'd never find us up there. I could get my wait-ressing job back and Thomas could keep working on his music and everyone could come visit."

"It's not a bad idea," Christine said.

"No," Kelorn said, "it's not. But anywhere that isolated is also going to be underpopulated. If they ever managed to find out where he was they'd have no problem whatsoever plucking him up. He'd be a fish in a barrel up there."

"I wish you'd both stop saying *him*," Heather said. "Thomas isn't going anywhere without me. Wherever he goes I'm going too. *We're* going wherever we go."

Kelorn patted the hand not at Heather's mouth. "Of course, dear. It's just that Thomas is the fugitive here, so naturally we're focusing on his situation." She turned back to Christine.

"What about Montreal? You have friends there, don't you?"

"Just my brother and his family."

"Might he be able to help?"

"He's an accountant."

"I see."

Outside, Yorkville was gearing up for another hot August evening. Crowd buzz, honking cars, and the faint strains of the Byrds' "My Back Pages" floated through the opened patio doors. But no sirens or fists pounding at the studio door. Not yet. The cops—Toronto cops—were out there, though; under the direction of city hall every weekend now parked a paddy wagon at the corner of Hazelton and Yorkville and strictly enforced an under-eighteen 10 p.m. curfew as a way of letting everybody know who was in charge.

"Let me talk to some people I know in Vancouver," Kelorn said. "There's a very active peace movement out there and a lot of American kids from the west coast are coming up and settling. It might be a good cover."

"But what about in the meantime?" Christine said. "He can't stay here."

"He can stay with me for now, but it's imperative that we get him out of town as soon as possible." Kelorn and Christine both stood up. Heather, too.

"I'm coming," she said.

"You're coming where, dear?"

"With you. To your place. With Thomas."

"If all goes well, it'll likely only be for tonight."

"I don't care, I'm coming."

"The sleeping arrangements at my house are quite limited, dear. I'm afraid there's only—"

"I don't care, I'm coming."

Kelorn smiled. "Of course. Not to worry. We'll find room."

Kelorn and Heather and Christine were nearly at the door before they realized they'd forgotten something.

"Thomas?" Kelorn said. "Coming?"

The entire time they'd been talking about him Thomas had been blowing smoke rings in the direction of the coming twilight, sitting there silent all by himself in the corner like a very bad boy waiting to find out whether he was going to bed without dinner.

"Let's go, Thomas," Christine said. "You'll be safer at Kelorn's."

Heather came over and took his hand. Thomas put his other hand around her waist.

"You go with Kelorn and Miss Christine, darlin'," he said. "Thomas is going to wait for it to get dark."

"That's actually not a bad idea," Kelorn said.

"It's not," Christine seconded.

"Then I'll wait here with you," Heather said.

"I can move quicker and quieter on my own. You get along and help get things ready. I'll be there soon enough."

"But—"

"No buts. You be a good girl, now, and do what Thomas tells you." He kissed her bare stomach, just below where her halter top stopped.

Heather wanted to cry but put on a shaky smile instead.

"That's my girl," Thomas said. He pulled a baggy out of his pocket and stuffed it into hers. "Be careful with this like I told you, all right? Just a little at a time."

Heather nodded.

"All right, then. Now give Thomas a kiss and off you go."

She did and was, and with Kelorn and Christine along with her. Slippery picked up his bottle off the table and got to his feet as steady as he could.

"I'm going for a lay-down," he announced.

Thomas and I watched him sway in place.

"But before I do I'm gonna tell you this," he said, pointing his bottle at Thomas. "I'm not saying I think what you're doing is right or not. That ain't for me to decide, and it ain't for you either." He uncapped the bottle and took a pull. "But if you're gonna run, Hoss, run. And wherever you go, always keep your back to the wall."

Slippery shut the door after him, and Scotty didn't look up when I grabbed one of the chairs from the table and sat down beside Thomas to wait for the night.

106.

I FIXED BECAUSE HE WANTED ME TO. When he took out his kit from the bag that the tapes were in and pulled up his sleeve, he didn't say a word. But I offered him my arm when he was done with his and he tied me off and slapped my forearm to raise a vein and slid the needle in slowly but expertly. By the time I'd barely made it to the bathroom at the end of the hall and vomited and come back, Scotty was gone. Before he left he'd watched us shoot up from his spot at the table. I nodded out on the floor and when I woke up Thomas was gone, too.

But that was all right. He'd be back. In the meantime I'd just keep having this continuous warm jet-stream body-and-soul orgasm I was having and wonder why Thomas hadn't let me in on the wonders of mainlining heroin until now. If acid solved the mind-body problem, heroin eliminated the question. How could something that made you feel truly comfortable in your skin for the first time in your life get such a bad rap, I wondered. I felt good for me but sad for the rest of my fellow human beings struggling day after day to achieve only a fraction of what I was feeling right now every tenderly pulsing second.

I'd nodded off again when Thomas returned, and when I woke up he was tossing slices of liver off the balcony. He had a white plastic bag full of it at his feet and was determined to deposit each and every piece onto the empty street. I joined him outside.

It was the middle of that hour that is the middle of the night and the beginning of day both, still thickly dark but ready to dissolve into slowly blooming light at any minute. Thomas plopped a bloody piece of meat on the windshield of a brown Ford Fairlane parked underneath us a few feet down. He picked up a fresh slice out of the bag.

"Do you know what I'm holding in my hand right now, Buckskin?"

I looked at the piece of meat for a second like I actually needed time to identify it. "Liver?"

"From what animal?"

"A cow?"

"That's right, from a cow. I have here in my right hand the liver from a cow." He pulled back his arm and flung the thing as hard as he could, shooting, I think, for the sidewalk across the street. It landed with a sticky slap a couple feet short of its target.

"And do you know what the purpose of a liver is?" he said. "Not just a cow's liver, any liver?"

I'd never really thought about it before. And now—a big beautiful butterfly delicately unfolding its elegantly embroidered wings and readying itself for takeoff in the pit of my stomach— definitely wasn't the time to start. "Um . . ."

"That's all right, don't be embarrassed. You'd be surprised at how many people don't." He seemed undecided about where to direct his next missile; kept tossing it up and down in his hand like a pizza pie while scouting the street. A yellow Volvo went by and tooted its horn. He let it pass.

"The liver performs many essential functions. It regulates blood volume. It stores up all sorts of important things a body needs like copper and iron and vitamin B^{12}. It metabolizes proteins and carbohydrates and fats and destroys old red blood cells. And"—he reached back and pitched the subject of his anatomy lesson side-armed, farther than the last but still not far enough to make it to the other side—"it also detoxifies foreign substances in the blood stream." He wiped his bloody hand on his jeans and looked at me for the first time.

"It keeps a body clean, Buckskin. Without it, there's nothing stopping something—*anything*—from stealing inside and spreading its poison and putting you down for good." He dipped his hand back in the bag and retrieved the final piece of liver.

This time I thought it was going over to the other side. He screamed and hurled the hunk of meat, and another six inches and it would have made it. It didn't echo, but you could feel Thomas's voice carrying on somewhere in the damp night air. He took in the carnage he'd created below, the thin slices of brown flesh splattered on the street, sidewalk, and dew-topped cars. He lit a cigarette.

"One more thing about the liver?" he said. "About the human liver?"

I nodded.

"The liver is the largest single organ in the human body. Most people, if you ask them, would say it's the heart, but it's not. The heart gets all the songs written about it and it's what everybody talks about, but the liver is the biggest thing in you. So how come you never hear anybody talking about the liver? Where are all the songs written about it?"

107.

THOMAS SENT ME OFF to Kelorn's to let her know that the cops hanging around near the studio that he'd made up and called her about when I'd passed out had gone, but that just to be on the safe side he was staying put for the rest of the night. By the time I was out of Yorkville and on Spadina the night was beginning to do its Houdini thing, and once I hit Harbord, yesterday was just a rumour. I was still high but felt like doing nothing so much as crying. When I couldn't put my finger on why, I wanted to cry even more. After I tried to and couldn't, I decided to sing.

Which was exactly as far as I got. I opened my mouth but something blocked the signal from my brain to my lips and plugged my vocal cords shut and nothing came out. I felt like I'd stubbed my toe, hard, on the sharp corner of a couch and couldn't scream.

I lowered my head and walked and walked and didn't stop until I found myself an hour and a half later in Etobicoke. When I heard a kid—a paper boy with an empty grey bag slung over his shoulder—kicking a can down the street, the sound of tin grating across concrete scraped my nerves and made me feel like yelling at him to cut it out and I knew I was going to be all right. I sang the first thing that came to mind, the chorus to Merle Haggard's "Sing Me Back Home," and wanted to run over and tell the kid how much I loved him.

I didn't, though. This was Etobicoke, not Yorkville. I started the long walk back instead and listened to him going his way still kicking his can, me going mine singing my song.

108.

THE NEXT DAY, that day, was hot. I think it was hot. Real warm, anyway. It had to be, it was August. August 20. The day Yorkville decided to strike its blow against the empire and the empire struck back.

Kelorn and Heather were taking tea on the front step when I finally made it to Making Waves. Heather must have stayed up half the night making a sizable dent in the bag of coke Thomas had given her, because it was all I could do to convince her that Thomas was fine and that we'd been up late talking and that he was probably sleeping and that for her to go by and wake him up wouldn't do anybody any good.

"Is he really okay, Bill?" she asked, pulling at the arm of my sweaty T-shirt.

"Sure he is. The poor guy just needs some sleep. You both do." I tried to give her my best I-know-of-what-you-sniff look of disapproval, but to no avail. She just kept holding onto my shirt until Kelorn gently put a cup of tea in her hand.

"You look like you could use some sleep yourself," Kelorn said, handing me another cup.

"I'm okay," I said, waving away the concern and the offer.

"Take it," she said.

I took both it and the space she made for me on the step after she sent Heather inside to make another pot. I sipped the hot tea. Chamomile. I immediately felt like curling up on the step like an old cat in the sun.

Looking straight ahead, "Vancouver looks promising," she said.

"Vancouver?" Maybe I already was asleep.

Kelorn turned to me. "You do remember what we were talking about last night?"

"Yeah, I just . . ."

"Yes, I know. There seems to be a lot of that going around." She returned her gaze to the empty sidewalk.

"I want to hear if Christine came up with anything," she said, "but I think the west coast is our best bet. Thomas would just seem like one more draft dodger out there."

"How long before he goes?"

"Depending upon what Christine has to say, he can and has to go now."

"What, like this week?"

"Like today."

"Today?"

She turned to me again.

"It's just that we're not done working on *Moody Food* yet," I said.

"Bill, do you know what the RCMP will do to Thomas if they get a hold of him?"

"Put him in jail?"

"Put him in jail. Correct. And not for the weekend, either."

I took another sip of my tea. "I can't imagine Thomas in jail."

"Exactly," she said. "Neither can I."

Heather poked her head out the door.

"What kind of tea should I make?" she said.

"Use the strong black tea, dear," Kelorn said. "Bill is going to bring Thomas back to us safe and sound. And it looks like he needs all the help he can get."

109.

ACTUALLY, WHAT BILL needed was to fire up a sizable piece of South American rock just to get his pulse pumping at a normal number of beats per second. But I resisted the desire to take some of Heather's stash with me on the grounds that I'd have Thomas up and around and back at Making Waves and myself horizontal on my cot in my old room by noon. The idea of pulling back the sheets, flicking on my ancient fan, and taking a short vacation from reality seemed as exciting an idea as I could imagine.

But it would be a long time before I got to have that sleep. And when I did, it wouldn't be a short nap. When I finally delivered Thomas where I was supposed to, I'd sleep the sleep of the dead. And there wouldn't be anything in the world of the living loud enough to wake me up again.

110.

"ALL RIGHT, think of it as my send-off into exile, then."

"I already know what I think of it," I said. "Have you lost it? A concert? Now? You might as well turn yourself in."

"I told you, we'll play under cover."

"Under what kind of cover?"

"I don't know. The International Donald Twayne String Band. Whatever. It's not important. The thing is, we'll tell everybody who's cool what's really going on and perform *Moody Food* from start to finish, the whole thing, exactly in the order it's going to appear on the album."

"With just the four of us? What about all the outside instruments we've used? Not to mention the studio effects you've—God, I can't believe I'm even talking about this."

I didn't have to get Thomas up; thanks to the block of coke and handful of reds on the table, he'd never come down. Which had given him plenty of time to plan his very own farewell party. He had his guitar around his neck and was stalking around the room as he spoke. He went to the table and inhaled a line in each nostril standing up and swung an arm around my shoulder.

"It's not about how close we can come to approximating the studio sound of the record," he said. "I know that's impossible, and that's what we're making the record for. But Thomas realizes now that we've left something out of what we've been doing."

"Oh, yeah, what's that?"

"Love."

"And you think that by putting your ass in danger of being incarcerated by playing a two-hour concert we're going to get that now?"

"People have to see what this music means to us, Buckskin. They have to see it up close and personal, in our eyes." He took hold of my shoulders so I couldn't look away. "Just like I can see it in yours and you in mine."

I didn't know what he was seeing, but all I saw was a road map of broken blood vessels and two ridiculously dilated pupils. Reasoning with him was useless, so I'd have to outsmart him.

"Okay," I said. "But this place is just too hot right now. Let's go downstairs and get Slippery and I'll call Christine and we'll all meet up at Kelorn's and work this thing out. But after that we've got to talk about where you and Heather are going to end up. How does Vancouver sound?"

"Vancouver, sure, whatever y'all say." He strummed his guitar. "But you gather up the girls and meet me back here. Thomas has got us a hiding place the devil himself would never find."

III.

THOMAS LED US ALL downstairs to the building's basement and stopped before a door marked FURNACE—KEEP OUT. He slipped in a skeleton key and, sure enough, there was the furnace. And, on the other side of the small cobwebby room, another door. He knocked—four times, slowly—and was answered by the door opening up on its own. He stepped aside and with a sweeping gesture bowed for Kelorn to enter first. She hadn't been happy about Thomas insisting on staying here and not at the store, but knew better than to argue. She looked at him and then at me, shook her head, gathered up her dress at her knees, and disappeared down the dark stairs.

"This is so cool," Heather said, following Kelorn, kissing Thomas on the cheek.

"I better wait upstairs for Christine," I said. "I left a message for her with one of her roommates. As soon as she gets here we'll come down."

"You sure you know the knock?"

At first I thought he was kidding. Until my eyes started to

adjust to the dull yellow light coming through the basement window and I saw he wasn't smiling.

"Four knocks, right?" I said.

"Four knocks with one Mississippi steamboat between each knock."

"Gotcha."

He handed me the key. "Take this."

"Right."

"And this." He reached inside his Nudie jacket and pulled out a pistol.

"What the hell do you want me to do with that?" I said, staring at the gun.

He slapped it into the palm of my hand. "I don't want you to do anything with it. It's only for using if you have to, you hear me? Only if you absolutely have to."

"Why would I have to use it?"

Closing the cellar door behind him, "Get your head out of the ground, Buckskin. There's a war on, in case you didn't know."

112.

I SAT AT THE CARD table with the pistol lying in front of me. The breeze from the balcony was warm, the gun cold and hard. I didn't notice Scotty shuffle into the room until he pulled back a chair and sat down. He rested his violin case and bag of papers on his lap and joined me in staring at the gun.

"I knew you weren't bright, but I never took you for stupid," he said.

"It's not mine."

"You think I'm just talking about that thing?"

113.

BY THE TIME CHRISTINE showed up I'd stashed the pistol underneath an overturned empty flowerpot out on the balcony and was relieved when Scotty unpacked his bag and set to work as usual.

"Where is everybody?" she said.

"It'll probably be easier if I just take you there."

"Let's just wait a minute, okay?" She sat down with her elbows on the table, rested her head in her hands.

"If it's about Montreal, don't sweat it," I said. "It looks real good for Vancouver. Kelorn's just waiting for a call and then Thomas and Heather are all set."

She looked up. "Good. That's good. I'm glad. At least something's going right."

"What is it?" I said.

Ever since I'd stalked her all the way home after the fracas at my place, Christine and I had barely spoken. I didn't even know if we were still officially a We any more.

"It's about Yorkville," she said. "You wouldn't be interested."

"Try me."

She thought about that for a moment.

"Okay," she said. "So finally Lamport agrees to debase himself and see us and hear what we have to say. About the traffic. About the pollution. About kids living out on the street and getting sick. About the constant police harassment."

"Great," I said.

"Yeah, great. And do you know what his response was?"

I shrugged my shoulders.

"That these sounded like pretty good reasons to him for us to leave."

"Geez."

"Yeah, geez."

Just then Scotty gave a little hoot and tossed aside his pen and took to his feet and brought out his violin and proceeded to lay down a poem-ending celebratory tune, a slow waltz.

"Give the fiddler a dram or a dance, you two," he said.

Christine and I smiled.

"What's it going to be?" I said.

"I don't even know what a dram is."

"I guess we better dance then."

And we did.

"Thomas wants us to perform *Moody Food* live before he leaves," I said.

"People are mad, Bill. When no one hears what you have to say, when no one even tries to hear what you have to say . . ."

"I told him he was crazy."

"People are angry, real angry. It's not good."

"I'm going to try to talk him of out of it, but you know how he gets."

"It's not good at all."

114.

ALL AFTERNOON WE planned Thomas's exodus and waited on the call Kelorn was expecting on the pay phone down the hall that Heather was dispatched to wait beside. And when the phone call finally came and the west coast was officially clear, spent the rest of the afternoon arguing with Thomas once he revealed to not just me but everyone how he was more than happy to skip town, but only after *Moody Food* got its moment in the setting sun.

"Thomas," Kelorn said, "listen to me, listen to me very carefully one last time. You cannot do this. You simply cannot do this." She'd started off shocked, moved on to patient frustration, and had now arrived at angry insistence.

All along, Thomas had remained the same. He smiled and reached over and squeezed her hand. "Everything's going to be fine," he said. "No one's efforts will have been in vain."

The room was minuscule enough to make Slippery's quarters seem like a suite at the Park Plaza. To top it off, the ceiling was so low we all had to sit on the dirty floor around an upside-down wooden crate that supported the room's only light, a single candle sticking out of one of Slippery's old bourbon bottles. Slippery himself, the phantom doorman of before, squatted on guard, filling the room with eyeball-watering smoke from his Marlboros and sipping from a fresh pint of Old Crow. His own pistol was stuck underneath his belt front and centre, behind the buckle, the same place Thomas wore his.

Kelorn looked at me across the flickering candlelight, but I'd already done my best and she knew it, had given Thomas my word that if he took the ride out of town she'd arranged for him and Heather the next morning, as soon as he got settled in B.C. we'd get the group back together out there and not only perform a live run-through of *Moody Food* but also finish up what needed to be done with the record. That was about an hour and a half before, around the time Christine bailed out to meet some friends at the Riverboat concerning the continuing fallout from the hippies' failed meeting at city hall.

Kelorn stood up, as much as she could, anyway.

"You know how I feel," she said. "I can't understand why you don't seem to care enough about your own future to do the only sensible thing, but I wish you'd think about the others around you who do." She cut her eyes Heather's way, but Thomas took Heather's hand and she gave him a big kiss and neither said a word.

Kelorn looked at me again. I lowered my eyes.

"Good luck, Thomas," she said.

"Thanks for everything, Kelorn," Heather said, Thomas's hand still in hers.

"Good luck to all of you."

115.

THOMAS LIT A FRESH candle and we listened to him talk about how the *Moody Food* showcase was going to be structured in terms of song selection and how we could compensate for the bare-bones instrumentation and lack of studio wizardry and what would constitute optimum club conditions and even what colour the backdrop behind us on stage should be. I felt like I was ten years old and sick in bed with the flu in the middle of winter and half-daydreaming, half-hallucinating endless summer days of schoolyard baseball and touch football games and glorious suppers of three hot dogs and two whole bottles of Orange Crush. I fell asleep to the sound of snorting noses and Heather's voice softly yesing Thomas's every sentence, thinking that none of us would ever get out of this room alive.

116.

THE POUNDING of someone's boots racing down the stairs ripped open my eyelids. Heather screaming and Thomas and Slippery whipping out their guns sent me scrambling on my stomach for the closest corner. I didn't have far to go, but before I got there I recognized Christine's voice.

"Everybody's in the street! You've got to see this! The hippies have taken over Yorkville."

Gun still at his side, "Miss Christine, I do believe I gave you precise instructions on how to gain access to the upstairs entrance."

"Everybody's in the street," she said, trying to catch her breath.

"What do you mean everybody's in the street?"

"Come see for yourself. They've shut down the village. You've all got to see this."

Thomas stuck his pistol back in his belt.

"Let's move, people."

117.

"PARK IT AROUND BACK. We can load up through the rear door." I flicked on the turn signal and did what Thomas said.

When a big party a bunch of hippies were holding at a warehouse downtown got raided, everybody headed over to Yorkville and decided that enough was enough and sat down in the street, effectively doing what the politicians wouldn't, stopping any cars from coming into the village. By the time we gathered on the balcony to check things out the avenue was swarming sidewalk to sidewalk with hippies chanting "CLOSE OUR STREET, CLOSE OUR STREET." There were so many people down there you couldn't see concrete any more.

"It's like a little country," Heather said.

"That's it," Thomas said, eyes roving over the crowd. "That's exactly what it is."

Of course I said no. No. No way. Forget it. Out of the question. Uh uh. I said it, but Christine was the one who walked away and into the street. I drove the hearse over to RCA to get our equipment while Thomas stayed out of sight by lying down in the back and rattling off instructions. Slippery rode up front with me, keeping his one good eye out for the bad guys.

There was some sense to it. Thomas said that if we did as he said, set up our instruments on the roof of our building and dished out *Moody Food* loud and clear to the starving masses, he and Heather would make their getaway in the morning and wasn't that just a fine plan.

"No," Christine said.

But there was some sense to it. There had to be. Otherwise, why else had I been sprinting between studio and hearse with all of our equipment, piece by piece, Slippery watching my back from the front seat, Thomas shouting out, "Hurry, Buckskin, hurry!"?

At a red light on the return trip to Yorkville I leaned my head back on the seat, could feel my wet hair sticking to the vinyl head-rest. An arm loaded down with a fat line of cocaine snaked into my peripheral vision. I shook my head.

"I'm all right," I said.

"Like hell you are," the arm answered. "Pick yourself up." I saw Slippery see it talking to me, too. He looked away.

"No, I'm okay," I said. "I'll grab a Coke at the studio."

"Coca-Cola isn't going to make the thirst you've got go away. Here." The arm slithered closer to my nose.

"No, it's okay." I could feel the hairs in my nose tentacling toward the white powder.

The arm disappeared and I took a deep breath. And then Thomas's face was beside mine, outstretched arm back again and sticking straight out and still coke-laden, Thomas's pistol hanging from the other hand.

"I don't know what you're thinking or plan on doing, but this is our moment and it will never come again and we're going to embrace it. And a sleepy drummer who loses track of the beat is not something we can allow to happen."

I put my nose to his flesh and inhaled. The light turned green and I hit the gas.

118.

HEATHER WAS WAITING for us where Thomas had told her to be, and she helped Slippery start to haul everything by foot through a dark alley to the back door of our studio. We didn't have to worry about the crowd thinning out; by the roar of it, it was even bigger than before. My job was to go into the belly of the beast and pluck out Christine so she could take her bass-playing place alongside the rest of us.

"Let me help carry some of this stuff," I said. "Even if I could find her, she won't do it."

"You'll find her. And she'll do it."

"She won't. I know her."

The intersection where I'd parked Christopher was deserted; the entire village was on Yorkville Avenue.

"She will," he said. "She has to."

I put my hands in my pockets and turned an ear toward the crowd. I'd walk around for a while and then tell him I couldn't find her and that we'd have to make do without her. So our sound would be a little thin on the bottom end. Nothing was going to stop him now.

"All right, we'll meet you on the roof," I said.

"Have you got your revolver?"

"My what?"

"The pistol I gave you, the pistol."

"Yeah, I've got it."

"Let me see it."

"I better go now."

"But you've got it?"

"I better go now," I said.

119.

THROUGH A FOREST of blue jeans the first face I saw when I hit Yorkville Avenue was Christine's. I cursed my good luck and squeezed my way through the crowd and squatted down beside her.

"Bill, c'mon, sit down," she shouted above the noise.

She looked happy. I was glad she looked happy.

"There's no room," I shouted back, taking in the sea of bodies that had swallowed me.

"Sure there is," she said, wiggling over a few inches on the street to let me in.

"I can't stay, I have to go."

She stopped moving. "Thomas is still threatening to play?"

"He is going to play. He says if we all help him he'll leave in the morning."

"If they don't arrest him before then."

Someone started up a "CARS, NO! PEOPLE, YES!" chant and there wasn't any use talking any more. I stood up, gave her an underhand wave, and pushed my way off the street. I went around back and climbed the stairs and stopped off at our studio, empty but for Scotty at the table working on a poem. He didn't look up. I climbed to the fourth floor and the door that led to the roof.

"Where is she?" Thomas yelled, looking up from adjusting his amplifier. Everything was set up near the edge of the roof, just like a regular show—Thomas's and Christine's mikes near the front, Slippery's steel guitar off to the side, my drums at the back, even Heather in a chair at stage right. My sticks were waiting for me on the snare.

"I couldn't find her," I shouted, heading for my stool.

"That's a lie," he said, standing up. "I saw you talking to her." He walked toward me, the black curly cord from his guitar trailing behind.

"No, I wasn't."

"Yes, you were. I saw you. What were you two talking about?"

"Christ, don't be so fucking paranoid. All right, so I talked to her. I told you she wouldn't play. This is *her* thing, man, this is her

Moody Food." I'd never thought of it that way before, but now that I had it made me feel good to say it. "Let's just play."

"Without a bass player? Without half our vocals?"

I pounded my snare, then my tom-tom. Slippery took my cue and ran a run on his steel guitar. You could barely hear either of us over the crowd. "Let's go, man," I yelled.

"Did you use every means possible?" Thomas said.

"What?"

"Did you use every means possible?"

"What are you talking about?" The wind was blowing my hair in my eyes and I brushed it away; was his, too, and he didn't.

"And now because you didn't, I have to."

"You have to what?" I said.

"Do what I have to do."

I stood up. "Let it go, man."

"I'll do what I have to do."

"I said let it go, man."

The door to the roof opened and Christine had one boot off and was working on her other as she hopped toward her bass. Heather jumped up and took it off its stand and put it around her neck.

"If we're going to play, let's play," Christine barked. Turning to Thomas, "And if I see your face in the village tomorrow I'm going to pay the Vagabonds to ship you off to Vancouver COD."

Thomas strummed his guitar.

"All right," he screamed, "'Some Good Destruction,' on four."

"Ain't we going to warm up first?" Slippery called out.

But Thomas was already counting off.

We played as hard as we could as loud as we could, but no one heard us. Everyone turned up their amps and Thomas and Christine sang at each other eyeball to eyeball so fiercely I saw blue veins in their necks bulge and threaten to burst. But what the wind didn't carry away high above the protesters' heads, the noise below suffocated like a heavy blanket of December snow. After every song Thomas kept moving us closer and closer to the lip of the roof. But if anybody did manage to hear anything, they probably thought it was just a radio left on playing in one of the cafés or maybe a record player in an apartment someone forgot to turn off in the excitement of getting down to the street.

"Till My Wet Fur Froze" ended the same way it began, with the chanting of the crowd the only thing any of us could really hear.

"Forget it," I screamed from behind my drums.

"'Isn't It Pretty to Think So,'" Thomas yelled out. Now we could hear police sirens wailing in the distance.

"It's no use," I shouted. The wind had picked up. Christine and Slippery and Heather were shielding their eyes and straining to understand what we were saying.

"On four," he yelled.

Maybe he thought that if he played even closer to the edge, right on the edge, more people might see him and listen harder and hear what he was singing. Or maybe he believed that the nearer he was to the people the louder his voice would be. I crashed my cymbal at the end of the chorus just like he'd taught me to, and when I looked up he was gone. We all dropped our instruments and ran to the edge. I watched Heather scream, but all I could hear were sirens.

As many dreams as there are reasons none of them ever come true. Everybody's got one and Thomas is no different. It's always the same and it happens a lot.

Thomas's is simple. He has to make a phone call—why, he never finds out, only knows he's got to make the connection—and every time he dials, over and over again all night, something goes wrong. Sometimes it's not the right number. Sometimes his fingers get jammed in the dial. Sometimes he forgets the number entirely. This last is the worst. Who forgets their own phone number? It's like forgetting your name. Who forgets their own name?

When he wakes up, Thomas sits up on his elbows and opens and shuts his eyes a couple of quick times just to make sure he's not still dreaming and swears that next time he'll remember. That next time he'll finally get through.

120.

IT HAD TO BE ME.

Sixty-one of Christine's brothers and sisters were punched in the face and kicked in the stomach and dragged off to jail and she had to be there to help sort through the aftermath. Heather wanted to come—sobbing, demanded to come—but cocaine and deep grief do not mix. And I will not talk about what that looked and sounded like. Somehow Kelorn managed to get her checked into the hospital and all she could say before I left town was that once Heather started to detox she wasn't as bad as before. Slippery, I thought, would want a ride at least part of the way home, but he turned me down flat.

We were standing outside his room. His opened suitcase was on the cot, a cup of steaming coffee in his hand. His patch was gone and he looked at me with two clear eyes.

"I can't take a chance getting mixed up in that," he said.

I nodded and ran a hand through my freshly cut hair. No matter how many times I did, there was no getting used to it.

"Take care," he said.

I shook his hand and remembered something and stuck my other hand in my pocket.

"Here," I said.

He took the roll of bills and began to slowly count them.

"It was in his bag," I said. "I'm sure he owed you something."

"Not this much. There's got to be more than five hundred dollars here."

"What am I going to do with it?" I said.

He looked back down at the money.

"I kept enough for gas and whatever else I'm going to need," I said. "Use it for your house. Another house."

He looked up.

"That haircut's a start, but you can't do what you're fixin' on doing in them clothes," he said.

I was wearing what I usually did—boots, jeans, a white T-shirt. He went inside and pulled his only other change of clothes, his other suit, out of the suitcase. It was identical to the one he was wearing, except blue, not brown. It also looked like the twenty thousand roads it had probably been down, but it made more sense than what I had on.

"Are you sure?" I said.

He stuck the money in his pocket.

"Looks like you just bought yourself a suit, Hoss."

121.

IT HAD TO BE ME. Because I'd promised him. There were credit cards and a birth certificate and ways of finding out who his closest relatives were and what they wanted done, but even if it took me several years to discover that "Uncle Pen" is a Bill Monroe song, I knew then that the Joshua Tree desert likely wouldn't figure into the final plans of any remaining family members. But it figured in Thomas's, so it had to be me. I changed the oil and filled up the tank and stuck a roll of toilet paper inside the glove compartment just in case my nose started to bleed. And got a haircut. I'd never actually seen one, but could only assume that hearse drivers delivering dead bodies across the U.S. border to grieving kin didn't have long hair.

I never went over the speed limit but only stopped for any length of time twice, once in Illinois to buy coke from one of our old connections, once in Wichita to sleep because I woke up in a cornfield to the *whap whap whap* of corn stalks pounding against the windshield. The guy at the border in Detroit had asked me what I had in the back and I'd told him. When he asked where I was going and I told him California he said he sure hoped I had air-conditioning back there. I told him I didn't and he said he was sure glad he didn't have my job.

122.

IT WAS AROUND midnight when I got to the desert. Although I'd had two days and nights to think something up, now that I was there I didn't know what was next. I got back on the highway and found the nearest all-night diner and ordered coffee and apple pie. I was only using enough coke to keep me awake, and my appetite was coming back. I had a refill and another slice of pie, this time with vanilla ice cream, and by the time I got the bill I knew what I had to do. I asked the waitress for directions to the nearest gas station.

"Regular or diesel?"

"It doesn't matter," I said.

123.

THE ENTRANCE TO THE PARK wasn't locked, or maybe there wasn't any gate, I forget which. Either way, I was surprised and relieved and killed my headlights and let the stars show me the way. I drove for about fifteen minutes, until I thought I was far enough inside that no one could see me, and pulled up beside an enormous, twisting rock formation and cut the engine. The smell in the hearse was only tolerable with every window wide open and going sixty miles an hour, so I didn't have time to sit there and think about what had to happen.

To help with the stench I'd wrapped him up in three layers of blankets, and when I drenched him in gasoline it didn't feel like I was doing it to him. So much so that I had to pull back the covers and make sure. It was him, all right. Grinning that goddamn grin. I dropped the match, and the heat and the explosion went straight up in the air and knocked me over on my back.

I picked myself up and watched the flame return to earth and turn into several smaller fires. I got back in the hearse and headed for the highway.

124.

THE REST IS JUST THE FACTS.

Thomas's first posthumous taste of glory was an Associated Press story picked up by a thousand dreary dailies about the grisly ritualistic sacrifice in California's Joshua Tree desert of an unknown rock and roll musician, Thomas Charles Graham, twenty-three, of Jackson, Mississippi, by one of his own band members, a Bill Ronald Hansen, Canadian, age twenty-one. Drugs, of course, were suspected, and the police were still investigating. The lawyer representing the deceased's family reported that the Grahams were in shock but in the process of bringing the remains of the body back home for interment in the Graham family plot. I was in an L.A. jail when they stuck what was left of him in the ground beside his mother, but what went into that hole didn't and doesn't matter and I didn't miss anything. Funerals are for the living and I'd already said goodbye.

The part the newspapers didn't write about was what they probably should have. How when Thomas hit Yorkville Avenue the police were so busy bashing noses and clubbing heads and the hippies so intent on trying to fend them off that no one noticed his body falling from the sky. When we collected him off the street there was a girl a few feet away on her knees with blood pouring out of her nose like water from a broken fountain. Compared to her, Thomas didn't look that bad.

They got me at the bus station. I'd flushed what was left of the coke down the toilet and scored enough Nembutals to numb me out all the way home before ditching the hearse and buying my ticket. I wanted to go to sleep and the downers would help see to that. When the cops busted me in the departure lounge they had to get a wheelchair to haul me out to the squad car, I was so weak kneed. They took away the Nembutals but couldn't make me stay awake.

My parents mortgaged their house and I got out on bail a couple of weeks later and eventually money and the truth got me off with a $700 fine for, get this, degrading a human body. I also couldn't apply to enter the United States for two years, the length of my American probation. They could have said I couldn't leave my parents' basement in Etobicoke for two years and I wouldn't have cared. Not counting trips downtown to score pot and stop in to see Kelorn, that's just about exactly what happened. My parents didn't complain. At least they could keep an eye on me.

I applied for readmission to U of T and when fall came around decided to wait for the spring semester and, with the arrival of it, the semester after that. I slept in and played solitaire in my room until dawn and took Snowball for walks late at night. I helped my mother do the housework and cut the grass and washed the car. I cleaned out the eavestroughs.

I also wrote Christine several long letters I couldn't figure out why I never mailed until I read one of them over the next day and realized I didn't have anything to say. When Kelorn told me Christine was going to Nigeria to do some kind of peace work with CUSO I finally did send something, just a short note saying congrats, and she wrote back saying thanks and to write and including her new address. I never did.

Except for what was playing on the radio in my mother's kitchen, I didn't listen to any music.

One book in the middle of the 80s, *Rock and Roll's Missing in Action*, and Thomas was on his way. I finally gave Electric Records *Dream of Pines* nearly twenty years late and it became a cult favourite, mostly among young musicians, and people started to call up once in a while wanting to know what this Graham guy who I'd torched in some desert was all about. They'd get about half of everything they wrote wrong, but I'd do my best.

Kelorn ended up back in England after someone broke into Making Waves one night, shit on the floor, and dragged as many books as they could through the mess once they found out there wasn't any money. Christine and Slippery and Heather, I don't know. After twenty years of nothing much, after moving down to Tilbury in '89 with the cash I got from selling my parents' house after they died, I was the guy, the only apostle who was talking.

Then I got drunk on some journalist's tab and let the lid off *Moody Food,* and Electric—which by now was owned by some monster company that made toothpaste and video games and a million other things—started to smell money but couldn't find the tapes and didn't even know where to begin looking. Soon enough they got wise and some lawyer would threaten me over the phone from time to time as Thomas's profile got bigger and bigger among the alternative music crowd, but I'd play dumb, which isn't real hard for me to do. Eventually I figured that, incomplete as it was, I was the best person to stitch *Moody Food* together and went online with my own CD. Naturally, the company decided to sue until I got somebody to check the contract and find out that Thomas had made sure that, except for *Dream of Pines*, all rights to all of his songs stayed with the band until a new contract could be worked out. They made me an offer and then another one, but eventually quit trying. After all, it was only music.

125.

BUT THE LEAVES are still on the trees, still change colours, still fall to the ground. And sometimes, when the kitchen is quiet except for the fridge motor coming on and the sound of Monty's soft snoring, I catch myself humming something I didn't even know I was.

I can still see it, but you can't.

So listen. Listen. *Listen.*

Acknowledgements

For debts past and present: Mark Boyd, Richard Currey, Lesley Grant, Tom Grimes, Nicholas Jennings, Andrew Johnson, Albert Moritz, Tom Noyes, Brad Smith, Miles Wilson, Nicole Winstanley, the Ontario Arts Council, and the Toronto Arts Council. The music of Gram Parsons was an inspiration in the writing of this book.

This is a work of fiction, and therefore of truth. Certain facts have been modified toward this end.

MARA KORKOLA

About the Author

Ray Robertson graduated from the University of Toronto with High Distinction with a B.A. in philosophy and later gained an M.F.A. in creative writing from Southwest Texas State University.

He is the author of the novels *Home Movies, Heroes, Moody Food,* and *Gently Down the Stream,* and a collection of non-fiction, *Mental Hygiene: Essays on Writers and Writing.*

He is a contributing book reviewer to the Toronto *Globe and Mail,* appears regularly on TVO's Imprint and CBC's Talking Books, and teaches creative writing and literature at the University of Toronto.